Dear Little Black Dress Reader,

Thanks for picking up this Little Black Dress book, one
of the great new titles from our series of fun, page-turning
romance novels. Lucky you — you're about to have a fantastic
romantic read that we know you won't be able to put down!

Why don't you make your Little Black Dress experience
even better by logging on to

## www.littleblackdressbooks.com

where you can:

- ♥ Enter our **monthly competitions** to win
  **gorgeous** prizes
- ♥ Get **hot-off-the-press** news about our latest titles
- ♥ Read **exclusive** preview chapters both from
  your **favourite** authors and from brilliant new
  writing talent
- ♥ Buy **up-and-coming** books online
- ♥ Sign up for an essential slice of romance via
  our **fortnightly email** newsletter

We love nothing more than to curl up and indulge in an
addictive romance, and so we're delighted to welcome you
into the Little Black Dress club!

With love from,

The *L*

Five interesting things about Julie Cohen:

1.  In high school in the USA, my best friend and I used to spend our chemistry lessons writing novels about us having sex with rock stars.

2.  Despite this lack of scholarly application, I graduated summa cum laude from Brown University. While I was there I wrote a daily comic strip about an Elvis impersonator and his pet squid.

3.  I came to live in England because of the Beatles, and because I fell in love with a guitar-playing Englishman.

4.  I have a postgraduate research degree in fairies in children's literature, which has very few practical applications.

5.  The Englishman and I have recently had our first child, who will be English as well, I suppose.

*By Julie Cohen*

# Nina Jones
## and the
# Temple of Gloom

Julie Cohen

little
black
dress

First published in 2010 by
LITTLE BLACK DRESS
An imprint of HEADLINE PUBLISHING GROUP

A LITTLE BLACK DRESS paperback

1

Cataloguing in Publication Data is available from the British Library

ISBN 978 0 7553 4141 2

Typeset in Transit511BT by Avon DataSet Ltd,
Bidford-on-Avon, Warwickshire

Printed and bound in Great Britain by
Clays Ltd, St Ives plc

Headline's policy is to use papers that are natural, renewable and
recyclable products and made from wood grown in sustainable forests.
The logging and manufacturing processes are expected to conform to the
environmental regulations of the country of origin.

HEADLINE PUBLISHING GROUP
An Hachette UK Company
338 Euston Road
London NW1 3BH

www.littleblackdressbooks.com
www.headline.co.uk
www.hachette.co.uk

To the Romantic Novelists' Association,
on their fiftieth birthday. You don't look a day
over twenty-five, darlings!

# Acknowledgements

Thanks to Woodkeeper Cindy Blaney of Highgate Wood for sharing her knowledge of bats and bat detectors, and to the Friends of Highgate Cemetery for the inspirational tour and for answering some rather bizarre questions. Thanks, too, to Cecilia Bainton for help with Spanish, and to Jan Sprenger for help with Spain, and to Kathy Love for always making me think about vampires.

My agent, Teresa Chris, was absolutely my fairy godmother while I wrote this book. Thank you so much, Teresa. I'm also deeply in debt to Anna Louise Lucia, Brigid Coady, Lee Weatherly, the Reading chapter of the Romantic Novelists' Association, and Helen Corner and all the students on the 2008 Cornerstones women's commercial fiction writing course. My editor, Cat Cobain, is eternally patient, wonderful and full of insight. Thanks too to Sara Porter and her fabulous eye for detail. And my family really do put up with a lot of my crap, too. Thanks, Dave and Nate and Mom and Dad. I love you.

# Prologue

I open my eyes. It's pitch black and I hear footsteps. I clutch the blanket and listen, holding my breath, until I realise they're above me, not in the same room.

It takes a few heartbeats more to remember I'm in a dead man's bed.

The footsteps walk back and forth. They're unhurried. I focus my gaze on the blank darkness above me, following them from one side of the ceiling to the other as if I could see them through the shadows and the plaster and lath. They pause, as if the owner is doing something, then start again, and fade away like a ghost disappearing into the mist.

It's impossible to tell what time it is. I can't leave. I have nowhere else to go.

Floating in the bed in the darkness, I close my eyes again. *Why why why?* sighs the wind through the eaves. *Why are you here?*

The rain is a thousand little footsteps around me.

# Part One:
# Fairy Castles and Prince Charmings

Anybody who knows anything about food knows all about Edmund Jett. He's got seven restaurants in London and Devon. He's got two Michelin stars, three best-selling cookbooks, a degree from Oxford, and a devoted and efficient personal assistant, who happens to be me, Nina Jones.

It's the best job I've ever had, not that I've had many, because I was lucky enough to be snapped up from the agency when Edmund's last PA got married and started popping out sprogs. In the three years I've been working for Edmund, I've met famous chefs, movie stars and even royalty. I've been able to afford (barely) the mortgage on a bedsit in Kensington. I've learned the restaurant business inside out and I've amassed a mouth-watering collection of shoes.

Jett, the flagship restaurant in Edmund Jett's empire, is located in the beating heart of Chelsea in a building that looks on a sunny day like an iced wedding cake, and at night like a magic castle. This afternoon, a prince is lunching in the restaurant with his entourage. This doesn't affect the staff, who move through their paces with the consummate professionalism that you'd expect in a top-rate London restaurant, but I must admit it gives a little lift to my step, because I'm the one who met him at the door and showed him to his seat.

I walk through the elegant, monochromatic, fully booked dining room of Jett, floating as effortlessly as the orchids that hover over every table. When I go through the door into the kitchen, heat and the steam immediately make my blond hair spring into curls. This happens every time. I might as well not bother straightening it every morning.

Then the reason why I bother spots me and waves and my heart springs up like my hair.

'Is he here?' Edmund shouts over the clatter of pans and whoosh of flames.

'Two minutes ago.'

He threads his way through the stations to me. His chef's whites are gleaming, his features classically perfect, his golden hair sexily mussed. Steam doesn't seem to touch it. Then again, his hair could be plastered to his head with sweat and cooking oil and everyone would think that was how he meant it to be. He could wear a fish for a hat. Nobody would care, least of all me, because he is Edmund Jett and there's nobody like him in the world.

'Nina Jones, you are a wonder,' he says and kisses me on the cheek.

For a split second I close my eyes. The noise and the heat and the armies of staff and customers, royal or otherwise, all disappear and it is me and Edmund, his lips on my skin. Then I open my eyes so quickly that he'll never know it isn't a normal blink.

'What about Nigel Dimmesdale from the *Telegraph*?' he asks.

'He's sitting two tables away.'

He nods, joyfully. 'It'll be in the Sunday magazine. You are a wonder. Pour yourself a drink.' He touches my shoulder and then leaves the kitchen, to shake hands with a prince.

I don't pour myself a drink, of course, because I've got work to do. Punters at Jett climb a grand spiral staircase to the bar upstairs; I go up the narrow staircase at the back, straight past the bar and on to the second floor, which holds Edmund's office and a tiny flat where he sometimes sleeps between services. The office is wide and spacious, and as the windows are quite small he's installed a skylight that floods the room with light, which gleams off the white walls and floors. His big glass desk with its several computers dominates the room. Mine sits beside it, small, wooden and squeezed tight with files and clippings, all organised according to my own special system.

I glance at the armchair in the corner. It's empty, though there's a hardcover book perched on the arm, and an empty coffee cup on the table beside it. With a grateful sigh I sink into my desk chair and toe off my Jimmy Choos. They are things of beauty – high, spiky, and very black. I bought them especially, when I heard I was going to be greeting a prince.

I'm a great believer in the power of high-heeled shoes. They're beautiful, they're stylish, they can rescue a so-so outfit, and they make you appear to have legs up to your armpits, especially if you have passably long legs anyway. Also – and this may be obvious, but it's really vital – the taller you are, the more people will assume that you know what you're doing. I read an article about it one time. I'm five foot ten in bare feet, so high heels make me taller than most women and quite a few men. Therefore I appear both more confident and more competent, merely by putting on my shoes.

Most importantly, they're uncomfortable. When you wear heels for every minute of your professional and social life, you're instantly proclaiming yourself as a person who is able to withstand blisters, pinching, and calf ache, because looking good is more important than pain. Besides, blisters can provide a handy distraction from an aching heart.

I rub the toes of my left foot against the aching arch of my right, and touch the spot on my cheek where Edmund kissed me. Who am I kidding? Blisters are no distraction from an aching heart at all.

But work always helps.

Tomorrow is one of the busiest days of the year in the restaurant industry and my to-do list is as long as my arm. Delicious odours and the sound of laughter waft upwards from downstairs, and outside the windows busy Chelsea clatters by. It's never quiet here, but that suits me fine, because I like to feel at the centre of things, directing traffic from the control tower of the Jett empire. I fire up my laptop and get stuck into the pile of emails and phone messages that have accumulated during my brief foray downstairs to meet the prince.

Some time later, I'm chewing on a pen and I have another one behind my ear while I sort the logistical nightmare of one day, one chef, seven restaurants and four media appearances. It's the sort of thing I love, but despite my absorption, the skin on the back of my neck immediately tingles when Edmund comes into the office. I shove my shoes back on.

'Try this,' he says. He's holding one of the big square plates from downstairs and his sleeves are rolled up to show his forearms. He pushes aside some of my paperwork and puts the plate down. This is yet another thrill of my job: witnessing a genius at work on his new creation.

I'm not precisely sure what this new creation is. It's heart-shaped and blood red, and it wobbles like a jelly. There are little fluffy white and red things around it, and a precise line of small cubes up one side of the plate. I can tell by the presentation that Edmund has made it himself. All of his cooking has a perfection that his kitchen staff train for hours to replicate. Even with the training, nobody does it like him. Eating Edmund's cooking is like eating a little bit of his personality.

'It's tomorrow's special.' He gives me a fork and knife, and stands there watching me.

I bite the inside of my lip. I know that Edmund's cooking is conceptual, and that surprise is an integral element of its appeal. But I would get a little bit less stage fright if I knew whether I was about to tuck in to a main course or a dessert. I sniff, trying to find a clue, but I can only smell Edmund: laundered whites, spices and warm oil. A strong note of coriander. Standing beside me, he's close enough that I could, if I let myself, reach across and brush the small dark smudge of something off his forehead.

'Go on,' he says.

'It's beautiful,' I say, stalling. He just smiles, so I pick up the fork, cut into the jelly, and take a bite. Whatever it is, I know it will have been sourced responsibly, raised humanely, and prepared with infinite care. Edmund is passionate about his ingredients.

The flavour explodes in my mouth: earthy, meaty, resiny. I swallow, and cross my fingers out of sight beneath my desk. 'Venison and juniper?'

Edmund beams. 'Close, it's gin. Do you like it?'

'It's gorgeous.'

He pulls over the big chair from his desk and sits down beside me, flipping through the letters I've printed out for him and picking up the pen I've recently taken from my mouth. I close my eyes for a split second, to savour and agonise and boost control all at once, and then take another bite of the food. I taste Edmund, swallow Edmund, help myself to some more of Edmund.

Close to me, he signs his name over and over with a large looping scrawl.

'Where's Caroline?' I ask, my glance flickering over to the empty armchair, the discarded book.

'Doctor's.' He reaches over and taps on my laptop to call up his schedule. 'How am I getting from my radio interview to my television spot in twenty minutes?'

'They're doing them both at Wood Lane. They've sent through a list of quest—'

'Oh my love.' Edmund's voice is drenched with adoration and my heart leaps, my stomach flips over. Immediately I sit up straight, tilting myself slightly away from him, and swivel in my chair to face the woman who's come in. She wears a swirling silk skirt and a velvet jacket, and her honey hair falls around her face in gentle curls.

Edmund scrapes back his chair and makes a bee-line for his wife, and then he takes her in his arms and kisses her. No peck on the cheek for the Jetts; even their hello-and-goodbye kisses are full of dear-God-I-love-you-so-much passion.

I pretend to be absorbed in my computer screen. My mobile goes and I answer it. 'Nina Jones.'

'Doll! It's Pet.' Her voice is both high and vehement, like a fairy with a loudhailer. 'Listen, are you coming out tonight?'

'Hi, Pet.' I speak quietly, even though the Jetts are unlikely to notice anything but each other for some time. 'This is my work phone.'

'I know, but you never answer your own mobile. You're coming, right? Nothing too special, just basically drinks at mine and then we're going to Lola's.'

Lola's is the hottest nightclub in SW3, and only Pet could describe it as 'nothing too special'. I met Petronella Lennox-Ward about eight months ago when she was doing one of her sporadic PR jobs for a charity ball Edmund attended; we got talking near the punch bowl and quickly discovered a mutual love of Emilio Pucci clutch bags. I'd heard of her before, a glittering heiress and gem of the twenty-something London social scene, so I was quite excited to meet her. She was incredibly friendly. We exchanged numbers, and since then I've gone to more stylish nightclubs than I can count on both hands. It's like she's got the key to some magic kingdom that most mere mortals can only dream about, and once she's your friend, you get to tag along through the doors she's opened.

'I'm so sorry, Pet, I'd really love to, but I don't think I can,' I tell her. 'It's really busy right now. Tomorrow is—'

'Valentine's Day, I know, that's why we're going out tonight. It's officially the best night of the year because you get to avoid the sickly couples. Oh please come, you can meet up with us later if you want. Your evil boss can let you off just this once, can't he?'

'I don't think so.'

'What about tomorrow?'

'Tomorrow is even more busy.'

'*Try* to bunk off, will you? Ring me when you know. *Ciao!*'

Shaking my head, I put down the phone. Pet's father is a shipping magnate of staggering wealth, and Pet works every now and then when it suits her. This would be sort of annoying, but she is so much fun, and so generous and cool, that you can't hold it against her.

'Cinderella can't go to the ball?' Edmund has wandered over, hand in hand with his wife.

'Oh, it's nothing, just a friend wanting to go out tonight.'

'And you said no because of work?' Caroline frowns.

'Edmund, it's bad enough that you're spending Valentine's Day working; can't you let poor Nina out tonight to have some fun?'

'Of course, my love. Nina, consider yourself free from this moment. I'll see you bright and early tomorrow.'

'But . . . I've still got your emails to sort for you, and those questions, and I need to pick up the cards from the printers . . .'

'Jennifer will do it. Go, and have fun. My wife commands it.'

I'm undecided, until Edmund gives Caroline another kiss.

Despite Edmund's edict, I still get everything possible sorted before I leave. Then I go home, straighten my hair, redo my make-up, and spend forty-five minutes deliberating over the perfect outfit to wear to Lola's. By the time I've settled on a little black dress and the red Fendi platform slingbacks, it's late enough that I might as well go straight to the club. When I step out of the cab, there's a queue running a good way along the pavement, but I go right up to the bouncer. 'I'm here with Pet Lennox-Ward?' I say.

It's like magic. He nods and waves me through. Behind me I can feel the other clubbers' stares as they wonder what special powers I've got. Once, about three months ago, I had my photo in *Hot! Hot!* magazine because some editor mistook me for someone quasi-famous. Of course, I am not pathetic and didn't cut out the clipping to save in a little plastic folder. Well, I did, actually. But wouldn't most people?

When you step into Lola's, you're supposed to feel like you're stepping into someone's front room, if that front room happened to be full of breathtakingly gorgeous people and a DJ playing an ironic selection of samba and easy-listening hits. Flocked wallpaper lines the walls and chintz covers the seating, most of which is in the form of three-piece suites. I stand by the bar and survey the room for Pet and her crowd.

And then I hear it: the DJ is playing the Carpenters' 'Close to You', the one about birds suddenly appearing and stars falling from the sky, et cetera, et cetera. The one you can only stand to hear if you're hand in hand with your loved one, and if you don't happen to have a loved one, or worse, if your loved one happens to be married to someone else and only thinks of you as his personal assistant, it makes you want to vomit.

My good mood evaporates into the lowlights. Pet was wrong: this place is packed with couples. They're draped over the three-piece suites, smooching and whispering in each other's ears. They're clinging to each other on the dance floor, swaying to the song as if it were written just for them. They're drinking from each other's champagne glasses and playing footsie across all the exit routes.

It's Valentine's Day hell.

I spot Pet. She's at a strategically placed table between the bar and the dance floor, surrounded by people I sort of vaguely know, all of them, of course, beautiful and rich. She's wearing a pink sequinned dress and is perched between two incredibly tall men of fashionable boyishness. One has his hand on her bare knee, the other has his hand on her bare shoulder. I've never seen either of them before, but this isn't unusual: Pet changes her men as often as she changes her clothes. Even knowing that these two will be forgotten by next week doesn't help me, because tonight I am the only person in this entire room who is single. There was really no point me worrying about my outfit. I might as well have come here in a hemp sack and a pair of plastic flip-flops, because all anyone is going to notice is that I'm lacking the ultimate accessory – a boyfriend.

I need a drink to face this, so I immediately turn to the bartender and order a very large glass of Sauvignon Blanc. While I'm waiting, the music changes to an instrumental version of 'A Taste of Honey'. It's Edmund's favourite song. I know this because one time we were at a charity ball and the band started playing it, and Caroline wasn't around for a moment so Edmund asked me to dance with him. And I did. I remember spinning in his arms, floating on a cloud, everything much sweeter than wine.

'Large Sauvignon Blanc,' the bartender says. I reach for my purse but he shakes his head. 'Gentleman over there has got it.' He nods towards the end of the bar.

At the end of the bar a man is sitting alone. He's dark-haired and muscular and tanned, and when I look over he holds my gaze and smiles.

Oh, great. The only single man in the club tonight has seen the only single woman and decided he's in with a chance. I nod and smile a thank-you and hotfoot it over to Pet's table before he decides to press his advantage.

'Nina!' Pet jumps up from her two men and stands on tiptoe to air-kiss me on both cheeks. She is about five foot tall in heels, and exquisitely girlie in every way, perfectly groomed from the top of her glossy chestnut head to the toes of her Louboutin boots. Next to her, I'm tall and too gawky for words. It reminds me of school, where I was always looking over the heads of my classmates, and stuck out like a sore thumb in photos. 'You got out of work!' Pet cries. 'Nina, this is everyone, everyone, this is Nina. Sit down, honey, tell me all about it!'

I look around the table. Every chair is being taken up by a couple. 'I'll just get—'

'Julian, Rupert, be sweethearts and go get Nina a chair, will you, and could you get me another mojito? Thanks!' The two model types get up and Pet pulls me down on to one of their abandoned chairs. 'You look gorgeous, love the shoes, what's wrong with your drink?'

'There's nothing wrong with it, why?'

'You look like you've just swallowed a pint of vinegar.' She sips prettily from my glass and shrugs. 'You're right, it's fine. It's the music, isn't it?'

'Mostly it's the couples.' I take my glass back and gulp as much as I can in one mouthful.

'Oh, I'm sorry, doll. I thought the lovey-doveys would be saving it till tomorrow. Chin up. Half of them will be split up by the weekend and they can join us in triumphant singledom.'

'You're not exactly a bitter old spinster yourself.'

'Oh, Julian and Rupert? They just showed up and it seemed rude to send them away. Hey, I've got an idea, do you want to borrow Rupert? Or Julian?'

I glance around for Pet's men. One is patiently hunting down a chair, and the other is patiently waiting at the bar for Pet's drink. 'I think they're both quite keen on you, Pet.'

'I'm happy to give one of them up for the evening for a good cause.'

'That's really nice of you, but I think I'll be okay.'

Pet rummages in her handbag for some lipstick and a mirror. 'Please don't tell me you're in love,' she says.

'What makes you think that?'

'Basically the drinking.'

I look at my glass. It's empty. How'd that happen?

'It's nothing, Pet. Just . . . just a crush.'

It isn't a crush. Even the first time I met Edmund, at our initial interview in the dining room of Jett, I felt something I'd never felt before. A shock, a pull, an attraction so powerful that I didn't even notice the individual aspects of his appearance, his hair or his eyes or his lithe, strong body. It was just *him*, and suddenly my world rearranged itself like metal filings around a magnet.

Pet purses her lips in the mirror. 'What do you mean, a crush?'

'I mean I fancy someone I can't have. You know.'

'Why can't you have him? You're gorgeous, single, fancy-free and I bet you're a firecracker in bed.'

'It's not as simple as that.'

'Of course it is. Unless he's married or something?'

I borrow her compact and check my own make-up, avoiding her eyes. 'You don't think I'd be so stupid as to fall for a married man, do you?'

'People do it, or so Mummy tells me on a daily basis. Tell me it's not that slave-driver you work for, is it?'

'Edmund's not a slave-driver. He's incredibly hard-working and he quite rightly expects the same devotion from his staff.' For a brief, crazy moment I consider confiding in Pet, but I dismiss that as soon as I've thought of it. Pet never had a hopeless crush in her life, and certainly never on her boss. 'Anyway, he's happily married.'

'No such thing.'

'Really, Pet, he is. The two of them are like newly-weds. A couple of weeks ago, for example? We were at Jett and his wife rang to say she was in bed with the flu. Edmund went straight down to the kitchen and stopped everyone in the middle of what they were doing and said, "I need chicken soup for Caro." And that whole kitchen staff, they're like a well-oiled machine, bent their entire concentration on making the most perfect bowl of chicken soup for Caroline, and Edmund got right in a cab and brought it to her.'

I have to stop, because there's a lump in my throat. It is just sodding rotten luck not only that I'm in love with a happily married man, but that I'm even more in love with him *because* he's happily married.

I cover it up by rubbing at an imaginary smudge on my cheek.

Pet snorts prettily in disgust. 'If that's happily married, I'll stay the bitter old spinster. Anyway, Nina, it doesn't matter who you have the crush on, there's no point mooning about. If you want a man, you get a man. It's that simple.'

'I'm sure it's that simple for *you*, Pet.'

'Do you really think we're that different?'

She frowns, furrowing her shaped eyebrows together, and I wonder if she can seriously be thinking that we're in any way the same. She's effortlessly cool, infinitely chic, rich and sexy and dedicated to fun, pulling people to her like moths fluttering around fairy lights. And I'm definitely one of the moths.

'Here you are, Pet.' Either Julian or Rupert stands in front of us, bearing a mojito. The other one appears behind him, carrying a chair.

'Oh, thank you,' she sparkles, and then she looks significantly between me and the mojito-bearer. 'Rupert, I want you to meet Nina. I think you two would like each other.'

'Hi, Rupert, nice to meet you, excuse me, I think I need another drink!' I jump out of the chair and head back for the bar. It's only when I'm already there that I realise that in my haste to escape borrowing one of Pet's boyfriends, I've forgotten that I ran away from the bar a few minutes ago to escape the single man. Fortunately, the bar is now occupied purely by canoodling couples being sickening. I order another large glass of wine and sneak off with it to a corner of the club. I find a chintz-covered armchair that doesn't have a happy romantic pair draped over it and slink down into it, out of sight and mind of everyone, to drink my drink.

I never wanted to be in love with Edmund Jett. My life would be so much easier if I weren't. I could concentrate on enjoying my job and having fun going out and shopping and doing all the things that a young woman in the city is supposed to have fun doing. But I can't help it. It's his power, his genius, his perfect good looks, his devotion to his wife and his career, his success. I've spent so many hours fantasising about what could have happened if I'd met him before Caroline did, if he were single and free to be mine. In the end, though, it's hopeless. Tomorrow is Valentine's Day, the day for lovers, and the man I love will only need me near him to manage his schedule.

I down my glass of wine. This place isn't so great to sit in after all; it seems to be the snogging corner. There are lips flapping all over the place. I can even hear kissing sounds above the soppy Barry Manilow tune that's playing. I put down my empty glass and get up, deciding to wish Pet a good night and go home and get some sleep before my busy day tomorrow.

Except I can't. I try to take a step forward, but my right foot is stuck.

I look down. My shoes fasten at the ankles with fabulous little golden buckles, and one of these seems to have got wound around with some threads from the chintz chair cover. I kneel, as far as I can with my ankle attached to the bottom of the chair, and tug at it. It's stuck fast.

'Oh, bollocks,' I say and sit back down. I bend forward, hanging my head between my bare knees, and try to untangle myself. The thing is, the light in Lola's isn't that great anyway, and in the snogging corner it's even more shadowy, plus my head is blocking what little light there is coming from the dance floor, so I basically can't see a thing. I try for several minutes to free my shoe, feeling my way around the buckle and the tiny threads, while the blood rushes and pools in my head. I probably look like I'm being sick, or trying to perform oral sex on myself.

I pull. I'm just as stuck as before, if not more so. I sit up and look around, but everyone seems too involved in lip-locking to notice my posture. I could ring Pet and get her to come over here and help me. I could slip off my shoe and walk to the bar through the fantastically well-dressed crowd with one shoe on, to borrow some scissors to cut the threads. Neither of these choices is particularly dignified. I bend down again and try to unwind myself.

'Please allow me to help.'

The voice is male and strongly accented. I sit up rapidly enough to toss my hair into my eyes. When I've shaken it out of the way, I see it's the dark-haired single man from the bar.

'I don't—'

'It is no difficulty.' He kneels in front of me and takes my foot in his hands. He's wearing a snug T-shirt that shows off the breadth of his shoulders, and his fingers are very warm.

'Really, I'm fine, I don't need any help,' I say to his back, which is all I can see.

'You have made an unfortunate entanglement, *si*?' I feel his hands working gently, and then I'm free. He puts my foot carefully down on the floor and smiles up at me. His teeth are white and dazzling in his tanned face.

'I'm . . . thank you.' I stand up, and he stands too.

'Would you like another drink?'

'I was just going home, actually. I have to be up early tomorrow.'

'Let me call a cab for you.'

'No, really, honestly, thanks for the rescue and everything, but I don't need a knight in shining armour.'

'Are you sure you do not?' His smile widens. He's actually quite good-looking, not the type you'd think hung around nightclubs being single.

'Good night,' I say, and make for the door.

'Wait!' He catches my wrist. 'You are beautiful. What is your name?'

'Nina Jones.'

Slowly he kisses the back of my hand. 'It is an honour to be your knight, Nina Jones.'

Then he drops my hand, and with a small bow he disappears into the crowd.

Early the next morning, Valentine's Day, I make myself the strongest coffee I can stomach and put two slices of artisan multigrain bread in the toaster. I check Edmund's schedule on my laptop so I'm ready to hit the ground running. There's an item highlighted in yellow as a reminder to me. My eyes still scanning the schedule, I reach for my mobile and autodial my father.

'Hello,' he answers, from the sound of it with his mouth full of breakfast.

'Morning, Dad.'

'Oh, Nina.' I hear some crunching and then he swallows. 'How nice to hear from you, dear. I was going to ring you a bit later on.'

'It's going to be really busy today. How's Imogen?' I ask even though I don't expect her to have changed much from the last time I talked with my father, two days ago.

'Well, she's still asleep. She'll be up in time for lunch, I imagine. She makes us the oddest sandwiches, things like peanut butter and pineapple, but quite delicious. Not sure how she thinks them up. You should suggest them to that chef bloke of yours.'

I strongly suspect that my younger sister belongs to the culinary school of what-to-make-to-satisfy-the-spliffmunchies. Then again, since the age of six, her favourite food has been pizza dunked in cold tea, so I should maybe give her the benefit of the doubt.

'Has she done any university applications yet?'

'Oh, not sure precisely; she's only just got her A-level results.'

'Six months ago, Dad.'

'Was it that long ago? How time does fly, as they say.' I hear him taking another mouthful of cereal. I hold the phone slightly away from my ear to muffle the chewing.

'Anyway, Dad, I was looking at the calendar and wanted to remind you that you have a dentist's appointment tomorrow at quarter past three.'

'Do I? Well that's nice to know.'

'I also noticed Maria's wedding a week on Saturday.' Maria is exactly my age, and used to live three houses down from us and be in my form at school, before we had to move to Holybrook. She's a barrister now, and she's marrying a partner in a management consultancy.

'Oh! Can you make it after all?'

'No, we've got a trade show,' I explain for about the thirty millionth time. 'I just wanted to know, have you got her a gift yet?'

'Well no, but surely there's time to—'

'You'll forget if you leave it till the last minute. Remember what happened at George's christening?'

'Yes, of course. Well I'm not precisely sure why we've been invited to the wedding in the first place; it's been so long now since we were neighbours, it's a whole different world.'

'That's why it's so important to get the gift right, Dad. Does she have a wedding list?'

'A list?' I hear a sound of shuffling paper. 'I think

there was something with the invitation. But that might have been directions to the church.'

'Can you check?'

More shuffling paper. While I'm waiting, I spread organic butter on my toast and pop it on a plate. I sit on a chair and curl my feet up beneath me. Polished floorboards are lovely and glossy and easy to keep clean, but cold on the feet in the morning.

'I must have thrown it away,' he says.

Since my father can't see me, I roll my eyes. At times like this it is almost impossible to believe that he was, once upon a time, a senior account manager for a large petroleum company. Sometimes I can't even figure out how he copes with his present job selling wall-to-wall carpeting.

'It's no problem, though,' he's saying. 'I'll pop into Debenhams in my lunch hour and get them a cheese grater or something. Your mother and I were given a cheese grater for our wedding; apparently it was very useful.'

Hmm, and look how well *that* turned out. 'Listen, Dad, don't worry about it. I'll get a gift and bring it round when I visit on Sunday. Okay?'

'That's very kind of you, but you don't need to. A cheese grater should be fine.'

'No, it's sorted. Really.' I check my watch; five more minutes before I need to get going.

'It's very busy around here, come to think of it,' my father says. 'That wedding, and then the week after, Arval's coming to visit. He's going off to America again.'

'Oh?' I try not to crunch my toast too loudly.

'Yes, he's bat-hunting in Colorado.'

My uncle Arval doesn't literally hunt bats. He stalks them. Or spots them. Whatever the term is for someone who hangs around in damp caves or wherever in the hope of catching rabies. He's my father's last surviving relative and yet more proof that the Jones men are prone to going off the rails in their middle age. Arval used to run one of the largest chartered accountancy firms in Wales. Then, twelve years ago, when his wife Claire died, he developed a sudden mania for bats. He cashed in his life savings and went jetting all over the world looking for rare species.

It shows you what my family has become, that no one except for me thinks this is weird.

'Arval would love to see you, dear,' my father says. 'Why don't you come up here for dinner?'

Hmm, how tempting. Imogen's odd food combinations and sulking, my father's execrable tea, and Arval's incessant talk about flying rodents. The last time I saw him he attempted to involve me in a conversation about guano. At first I thought it was some exotic fruit he'd encountered on his travels, but it turned out it's bat poop.

'I'll put it in my diary. Got to go now, Dad. Give Immy my love.'

'Oh I will, dear, thank you. Oh, and happy . . . it's some holiday today, isn't it? On the news this morning.'

'It's Valentine's Day.'

'Of course it is. Well I hope you have a very romantic time.'

I hide my empty Frappuccino cup in a bin down the street from Jett before I report to work. Caroline is in her armchair in Edmund's office on the top floor, reading the newspaper. She looks up at me when I come in, and smiles. Her pretty green eyes light up. Sometimes – quite often, to tell the truth – I envy Caroline, but I can't help but like her, especially when she smiles so warmly and easily. And how can you begrudge true love, anyway?

'You look so lovely today,' she tells me. 'That's a beautiful dress.'

'Oh, this old thing?' I run my hand over my pink Jackie O dress, bought three weeks ago especially in preparation for Valentine's Day. 'I picked it up in a sale somewhere.'

'You're always so well turned out.'

'No, *you* are, Caroline.' Caroline has a style of her own, a genuine soft, feminine beauty. Me, I've got some good assets – I'm tall, I'm blonde, my skin isn't bad – but I have to work hard to make the most of them. I've been up since six, cleansing and polishing and making up.

'What's in the bag?' she asks.

'Oh, I stopped into Harvey Nicks for a vase. A friend of the family is getting married.' I put it carefully in a corner. It gave my credit card a little bit of a workout and I don't want to see it smashed.

'Coffee?'

'No thanks, I'm already on caffeine overload.' I leaf through the papers on Edmund's desk to find the list of questions the BBC sent over. My phone beeps, and I check the text message. It's from Pet: *All u need is a gd shag 2 forget all about crush. Let me no if u want rupert 4 vd. Pxx*

I have to smile at that. 'Thanks for making Edmund let me go out last night,' I say to Caroline.

'Oh, my husband never does anything he doesn't want to, believe me.' She goes back to the news.

Caroline spends quite a bit of time in the office, which I think is very sweet. She likes to be there to support Edmund, and they like to snatch every moment of time together that they can. Usually she can be found curled up with a book or the newspaper in her armchair, which has its own special corner of the room. I'm used to working with her nearby, and fortunately she's easy to be with and doesn't demand attention when she knows I'm busy.

'Now that's what I like to see in the morning: two beautiful women at my beck and call.'

Edmund comes in, wearing a tailored suit and bearing a bouquet of at least two dozen roses. Each one of them is a furled crimson heart. 'Oh, they're gorgeous. Lucky you, Caroline,' I exclaim.

'Caroline's had her roses; these are for you.' Edmund hands them to me. They're heavier than they look.

'You shouldn't have.' I inhale their scent and try not to look at him.

'I didn't. They were delivered just this minute. This was attached.'

I take the card and open it. *For the beautiful Nina Jones, with respectful admiration. Your knight in shining armour, Juan Esperanza.*

I must look as astonished as I feel, because Caroline asks, 'Who are they from?' I hand her the card, and she reads it, raising her eyebrows, before passing it to Edmund.

'Juan Esperanza?' he says. 'He's not trying to poach you, is he?'

'You know him?' I ask in surprise.

'He's head chef at Asparagus. Remember his tapas, Caro?'

'Mmm,' she says. 'Very good looking, isn't he?'

'Rumour has it he's looking to start up his own restaurant. How do you know him?'

'I ran into him last night at a club, by accident. He saved me from an armchair.'

His brow furrows in mock concern. 'I'm not sure I want you being wooed by good-looking Spaniards.'

'Don't worry, I'm not planning on being wooed.'

'Good.' Edmund playfully kisses Caroline on the forehead, then takes her hand. 'You've had your fun, Nina Jones, but now it's Valentine's Day, and Valentine's Day belongs to me.'

'Believe me,' I say, 'I know.'

3

On Friday, a dozen pink roses turn up on my desk, with a card bearing Juan's mobile number.

Edmund doesn't even see the roses; he's out for a long lunch with his truffle supplier and won't be back for another half an hour. Just in case, I hide them under my desk. I'm not going to ring Juan. I don't have time, and no matter what Pet says, a mere shag isn't going to erase my feelings for Edmund. Lovers may come and go, marriages may end. Most of them do. But I have to believe in happy marriages, everlasting love, or else I'd go mad.

I did actually try to forget Edmund once, by getting off with someone else. His name was Ben and I met him at a dinner party given by some university friends in Notting Hill. He was some sort of a film-maker, I think, though I had enough red wine so that I'm not really sure now. I do remember the next morning, though, when I woke up, mouth tasting of sour grapes, and turned over to see a head of tousled golden hair on the pillow next to mine.

'Edmund?' I murmured sleepily, and then Ben turned over. 'Who's Edmund?' he asked.

I was so appalled that I jumped out of bed, pulled on my clothes and ran downstairs to the street to get a cab with my shoes in my hand. I see Ben sometimes, from a distance, or someone I think might be him, and have to scurry for cover before he can see me and I have to recall the whole sordid episode.

The worst thing about it wasn't saying the wrong name, or being such a pathetic wuss the next morning. The worst thing was the creeping sense of shame, as if I'd cheated on Edmund. Betrayed my true love for a bottle of wine and a one-night stand.

I can't throw away my roses from Juan, though, even though I don't want Edmund to see them. They're beautiful. And it feels good to have someone noticing me for *me*, not my organisational capabilities.

Right. I give up on my spreadsheets, gather up my roses and sneak down the narrow stairs in the back and out the door, where I hail a cab. I ask the driver to wait at my door, run the roses upstairs to my flat, safely out of sight, and then nip back down. All the way from Kensington to the King's Road I debate with myself, but when we pass the third Starbucks I know I'm too weak and tell the driver to stop. After I get out, I look both ways down the street to check the coast is clear before I nip through the door into the coffee-scented, light-jazz-playing café.

It's wrong to have a Frappuccino habit when you work for Edmund Jett. Last year Edmund found half a cup of McDonald's coffee in the staff room, and he called all of his employees together to watch as he poured the contents down the toilet, and then doused the cup with cleaning fluid before setting it ablaze with his chef's blowtorch. He then delivered a twenty-minute lecture on the soullessness of fast food and beverages.

And I agree with him, I totally do. My food shopping and eating habits have revolutionised themselves since I got this job. But there's something about the shocking cold and the sweetness, the caffeine and the chocolate, and mostly the little lift it gives me when I feel like I'm treating myself. Edmund won't even notice I'm gone – when he's talking truffles, he can lose track of time. And I already feel guilty about the roses and the remembered one-night stand.

I pick up my Frappuccino under the red lights. The only free table is near the window, so I take it and scroll through my BlackBerry to make sure I'll have everything in hand for when Edmund comes back from lunch. I'm just ticking items off my to-do list, slurping happily at my frozen mocha, when I glance up and I see him.

He's wearing his brown suit, collar open at the throat, and he's stopped on the pavement and is staring at me. I stare back, open-mouthed, open-eyed, frozen stiffer than my Frappuccino. He pushes open the door.

Shit. I shove my drink to the side, but there's no point hiding it; he's already seen it. I jump to my feet. 'Hiya,' I say, feigning nonchalance.

'Nina Jones,' Edmund says, 'are you ruining your palate with a mass-produced coffee-flavour beverage?'

He's tall and godlike and the faint musky odour of truffles clings to him. They smell like pigs in heat, apparently. On Edmund they smell of sex and power.

'Um. Well, yes.'

There is a long moment when I can hardly breathe and my heart thuds so loudly I swear he can hear it.

Then he smiles, and my world is all right. He pulls out the chair opposite me and sits down.

'You should see how guilty you look,' he says. 'Am I really that much of a tyrant?'

'Um. No, of course not. I mean, I know you don't approve of fast food and chain restaurants and all that, and I agree with you. But I just like Frappuccinos.'

'Hmm.' He taps his fingers together. 'It makes me wonder what other little secrets you might have.'

'None,' I say quickly.

He watches me. I fumble with my BlackBerry. 'Anyway I was looking at the meeting schedule for next week, and—'

'You should have an affair.'

'Uh. What?'

'You should have an affair,' he says. 'You work too hard. Caro agrees.'

'I don't have time for an affair,' I say as briskly as I can manage. Which isn't particularly briskly, because my voice is shaking.

'No, you're too busy sneaking off to Starbucks during work hours.' His eyes crinkle and he holds out a hand. 'Give us a taste, let's find out what's so great.'

I give him my Frappuccino. He sips it, through the straw where a moment ago my lips have been, and grimaces.

'I like it,' I say, and I stand up. 'I was on my way back to Jett anyway.'

Edmund stands up too. 'Don't forget your drink,' he says, and he reaches for it the same time that I do, and his hand closes over mine. Our eyes meet.

'Are you happy with me, Nina?' he asks me, in a low voice.

His eyes are bright blue and so many times I've imagined drowning myself in them. The customers, the baristas, the light jazz music all vanish, I catch my breath, and at that moment I know that my emotions are stark on my face for him to read as he will.

'Yes,' I whisper.

I see him see it. I see him understand. His fingers tighten on mine. I tilt back my head, without meaning to, as if to present my lips to him, and if I didn't know better I'd think that he's beginning to lean towards me, into a kiss.

I should blink. I should look away. I can't. This is the moment when in a film, the hero and heroine would be shown close up on the screen, their eyes full of awakened passion and the knowledge that whatever happens because of it, the tragedy or the happily-ever-after, this one moment has been perfect.

He looks down, and he takes his hand from mine. My face burns.

'Sorry,' he says.

'Sorry.' As if I'm talking about the accidental brushing of hands.

On the way back to the restaurant, we talk about truffles.

On a Sunday afternoon, Lola's is nearly deserted. Coming in from the watery February sunlight, it's more apparent that there are no windows. The only light comes from the tasselled lamps; it shines on the chintzy sofas, which are duller by day. The flowers don't quite hide the occasional red wine stain. The air smells of lemon cleanser and alcohol.

Juan Esperanza is waiting at a table in the corner, flanked by flowery armchairs. A silver wine bucket sits beside him and two glasses are on the table. He stands up when I approach, puts a hand lightly on my elbow, and brushes a kiss on each of my cheeks. His stubble rasps against my skin.

'Thank you for the flowers,' I say.

'I am very glad you called me.' He lingers with his hand on my elbow; my practised eye tells me he's about two inches shorter than I am.

I sit in an armchair. 'Why did you want to come here?'

'Because this is where we met. I like to observe such things.'

'It's not because you're hoping I'll get stuck to a chair, is it?'

'It is because I wanted to see you again.' He pours the wine and then lifts his glass in a toast. I don't usually drink in the afternoon, but it's my day off and I'm a little bit nervous, so I touch my glass to his and take a sip. It's delicious, but then chefs do tend to know their wines.

'How are things at Asparagus?' I ask him.

'Very good. So you do know me after all.'

'Edmund thinks you're going to open a restaurant of your own. He thinks you're trying to headhunt me.'

'*Muy interesante*. Does this mean you're not happy with Jett?'

'I'm very happy with Edmund Jett.' I take a glug of wine to prove it. Juan pours me some more. Cannily, he has worn a white shirt to contrast with his dark skin, and he has rolled the sleeves up to his elbows. Chefs have muscular forearms, and they know it. His are covered with black hair.

'So are you planning on opening your own place?' I ask.

'I have my eyes on some premises in Spain. But I have no plans. I am not headhunting you. I merely wished to see you again.'

'Why?'

'I think you are an intriguing woman. They say that you don't have any boyfriends. I wonder why?'

'You've been checking up on me?'

'I am curious.'

'If you've been checking up on me, you should know that I don't have time to date.'

'Or, perhaps, the inclination.'

The wine has made its way to my knees. 'I don't see the point of dating random men, to tell you the truth.

Seems to me that if you're going to fall in love with someone, you'll know it more or less straight away.'

'Ah, so you believe in love at first sight, like *Romeo y Julieta*.' He pronounces the 'J' as an 'H', the Spanish way. 'You are a true romantic.'

'*Romeo and Juliet* isn't a romantic story at all. They never get to be together and they both commit suicide.'

'They would do anything for love. As would I.' He pours us more wine and waits to clink his glass with mine again, but I'm not interested.

'Killing yourself is just stupid,' I say. 'That's not love, that's cowardice. Look at all the people they left behind who loved them, like their families, for example, who had to suffer and think about how it was their fault. I have no idea what Shakespeare was thinking with that story.'

Juan has put his glass down and is waiting for me to finish my rant. 'So what stories do you think are romantic?'

'Oh, you know, the ones where the heroine and hero fall brilliantly in love and get to be together for ever.'

'You like a happy-always-after ending.'

'Happy-*ever*-after. Yes. Life's too short and too busy to read things that are going to make you depressed.'

'So you are only interested in falling in love at first sight and living for ever in love.'

I shrug. 'Something like that.'

'I will have my work ahead of me then.'

I drink my wine, because there's really nothing to say to a comment like that.

'Where are you from in Spain, anyway?'

'I was born on the Costa Blanca, the fifth of six sons. Every one of them but me is a farmer. London is a great city but I miss the earth and the sun on the olive trees. Here I cannot taste the sky in the rain.'

'Very poetic.'

'It is the truth. I am a Spaniard. You, on the other hand, are an English rose. You did not grow up in London, no?'

'I grew up in Berkshire. You can't really taste the sky in the rain in Berkshire. It's just rain.'

'It is never just rain.' His Spanish accent is becoming more pronounced the more wine we drink. 'Where is it that you love best?'

'Here,' I say firmly. 'I love Chelsea. I love London. It's the centre of everything.'

'Ah. I see.'

'Why did you come to London if you miss Spain so much?'

'Because it is the centre, as you say. But really, I came here to forget.' He smiles, his teeth very white, his expression a little bit sad.

'And have you forgotten?' I swirl the wine in my glass, catching the golden glints from it and realising that I'm flirting.

'At this moment, yes I have. And you?'

'What makes you think I have something to forget?'

'I saw it in you from the first time we met.' He brushes his thumb across the back of my hand, the same place where he kissed it a few days ago. The same place Edmund touched me, right before I showed him that I loved him.

'I think we can help each other,' says Juan.

There are some things you just never forget. For example, with me one of the things is fifty-pence coins. They have a metallic smell, the scent equivalent of biting on aluminium foil. These days they're smaller, but when I was a teenager they were thick and heavy. When you have lots of them together in a bag, they clunk and weigh down your arm. It was one of my jobs, after our mother left us and we moved to Holybrook, to collect fifty pences and hoard them to feed, one by one, into the electricity meter.

I had to hide them from my sister Immy. She was too young to understand the concept of running out of electricity and would want to spend the money on sweets. Sometimes we didn't have any fifty-pence coins and I'd have to scavenge around the house for pennies and ten- and twenty-pence pieces, looking in pockets and behind couch cushions, so I could take them to the corner shop. I would walk past all the colourful packets on the shelves, straight to the till to ask the woman behind it to change the tuppences for fifty pences. I could hear the meter ticking down in my imagination, hungry for money, and I would bounce up and down impatiently in my plimsolls waiting for the woman to count out the coins. I couldn't stand the idea of the bungalow going dark.

The most expensive pair of shoes I've ever bought was a pair of Manolo Blahniks in New York, when I was over there with Edmund last year. Even with the pound stronger than the dollar, they were eyewateringly expensive. My credit card, as I handed it over, was slim and light, and though I was thousands of miles and many years away, I thought *that would be a heavy bag of fifty pences*.

The week after I meet up with Juan, Edmund and Caroline have one of their dinner parties. This is held in the gorgeous newly decorated dining room of their gorgeous Chelsea home, a stone's throw from Jett. Although it's largely a social occasion, I'm here because two of the other guests are a Channel Four television executive and a documentary producer. There's been quite a bit of talk about doing a fly-on-the-wall series about the realities of running a phenomenally successful restaurant empire. Mostly this is a pretty informal discussion, bandying ideas around, but every time the topic comes up I can see in Edmund's eyes how keen he is on the project. He's been on TV before, of course, but that was a studio show tied in with his third cookbook, *Jett Sett Menus*. This programme will be more in-depth, more far-reaching, more reflective of his true abilities.

After the main course, I slip out with Caroline to help her carry the dishes and plate up the dessert. The Jetts' kitchen is large and impressive, all stainless steel and glass, almost like a laboratory, which is fitting, really, as this is where Edmund comes up with many of his creations.

Caroline, in her velvet dress, stacks the plates in the dishwasher. 'Did you like dinner?' she asks me.

'It was incredible. I can't believe Edmund got

everything into perfect cubes like that. Even prawns! They were prawns, weren't they?'

'I'm not sure.'

'It tasted amazing, anyway. I don't know how he does it. I can just about manage shepherd's pie.'

'I wouldn't mind a good shepherd's pie now and then,' Caroline says, and she laughs. 'Anyway, you should be able to handle the dessert fine. Edmund's given me extensive training. Would you get the trays out of the freezer?'

I open the enormous freezer and take out two aluminium trays, one lined with green cubes and one with pink. 'Are they ice cream?'

'Knickerbocker glory. In cubes.' She lays out frosted glass plates and hands me a spatula. 'Just put one of each colour on each plate, with two centimetres between them.'

'Okay.' This takes some concentration, so we don't speak for a moment. Caroline has found two plastic bottles and as I hand her each plate, she squeezes out precise lines of yellow and red around the cubes.

'Edmund's very excited about the show,' I say when I've got the hang of it enough to trust myself to talk.

'Hmm.' Her pretty mouth twists and her lips thin. 'I'm not so keen on him doing more television, to tell you the truth.'

'Why not? He's been hanging back waiting for the right project. And he's a natural on TV, with his charm and—' I remember the moment in Starbucks, a few days ago, and my cheeks flush. 'He'll be very good.'

'Yes, he'll be great. It's the time I'm worried about. He's spreading himself too thin as it is. Don't you think?'

Her green eyes meet mine and my blush gets deeper. 'I . . . I wouldn't know. I mean, he certainly works very hard, but that's what it's like.'

'Yes. It is.' She sighs and squeezes the last bit of sauce on to the last plate. 'There, perfect. Thank you. Any more flowers from your admirer? The charming Spanish chef?'

'Roses,' I admit. 'He says I'm an English rose.' He's started sending them to my flat now, though. I've run out of vases. My flat smells like heaven.

'Very nice. And have you seen much of him?'

'We've had a drink. It's only a bit of fun, though, Caroline.'

'You might think that, but chefs are very serious. Every little detail means something.'

I put on water for filter coffee and wonder if this is true. I can definitely see it with Edmund, but Juan's statements about romance and tasting the rain seem a little bit too much like a heart-shaped box of chocolates. But maybe that's his passionate Spanish nature. There's certainly nothing wrong with hearts and flowers.

'It's nice to be pursued,' I say. 'He's very handsome, and very flattering. He reminds me of Edmund that way, how he's always giving you compliments and sending you little gifts.'

Caroline lines up the dessert plates on a tray. 'Could you please get down some glasses for dessert wine?'

'Should I get one for you too?' Caroline never drinks during Edmund's dinner parties even though the wine is flowing; she says Edmund can do this sort of thing in his sleep, but she can't, so she wants to be fully compos mentis. I think it would be more fun if she relaxed a bit more. Sometimes the talk can get bogged down in business, and when Caroline's had a few she's an absolutely wicked storyteller, especially about some of the hilarious things that happened to her before Edmund's career took off, when she worked as a trader, surrounded by men in a men's world. She's so sweet and feminine now that it's hard to believe she was once this tough-as-nails force in the City.

'No thanks,' she says, and pauses while she's adjusting a last plate. 'Actually, Nina, there's something I should tell you.'

I freeze, my fingers around the stem of a glass. Has Edmund told her about my feelings for him? They share everything, I know they do. I can't imagine Caroline yelling at me, warning me off her man. In her place I would defend Edmund tooth and nail, but she's not that type of person. She will probably tell me she understands. She will probably be kind.

Kindness will be worse.

'What's that, Caroline?' I force out.

'I'm not drinking because I'm trying to get pregnant.'

I put down the hand-blown glass. 'Oh.'

'You seem very surprised.' Her lips turn up in half a smile.

'No, I'm . . . well, yes, I am a bit. You both seem so focused on Edmund's career, I just never thought . . . but it makes sense. I mean, of course you want a baby.' I shake my head and put on my brightest smile. 'You two will be brilliant parents. I can't imagine a better family to be born into, lucky baby.'

'You're so sweet, Nina.' She comes over to me and gives me a fragrant hug, and kisses me on the cheek. I keep my smile on my face, though my sinking stomach tells me I don't deserve her compliment or her kiss.

'I'm wildly jealous.'

'Of the baby, or of us for having it?'

'Both, a bit.'

'Poor Nina, you didn't have the happiest of families, did you? How are your father and your sister?'

I never talk about my family, but it's typical Caroline to notice and remember that I visit my father often and never speak of my mother. This makes me feel even guiltier. 'They're well, thanks.'

'Good. Listen, Nina, this isn't common knowledge yet, that we're trying for a baby. It will obviously affect a lot of things, so we're keeping it to ourselves for now. And of course it may never happen.'

'It will,' I say. And I know it will. Edmund and Caroline's marriage is so perfect that it couldn't possibly go wrong in any way. 'This time next year you'll be changing nappies and wondering why on earth you wanted the thing.'

She laughs. 'Quite possibly. Or watching Edmund on television and wondering why on earth I wanted anything else. Come on, let's bring this through.'

When we come back into the dining room, Edmund and Doris the producer are deep into brainstorming ideas about show formats. As I give Edmund his dessert, I catch his eye for a split second, and I can't help smiling to let him know I know his secret. He returns my smile with a private one just for me.

My own knickerbocker glory sits on my plate, a cubist sweetness I couldn't possibly swallow.

Something needs to change.

'I'm going to fall in love with Juan,' I announce to Pet.

We're in adjacent changing rooms in a boutique she knows. I've read a magazine article recently that said that every woman should own a perfect pair of black trousers, so I have several pairs to try on. Though I'm also trying on three skirts and a jacket, because I got a little distracted. Edmund Jett pays me well for my services, but I rarely seem to have much left over at the end of the month, probably because I can never resist temptation. But it's good to boost the local economy, right?

'Why are you going to fall in love with Juan?' she asks.

'Why not?'

'I can think of several answers to that, but I'm more interested in your reasons first. Damn, this white thing is too big.'

'He's very good looking, for one.'

'That's no reason. There are millions of good-looking men out there; if we fell in love with all of them, we'd be exhausted.' I hear her poking her head outside the changing room to speak to the assistant hovering nearby. 'Can I have this in a six?'

'He's also incredibly romantic,' I say. The current trousers are too short, so I take them off and try another pair. 'I've never had so many flowers. He's started writing poetry on the cards.'

'Please say it's not his own.'

'It's by someone called Pablo Neruda.'

'Well, that's not so bad. Though I don't quite understand why they do that; it's like they copy something out of a book and they expect you to swoon all over the place? And the ones who write their own are even worse. They expect you to spend hours appreciating how deep they are, which is basically a free ticket to acting moody, as far as I can tell.'

'I thought it was nice.'

'What's he like in bed?'

'I don't know.'

'God, you mean you were too drunk to notice?'

'I mean I haven't slept with him.'

Pet comes round to my booth and opens my curtain. She is wearing her skirt but only a bra on top, and she stares at me with an incredulous gaze.

'You haven't slept with him? Why ever not?'

'Well, I've only met up with him the twice.'

'That's one more time than it takes. Is he gay?'

'No.'

'Are you sure? The poetry sounds suspicious to me.'

'It's . . . not like that. It's just the way he is. He's much more about love and happily-ever-afters than jumping into bed.'

'Have you even kissed him?'

'He kissed my hand.'

Pet's eyes are wide. 'Dear Lord.'

'It's old fashioned. And romantic.'

'It's an act. There's no such thing.'

'There is, Pet. Juan is perfect for me. He's sweet, and considerate. And talented, and successful, and good looking, and he has the sexiest Spanish accent.'

'Sounds like you're trying to convince yourself.'

I put down the trousers and sit on the little padded stool in my knickers. 'Pet,' I say, 'I'm sick of being single. I'm sick of not having anyone special of my own.'

'I keep telling you, you could have several special someones if you spent less time at work and more time in bed.'

'I want more than sex. Look at Ed— Look at Caroline and Edmund, for example. They're always together, they share a dream, they're both beautiful and generous, and when they look at each other, you can just see love in their eyes. They'd do anything for each other. And now . . . and some day they're going to have these gorgeous children and they'll just—'

I have a lump in my throat.

'So you think that this fella could be this for you? A soulmate or whatever?'

'I'll never know if I don't try, right?'

'Hmm.' She pushes her hair, which she's had highlighted, behind her ear. 'I still think it's one of the strangest things I've ever heard, deciding you're going to fall in love with someone you haven't even tried out yet. What if he's horrible in bed? Then you're stuck.'

'Miss Lennox-Ward?' says the assistant's voice from outside. 'I've got the size six.'

'Brilliant.' She sweeps out of my cubicle and I hear her going into hers. I get up and try on the third pair of black trousers.

'What did you say his name was?' Pet calls. 'José?'

'Juan.'

'Well, it takes Juan to know Juan.' She laughs.

'Juan Esperanza,' I add. I try it out, mouthing it without giving it voice: *Nina Esperanza*. It sounds quite exotic.

'Oh, isn't he the chef at Cabbage or wherever? I've seen him. He's been around for nearly a year and never gone out with a single woman.'

Really? And yet he's interested in me? My heart does a pleasant flip.

'Bunny had a massive crush,' Pet continues. 'She was dragging me to his restaurant to eat all this garlicky stuff and then she'd practically follow him everywhere, but he wasn't interested.'

'Who's Bunny?'

'Bunny Atherington? She's the one with the boob job?'

'Oh, yeah.'

'She told me all about it one night after we'd basically stuffed ourselves with tapas. I think he told her that he was nursing a broken heart or something. His childhood sweetheart back in Spain ran off on him. He could have been lying his head off, of course.'

'He told me he came to England to forget.'

'Well, he's the first man to turn Bunny down since the op. Are you really sure he's not gay?'

'Of course he's not gay.'

'Fair enough. Well, good luck to you, babe.'

'Thanks.'

The third pair of trousers aren't bad. The fabric is nice. They're even long enough, which is pretty rare for me. I turn around in the mirror and inspect them more closely.

'Be careful with the poetry, though,' Pet tells me. 'Honestly, I once slept with this guy who wrote his own poetry in these beautiful little handmade books. He illustrated them himself and prided himself on being very sensitive and everything. The minute we were naked in bed, he started reciting the damn stuff and wouldn't stop. He even paused in the middle of thrusting to point out a clever couplet or whatever. I fell asleep halfway through.'

'I'll watch out for that.'

'Do. And let's go to Harvey Nicks after this. They've got new bags in.'

I finish my three-hundred-and-sixty-degree turn in front of the mirror. The trousers are a little big in the waist, and I'm not sure I like the pockets, but they'll do. I poke my head outside the curtain and speak to the assistant. 'What have you got for belts?' I ask.

The afternoon following this conversation with Pet, I ring Juan on his mobile. I've decided to ask him to my flat for dinner. A proper couply dinner. With a few candles on the table, for romance.

The phone rings and rings, and I get his answering message.

I ring him again later, but no luck. And the next morning. And the next afternoon. I have vivid images of him lying dead in his flat having choked on an olive or similar, and so I call his restaurant, Asparagus.

'May I speak with Juan Esperanza, please?' I ask, making my voice a little husky, because I don't want to appear to be a desperate would-be girlfriend.

'He's on holiday,' the girl at the end of the line tells me.

'On holiday?' I'm relieved that he's not dead of an olive, but at the same time I frown. He never mentioned a holiday; he keeps on sending flowers with notes asking me to ring him. Maybe he's not as expedient to fall in love with as I thought.

'Do you know when he'll be back, please?'

'He's back here on Monday,' the girl tells me. I hear a bit of amusement in her voice, which means there was a bit of panic in mine. I thank her as coolly as I can and put down the phone.

On Friday night I go out with Pet again, to a new club called Charleez. It's all sleek minimalism and it's clearly *the* new place to be, this week at least. The spindly stools are full of famous people; Rupert and Julian have been exchanged for a tall, broad, dark fellow called Ignatius who dances like a pro and keeps Pet on the floor. He twists and twirls her, his hands all over her, and I wonder whether Juan's gentleman act was a fraud after all and he's decided he's not interested in a woman who won't put out after half a dozen bouquets of roses. I drink too many martinis and slip off home early.

Saturday morning my head is fuzzy. I'm behind on Edmund's press clippings, so I bring my big folder to bed with me and spend a couple of hours under the duvet cutting and sorting. It's quite peaceful, really; just me and the newsprint. When my phone rings I answer it without looking at the number.

'Good morning, sleeping beauty,' says a smooth Spanish voice.

I sit up abruptly, clippings fluttering to the floor. 'Juan! Where have you been?'

'Have you missed me?'

He knows I've been ringing him, because it's recorded on his mobile. 'I might have,' I say.

Juan laughs. 'I missed you too, my angel.'

'Listen, do you want to come round for dinner?'

'Tonight?'

'Why not?' I say. After all, if I'm going to jump into the depths of this Juan-love, it's no use lingering by the side of the pool.

What do you cook for a chef who you're trying to seduce?

I have, of course, given a lot of thought to this question in the past, in a completely idle and fantastical way, of course, but in my fantasies I was cooking for

Edmund, and not Juan. I know Edmund's tastes like the back of my hand, and so I devised this elaborate menu that included both saffron and nectarines, which are his favourite ingredients. Juan, though, is different. Which is the entire point. So I can't use Edmund's menu for him, and I've been too preoccupied with deciding to fall in love with him and then trying to reach him to actually think through what I am going to cook.

I dunk my head under water, scrape back my sodden hair, throw on some jeans and knee-high boots and go to the supermarket to look for inspiration. I stand in front of the fruit and veg, vacillating. I can cook, after a fashion. At least I never killed Dad and Immy. But my repertoire is limited. I'm good at toad in the hole, inexpensive vegetable stews, one hundred and one things to do with beef mince. None of those are remotely suitable.

I could go with the all-out seduction routine, ringing Jett's suppliers and calling in some favours to get some fantastic oysters and champagne. But does that make me look like a hussy, or even worse, like a cliché?

I want to appear in control, and yet alluring. Exotic, and yet English. Feminine and gutsy and romantic.

If I rang Edmund, he could tell me exactly what to cook. He would also tell me to get the hell out of the supermarket. He hates supermarkets.

I finger my phone in my handbag and decide this is ridiculous. I buy some likely-looking steaks and the best red wine I can find. Several bottles, in case the steak's no good. I throw in some cheese and biscuits and a fresh pineapple, which I've heard has some aphrodisiac qualities but isn't quite as obvious as an oyster, and rush home to clean the bedsit top to bottom.

It's only when I'm changing my sheets that I have to pause again to think. I haven't had visitors for some time now and I'm not sure that one or two revealing things haven't crept into full view. For example, the three little pink porcelain sheep that my auntie Claire gave me before she died. They're sitting on my bedside table, so I can look at them every now and then before I go to sleep. They're comforting, almost as if Auntie Claire is stroking my forehead in that way she used to do when we visited her and Arval in Wales, back when my family was whole and I thought nothing could ever go wrong.

But porcelain sheep aren't exactly chic and upmarket city-girl things. I sweep them carefully into my sock drawer. I also hide my MP3 player. I have quite embarrassingly bad taste in music. It's loaded with prog-rock, mostly Rush but some Yes and early Genesis and Jethro Tull too. I have this nasty habit of listening to *2112* over and over whenever I'm a bit stressed. I blame the teenager who lived next door to us when I was about ten; he was called Ricky and I had an enormous crush on him, and he used to play this stuff from the stereo of his car every weekend while he washed it.

Anyway, again – not upmarket city-girl music. I don't even listen to it with earphones in public, for fear of being found out. Into the sock drawer it goes.

Then I open my underwear drawer, and first do a bit of careful rearranging so that the best items are near the front and top, and the more workaday cotton bits down at the bottom where they're not available to casual scrutiny. I have some good underwear. Even though nobody sees it but me, I believe that underwear serves much the same function as high heels; it gives me a confidence that I can naturally project to others.

I'm not really sure what underwear would portray the best image to Juan, especially on our first night together. White is too virginal, pink too girlie, cream too demure, black too knowing, red too sirenish, leopardskin too ironic. In fact, it's probably best if I start all over for Juan, with something completely new. That's perfect; I can tell him I bought it just for him. And there's a lingerie boutique not far from here. I put my boots back on and go out.

Far too much money spent later, I return with a slim bag mostly filled with tissue paper. The bra and knickers are blue, as blue as the Spanish sky and as blue as my eyes, and the assistant assures me that any right-thinking man would salivate as soon as he clapped eyes on them. I thought about showing them to a couple of random men on the street just to see if this is the case, but fortunately sanity, on that point at least, still rules.

Showering, dehairing, moisturising, perfuming, make-upping and hairdoing take far more time than they should, but by half past six I'm in the kitchenette, looking fairly gorgeous in a short dress and blue heels that match my underwear (in case Juan wants me to keep them on), potatoes in the oven, a bottle of wine open and breathing and my hands full of salad. This is when the phone rings.

I shake the rocket off my hands and rush to the phone. I'm actually quite proud that my first emotion is panic and fear that Juan wants to cancel. If I feel this way, I must be halfway close to falling in love with him already. 'Hello?' I answer breathlessly.

'Nina? I wasn't sure I'd catch you.'

It's my dad. 'Are you all right?'

'Fine fine, everything going as planned. When are you getting here, or were you thinking of coming tomorrow?'

'Tomorrow?' I raise my wet hand to my forehead.

'Yes, Arval's arriving any minute now, but if you'd prefer to come to Sunday lunch, then—'

'Arval! Shit!' With the whole Juan thing, I've

completely forgotten I've promised to go to Dad's to see his brother. 'Oh no, Dad, I'm really sorry. Something came up.'

'Oh. Well, that's all right. Immy's here.' He sounds resigned rather than disappointed, which should make me feel relieved but instead makes me feel worse. 'Is it work?'

'Well no, not exactly. But I can't cancel. It's sort of . . . a date.'

'Oh. Oh well then, that's nice. Much more fun than hanging around with a couple of middle-aged men.'

This is true, so I bite my lip. 'I'm sorry. My date's been away, and this is the only time we can get together. I think it could be important.'

'How about tomorrow then? Immy's cooking lunch.'

'I . . .' I picture waking up in bed with Juan after a wonderful night, lazy and ready to make love again but having to kick him out instead so I can get a train to Holybrook to see my dad. Or even worse, what if Juan insists on coming with me? Would he be romantic enough to want to meet my family?

'I really can't,' I say. 'Will Arval be visiting again soon? I'll put it in my diary way in advance.'

'I'm not sure. He's going to America for the summer, don't you know. He might get back here before that, maybe.'

'Summer's a long way away. I'm sure he'll get back. Give him my apologies, will you?'

'Yes, yes, of course. Listen, speaking of Arval, while I've got you, I was wondering if you remembered what he was allergic to. Imogen thinks it's cinnamon, but I thought it was cheese.'

'He's allergic to cat hair. It gives him a mild rash.' I wrote this down years ago, because my father has a similar kerfuffle every time he sees his brother.

'Oh, that's fine then. Only we have cinnamon break-fast cereal and I didn't want him to get ill. And Imogen likes cheese sandwiches, so we've got about seven kinds of it.'

'I think he will be fine with cereal and cheese. Listen, Dad, I'm sorry but I really do have to—'

'Who's your date with?'

I stop, mid-excuse. This is the first time in recent memory that my father has asked me a question about my own life.

'It's . . . someone I met recently,' I say cautiously. I might have great hopes for Juan, but I don't want to disappoint my father if they don't work out.

'Well that's nice. Imogen seems to have met a nice young man too, though of course I don't like to ask. He might be coming here this evening. Do you think the neighbours' cat will bother Arval? It came in here last week and rubbed against the curtains.'

'You'd better give them a hoover just in case,' I say. I'm not sure why I'm disappointed at my father's lack of curiosity, since I've just done my best to defeat it anyway. 'Whoops, I think that's my date at the door. Gotta go! Love you, Dad, bye!'

I hang up and stand in my empty room, with no one at the door. It's quarter to seven, and no Juan yet. I wonder, for a moment, if I'm doomed to follow in my father's footsteps and end up single and middle-aged and worrying about cheese.

Neither my father nor my uncle has seemed the slightest bit interested in getting remarried. Since Auntie Claire died, Arval's been too busy chasing rodents, and Dad— well, I can't blame my father for being reluctant to try it again. Anyway, I don't think he's been overwhelmed with offers. Women don't want men like my father. Women want strong men, capable men. Men who haven't been shattered by their ex-wife's betrayal. Men like, for example, Juan.

Who is fifteen – no, twenty minutes late, and has been gone for a week without telling me where he's been.

The doorbell rings and I rush to answer it. Juan is standing there all dark and handsome, with a bunch of flowers in one hand and a bottle in the other, and I'm so glad he's turned up and I don't have to rethink this whole decision that I immediately kiss him. He tastes of wine.

'If this is my reward, I am glad I went away,' he says when we've finished. I was in such a hurry to get ready that I forgot to use the stay-on lipstick, and his lips are touched with glossy pink. I rub it off with my thumb.

'I'm really glad to see you. These are gorgeous.' I take the flowers from him, more roses of course.

'This is a very nice flat,' he says.

My bedsit is part of the top floor of an Edwardian mansion house in Kensington, originally servants' quarters but expensive enough now to eat up a major proportion of my salary. It's small, just room enough for a double bed, a table and a kitchenette, but I've got white walls, white furniture, polished floors, and the whole thing feels like being inside a shiny, clean cloud. The proximity of the bed to everything else can't hurt the evening's prospects, either.

'So where have you been?' I ask casually, handing him a glass of wine.

'I hear you rang Asparagus.' He's smiling the smile of a man who thinks he's probably caught what he's been chasing. Which is fair enough, because he has.

'Well, you never told me you were going away, and I had visions of you dead in an alley somewhere.'

'So you were checking to see if I am alive. That's all.'

'Maybe.'

He smirks again and takes a sip of his wine. I finish up making the salad, though to be honest I don't like to do it while he's watching. I keep on thinking I might be handling the lettuce wrong or something. I wish I'd noticed more carefully how Edmund deals with vegetables instead of watching his masterful hands all the time.

'You are breathtaking, Nina.'

Now this is more like it. This would be one of the nice things about having a relationship with Juan; he would always be giving me compliments. I smile at him flirtatiously. 'So where have you been?'

'I'll tell you over dinner.'

'In that case, why don't you sit down and relax. Choose some music to listen to. Something to get us in the mood.'

He tops up our wine and turns his attention to the CD player. I'm glad; it's much easier to cook without him watching, and I am actually very hungry. This could be because Juan Esperanza has awakened all my senses. Or possibly because I haven't eaten anything all day.

I drink more wine and set about preparing the steaks. The music selection on display is much more suitable for public consumption than my private collection, though I'm sort of thinking I might have left *Aqualung* on the CD player by mistake. Fortunately, instead of the manic flute stylings of Ian Anderson, I hear some soft, sultry jazz, a CD that came free with a Sunday newspaper. I've never listened to it all the way through before, but it's the predictable choice for Juan.

That will be nice, too, I think, to have a boyfriend who's predictable. No nasty surprises. Then I remember that he's been missing for a week and I quickly slap the steaks on a couple of plates, add hot jacket potatoes from the oven and scatter salad in a way that is hopefully appealing. When I bring them to the table, Juan is perusing my bookshelves. These have also been pruned. I leave most of my more embarrassing choices on trains.

'*Learn Spanish In Two Weeks*,' he reads from the spine of one of the books. I actually got that one by mistake in a box of second-hand romance and fantasy novels, but from Juan's pleased expression I made a good choice to leave it on the shelves. I smile mysteriously and put the plates on the table.

'*Muy delicioso*,' he says and holds out my chair for me.

'*Gracias*.' He sounds very sexy speaking Spanish, but I hope he's not going to say anything more difficult, as I've just used up one third of my Spanish vocabulary.

'*Un poco de vino?*' with the bottle poised over my near-empty glass.

'*Si*.' And that's the second third of my Spanish; his next sentence had better be about sangria or I'm lost.

'Thank you for inviting me to your home, Nina,' Juan says.

'Why didn't you tell me you were going away?'

I hate the way that question sounds. I meant it to sound intimate, but it sounds needy instead. He doesn't seem bothered at all; he slices off a bite of steak and chews it appreciatively.

'I didn't know you would care,' he says when he's finished.

'I don't.'

'You are a poor liar.'

'Don't tell me where you were, I don't mind. Be a man of mystery if you prefer it. But I warn you, you might not get dessert.'

'What's for dessert?'

'You'll find out if you tell me where you've been.'

'I have been in Spain,' he says.

'Visiting family?'

'No, I was looking for something else.'

'Did you find it?'

He eats some more of his steak. He's sexy when he eats, I decide. Not as sexy as Edmund, who puts his entire being into his taste buds, but still sexy. Dozens of women would kill to be sitting where I am right now. Probably hundreds.

'On a cliff,' he begins, 'she stands like a faded beauty, surrounded by orange blossom and sea air. Her eyes gaze for ever out to sea, shimmering turquoise and boundless.'

What is this? More poetry? Have I missed a vital part of the conversation? I think back, but still haven't got a clue. 'Are you talking about a woman?'

'I'm talking about a gracious lady, who has passed through her days of glory, but could be restored to her former beauty with loving care.'

'Your mother?'

'El Flor Anaranjado,' he says, and I must be looking as bewildered as I feel, because he laughs and says, 'The Orange Blossom. It's a restaurant on the cliffs of San Nasareo, on the Costa Blanca.'

'Oh. You ate there?'

'I did, though that is not the reason I visited it. It's owned by a very elderly man, Señor Solorzano. His sons have emigrated to America and he has no one to run the business for him. But the place, Nina. It is sublime. The terrace is a hundred metres above the ocean, and yet it is so quiet that you can hear every wave break on the shore. And when the sun sets, it gleams into the windows of the restaurant and turns the tiles to molten gold.'

He goes on in this vein for quite some time, describing the cracked yet creamy stucco on the outside of the building, how it is surrounded by orchards and

fields, how bougainvillea grows unpruned over the
northern wall, the smells of blossom and warm earth and
sea. I listen quite happily, not least because this gives me
time to eat my dinner, but then a disturbing thought
creeps up on me and I put down my fork.

'You're not thinking of buying this place and leaving
London, are you?'

'Oh, no no no. There is far too much for me here.' He
smiles with this romantic glint in his eye. I don't trust it.

'But you want to, don't you? Nobody talks about a
place like you're talking unless they really want to be
there.'

'It is a fantasy. I am a chef, not a restaurateur. She
needs so much work, and I cannot do that by myself.
Besides, it is true what I said. There is so much for me
here in England. I am only just beginning to discover it.'

'That's true,' I say.

'And I like very much what I am discovering here,
Nina Jones.' He toasts me with his wine glass and gives
me a long, smouldering look. My heart beats faster. I love
intensity in a man.

'I heard something interesting about you, Juan,' I say.

'What is that, *querida*?'

'I heard that you haven't dated anyone in London
because you had a girlfriend who broke your heart in
Spain.'

He stands. 'Come and sit with me,' he says, and takes
my hand and leads me to my own bed, which is the only
other place to sit, besides the table. He settles me on one
end, and I curl up my legs as he sits on the other. We're
close enough, though, that my foot touches his thigh, and
I let it linger there.

'Her name is Juanita,' he says. His voice is soft and
sad. 'Her father owned the farm next to my father's. We
were born the same week and our mothers named us the

same. Every day from when we were little children we were together. We went to school together. Our fathers taught us to farm and our mothers taught us to cook. When we were both old enough, we went to Barcelona together. She is a biochemist.'

'And very beautiful.' Because they always are, the true loves who aren't me. I think of Caroline.

He smiles sadly. 'Nina, she is the opposite of you. You are so tall and bright; she is small and dark, with black hair like a raven's wing.'

'Did she . . . did she die?'

He shakes his head. 'But I have not seen her for over a year.'

'What happened?'

'It was her birthday. I booked tickets to see *The Barber of Seville* at the Gran Teatre del Liceu. Juanita loves opera. She loves the music and the passion. Like me, she has . . . she had the romance in her veins.'

I'm not sure how romantic my veins are. 'Go on.'

'I brought the tickets to her laboratory in the afternoon to surprise her. The door to the lab was glass, and through it I saw her. I spotted her long black hair. And then I saw she was not alone. Diego, her supervisor, was with her. I was disappointed we would not have our private moments, but these things cannot be helped. I raised my hand to knock on the door, and then I saw my Juanita step into Diego's arms and the two of them began to kiss with passion.'

'Oh no. What did you do?' I have visions of Juan crashing through the window and challenging Diego to a duel with the swordlike shards of broken glass.

'I went home and waited for her. When she appeared, many hours later, I told her what I had seen. She confessed that she had been having an affair with Diego for months. We had a fiery argument. After all our arguments in the past we had ended by making love. This time, we ended by her leaving.'

'She wasn't worth it,' I say vehemently. 'Anybody who can cheat on someone who loves her more than anything doesn't deserve to be loved.'

'I loved her nevertheless. I pleaded with her not to go. I forgot I was a man and I begged her. But she said she loved Diego more than me. And so I lost my Juanita.'

There is so much pain in his voice that all I can do is to scoot up on the bed and take him into my arms. I stroke his shoulders to soothe him.

'Have you seen her since?' I ask.

'No. I resigned from my job and I came to London to work and to forget. And I have built myself a new life here.'

'Yes, you have. I think it's wonderful.' I really do. Juan is a real man. When his heart was broken he didn't crumble and become a shell of himself; he didn't let everything slip away and allow his family to pick up the pieces. He didn't act like my father. Instead he kept it together, moved somewhere new, made a new life. I have new admiration for him.

'You were right,' I tell him. 'We can help each other.'

I turn my head towards his, sink my fingers into his hair, and kiss him.

He responds instantly, and with quite a bit of heat. A little part of my brain wonders if he's told me this story in order to win my sympathy and therefore get me to sleep with him, but I reject that idea. He's got more honour than that. Otherwise he would have slept with Bunny what's-her-name, and all those other women who have been chasing after him. He can't be short on offers. He wants me.

I wonder why.

Juan kisses my lips, my face, my neck. I close my

eyes. I don't have to wonder why he wants me. It's chemistry. He's a man, I'm a woman, I'm wearing good underwear and high heels. We're here on this bed together, quite a bit of wine has been consumed, and we're going to make love because it's the right thing to do. And I want to.

I pull away from him slightly and ask, 'Why do you want me, Juan?'

'Do you not know that special thing that makes you different?' He runs his thumb along my bare calf. It feels good.

'My shoes?'

'Your heart.'

'I don't understand.'

Juan nuzzles my neck, just underneath my ear. 'Listen to yourself. You say you don't understand, and yet when I told you Juanita's story you were instantly angry. You know how it feels to love and to lose. You have your own broken heart to forget.'

'You can see that about me?' Oh, dear God. Am I that obvious? Have I been walking around London with my broken heart on my sleeve? Does Caroline know?

He taps his chest with his index finger, and then taps me above my left breast. 'One broken heart knows another.'

I bite my lip, so recently kissed.

'Nina, don't worry. It is not written on your face. But I knew, as soon as I saw you. There was something inside you that drew me to you. I knew that you would value love. You would not throw it away like a child who has tired of her toy.'

'No,' I say. 'I wouldn't do that.'

'We are meant for each other.'

Juan's mouth meets mine again, and in his fervent kisses I see that he's right. We're kindred spirits, both hopelessly in love with someone we can never have. We can heal each other; we can discover love again.

We're a perfect fit!

He goes back to kissing my neck again and I pull away slightly to look into his eyes. 'Are you ready for dessert?' I ask.

'What is it?'

I lie down on the bed. I keep my shoes on, but I lean back on my elbows and prop myself up, giving Juan a seductive smile, which I might have practised a few times in my mirror this afternoon whilst getting ready.

'I'm dessert,' I tell him.

'Oh, my Nina,' he sighs, by which I deduce I've done a good job with the smile. He stays still for a moment, looking at me, and I feel like a goddess. Then he lies down beside me and cups my face in his hand.

'I am going to make this wonderful for you,' he says.

I tilt my head and shake my hair back, loose, on to the pillow, and we begin kissing again. I can still hear the light jazz, which is a good touch, I think. We kiss gently, and sensuously, and Juan runs his hands up and down my dress. Each time, he pulls the skirt up a tiny tiny bit more.

I'm not sure why he's being so subtle about it. It feels as if he's trying to sneak my dress up around my waist without my noticing. But since I've pretty much told him I'm his for the taking, it seems a pointless subterfuge. He could flip my dress up or rip it off, that would all be fine. Well, maybe not the ripping, because it was an expensive dress. But it might be a nice display of his passionate nature, a little alpha-maleness.

But the hem creeps up instead, inch by inch. I wriggle downwards on the bed a bit, trying to hurry up the process.

I shouldn't be in a hurry. I imagine myself saying

breezily to Pet, 'Oh, Juan and I made love all night.' That sounds like a promising start to a relationship. And in the morning he can make me breakfast. If I remembered to buy some eggs, that is.

'You are so beautiful,' Juan murmurs to me, which brings me away from breakfast and back to the present. I unbutton his shirt, not too fast but quickly enough to maybe express that I am willing and eager to get on with making love with him, and run my hand over his chest, which is hairy. I like a hairy chest on a man, it makes him seem manly, although perhaps not quite as hairy as this; but then again Juan is Mediterranean and very manly, so I should make allowances.

Juan is still working on my dress. It's now nearly all the way up my legs, which means that any moment he'll encounter my pricey and specially chosen blue underwear. I hold my breath in anticipation. But I have to let it out again when it becomes clear that I'll probably pass out from lack of oxygen before he touches a single bit of blue silk.

I close my eyes. This will help me to be fully here in the moment, to appreciate every little nuance of Juan's lovemaking. I am putty in his hands, a fierce ball of sexual longing. Besides, I hear women all the time complaining about how their men rush through sex without bothering to take the time to pleasure them. It's practically a cliché. I, on the other hand, have found a man with finesse. Who likes to play a woman's body like a fine instrument.

'Ohhhhhh, Juan,' I moan encouragingly. He takes this as his cue to speed up, and I am delighted when he unbuttons the top of my dress, pushes it aside, and exposes my blue bra, all in one go.

Now we're getting somewhere. He roughly mutters something in Spanish (though as it definitely isn't about sangria, I can't be sure what it is) and begins to kiss down my neck towards my chest. His crotch is against my hip, and I can feel his erection pressing into me. Not in a gross way, like he's humping my leg or anything; in a nice way, as if he's letting me know how much he wants me.

His hand moves upward, to the peak of my breast, and his fingertips begin to circle my nipple through the fabric of my bra. He doesn't actually touch the nipple itself, but just around it, gently, as if he's tracing the rim of a wine glass. Meanwhile, he's spending a lot of attention kissing my collarbone. It's a good little technique, refreshing compared to those men who stampede in there grabbing breasts left and right. Subtle. I've still got my eyes closed so I imagine what he looks like, with his big hand on my chest, his body curled towards mine, his lips on my skin and his blond hair like the sun—

Wait a second. My eyes bolt open and I stare at Juan's hair, the ends of it ticking my chin. It's as black as night.

I'd been picturing Edmund, not Juan.

No. This *cannot* happen again.

'Juan,' I say out loud, in such a way that it could be a moan of ecstasy, but really to remind myself who I'm with. Juan. Juan Juan Juan. Not Edmund.

Juan is still circling my nipple and licking my collarbone. He hasn't made a move towards the other breast or any other part of me yet. If I'm forgetting who I'm with even with this minimal stimulation, what's going to happen when I'm out of my mind with passion, passion that Juan has brought me to with his patient and thorough lovemaking, and I scream out 'Edmund!'?

'Ohhh, Juan, that's so good,' I say. I bury my fingers in his black hair, to remind myself. I also keep my eyes wide open. I can't afford to drift off into another daydream. 'Juan, you are so sexy, I can't stand it.'

Around and around and around. I glance downwards

to see if maybe he can't see where my actual nipple is because of the bra. But no, it's obvious, sticking out in stark outline against the silk.

Then suddenly his hand makes a move, travelling across the valley of my cleavage to where my right nipple is also in plain sight, skimpily covered by silk. His head moves downward to kiss and nibble at my chest. 'Juan, oh Juan, I want you so much,' I say, hoping that we're about to get some nipple action.

He begins to circle, slowly, around and around and around.

I wonder how Edmund is with breasts. I've seen him knead bread and he seemed much more energetic than this. Still sensual, of course, but with more of a grabbing and caressing action, more friction and muscle, less tickling and stroking.

*Must not think about Edmund.*

I've got too much time to think. Maybe if I'm more encouraging, take matters into my own hands, as it were, Juan will follow suit. I reach downwards, sliding my palm down Juan's body, and grasp his erection through his trousers in a firm yet gentle hold.

'Oh Juan,' I say, 'you're so hard and throbbing.'

Juan raises his head and smiles at me. 'Be patient, *mi querida*,' he says. 'This will take all night.'

'Yes,' I say, 'I was thinking that too.'

He takes my hand in his and moves it away from his crotch. Then, tenderly, he unbuttons more of my dress, then all of my dress, down to the bottom. He opens it, baring my body and my underwear to his gaze. Then he dips his head downwards.

I hold my breath. At last. He'll take off my blue knickers and get down to business and then all I have to worry about is thinking of more things to say starting with 'Juan', because I'm not much of a sex-talker and I was sort of scraping the bottom of the barrel there with the hard and throbbing comment.

Soon, though, I won't have to worry, because I'll be beyond rational speech anyway. Moaning, groaning, panting, screaming, all that is good. Probably once I get past this first orgasm, I'll have forgotten all about Edmund and will only have eyes for Juan.

He pauses tantalisingly over my body. 'Juan,' I whisper.

Softly he begins to lick my belly button.

I close my eyes and try to relax. He's bound to hit an erogenous zone soon. All I have to do is not think about Edmund. Not fantasise about Edmund. And not, absolutely not, open my mouth and say—

My mobile phone rings. I sit up, gasping an apology to Juan, and hurry, half clothed, to fetch it. I recognise the number right away.

'Edmund,' I say.

'Nina, I hope I haven't interrupted anything.' His voice is smooth as honey.

'Of course not.'

'Good. Listen, I have some news. Channel Four have come through with an offer and a contract for the programme.'

'Edmund! That's fantastic!'

'Isn't it? I'll see you at the house in half an hour. Unless you're busy.'

I look down at myself and see that my nipples are still standing out like sore thumbs. Or rather, neglected thumbs. 'Will . . . will Caroline be there?'

'Why wouldn't she?'

I blush furiously. I glance at Juan, who has got up too and is standing, shirt open, at the foot of the bed.

'Oh, it's just that I have something to tell her, that's all.' Which is true; Caroline is going to be thrilled about my budding relationship with Juan. She wants everyone to be as happy as she is.

'We'll all be there. One more thing, Nina, keep this under your hat, all right? I don't want word getting around until we've signed the contract.'

'No problem.' I hang up and turn to Juan. 'I'm really sorry, Juan. It's an emergency at work.'

'What happened?'

'I've actually been sworn to secrecy.'

'And you must go now?'

'Yes. I'm sorry.'

He crosses the room and kisses me. His hand rests on my bare waist and his warm chest presses all against my front. My skin sings out with frustration.

'Soon,' I say to him.

He buttons his shirt. 'Next time, there will be no interruptions. I will take all the time that I want with you.'

'Can't wait,' I say.

I wonder how I can grow more nerve endings in my belly button.

We work until early Sunday morning around the Jetts' gleaming dining room table, Edmund and his lawyer and his PR guru, who have apparently also never heard of nine-to-five jobs with weekends off. I don't mind, though; Edmund is so excited, he's like a little kid with sweets and I have to keep on looking down at my notes to keep from jumping up and giving him a hug. Every hour or so I help Caroline make coffee and replenish the tray of sandwiches and pastries.

The sky is beginning to get light when I get back to my bedsit. I walk straight past the remains of my dinner with Juan, crawl into bed, and fall asleep.

My mobile ringing wakes me up and I turn over with a groan. The clock says it's half past one in the afternoon, too late to get to Holybrook for lunch with my father and Arval. I grope for the phone, expecting it to be Edmund with more work, or Juan with another date, or my father with queries about cheese.

It's Pet. 'You're up early,' I say.

'Good morning! What are you doing?'

'Sleeping. I was up all night.'

'Ooh, that's good news! Are you alone? Do you fancy doing something?'

'I'm alone. To be honest, though, Pet, I don't think I

could do anything if I tried.' I hoist myself up on my pillows, and that's an effort.

'Oh, it doesn't need to be anything special. I need to get out of here. My phone is ringing like crazy and it's driving me mad.'

'I don't even think I could do shopping today. I was just going to curl up and read or something.'

'That sounds great! I'll be round in five. What's your address?'

I give it to her, all the while zooming through the list of what I need to do to make my flat presentable. Fortunately I've done most of the work already for Juan, so I force myself out of bed and do the washing up and cut up the uneaten pineapple.

Pet arrives quarter of an hour after she's put the phone down. She's gorgeous in teensy tiny jeans and teensy tiny top and very expensive boots and handbag, and she's carrying an enormous organic cotton shopping bag. 'Lovely flat.'

I've been to Pet's mews house in Knightsbridge. She has a working fireplace, designer furniture and a signed Damien Hirst on the wall.

'Thanks. Uh . . . would you like some coffee?' It seems such a mundane thing to offer to Pet. I should be breaking out the champagne or something. 'Or I've got red wine.'

'It's all sorted.' She puts the carrier bag down on my table and spreads out the bounty. A stack of glossy magazines, two thick Sunday papers, two Frappuccinos, a box of chocolate hazelnuts, and a litre bottle of something very green from the juice bar down the road. She selects the *Vogue* magazine and one of the Frappuccinos, and collapses attractively on one side of my bed.

I take the other Frappuccino and a *Cosmo*. 'Thanks

for bringing all this,' I say guiltily. And here I was going to offer her second-hand aphrodisiac fruit.

'Least I could do.' She waves her hand and opens the magazine.

And then it's quiet. I've never been quiet with Pet before. Usually there's chatter, gossip, music, laughter. I peek over my magazine and she's seemingly engrossed, so I go back to reading. The people in *Cosmo* laugh and pose, as if they never have to worry about anything. Everything would be so easy if I could slip into the polished pages of perfect clothes and beautiful interiors.

Surely Pet's bored? Stuck here on my bed being quiet, having to bring her own provisions? I picture her rolling her eyes and saying to someone tomorrow, 'Oh, basically we just sat there on her bed for hours, but she refused to go out so what could I do?'

'We could go and see a movie,' I suggest.

'Oh no, this is great, it's what you said you wanted to do. I suppose you had one of those families who all gathered round and shared the newspaper every Sunday over a huge lunch? A companionable silence sort of thing?' She pronounces the words 'companionable silence' as if they're an exotic phrase from a foreign language.

'Uh. Something like that.'

'Lovely.' She flips a few pages on her magazine. 'So what brilliantly exciting thing were you up to last night that you're so exhausted?'

'I was with—' Then I remember that Edmund has sworn me to secrecy. 'I was with Juan.'

'Oh? And how was that? Did he read you poetry?'

'No, no poetry.' For a moment I'm tempted to tell her what happened. How I was scared every minute that I'd call out the name of the person I'm in love with. It would be nice to tell someone how I feel about Edmund, to admit the desire and guilt and sadness. They say that sharing your secrets makes them easier to handle.

But if I went into my feelings for Edmund, I'd have to explain why I love him. Why I'm attracted to powerful men. Why I envy happy marriages.

And besides, that's the past now. The future is all about Juan.

'He knows how to play a woman like a fine instrument,' I say.

'Nice. So this whole falling-in-love lark is totally working out.'

'It really is.'

Pet takes a long sip of Frappuccino. I do the same. We both go back to our magazines.

'Another drop to finish it off?'

Edmund holds up the bottle. I shrug and say, 'Might as well,' so he sloshes another dollop of rich, dark red wine into my glass.

Sometimes we open a bottle when we have to work late; Edmund says it helps him relax and wind down, and pathetically, I enjoy sharing this little indulgence with him. Tonight, the wine is supposed to be a crutch to help me seem more normal, because this is the first time I have worked alone with Edmund since the Starbucks moment, and I feel like my skin is about to jump off.

It hasn't been difficult to avoid being alone with him. He's constantly surrounded by people anyway, and of course Caroline is always around to give help and support. But he let me have tomorrow off specifically so we can blast through a load of work tonight after the dinner service at Jett. I've been sitting here at his big desk with my laptop, while Edmund walks around the office. He says it helps him think. About twenty minutes ago Red, Edmund's sous chef, came up to tell him everything was wrapped up and he was going home.

There's nobody in the building but the two of us. Now that the clatter of the work below us is gone, the night city noises from outside seem far away. Rain patters against the windows. I concentrate on typing the words he's dictating to me, not on hearing the smooth velvet of his voice.

'So with regards to the property in Devon, according to the current . . . do you fancy a brandy?'

I'm halfway through typing 'brandy' when I realise he's asking me a question. 'Oh . . . uh, sure, why not?'

I know damn well why not. But I can't say no to Edmund.

He fetches a bottle and two glasses from a cupboard. He's got all sorts in there; sometimes he stocks it with Gianduja chocolate for me, because I said one time that I liked it. 'I can't seem to concentrate tonight,' he says, pouring a finger into each glass.

'You could probably do with some rest.'

He rubs at the faint blue rings under his eyes. I actually think he's sexier when he's tired; the small vulnerability only emphasises how masterful he is. 'I haven't been sleeping well,' he admits.

'I don't blame you. You and Caroline must be so excited.'

'What's your opinion of the TV show, Nina?' He's focused right at me, a small line between his eyebrows. This is the sort of intense, full-minded attention he gives to everything he does, and it makes my heart beat faster.

'I think it's absolutely fantastic. You'll be a big hit. It's going to make you huge and you'll reap the benefits across every part of your business.'

He sighs. 'Caro doesn't like it.'

I'm not comfortable with this criticism of Caroline, and especially not when I'm alone with Edmund. 'I'm sure she's just worried about you, whether you're looking after yourself . . .'

'No, she doesn't want me to do it at all. She wants to have a baby. Aren't you drinking your cognac?'

I gulp at it, tasting pure alcohol and mellow wood. Edmund pours us both some more.

'Caroline told me you were trying for a family,' I venture.

'Did she?' He frowns. 'I'm not convinced. A baby takes up so much time and money and energy. Why can't we just be happy together?'

'Men always say that.'

'Really? Have you been asking men to have babies with you lately?'

'No, I just . . . read about it in some magazines.'

Edmund laughs. 'It's good to hear I'm nothing out of the ordinary.'

'You're probably worried about having children. It's a big step.'

He pulls out the chair beside me and sits down, cradling his brandy glass in one talented hand. 'You might be right. Maybe I've got cold feet. My own father wasn't the best role model. He was a tyrant and he was pretty handy with his fists.'

His honesty makes my throat constrict. Edmund never talks about his past; in media interviews he insists the questions focus on the present and future. The idea of him as a scared little boy is almost too much to bear. I put my hand on his arm.

'None of us is condemned to repeat our parents' mistakes,' I insist. 'We can't be; there has to be more to life than that. And Edmund, you're going to be a wonderful father. Your child will worship the ground you walk on. They won't be able to help it.'

His blue eyes soften. 'It means a lot to hear you say that.'

'It's true.' His sleeve is warm beneath my fingers, and the muscle of his arm is firm. Suddenly I feel the effect of the wine and the brandy, because my head is spinning. I pull my hand away, but he lays his on top of mine to stop me.

'I promised myself I'd stay quiet,' he says. 'But I can't. I need to ask you something, Nina.'

'What magazines I read?' I try for a joking tone, because I've got alarm bells clamouring in my head.

'No. It's about the other day, when you and I were in that coffee shop. For a minute there I caught you looking at me, and you looked like—'

'Edmund, let's not—'

'Like you really cared about me. Like there was some spark there between us.'

'I . . .'

I can't believe he's said it. My heart is hammering. My eyes fill with tears. My body tenses, ready to bolt from the building or maybe, so so wrongly, to fling myself into his arms. 'I don't . . . Edmund, I . . .'

'I didn't imagine it, did I?'

I try to tug away from him. I can't. I'm pinned by his loose grip on my hand, by the force of his eyes, by the strength of my own emotions. I open my mouth to deny everything, to back out of this dream coming true before I ruin my entire life. But nothing comes out, not even air, because I can't breathe.

'I didn't imagine it.' His voice is a low, warm murmur that bubbles the two of us together. 'You do love me. Very much.'

The word 'love' does it. It pushes my panic to the surface enough so that I can pull away from Edmund.

'I've got to go,' I say, and head for the door as fast as my heels will let me.

I haven't taken two steps when his hand touches my shoulder. 'Nina,' he says behind me and stops me in my tracks. 'Tell me if it's true.'

I don't turn around but I can see his face in my mind's eye, because I've memorised every feature, every expression, everything about him.

'Yes.' I whisper it but it's loud.

'This changes everything.'

'I know.'

So here it comes. I'm going to be sacked. I turn around to face him, and try to stand as tall as I can. 'I give you my word, Edmund, I never meant for you to know, and I would never, ever do anything to hurt you and Caroline, and I don't blame you if you don't think you can work with me any more, but I swear that I won't let it affect . . .'

Then I see how he's looking at me. He isn't the powerful leader, the indulgent boss. He's looking at me like a man looks at a woman, and in his eyes I see a reflection of my own desire.

'I haven't been able to get you out of my mind,' he says.

*Oh my God.*

I don't know how it happens. One minute I'm standing with my life tumbling down around me, and the next I'm in Edmund Jett's arms and my lips are on his. I'm touching his hair and his face and my heart is beating so fast and I've imagined this moment a million times and I cannot believe that it is coming true.

It shouldn't come true. I push away, blood pounding in my ears, stars bursting in front of my eyes.

'I am so sorry,' I gasp, stepping backwards. One of my heels catches on the rug and I stagger. Edmund reaches forward to catch me but I twist away before he can touch me again, before I'm even more tempted. I can't look at his face; I focus on his glossy shoes and the cuffs of his trousers.

'You have nothing to be sorry for,' he says.

'I'm not . . . I didn't mean for that to happen.' I sidle towards the door, talking fast. 'You love Caroline, I know that, I know we can't be together, you're not really interested in me, it's just because you're freaking out about being a parent and I shouldn't be taking advantage of that.'

'You didn't take advantage,' he says, his voice so calm that my chest aches. 'Stay here. Let's talk this through.'

I've reached the door; I grab the handle.

'Nina.'

The room is too bright, the air too close. I think I might faint. 'Goodbye, Edmund,' I say, and run out the door, down the stairs, through the darkened restaurant and out on to the street.

The sounds and smells open up to wideness, to a whole city that was out here all along. I take three steps, and the skies open and rain pours down.

I want Edmund to come after me, to sweep me up into his arms and carry me away, to kiss me so hard that I'll forget about all the reasons we shouldn't be together, forget everything except for the fact that I love him.

I hurry down the street. I don't see where I'm going, don't register the direction, except that it's away. A cab splashes towards me with its For Hire light on, but I don't raise my hand to hail it. The cold rain trickles down my face and drips on my neck.

*What have I done? What have I done? What have I done?*

Nothing is going to be the same ever again. I can't work for Edmund any more, not after this. I can't face him again. I could certainly never be alone with him. And what if Caroline finds out? What if Edmund confesses?

I can't imagine him lying to her. It'll be late one night, he'll be racked with guilt, and he'll turn to her in bed, where she's reading one of her thick books, and say, 'Caro, I've got something to tell you. Nina's in love with me. And we kissed one night when we were drunk.'

Or more likely, '*She* kissed *me* one night when she was drunk.'

I moan with pain thinking about it.

'Lighten up, love, it might never happen,' says a jovial drunken chap, staggering about with his arms around his mates. They all have sodden newspapers over their heads to keep off the rain. I keep on walking. Everything around me – the darkened buildings, the landmarks, the pedestrian crossings – seems familiar yet strange, as if it has changed since the last time I saw it. Transformed by a single kiss.

How did it happen? Did he kiss me, or did I kiss him? Suddenly this seems very important. I think back to those few seconds. He asked me if I loved him and I said yes. He said he couldn't get me out of his mind. But then I turned around. I shouldn't have turned around. Who made the first move? All I can remember is the attraction, how we were pulled to each other. Or maybe I was just pulled to him. I probably aimed my lips at his. But he bent his head, didn't he? He touched my shoulder? He didn't pull away?

I stop on the pavement and stare around, as if the answers are in the air. I've been walking for longer than I realised, and somehow I've managed to get to Kensington, across from the pointed tower of the Albert Memorial. In the light from the street lamps it looks like the dark shadow of a fairy-tale castle. Filigree and gold and shadow, a precious casement for a statue of one man. A monument to a marriage so strong it didn't fade after death.

'Shit,' I say aloud.

It doesn't matter who made the first move. Edmund is a married man. All of this is my fault. I'm the one who fell in love. I let him see how I feel. I let myself be alone with him. I didn't run out of the room. When he asked me if I loved him, I didn't lie or laugh. I harboured secret feelings for months and years, keeping them safe, letting them grow. I built a castle around Edmund and lived in a fantasy fairy tale.

And now I get to live the unhappily ever after.

My legs are shaky. I walk until I find a bench and sit on it, curling my wet legs up beneath my wet dress. The wood is slightly warped, so that rainwater has accumulated in the middle of the seat and formed a cold puddle. The water seeps through what's still dry of my dress and knickers and chills my skin.

Edmund is probably pacing the office now, cursing himself for giving in to easy temptation. He's probably re-pledging himself to his marriage. Washing his face again and again to get rid of traces of my lipstick and perfume. Or maybe he's already home, crawling into bed next to an innocently sleeping Caroline, wrapping his arms around her and pulling her close, thinking how precious she is, how miraculous their child will be, how lucky he was to escape before he made a colossal mistake.

While I, the colossal mistake, sit on this park bench, squelching every time I move.

I should go home. I should get out of these wet clothes, and take a shower and go to bed. But I won't sleep. And what am I going to do after tomorrow?

I stare up at the yellow street light above me. The

rain is coming down in a steady stream, and the light shines off the drops in such a way that it seems almost as if they're going upwards, from the ground to the sky. All this time I've thought I was being realistic, that I'd resigned myself to unrequited love for Edmund, and that I've never told anyone about it because I was too ashamed to have fallen for a married man.

But that's not it. I've been keeping it secret because I've been clinging on to hope and I didn't want anybody to shatter my illusions. I've been hoping, somehow, that everything would change and that I would have Edmund for my very own. Otherwise, why would I have been thinking of him that whole evening with Juan? Why wouldn't I have seen what was good in front of me, and stopped longing for something impossibly out of my reach?

I stand up from my sodden park bench and walk towards Kensington High Street. My wedges squish with every step I take. My hair drips down my back. When I reach the road, I hail a cab.

'Goodness, love, you forget your umbrella?' the cabbie says to me as I climb in the back.

'I've been in the wrong place,' I tell him. 'But I'm going to the right place now.'

I give him Juan's address.

I have to lean on Juan's doorbell before a light comes on, and then it's still ten more minutes before he comes to the door. I hear him pause as he looks through the peephole, and then the chain slides back.

'Nina,' he says, concern balanced with surprise. He's bare-chested, wearing only a pair of trousers and no shoes, and his face is rough with stubble. He probably just came home from work. I feel a vast surge of gratitude that he found me, that he wants me, that he's given me a chance to pull myself out of this great big mess.

I wrap my wet arms around him and kiss him, hard, there in the doorway, with the light spilling out on to the street.

For a moment he's too surprised to react. Then he embraces me, kisses me back, pulls me into the house. I kick the door shut behind us.

'*Querida*,' he says. He doesn't ask me where I've been or why I'm here at nearly four o'clock in the morning. He doesn't ask me why my clothes are soaked through, and he doesn't say a word as I begin to strip. My hands are shaking and it's difficult to get my dress off because it's clinging to my body.

'Make love to me, Juan,' I say. 'Right now.'

I pull him down to the floor.

I wake up in Juan's bed, with light streaming in through the windows. I'm alone, but I can smell coffee and toast from the kitchen. I stretch my legs underneath the duvet, poking my feet out the bottom.

Taking a man by surprise and demanding sex is definitely the way to go. No nipple-circling, no belly-licking, just pure animal passion on the living-room carpet. It was hot. I wiggle my toes in satisfaction. I think I even have a bit of a rug burn on my back, which is a good thing. It reminds me this is a real relationship, not a fantasy.

Juan comes into the bedroom, holding a tray of coffee and toast and eggs. He's wearing nothing but a pair of red Y-fronts, which is something I've never seen on a British man, but he can pull it off. He sets the tray down on the bed and then sits down beside me and kisses me on the cheek. 'Good morning, my beautiful girl.'

I rub my eyes and pretend that I'm sleepy. 'Morning. What time is it?'

'Eight o'clock,' he tells me, pouring me coffee. He begins to butter some toast. 'I wish I could spend all day in bed with you, but we both have to go to work.'

The word reminds me of everything, and my satisfaction disappears.

'I don't. Edmund let me have a day off.' Saying his

name makes my stomach twist. I try a bite of toast, but that doesn't help. I'm waiting for Juan to ask why I appeared in the middle of the night, soaking wet, and made him have fast, furious sex with me without speaking a word. Or why I have the day off.

'You're lucky,' he merely says, and takes a bite of his own toast. 'What will you do?'

'I don't know,' I say miserably.

Juan smiles. 'Your clothes are all wet. You could stay here in my bed naked and be here waiting for me when I come home.'

'I might,' I say. It would be a good way to hide. My mobile is off, but maybe Edmund has rung my home phone. Maybe I've been fired already.

Or what if I haven't been fired? What if Edmund wants to carry on as if nothing has happened? I'll have to resign. But then what am I going to say when I apply for new jobs?

'I probably will stay here, if that's all right,' I say.

'Of course. *Mi casa es tu casa.*'

Whoops, I was wrong, I know that Spanish too. '*Gracias.*'

'*De nada.*'

Juan climbs into bed beside me, and we eat for a little while in silence. I like how he is not asking me questions. I like how easily he accepts me into his life. I'm even learning more Spanish. And he's a brilliant cook. I don't know what he's done to these eggs, but they're great.

When we're done, he takes the plates into the kitchen, and then he comes back and I watch him get dressed. It feels intimate and I like that too. Or I would if I didn't have this horrible sense of impending doom.

'Do you mind if I borrow a T-shirt and a pair of your jeans or something?' I say. 'I think I might nip out and do a little shopping.'

He gestures to his dresser, and says, 'There are spare keys hanging in the kitchen. I will see you when I get home, *cariño*.' He blows me another kiss and I listen as he leaves.

I roll over and over again in the bed until the duvet is wrapped around me like a pancake. I will definitely go shopping, I think. And I'll chuck what I was wearing last night into the bin. Even the shoes, which are probably ruined anyway.

Maybe it will help me forget about Edmund for a few minutes.

I don't go shopping. Or rather, I try to, but I catch a glimpse of myself in a full-length mirror in the first shop I go into, and I shudder. My hair is frizzy, my make-up smudged. They say bed head is sexy, but that's the kind of bed head you get from a trained stylist, not from an actual bed. Juan's T-shirt is too big for my shoulders, and his jeans are fully one inch too short. I look like some sort of horrendous echo of the person I'm supposed to be. I turn around and go straight home.

I mean to have a shower, but the minute I walk in through the door, I see the files of cuttings about Edmund, and the newspapers and magazines I haven't gone through yet. I was going to do that today. There's a Sunday supplement on the top of the pile, and it's got a photograph of Edmund leaning against the entrance to Jett, looking handsome and stylish and famous.

First I remember how it felt to kiss him. Heaven on earth, too good to last.

Then I think about how life will feel without him. After years of circling around him, I'll be cut adrift.

God, what will I do?

I walk around the flat, straightening things as I go. This whole situation would be so much easier if I had another job to step into. Something new and exciting, so nobody will ask any questions about why I'm leaving a job I love. But I have to go back into work tomorrow.

Ugh. My stomach turns over with dread. I check my phone, but there are no messages. So I go and take a nice long shower, and dry my hair, and get dressed, and do my make-up, and when I look at the clock, only forty-five minutes have passed and there's still a photograph of Edmund on my table.

This is what life will be like when I'm not working for Edmund. It'll be torture.

I throw a towel over the stack of papers and lie down on my bed. How can I find a new job in less than twenty-four hours? Not just a new job, but something really, really great, something that will fill up my time and my thoughts and make it feel as if I've never known Edmund Jett.

Thank God I've got Juan, at least. Though if I keep on seeing Juan, I'm going to be reminded of Edmund, too. He's a top chef, and London's not such a big place. If we could only escape, somewhere far away. Even Spain would be—

I raise my head from the pillow. Then I jump off the bed and grab my mobile and dial Juan's number. He answers it after half a ring.

'*Querida*,' he says. 'I cannot stop thinking about you.'

'I can't stop thinking about you either.'

'I will try to be home early.'

'That's great. Listen, Juan, I've had this crazy idea. What is the name of that restaurant you were talking about in Spain? The one that's for sale?'

'El Flor Anaranjado.'

The name sounds so beautiful, tripping off his tongue like that. As if it's an orange blossom itself, fragrant and sweet.

'What would you think about buying it, you and me?'

He laughs.

'I'm serious.'

He doesn't say anything, but he's stopped laughing.

'Think about it,' I continue. 'We'd be perfect. You could handle the food side, and I'd handle everything else. I've learned a lot about the restaurant business over the past three years. We could restore the place, advertise it, we could pull in British holiday trade as well as local clientele.'

'I don't know,' he says. He sighs. 'It would cost a lot of money.'

'The building can't cost much, can it?'

'No. It is not expensive.'

'So the real outlay would be in restoration and buying equipment.'

He pauses. 'I have a little money put aside.'

'I could sell my flat. And there are business loans.'

'I don't know, Nina. It is all a lot of commitment and money. It is also very fast.'

'You're the one who said we could help each other,' I remind him. 'This would be a whole new life. An adventure, Juan.'

There's another silence, and I can hear the clatter and talk of the Asparagus kitchen behind him. I picture him standing there, swarthy and sexy in his whites, that romantic gleam in his eye.

'I will think about it,' he says at last. And I know I've got him.

'I'll see you tonight and show you exactly how exciting it will be,' I tell him.

I put down the phone and grab my jacket and handbag. I think I'm up for some shopping after all.

*

'Pet!'

'Mmmmmmmm?'

Her voice over the phone is husky with sleep.

'Have you just woken up?'

'Mmmmmmmm.'

'Well, I have some big news, so I hope you're awake.'

I'm sitting in a café, wearing my new outfit, which is a white linen skirt and jacket with a cute little flowery top and pink strappy shoes. Exactly the sort of thing I'd expect a successful yet hip restaurateur to wear in Spain. Juan's T-shirt and jeans are carefully folded in one of the many carrier bags at my feet.

Five minutes ago, he texted me a single word, three times: *Si, si, si!*

I hear a rustling on the other end of the phone, which is obviously Pet sitting up in bed. There's a distinctly male grunt in the background.

'Who've you got there?' I ask.

'Not quite sure,' she says. 'Okay, I'm ready. Hit me with it.'

'Well . . .' I pause for effect. 'Juan and I are buying a restaurant together and moving to Spain!'

There is a long silence.

'Pet?' I say. 'Pet, are you still there?'

'What? Of course I'm still here. Just distracted for a moment. Well, that is fantastic news. How exciting. When did you decide this, last night?'

'This morning. It's called El Flor Anaranjado, which means the Orange Blossom. It's on a cliff overlooking the sea on the Costa Blanca. Juan says it's the most beautiful place he's ever seen.'

'What about your job?'

'I'm resigning. And I'm selling my flat, because we'll need the money to invest. And' – an idea has just struck me – 'I'm giving all my winter clothes to charity, because

I'm always going to be warm! A whole new beginning, from the wardrobe up.'

'Well. Wow.'

Another great idea strikes me. 'Hey, will you organise my going-away party for me?'

'Of course I will.'

'It will be so great, Pet! You can come to the Costa Blanca as easy as anything. We'll take Spain by storm. Listen, come and meet me at the Moët bar in Selfridges in an hour and we'll celebrate properly.'

'Now you're talking.'

I put the phone down happily. Everything is perfect. Juan is perfect. Spain is perfect. Everything is going to be sunshine and orange blossoms from now on.

Only three clouds blot the horizon, the three things I have to do before my dreams become reality. Resign from my job. Avoid being alone with Edmund. And tell my father.

Holybrook lies directly under the flight path of a busy airport. When I was fifteen years old and what was left of my family moved here, I was regularly awakened at four o'clock in the morning by charter flights roaring over my head on their way to cheap holidays in Ibiza or wherever. My GCSE and A-level teachers punctuated their lessons with pauses while they waited for the plane noise to fade enough so that we could hear what they were saying; this was, of course, a perfect time for the disaffected youth at the back of the room to chuck various lethal and pointed instruments at each other.

The aeroplanes create a vast white noise that seems to pierce right through your ears and into your brain, like headlights startling a deer. If you're not used to it, it's nearly impossible to think about anything else during the moments while the plane is directly overhead. And then, in between planes, it feels as if you're just waiting for another one to come. A whole community living a life of pauses. Still, house rentals are relatively cheap.

The cab lets me out in front of 34 Halcyon Close. My father's pebble-dashed bungalow seems smaller every time I see it. The grass is overgrown, again, and I'm wearing a pair of alligator court shoes. Maybe I can borrow a pair of Imogen's Jesus sandals later, to mow it.

I walk up the short path and stop to pick up a damp newspaper lying on the concrete.

I knock on the door. I always do. It's not that I think my father's going to be doing anything inside that requires privacy; it's more to do with my feeling that even though I spent three years of my life here, this house has never been mine. It's never been home. Home was years ago and miles away, with four bedrooms with walk-in wardrobes and a green lawn that my father used to ride a lawnmower over on Saturday afternoons and a patio where Mummy sipped cold drinks while I helped Immy hide her dollies in the flower beds.

Home was a big detached red-brick, double-glazed lie.

The noise of an aeroplane swells in the sky and has built to a proper roar by the time my father opens the door. I see but don't hear his greeting to me. 'Hi, Dad,' I say, though I know he can't hear that either. I hug him. He's shorter than me. Like the smallness of the bungalow, I've always known this, but it's a bit of a shock every time. My nose touches the grey, thinning hair of his comb-over before we end our embrace.

He gestures at me to come in, and I can tell by his lips that he's asking me how my journey was. 'Good, good,' I say loudly, nodding my head in an exaggerated way, though I never answer anything else to this question and really it makes no difference that we can't hear each other, since there's no meaning to it anyway. I consider yelling, 'I'm moving to Spain!' while he can't hear it, but that's the coward's way out. Besides, he's talking already and the plane noise is fading now.

'. . . gen's put the kettle on,' he finishes, his voice suddenly loud. 'Or I think she has. Imogen, your sister is here!'

There's dub music blaring from the right-hand side of

the hallway, where my sister's bedroom is located. Once, the two of us shared that room, and I remember many squabbles about which of us got to play her music on the single boom-box. I wonder if Imogen thinks of those arguments when she plugs in her iPod these days, and I wonder who she thinks won in the end.

The kitchen, at the back of the house with a view of the back of the bungalow opposite, is empty when we get there. I touch the kettle. It's cold. I fill it and put it on and begin getting out mugs and the tea canister. There are only two tea bags, sitting half buried in a mound of brown dust. I drop them into two mugs; I'll have to squeeze three cups out of them.

'So what have you been doing?' I ask my father. He stands, ill at ease in his own home, with one hand resting awkwardly on the kitchen table.

'Oh, this and that. A bit of sorting and tidying. Oh, and I wrote a letter to the local paper, about the state of the roads around here. Shocking.'

My father writes a lot of letters to the local paper, in fifteen-year-old business jargon, many of which get printed. I think it makes him feel as if he's doing something. He used to fire off bundles of letters in his old executive job before he lost it. I've tried pointing out several times that if he really wants something changed, he should go direct to the council, or speak with the people responsible for the problem. All a letter to the paper does is use up some ink. He always shakes his head and starts talking about freedom of the press and democracy, as dreamy-eyed as any American on the topics.

I'm not going into that today. 'How was the dentist?' I ask instead.

'She says I have the teeth of a thirty-five year old.'

'Doesn't he miss them?'

Dad laughs and for a minute I catch his eye and we're transported back, way back before anything happened, when we were happy and together as a family, when he was the best father a girl could have.

'What's so funny?' Imogen slopes into the room. She's wearing a tiny T-shirt and extremely baggy jeans, which expose her pale, flat belly. Her navel is pierced with a single glittering jewel. For some reason I'm immediately irritated by this.

'Just an old joke,' I say, turning away to make the tea. I throw away one of the tea bags before I remember it has to do double duty, and so I have to make two cups from the single remaining bag. When I put the milk in, I can see tea dust floating on top of the liquid in brown flecks and clumps.

'So what do we owe this visit to, sis?' Imogen takes her tea and curls herself into a pine chair. She has this ability to look half asleep in any situation. During hockey matches at school she used to stand in the field dangling her stick in one hand, yawning.

'What do you mean? I was here a couple of weeks ago, when I brought the gift for Maria's wedding.'

'I think it was last month.'

'Well, I'm *very* busy. With work.'

'Oh, I *know*.'

I'm amazed that she knows what 'busy' means, since she obviously can't be bothered to go shopping or help Dad with the garden, but I don't say anything. Imogen already treats me like I think I'm God's gift to the world, just because I have a career and try to help out around here the best that I can. I don't need to give her any more ammunition by lecturing her.

I'm seven years older than Imogen, but I feel ancient when I'm with her and Dad, as if all my youth and fun have been drained away. I suddenly long to be out in a nightclub with Pet, laughing and dancing and acting like I'm in my twenties, which I am. With my whole life in front of me.

I bring my father's and my weak, dusty tea to the table and sit down. Dad sits across from me and watches his thumb rubbing over a stain on the oilcloth. He's had the same cloth on there for as long as I can remember, with faded blue flowers on it. I think it came from our old house, which means my mother bought it.

Quite suddenly I wonder what Pet would say if she could see this house, my father, the stained oilcloth. Or what Edmund would think.

'So, what else is happening in sunny Holybrook?' I ask brightly. 'What have you been doing with yourself, Imogen? Any word on university applications?'

She shrugs. '*Emerly Street* has been really good.'

'Emerly what?'

'*Emerly Street*. The soap opera? Deeanna's taken in this mysterious stranger called Aloysius and Walter and Beryl are sure he's up to no good. Word on the street is he's after her money. You should watch it.'

'I don't get much chance to watch television.'

'Oh yes. You're too busy jumping whenever Edward calls your name.'

'It's Edmund,' I snap. 'And at least I'm doing something constructive with my time. Not lying around the house watching the days go by. Are you even going to apply to university? You can't hang around, it's only going to get more expensive.'

'There are other ways besides your way, Nina. Not all of us feel the need to get a degree just so we can have some man ordering us around.'

'You mean it's better to hide away from reality?'

'You missed a smashing visit with your uncle,' my father cuts in quickly. 'Still, he says he'll come back again before he goes to the States. How's next month for you?'

'Actually, Dad, I'm not sure I'll be around. I've . . . got some news.'

'Do you, dear?'

I say it as quickly as I can, to get it finished. 'I've met a wonderful man called Juan and we've fallen in love. And we're buying a restaurant in Spain together and moving there.'

My father blinks. He looks like a baffled rabbit.

Immy says, 'I don't believe it. You've given up the best job in the universe? How will Mr Big Chef survive without his Girl Friday?'

'He'll be fine. I've started training Jennifer already; that's one reason I've been so busy.' I chose my moment carefully to give Edmund my resignation letter: in the morning, before a day full of meetings and interviews when I knew we wouldn't have a single second alone together. He read it in front of me, his face growing more and more grim. I held my breath and pretended to be checking my BlackBerry, to hide any sign that my heart might be breaking. Because it wasn't.

'Dad?' I say gently. 'What do you think of my news?'

He blinks again. 'You're really moving to Spain?'

'Yes.'

'Er . . . where?'

'The Costa Blanca. The restaurant is called El Flor Anaranjado, which means the Orange Blossom, and it's in an orange grove overlooking the ocean in a place called San Nasareo. I've got a photo.' I flip open my mobile and click on a picture file. On a mobile phone it's hard to see details, but the colours are clear enough: the low building is covered with creamy stucco and roofed with red tiles, against a sky of incredible blue. 'Juan took it yesterday afternoon,' I tell them, showing them the photo. 'He flew over to make an offer on the building and it was accepted this morning. Isn't that great?'

Immy takes the phone, glances at it and hands it to our dad. 'You didn't go with him?'

'I had to work yesterday so we thought he might as well go by himself. Since he's the one who speaks Spanish he can sort it out for both of us. And I wanted to come and tell you about it as soon as I could.'

Also, this way I didn't have to bring Juan back here to Holybrook, but I won't mention that.

My father squints at the phone. 'When are you going?'

'I've handed in my resignation for my job, and I put my flat on the market last week and I've already had an offer. It will be busy, but we're planning to go in about three weeks.'

'Oh,' says my father. Just that one word. His shoulders are slumped and his hair is grey.

'My phone works in Spain,' I say. 'We can talk any time, still. And it's only a three-hour flight. That'll be one good thing about being so close to the airport, right?'

As if to answer my question, another plane flies by overhead, though on a more distant flight path, because the roar is more muted.

'Yes, maybe I can come over,' my father says. 'A bit of sunshine, eh?'

He won't come over. Ironically enough, though he practically lives in the underbelly of an aeroplane, my father hasn't flown in years. But I'm grateful for the pretence, for the excuse it gives me to do this to him, to leave him like my mother left him all those years ago.

But it's not like that. It's ridiculous to feel guilty. I'm not abandoning him, I'm just going to Spain. To live my own life. Surely I'm allowed to do that, after everything?

'That would be great!' I say, and then stand up. 'Right,

can I borrow a pair of your shoes, Immy? I'll get the lawn mowed. And what have you got in the house to eat?'

After dinner, which has been filled with careful conversation about television shows I haven't watched, news I haven't had time to hear, and catch-ups on mutual friends I don't see any more, I hug my father and say goodbye. Imogen walks with me to the front door and steps outside to wait for my cab with me. We stand on the path, which is strewn with cut grass. Immy said she'd rake it up after dinner, but she's not making a move towards the shed. Somewhere, someone very optimistic is having a barbecue.

'You should watch *Emerly Street*,' my sister says to me, crossing her arms in the chilly air. 'It's really good.'

'I'll try to record it.'

'It's not so bad here, you know,' she adds. 'Dad and I have fun.'

'You do?' I try to keep the disbelief out of my voice, but a little bit creeps in.

'Yeah. We do. For example, when Arval came to visit, we went up the spire of St Barnaby's at midnight to see the pipistrelles.'

'You . . . you took Dad up the spire of a church at night? He's blind as a bat in the dark, you know that!'

'Bats aren't blind in the dark. Arval told us all about it.'

I squeeze my eyes shut, tight, for patience. 'I can understand Arval dragging people up church spires at night, because he's obsessed. But Imogen, you're meant to look after Dad. We talked about this.'

'*You* talked about it. I didn't talk at all. And he's a grown man, Nina; if he wants to go look at bats with his brother, he can.'

'But he ...' I take a breath, and speak slowly and rationally. 'You don't understand, Immy. You don't know how easy it is for him to come to harm. You were too young to remember what he was like before Mum left, how much stronger he was. Or what it was like when he ...' I swallow. 'When she did leave.'

'I know what he's like now, and that's all we've got. Anyway, don't you have to catch a flight to Spain or something?'

'Don't be like that, Immy. It's an amazing opportunity, and I'm in love with Juan.'

She pauses. I sense she's about to say something else, but she doesn't. Then she sighs and says, 'I don't blame you. Get as far away as you can, while you've got a chance.'

'That's not what's happening, Immy. I'm running towards something, not away.'

My cab pulls up. It's the same purple one that I came here in.

'Sure. See you, sis.' Imogen heads for the house.

'Immy?' I say. She turns at the door. 'Please take care of Dad. Please.'

'Whatever.'

'And you should come and visit me in Spain.'

'See you later.' She closes the door behind her.

It's not quite twilight; I can hear a strimmer buzzing one or two houses down, and the hum of the idling cab. I stand on my father's path and look at the pebble-dashed bungalow, with its windows spotted by dust and rain. I hear yet another plane approaching to drown out all the noise and the music and the communication. A doll's neighbourhood, hemmed in and grey-washed and far from everything new.

This is what my father has left, after he's lost everything. And Immy might be right: he might be doing well for now, but compared with what he's had, it's so, so small.

I say aloud to the evening, 'It's never going to happen to me.'

I loop the carrier bags over my arms and take the two suitcases by the handles. By the time I've lugged it all down the stairs from my flat, down the street, around the corner, up the next street and to the door of the charity shop, I'm breathing hard and beginning to sweat. I prop the glass door open with my backside and shove the suitcases into the shop. They make a loud *whsssh*ing sound against the linoleum.

The woman behind the counter looks up above her reading glasses. She's a large lady, with grey roots in her hair, and she's reading *A Brief History of Time*. 'Goodness, are you moving in?' she asks.

'I've got a donation.' I shrug the carrier bags off.

The woman doesn't put down her book. 'It doesn't matter how many times he's cheated on you, we won't take your ex-boyfriend's entire wardrobe. We're volunteers here and we don't need the aggro. If you want to get back at him, you'd best just cut it up with a pair of scissors.'

'It's not my ex's stuff, it's mine.' I haul the suitcases past the racks of clothes and open the first one, stuffed with my entire winter wardrobe, from woolly tights to knitted hats. The woman raises one eyebrow. Then I open the second suitcase, which is filled with stacks of shoeboxes.

This makes her put down her book. The movement jiggles the spare flesh on the tops of her arms. She struggles to her feet and reads the names on the boxes. 'Are these . . .'

'They're my shoes, and yes, they're what they say on the boxes.' I open a pair of Valentinos for her, and a pair of Stella McCartney platforms. 'I need to get rid of them.'

'Why?'

'I'm moving to Spain; it's too hot there for this kind of shoe. It's all sandals and espadrilles and things.'

She scrapes back her chair and lumbers around the counter to stand directly in front of the suitcase. Slowly she inspects the outside of each box.

'These must be worth a lot of money,' she says at last.

'Well, they're used.' Every shoe has its own memories, of where I bought it, when I wore it, how it made me feel. I had to pack them up quickly, with Rush on the stereo full volume, or else I'd never have got them here.

She picks up the platforms, which are very slightly scuffed on one toe from dancing last New Year's Eve, examines the damage, and then replaces them in the box. 'It seems to me that you could put them in storage or something.'

'I want to make a whole new start,' I tell her. 'From the wardrobe up.'

'And it does get cold in Spain eventually, I hear. You could use these again.'

For God's sake, how difficult is it to accept a charitable donation? 'I don't need them. I don't need anything. I'm going to make a new life for myself. Can you use them, or should I find someplace else to take them?'

'We can use them.' She goes back around the counter and picks up her book, though she doesn't start reading it again. 'Bring them to the back of the shop, will you?'

'Thank you very much for your donation,' I mutter under my breath, and push the whole shebang to the back of the shop. There's already a big pile of stuff there, most of it in bin liners.

'Do you want the suitcases back?' she calls. 'For your trip?'

'You can have them. I'm not taking much with me.'

She's watching me as I come back through the shop. 'If you're going to change your mind, I'd hurry up and do it now. Our donations get spread all over London, and it might take you a while to get your things back.'

'I'm not going to change my mind. This is the best decision of my entire life.'

'A man?'

'It was my own idea, actually.'

'Well, there's a first for everything, I suppose. Still, you want to be careful. Huge, rash, life-changing decisions like this rarely come to any good, and you don't want to end up coming back here with your tail between your legs.'

I clench my fists and swallow down my fury. I am not going to get angry at an old woman. She's obviously disappointed and bitter about her own life, and probably jealous of my youth and the fact that I'm starting off on a new and exciting adventure.

'Right,' I say. 'I'll be back in ten minutes with a couple of boxes.' Unfortunately this is by far the closest charity shop, otherwise I'd choose somewhere manned by a less cynical volunteer.

'More shoes?'

'No, this is household stuff. Pots and pans and some books.'

She brightens up. 'Ooh, books? You haven't got any Mills and Boons in there, have you?'

'No.'

'That's a pity. I've been waiting for some Mills and Boons to come in. This astrophysics business is all well and good, but I'm a sucker for a happy ending.'

My going-away party is at Jett, of course. But since I gave Pet the job of organising it, I haven't had to talk with Edmund. All I've had to do is walk in at the appointed time on Juan's arm.

Pet went shopping with me for the outfit I'm wearing, which is a light silk floral dress, one of the first of the summer collections to hit the shops. She also helped me choose Juan's clothes: a cream linen suit and a red shirt, which set off his colouring. As soon as I walk in to Jett, I know why she insisted on this particular dress, Juan's particular outfit: everyone else is dressed in black and white. In Jett's monochromatic dining room, they look like walking, talking extensions of the beautiful decor, and Juan and I stand out like exotic flowers.

I don't know all the people, but that's what the best parties are like. I have orange blossoms in my hair and Juan and I circulate, our arms around each other like the lovers we are. Edmund is wearing a black suit and a snow-white shirt, and every time I'm tempted to look at him, I squeeze Juan's hand and kiss him on the cheek. Then I have another glass of champagne.

I remember the first time I walked in this door, when I was sent from the agency to cover for Edmund's last PA. The orchids, the gleaming crystal, the flawless silver, the white linen, the precise and perfected food. I understood immediately how, for Edmund, this place isn't just a building where he and his team create and serve meals. It's his castle and he's its golden king. I borrowed it for a little while, but now I'm going to make my own castle home.

'Yes, El Flor Anaranjado is so gorgeous, I'm so happy, yes we're off tomorrow morning, you must come and visit,' I say about a million times, and I mean it. I really do. Beside me, Juan echoes what I say in his lovely accent, and between sentences he whispers in my ear about how beautiful I am.

I excuse myself to go to the ladies' and reapply my lipstick, which has worn off from all the kissing I've been doing. As I'm blotting, the door to one of the cubicles opens and Pet steps out. She's ridiculously elegant in a white suit with black jet jewellery, her hair tumbling down her back. But her nose is pink, and her eye make-up is smudged. She's obviously startled to see me, because she takes a step backwards, as if she's going to retreat into the cubicle.

'Pet? Are you all right?'

She laughs, exactly the same high, loud laugh as usual, and steps forward. 'Someone is wearing that horrible perfume I'm allergic to,' she says, and comes to the mirror to repair the damage. She wrinkles her nose and frowns at her reflection. 'Ugh, this requires major surgery.' She rummages in her bag, pulls out concealer, powder, eyeliner and mascara, and gets to work.

'I didn't know you were allergic to perfume.'

'Only the cheap stuff.' A practised swipe with the concealer removes the dark smudges, and Pet begins to rebuild her proper image.

'Are you sure that's what it is?'

I've never questioned Pet before, but this is my party, and the champagne has made me bold. She stops, mid-sweep with the mascara, and meets my gaze in the mirror.

'Do you know how many men I've slept with this year so far?' she asks.

'Um . . . five?'

'I slept with that many in February alone, and that's a short month. Do you know how many of them have asked me to run off with them to start a new life together?'

'All of them?'

'None. And that is because I'm not the kind of woman that men build a new life with. I'm the kind of woman that men have a very good time with.'

'I thought you liked being that kind of woman. I thought you didn't believe in all this love stuff.'

'I don't. My mother has been married three times, Nina, and my father was married twice before he even had me. They both believe in love, and look where it's got them. No, I can totally do without love. It's just . . . it would be nice to be asked.'

She sighs. Then she goes back to her mascara and eyeliner. 'Basically I'm jealous as hell,' she says.

Petronella Lennox-Ward is jealous of *me*? I'm tempted to pinch myself to see if I'm dreaming, but I don't think I could be that audacious even in my sleep. 'If you want to be asked, Pet, I'm sure you will be,' I say. 'All you have to do is believe in it.'

'Ah, well that's the problem, of course.' Her voice is light again and she snaps her handbag closed. 'Let's go get some more champers.'

I put my arm around her delicate shoulders as we leave the loo. 'You're going to come and visit me in Spain, right?'

'Couldn't keep me away. Oh look, Boris is here, you must meet Boris.'

*

Some time later, buoyed on a cloud of everything, it suddenly occurs to me that my father may have rung me with his own congratulations. I leave Juan talking a mile a minute about the qualities of champagne versus cava with Jett's mixologist Gretchen, and find the chair at the back of the room where I dropped my handbag earlier. I'm not quite aware of how tipsy I am until I find myself fumbling the catch of the bag.

A warm hand touches my bare arm. Drunk or not, I know it's not Juan. I know who it is, because the warmth floods over every inch of my skin.

'Nina,' Edmund says quietly behind me.

We have not been alone for a single moment since we kissed. We are not alone now. But of course, when he speaks, everyone and everything else disappears.

'We have to talk,' he says.

I bite my lip. If I didn't know already that I had to leave, how I feel right now would be all the reason I needed.

'I don't want to talk,' I say to the clasp of my handbag.

'But you're leaving because of what happened between us that night, and that's wrong.'

'I'm leaving because I'm in love with Juan and we want to open up a restaurant together.'

'I think that's a lie. I think you still care about me.'

My heart is beating so hard that I can barely hear my own thoughts. I shake my head, but it's a flimsy denial, and I know he can see it.

'You made me see so much that night,' he says. 'Things I never understood before about you, and about me. We need to talk about it. I need to know exactly what you feel. Come away with me for a minute.'

'No,' I say, and I pull out of his grasp. I'm close to tears. Instinctively I look for Caroline, but I can't find her.

'At least tell me the truth about why you're leaving.'

'I did. It's because of Juan. Just . . . just please be happy for me, Edmund.'

'I can't . . .' he begins, but I don't stay to hear it. I go back to Juan and my party.

# Part Two:
# A Land Far, Far Away

I roll down all the windows in our rental car to smell the Spanish air as we drive up the twisty roads towards San Nasareo and our restaurant. Juan is talking non-stop, pointing out landmarks, local flora and fauna, recounting memories. He grew up about twenty miles from here. On our right, stretching ahead of us, are brown rocky cliffs topped with fluffy green trees, and the turquoise sea. Rocks and islands jut out from the water and the morning sunlight turns them into gold.

'It's the most beautiful place I've ever been,' I tell Juan.

'Did I not tell you, *amor mío*?' His teeth flash brilliant white in his face.

White and cream buildings, with their terracotta roofs, signal the beginning of San Nasareo. Juan turns the car into what I assume is the main street, running alongside the seafront. Boats bob in the harbour, and cafés and market stalls line the pavements, with the traffic twisting through them. I breathe in salt air and petrol and read the unfamiliar signs. *Fortuna. Damm. Sin Salida.*

'Sergio!' cries Juan suddenly, and stops the car half-way up the pavement. He gets out and greets a stocky man sitting at one of the café tables. They embrace each other and speak in rapid Spanish.

I hesitate, unsure whether to get out or not, unsure how to behave in general in this brand-new place, but Juan catches my eye and gestures for me to stay put. In a moment, he pats the other man on the back and comes back to the car. He's beaming.

'Sergio is going to do some work for us. You will meet him properly later, but I told him we were eager to see our new home.'

'Our new home,' I say. 'How do you say that in Spanish?'

'*Nuestra nueva casa.*'

'*Newestra neweva casa.*'

'*Muy bueno.*'

I repeat the phrase over and over again, trying to make it familiar in my mouth. Juan starts the car again and drives through the town and out the other end, turning up a steep road lined with orange trees.

I stop trying to speak Spanish and hold my breath.

I see the sign first. *El Flor Anaranjado*, it says, in peeling paint on a crooked board, weather-beaten and dangling from the dead branch of one of the biggest trees.

Juan stops the car and gets out. I see the building now, low and covered with creamy stucco. The roof tiles are brightly, shockingly red, redder than roses. The photographs have made it look smaller. They've also made it look like it's in better shape. Here I can see how the stucco is falling off in places, how the windows are dirty. Barrels of cooking oil rust behind some scrubby bushes at the side.

Juan opens my door for me. I smell sea air. Below my feet, the ground is gravel and dust. I take a step, and my heel clinks on something. I look down to see I've stepped on a San Miguel beer bottle cap. They're scattered everywhere, like worthless coins at the bottom of a wishing fountain.

'We will clear this out easily,' he says. 'It is no work at all. But *mi amor*, you must see the best part.'

He takes me by the hand and leads me to the front of the building. There's a veranda, lined with colourful hand-painted tiles, scattered with cane chairs and scarred tables, some of them occupied by men in dusty clothes nursing tumblers of drink. The veranda stops at a low wall, and just beyond it, the earth ends and the sky and sea begin, two infinities of flawless blue.

'Oh my God,' I whisper. 'You could jump off and fly.'

'It is what I said to you, a beautiful lady waiting to be rescued, no?' He kisses my hair. 'Like my Nina.'

'Juan!'

A man in a smudged apron appears in the doorway to the restaurant. Juan raises his hand to him and shouts a rapid greeting in Spanish. Cigarette smoke laces the intoxicating air. A sea breeze flirts with the hem of my skirt and the sun caresses my skin.

*I'm going to be incredibly happy here*, I think.

In its unintelligible language, a gull screams.

We go to meet Juan's family the next day. Although Juan acted very excited about bringing me to the restaurant, we drive to his parents' farm in near silence. Possibly he's tired from last night; we stayed in a hotel in San Nasareo, because we don't have any furniture yet for the little flat above the restaurant, and we spent most of the night making love. This morning I feel more connected to him than I've ever felt. We're starting our new life together.

He's so quiet. He's probably worried that I won't like his family. I want to ask him some questions about what they're like, but I know that if Juan were meeting my father and sister and uncle, I wouldn't want him to ask questions through the whole journey. I'd just want him to accept them as they are. So I keep my mouth shut, try to hum along with the unfamiliar music on the radio and watch the new scenery going by.

He's told me quite a bit about his family already, anyway. He has four elder brothers and one younger, all of them married and working on nearby farms, all of them with varying sizes and numbers of children. Six nephews, four nieces, I repeat to myself; two sisters, three aunts, twelve cousins. What fun it must have been to grow up in a big family. His mother is a brilliant cook, and Juan inherited his passion for food from her. I imagine the big, noisy Esperanza horde gathering around an outside table laden with food and wine, teasing each other, kissing each other, sharing the little sorrows and triumphs of the day. I picture them welcoming me with open arms. His mother will be a big, comfortable woman with white hair; she will embrace me to her soft bosom and thank me for bringing Juan back to Spain.

Fortunately, I'm wearing the perfect outfit for it: a long, gauzy white dress, which is both modest and sexy, and high white espadrilles. I thought about higher heels, but I don't want to tower over Juan too much. We pull into the rutted road leading to the farm and I admire the neatly planted green fields.

The farmhouse is big, made of stone with tiny windows, and the farmyard is dirt and scrubby grass. Juan opens my door for me, but as I step out, a tiny wiry woman with a mass of curly black hair flies from the open house doorway and embraces him, talking a mile a minute in Spanish. She takes his hand and immediately begins to lead him towards the house.

I follow them, wrinkling my nose against the smell of manure and straw, and avoiding the more dodgy-looking piles of dirt. We go through a heavy wooden door into a narrow corridor and then into a dim, low-ceilinged room, which is filled with a crowd of people sitting around a vast table laden with huge plates of salad and bread and cold meats. The odours of garlic and onions from elsewhere in the house overwhelm the last vestiges of manure. When Juan enters, a cheer arises and they flock to greet him, touching and kissing and exclaiming in Spanish.

Though Juan's family are of various ages and builds, they are all dark-haired and quite short. I stand in the doorway, watching the reunion, feeling pale and blonde and very tall. I understand about one word in a million. I smile, waiting for someone to notice me.

Everyone starts to take their places again at the table; Juan's mother directs him to a seat near a grizzled, brawny man who I guess is his father. With nearly everyone sitting down I feel even taller. 'Um, hi,' I say.

Juan's hand reaches for me, and he pulls me to his side. *'Mamá, Papá, os presento a Nina Jones.'*

All eyes in the room snap in my direction. *'Hola,'* I try.

Juan says something else, in which I catch *El Flor Anaranjado*. His father nods slowly, and several other members of the family nod too. Mrs Esperanza scurries off to fetch another chair and a place setting, which she puts next to Juan's. *'Gracias,'* I say gratefully and sit down.

Conversation immediately resumes, and the dishes of food are passed around. Mrs Esperanza hovers between me and her son, making sure he is served first with the tastiest bits, and that I'm served second. The room is so close, and there are so many people, and the courses of food keep on coming, carried in from the kitchen by endless female cousins. I feel dizzy and overwhelmed, but I make sure I smile at Juan's mother and thank her each time she adds something to my plate.

It's delicious, fresh and punchy, and Juan nods at me encouragingly whenever I lift my fork to my mouth, but I can't manage more than a few bites. I might as well be a space alien for all the resemblance I have to this family. I should have learned more Spanish, and then I could have tried to join in the conversation. It's my own fault; if I'd made more of an effort, I'd blend in better.

Juan smiles at me. 'You are doing well,' he whispers, and takes my hand under the table. Then he joins in a rapid-fire volley of Spanish with the man across the table from him, who from the looks of it is one of his brothers.

I smile, and nod, and take another mouthful. I'll do better next time. I'll practise Spanish every chance I get. I'm sure that, eventually, they're going to love me.

# Five months later

Sunlight beats against my eyelids with the ruthless good cheer of a gaggle of girls on a hen night. I turn over, and fall out of bed.

'Ow.' I sit up, rubbing my nose. The wooden floor of our flat is dusty from the renovations going on downstairs, and my knees are smeared with grey.

I look around for Juan. Our flat, upstairs from El Flor Anaranjado, consists of a bedroom and a closet with a sink in it; all the other rooms are full of furniture and building equipment. You don't need a hot bath in this weather. When we first got here, Juan set up a barbecue outside, and we used to sit on the ground eating and looking out at the sea, talking about our plans under the stars.

Juan isn't in the bed, a battered narrow double that we rescued from his family's barn, and which still smells slightly of goats. In fact, I was sleeping on his side of the bed, which is probably why I fell out. There isn't really enough room for two in it, especially when the nights are so hot you can't bear the thought of getting within half a metre of someone else's body heat. Usually Juan sleeps outside in a hammock he's strung up between two orange trees, leaving me to stretch out and sweat in the bed alone. It doesn't sound terribly romantic, but when it's that hot, you're glad of the space, believe me.

He's probably up already, supervising the workmen, who slope in when they're good and ready every morning, and slope out when it gets too hot. I stand up and stretch. It's another sunny day, and the heat simmers along in the background, waiting to get fierce. San Nasareo has the best weather on the planet. Day after day of brilliant sunshine, each one more perfect than the next. You hardly ever have to think about what to wear, because most clothes look good with a tan. This is the place that little floaty summer dresses and halter tops were invented for.

I wander off to the closet to have a wash. Even though I haven't had much time to do things like sunbathe or swim in the balmy sea, the mirror above the sink shows that my skin is tanned and my hair is bleached more blond from the sun and the salt air. It happens practically by osmosis out here – you move to Spain and bingo, you're more attractive. I brush on some make-up from my case, hung from a nail pounded into the unfinished wall, and then go back into the bedroom to pull a floaty summer dress off the neat pile of clothes on a packing crate. I slide a pair of Dolce & Gabbana sunglasses on to my head, slip my feet into a pair of open-toed heels and go downstairs to the restaurant.

As always, I have to pause before entering the dining room, to appreciate its perfection.

It's empty, except for some tools and spare wood leaning against a sawhorse-type contraption that the workmen have left. But the walls are smooth, newly plastered and painted; the floor is hand-fired tiles, gleaming richly in the sunlight. The ceiling is gorgeously rustic, crossed by ancient beams and with no trace of the large damp patches we found when we first came here. Or the dodgy wiring, or the termites, or the mice. Along one wall is the bar, hand-carved from mahogany, topped with Alicante marble, and bought from a colonial Valencia hotel that was going out of business to make way for executive flats. The main wall is nearly all glass, looking out at the spreading Mediterranean. Outside I see seagulls soaring, hear cicadas buzzing.

I made this. It's mine. Mine and Juan's.

'I completely made the right decision,' I say out loud. I say it every day.

Then I draw in a deep breath of paint, varnish, salt air and cigarette smoke. There's always cigarette smoke, but it's strongest from the direction of the kitchen, and I can hear male voices too, so I go there next.

Juan is standing with three other men, all of them wearing sleeveless T-shirts and smoking. They're talking in Spanish, too rapidly for me to follow, though from deduction I suspect it's something about the installation of the big stainless-steel ranges that are standing in the middle of the floor. Nobody's making a move to do anything, but this isn't unusual. I've learned that in Spain, any piece of work requires substantial prefatory discussion, along with many cigarettes smoked and much coffee consumed. That said, when they get down to it, they work very hard, at least until the next break, when they go and sit in the shade and argue over . . . whatever they argue about. Even though I've been here nearly five months, my Spanish still isn't good enough to understand a lot of it, aside from the occasional calls for *café* or *agua*. Fortunately Juan deals with all of the local workmen, and also most of the local merchants, estate agents and bankers. If it were down to my communication skills, they wouldn't get any further than coffee and cigarettes.

'*Buenas dias*,' I say cheerfully. All of them, including Juan, laugh.

'Is my accent that bad?' I ask.

'It is very endearing,' he says, and kisses me on the cheek. His own accent has become more pronounced, and the Spanish sun has darkened his skin. For a while he was growing a bit of a beard, because of the inconvenience of shaving in our little closet, but lately he's been perfectly clean-shaven. He's had a haircut recently, too. I think it's because we're getting closer to finishing the restaurant after months of dusty, dirty, costly renovations, and he's feeling the need to smarten up to match.

I hook my finger in his shirt sleeve and draw him a little away from the others. 'Where were you last night?'

'I finished late,' he says. He holds up his hand and one of the workmen passes over a cigarette. He never smoked in London, but here he's taken to Fortunas. An old habit, picked up again, he says. 'I came up and saw you sleeping there like an angel, and could not disturb you. I slept on the hammock.' He lights the Fortuna and exhales a curl of smoke. His eyes wander to the new stoves.

'Why were you so late, anyway? You said you had a meeting about a dishwasher . . .'

His voice lowers. 'Even with a dishwasher you must be careful. I do not want to hire some raw new person who has never been in a kitchen before. But to get someone experienced, you must find them in another restaurant. I have to meet these people out of work, on their nights off, places where we will not be thought to be doing business.'

'Where? Back alleys?'

'Bars. Nightclubs. Sometimes miles away. We have been through this before, you and I.'

'But it sounds so ridiculously clandestine, to get someone to wash dishes. Can't you just make some phone calls?'

'It does not work that way. And it is not ridiculous. It is how I met you.'

'But . . .' I remember Edmund talking about Juan poaching me, and I shake my head. 'But we're more than that.'

'Of course we are, *corazón.*' He kisses me on the cheek, and I smell his cigarette. Then his phone rings, and he checks the number. '*Perdóname,*' he says, and goes with the phone out of the kitchen into the dining room. I hear him speaking softly in Spanish, and then he goes outside or speaks even more softly because I can't hear him any more.

'*Café?*' I say to the other three, and they give me a chorus of *sís*. I go to the espresso machine, one of the first things we had installed, and make us all the super-strong, super-sweet coffee that this country runs on. So much more exciting than bland old English tea. Everything in Spain is so much more exciting, so much more vibrant, so much better.

So much more lonely.

I shake my head quickly and stir sugar into the coffees. I'm not lonely; I'm busy. So is Juan. We're working hard and we like it. I'm sure Edmund and Caroline barely saw each other when they were getting started, too. Long hours are part of the job. Underneath, our lives are entwined.

And there are people around here all the time, working, talking, observing. People from the town come up constantly to see what's going on; sometimes they bring food and drink and picnic while they're watching the walls being plastered or whatever. We practically had all of San Nasareo up here to watch the bar being installed. Pet's rung several times asking when she can come over, though I'm not ready to have her here yet, not until the restaurant is finished. And I've met a few British expats. There's Amanda, the interior designer, for example. We've been out shopping a few times, and I'm meeting with her this morning, to go through tablecloths.

Whoops. *'Cuándo es?'* I call to one of the men, who have all lit fresh cigarettes and are contemplating the ovens again.

*'Son las diez.'*

Yes, I'm late. I deliver the coffees and gulp mine, which is hot enough to scald my throat. I run out to our battered Jeep as fast as I can over the gravel and tufty grass. Juan is under an orange tree, gazing out to sea, still on the phone. I wave at him, though I'm not sure he sees me, and start up the Jeep.

The sun shines on my shoulders and the warm wind lifts my hair and plays it around my face as I drive down the hill and into the town of San Nasareo. I dodge around scooters and pedestrians, who spill out over the pavements and walk in the roads. If you did that in London you'd get sworn at by all the cab drivers, but not here. Spain is so much better than London in so many ways. For example, here, I'm not mooning around after someone else's husband. I've got my own man. In fact, I'm pretty much completely over—

'Edmund!'

He's tall, blond, walking in the street directly in front of my car. I slam on the brakes and throw it into neutral. Behind me, I hear loud Spanish cries and horns blasting, but I don't care. He's here, somehow, in front of me, back on the pavement now and rounding the corner into a steeply climbing cobblestoned street. My mind is racing as I jump out of the car and hurry after him.

How? Why? Are he and Caroline here on holiday?
He's alone, but she could be off somewhere. But they'd
ring, wouldn't they, if they were coming here? Unless . . .

Unless he's come here just to see me? Alone?

*Nina, we have to talk*, I hear him saying on the night
of my party.

I gasp, and run the last little bit and put my hand on
his shoulder. 'Edmund?'

He turns around. *'Ja?'*

And it's not Edmund. He's built the same, and has
similar hair, he moves the same way, but his face is too
long, his chin too weak, his eyes too pale. He has a little
peach-fuzz moustache, and he smiles when he sees me.

'I'm . . . I'm sorry, I thought you were someone else.'

'Hello? That is fine, what is your name?'

He's German, not English. Not even close to
Edmund.

'I'm sorry,' I say again, and turn to go back to my car,
feeling sick.

The crickets chirp behind me. The waves kiss the shore
below me. Ghostly moths flutter around my single
candle.

I pour another glass of Rioja.

In the distance, from the town sparkling down the
coastline, I can hear the throb of dance music. The night
breeze catches the hem of my silk dress and bumps it
against my bare legs. It was far too expensive for my
depleted bank account, but I bought it especially for
tonight, which is the five-month anniversary of my and
Juan's arrival at El Flor Anaranjado.

On the first-month anniversary, Juan surprised me
with a single red rose and a handmade local silver
pendant in the shape of an orange blossom. On our
second, he arranged a midnight sail in the harbour. Our

third was another red rose. Our fourth-month anniversary happened while we were mid-negotiations for buying the bar and also when we discovered the termites were further afield than we'd suspected, so that sort of got lost in the shuffle.

This time, I want to surprise him. We've been so busy, we deserve a treat. This morning, in between the noise of the digger we've hired to get rid of the rocks in the lawn so we can lay down turf, I told him, 'Make sure you're back by eight tonight, okay?'

He nodded, and gave me what is becoming his usual goodbye to me, a kiss on the cheek. In the wake of the not-Edmund-but-really-a-German disaster, I'm thinking about why I reacted so strongly to someone who resembled my ex-boss, and I've concluded it's because I'm not seeing enough of Juan to distract me from my self-destructive urges. I stood among the dug-up lawn this morning and counted how many times we'd made love in the past few weeks. The best I could come up with was half a time, when we'd both fallen asleep in the middle of it.

Thus the dress. And the lingerie. And the Rioja, and the lobsters, and the cake ordered in secret from the bakery in town. I'm going to treat Juan to a taste of his own romantic medicine, and then I'm going to take him to bed and blow his mind. Among other things.

That's the plan, anyway. Except that Juan hasn't shown up. I check my watch again, in the feeble light from the candle: nine thirty.

I think he was meeting a meat purveyor. That could take a while, I guess. But he did say he'd be here for eight.

I dial his number on my mobile, and it goes straight to his answerphone. This means that either he's turned his phone off, or he's using it. Maybe he's ringing me. I hang up quickly.

Usually if Juan says he'll be somewhere, he is. Reliability is a hallmark of a good chef. In fact I can only remember one other time he was late, that time when I made him a special dinner at my flat, on what was almost our first night together. Come to think of it, that was the last time I was the one to make the romantic gesture, too. It's almost as if he likes being the pursuer, rather than the pursued.

But that's ridiculous. We've gone beyond that; look at all we've achieved together here. Meat is important for a restaurant. He needs to find the best purveyor, and that takes time.

I slide a Fortuna from the pack I bought for him and light it from the candle. I take an experimental drag, remembering secret Silk Cuts behind the cricket pavilion at school. That was at my first school, St Hilda's School for Girls; Holybrook Comprehensive didn't have anything grander than a bike shed made of corrugated plastic, and there was never any room back there anyway with all the eleven-year-olds puffing away.

Ugh! The smoke is thick and tarry and even more foul in the mouth than it smells.

I take another drag.

The phone rings, and though I've been hoping for it, I jump. I drop the fag on the ground and grind it out with my heel, then press 'answer' on my phone without even checking the number. 'Where are you, darling?'

'I'm in Holybrook, oh love of my life, where are you?'

It's my sister. I sit back in disappointment. 'Oh, hi, Immy.'

'What's up?'

'Not much. I'm sitting here on our terrace overlooking the sea with a glass of Rioja.' I pick up the bottle. It's empty. Whoops.

'Very nice. Surrounded by Spanish studs?'

'Something like that.' Imogen never calls me off her own back; I haven't spoken with her for weeks. I suspect she hides when I ring Dad. This isn't an emergency, or else she wouldn't be making wisecracks. Probably she's opened a bottle of sherry, had a few tokes off a spliff, and feels like chatting before she gets stuck into the contents of the breadbin. 'How's everything there?'

'All right. Dad asked me to call you.'

'He did? He wants his girls to be closer to each other, huh?'

'No, he wants me to tell you that Arval died.'

I sit bolt upright. 'What?'

'He was spelunking in the Ozarks looking for *Corynorhinus townsendii ingens*.'

'Speak English, please, Immy.'

'He was in a cave in America looking for big-eared bats. He had a heart attack.'

I flinch. 'My God.'

'It was instantaneous, apparently. One of his bat friends rang Dad and told him. I mean his bat-loving friends, not a friend who's a bat; bats can't use the telephone, obviously. This guy was there with him and saw it happen. They're doing some sort of inquest, though, so it's going to be a while before the body can be shipped back to England.'

'How's Dad?' Panic rises in my throat as I finally realise the implications of this news. 'Immy, Arval is Dad's last relative besides us. How's he taken the news? Is he all right? Put him on the phone, I need to talk to him.'

'He's all right.'

'He can't be. Immy, put him on the phone.'

'I can't.'

'Why not? What's he doing?'

'He's in the bathroom.'

'He's in the *bathroom*? What is he doing?'

'Taking a shower, I guess. Or using the toilet. He asked me to call you and tell you about Arval.'

'Why? Why doesn't he want to speak to me?'

'He didn't say why, but I assume it's because you were going to freak out, like you're doing now.'

I take a breath. I wish I hadn't stubbed out the Fortuna. 'I'm not freaking out. I just need to speak to Dad. I need to know that he's all right.'

'I told you, he's fine. They're going to cremate him, apparently, so he won't go off.'

'*What?*'

'Arval. They don't want him stinking up a plane. It's sad. I liked Arval. He was cool.'

'Imogen, I'm worried about our father. Are you sure he's in the shower?'

'I suppose I could go and turn on the hot water in the kitchen and see if he screams.'

'Immy!' I am not getting anywhere with this. I stand up and go inside, heading for the stairs to our bedroom. 'I'm flying back to England.'

'No. Don't. Dad said he didn't want you to.'

'Don't be silly, he needs me. I can probably get a flight out of Alicante tonight or early tomorrow morning.' Once in our bedroom, I get on my knees and reach under the bed for my carry-on suitcase. Then I remember about all the dust. No matter how many times you clean, it comes back. 'Oh shit, my dress.'

'What?'

'It doesn't matter. Not important, anyway. Listen, I need to get off the phone and call the airline.'

'Nina, you really don't have to . . .'

'Don't worry, there are loads of flights. I'll rent a car at the airport and go straight there. You just hold on there, okay? I won't be long.'

'Nina, don't—'

'Just please go and stand outside the bathroom, will you? Knock on the door. Make sure he's okay.' I hesitate, caught between my need to hear that Dad's all right and my need to book a flight, to be on my way, to be there *now*.

'This is so stup— Oh, he's just come out. He's all wet, he's been in the shower like I said.'

I put my head on the goaty bed, sagging with relief. 'Is he all right? Put him on.'

'He's got a toothbrush in his mouth.'

'Just . . . hold on till I get there, will you, Immy? Bye.'

I pull the carry-on out, shake the dust off it, and put it on the bed. Then I start scrolling through my mobile contacts for the number of a taxi. Juan has the Jeep, and it'll be quicker to go straight to the airport and buy the first flight when I'm already there. While I'm thumbing the button, I look out the window to see if Juan's shown up yet. I see the faint flickering light of my single candle on the terrace, and the inert black shadow of the digger. No Juan. I don't have time to wait for him.

I order the cab, and then I write a note.

12

I park the rental car in front of my father's house and jump out into the grey morning. I couldn't get on anything but the very last flight, which went to Gatwick, and which was also delayed for two and a half hours. When I finally got to Gatwick I had to wait for the car rental desks to open, pacing the polished floors, cursing at the featureless shuttered shops and cafés. And then there were the pre-rush-hour traffic snarls on the M25, when I pounded my fists on the steering wheel and wished for the narrow streets of San Nasareo. They're a deathtrap, sure, but at least you can move.

Now it's nearly eight o'clock. Anything could have happened. While I've tried to distract myself from worrying by mentally checking inventory lists for the restaurant, practising Spanish phrases, and going through every note of Rush's entire *2112* album in my head, for the last hour table linen, *Que aproveche!* and the Priests of the Temples of Syrinx have not been helping me. I've been ambushed by memories of those first few weeks after Mum left. If that happens again, Imogen just could not cope. She hasn't got the commitment or the mental strength, and because she doesn't remember what it was like, she's been lulled into a false sense of security. Sure, Dad's been relatively fine for the past few years, but another huge shock like this could send him spiralling back downwards.

A plane is mid-flight overhead, filling everything with its noise. I run to the bungalow door and fling it open. No point knocking. I can't hear anything, of course, but there's a light on in the kitchen, so I hurry there first.

Dad and Imogen are sitting at the table, eating Frosties.

'Dad!' I hug him. He smells of shaving cream and sugary cereal. I hold him as tight as I can while I'm standing up and he's sitting down, thanking whatever's up there to thank that he's okay. The plane noise fades, then disappears.

'Nina,' he says. 'You really didn't need to come, love.'

'Of course I did. You can't be alone at a time like this.'

'Well, Immy's here, and we rub along pretty well. All that expense – flying over here at such short notice, and renting a car – it's really not necessary.'

'It wasn't that expensive,' I lie. 'Anyway, that's what credit cards are for.'

'Well, you're here now; you might as well sit down and have some cereal.'

I finally let him go. 'I'll . . . uh, I'll get a bowl.'

Imogen keeps on spooning cereal into her mouth. 'Hey, Nina,' she says through Frosties. 'Good thing you're here so you can stand outside the bathroom door.'

'Good morning, Imogen.' I get out a bowl and pour myself some cereal for something to do, though I haven't touched anything like Frosties for years. Edmund says sugary breakfast cereal is just one of the ways that the big food companies indoctrinate children and stunt their taste buds. I pour milk on it and then examine my father.

He looks fine. He looks completely normal, in an ineptly ironed shirt and a bland tie, eating his breakfast and drinking his tea. But appearances can be deceptive.

'I'm really sorry to hear about Arval,' I say carefully. It's hard to know whether to talk about it, or whether it's best to avoid the subject. I'll test the water, and see how he reacts.

'I know. It was quite a surprise to get the phone call. He told me to say hello to you when he was here last, did I tell you that?'

'I'm not sure,' I say, and then realise that this was Arval's last message to me, and that Dad would feel bad if he hadn't passed it on. 'Actually I remember, you definitely did.'

'They say he was looking for an Ozark big-eared. He'd hoped to see one this trip. They say that's the last thing he saw.'

He looks down at the table for a minute, then takes a sip of tea. I feel a wave of sadness, for Arval and for what Dad has lost. It's the first time I've really had time to think about it in itself, not buried under worry and panic and travel.

'Oh, Dad, I'm so sorry.'

'Thank you.' Our eyes meet for a second, then he looks down at his cuffs and fusses with the buttons. I remember him doing this a long time ago, in the mornings on his way to work, except then it was gold cufflinks my mother had given him. It's yet another reminder of how things have changed, how things can look fairly normal on the surface but hide a depth of loss underneath.

'Well, it's nice of you to come all this way because of Arval,' he says. 'Will you be staying long?'

'As long as I need to. Juan can hold the fort with the building work, and I'll get on the phone this morning and cancel my appointments.'

'Whatever you like. Of course you're always welcome. I think the camp bed is still in Imogen's room from Christmas, isn't it, Imogen?'

'I've been keeping my shoes on it.'

Ugh. Nice. 'That will be fine,' I say.

'Well, that's good then. I'll be off to work.' Dad scrapes back his chair and stands up.

'You're not going to work today, surely?'

'Of course I am. Why wouldn't I?'

'Well . . . you've just had some awful news. It seems like you should have some time to get used to it.'

'They're expecting me in today.'

See? This is the sort of thing I'm talking about. My father can't even stand up to his employers when he needs a day off. As if they'd even notice if he were gone. 'Dad, that's ridiculous. They can spare you for a few days when you've lost your only brother.'

'Nina, I'm surprised to hear you talk like that. You know what it's like to have responsibilities. I've had that one day last week when I got the news, and that's more than enough.'

'You've had . . . what? You mean you heard about Arval last week?'

'Yes, last . . . when was it, Immy?'

'Last Monday evening,' she says. 'You took Tuesday off.'

'That's right. I took Tuesday off. They were very nice about it.'

'You got the news last Monday and you waited *over a week* to tell me?'

'Well, as I said, there's not much to be done, and we know you're busy.' He brushes a kiss on to my gobsmacked face, and then kisses Imogen on the top of her messy hair. 'I'm off, then, see you when I get home.'

I watch him leave. I hear the front door close. Then there's no noise except for Imogen chewing.

'You like your cereal soggy, huh?' she says at last.

'You got the news *last Monday*?'

'Your habit of repeating yourself has got a lot worse. Is it a Spanish thing, do you think?'

'I just can't believe that you didn't tell me. You knew I'd be worried.'

'Yes, we did, and that's why we didn't tell you. I told you, Dad is fine. Everything's fine. Arval's dead, and that's sad, but that's it. If you don't want your cereal, I'll eat it.'

I go into the living room and ring Juan, but it clicks straight to answerphone again. He'll be working, twice as hard because I'm not there. 'Love,' I say, 'I've made it to England safely, but I'm not sure how long my fath . . .' I hesitate. I've never really discussed my father and his foibles with Juan, and there's no point going into it in a phone message. 'I mean, I'll probably be sorting out funeral arrangements, so I might stay here for a few days. Ring me with anything about the restaurant. And . . .'

Again I pause. I'd like to ask where he was last night, when I was waiting for him, and why he hasn't called yet. He'll have a lot to do, but surely he can take a few minutes to make sure I'm all right. Then again, maybe he's annoyed with me for taking off so quickly and only leaving a note.

Funny, one of the reasons I decided to fall in love with Juan was because I was assured of his devotion to me, whatever I did.

'Just give me a ring,' I finish. 'Okay, talk to you soon.'

Then I spend quite a bit of time with my BlackBerry ringing all the people I had appointments with and cancelling them. They're all quite cheerful about it, and I clear several days. For a moment I'm a little disconcerted at how easy it is to drop out of my own life, but then I shake my head. It's this yellowing magnolia woodchip on the walls, and the carpet patterned with unnatural twists of dead blue foliage; it instils instant despair.

When I go back into the kitchen, Imogen has disappeared, but thumping music from her room tells me where she's gone. No chance of a nap for me after my sleepless night, then.

But there's too much to do anyway. I need to take an inventory of the fridge and cupboards and go shopping to stock up with fresh, healthy, tasty food, and then I need to attack this bungalow with a duster and a scrubbing brush. Anybody would be depressed here, even if they hadn't lost their only sibling. Look at me: I've got a great life and a brilliant boyfriend and even I am ready to throw myself out the window because of the decor, though as it's a bungalow I wouldn't inflict much damage on myself.

I make it through three days of cleaning and cooking and being upliftingly cheerful and watching insipid television in the evenings and then listening to Dad and Imogen discuss it in detail the next morning. I've been watching Dad with an eagle eye, but he doesn't seem any different from normal. I have no idea whether this is because it's the calm before the storm, or if it's because my presence is helping him keep his mind off things.

Tonight I've made them Juan's special tortilla and I serve it with the only bottle of Rioja I could find in the local Tesco. There's nothing wrong with Dad's appetite, anyway; he shovels it down while speculating with my sister about whether Jamila off *Emerly Street* is going to run off to Portugal with Bryan despite being best friends with his wife Nicky.

'Nice omelette, Nina,' he says as he scrapes his plate clean.

'Tortilla. Thanks.'

'I thought tortillas were those things you wrapped around burritos,' Imogen adds.

'That's Mexican. This is Spanish.'

'Mexicans speak Spanish, don't they?'

'Yes, but it's different.' Actually I don't have a clue, but I seem to be the voice of authority in this house.

'I like burritos, we got a kit once.'

Would it be so hard for her to thank me for cooking? My father is never enthusiastic, but he's not enthusiastic about anything in particular these days and at least he's appreciative enough. But Imogen just appears in the morning for breakfast, then goes back into her room and doesn't re-emerge until lunchtime, when she makes herself a sandwich and takes it back into her room again. I have no idea what she's doing in there for the entire day; she claims to be working, but I haven't seen any evidence of work going on. The room's so cluttered that she could be hiding an oil painting in progress in there for all I'd know, but the few times I've gone in during the day to get something from my bag, she's been hunched in a chair in front of her laptop. She quickly minimises what she's doing as soon as I walk in, leaving me with only the view of her desktop wallpaper, which looks like one of the spotty teenagers off that soap opera she's crazy about.

I haven't caught any whiffs of illegal substances, so thank God she hasn't been doing that, not since I've got here anyway. Not that I mind so much in the abstract if someone has a few puffs on a joint to relax, but I'd prefer my sister to have a clear head in case I need her for an emergency.

At least she doesn't talk in her sleep any more like she used to when we shared this room when she was a kid. Mutter, mutter, mutter, she'd go all night, not even in real words but in something that sounded vaguely

Swedish. I used to have to sleep with my head under the pillow. Even though these days she's quiet at night, I've hardly slept, because I keep one ear cocked in case my father does any midnight wandering. All I've heard is the jets, flying off to wonderful distant places.

After dinner I do the dishes and then pop outside to try to ring Juan. All I've had from him is a single text, *Hope all is well*, which I received yesterday morning. Nothing else, nothing asking me when I'll be back or saying that he misses me or filling me in on the restaurant's progress, and I'm wondering if his mobile has conked out. Or maybe he's visiting his own family; mobile reception is tricky at best at their farm. Still, I wish he'd get in touch and let me know if our lawn is still a quarry.

I get his answerphone again and don't bother to leave a message. I join my family inside just in time for the closing credits of *Emerly Street*.

'I can't believe she's pregnant,' my dad is saying.

'Who's pregnant?' I ask. I'm not interested, really I'm not, soap operas are for people who haven't got lives of their own, but I can't help asking. I might as well know anyway, because that's all anybody ever talks about around here.

'Deeanna,' my dad answers. 'That Aloysius is a bad 'un.'

'Did Jamila run off with Bryan?'

'Not yet. She's packing. Bryan's writing Nicky a note.'

'Well, at least he has the decency to do that.'

When my mother ran off, she didn't leave a note. My father didn't have a clue what had happened until he found that the bank accounts had been cleared out, and then later, when we heard that our tennis instructor had gone missing too, we put two and two together. I quickly glance at my father to see if he's also made this unfortunate connection between our real life and a tacky soap opera plot, but he's turning over to a motoring programme.

'Well, I'm off,' Imogen says, getting up from the couch.

'Where are you going?' I ask.

'Pub's got wi-fi. See you later.' She grabs her coat from where she's draped it over an armchair, tucks her laptop under her arm, and leaves the room before I can say anything else.

Typical. She's going out to have fun, leaving me with Dad and a show about cars. I wouldn't mind the pub, though the places around here are pretty ratty. It would just be nice to have a drink and not worry for an hour or two. Not have to watch what I say, or pretend to be cheerful.

Then again, if Imogen's gone, this is my chance to talk to my father one-on-one, and really figure out what's happening with him.

I'm formulating the best way to tactfully and cheer-fully broach the subject when my dad turns down the volume on the telly with the remote and says, 'So, Nina, how much longer were you thinking of staying?'

'I'm . . . I'll stay as long as you need me to, Dad.'

'Well, as I said, I appreciate the cooking, and the place has never looked better, but you've got a job out there in Spain, hey?'

'Juan hasn't called with any problems, so everything's fine. You need me more, Dad.'

'Well, I love having you here of course, but you'd probably rather be with that young man of yours.'

'There's nowhere I would rather be than here with you.'

'Very kind of you, but I'm sure that's not true.'

'Of course it is.'

We watch cars race around a track for a moment. I'm thinking I didn't sound very convincing, so I try again.

'I'd like to do more than cooking and cleaning, though, Dad. What about the funeral arrangements? Can I make some phone calls for you?'

'There's really no need. We can't have the ashes until October, and I've spoken with the vicar in Hedegogllygoden, so there's plenty of time to work things out.'

A plane goes by and my dad waits, his eyes on the television. When the noise dies down I say, 'But how *are* you, Dad? Really? Are you okay?'

'Well, I'm sad. I'll miss Arval. He was a good big brother to me. And he and Claire were like second parents to you girls too, you know. Before.'

'He wasn't much good when Mum left.' It comes out before I know it's going to.

'Don't be too hard on him, Nina. He'd just lost Claire, you know. He did the best he could for us.'

*Yes, Arval going batty helped us no end*, I think, but I don't say it.

'But are you okay? Are you . . . do you feel maybe you can draw a line under it and move on?'

'You don't draw a line under your brother's death, Nina. It's not something you can say: here, it's over, I'll forget all about it now. You can't mark off so many days for mourning, or decide how you're going to feel. Life's not like that. It's never been like that.'

'It's just that . . . you know, when Mum left . . .'

Another plane. I'm sort of glad of the interruption. My father hasn't looked away from the telly this whole conversation.

'Cup of tea?' he asks when the plane's gone over, and gets out of his armchair.

'Yes please. But Dad, I'm just . . . I worry about you.'

He stands with his hand resting on the back of his arm-chair, and sighs. 'It's not the same,' he says. 'Your mother left me, but Arval just left. There's quite a difference.'

'I . . . I suppose so.'

'There is. And I can't help but think Arval had exactly the death he would have wanted. Face to face with an Ozark big-ear; you can't ask for better than that.'

I think I could probably ask for better than that. But I'm not Arval, that's for sure.

'So what you're saying is, you're fine.'

'Not sure about fine. But okay, yes.' He goes into the kitchen to make tea.

On the television, the presenter is gesturing enthusi-astically over some low-slung sports car. I've never had a desire for a sports car, but right now I wouldn't mind being that presenter, bad style sense and all, because at least he knows what he's doing. He's being a car fanatic, talking to other car fanatics about cars.

Whereas I have very little idea how I should talk to my father about any of this. How can I make sure he really is okay without bringing up all the reasons why I can't believe he is?

My father comes back with two mugs of weak tea, gives one to me, and sits back down. 'Isn't there anything you'd like me to do for you?' I ask. 'There surely must be something more to be sorted out.'

Dad turns the remote control around in his hand and thinks. 'Well, someone will have to go through Arval's flat in Highgate.'

'Has he left it to you?'

'He left all his money to the Bat Conservation Society, but the flat to me, yes.'

'We should get that done, then. It must be worth a fair bit, or we could rent it out. The money would come in useful, wouldn't it?'

Dad shrugs. 'No hurry about it. No, Nina, you should go back to Spain and your young man. You must have so much to do there.'

'Well, we've finished the renovations more or less, but now comes the hiring and promoting. I've been practising my Spanish, and Juan's been . . .' Actually, I don't know what Juan's been doing. Suddenly I have an urgent need to get back to Spain, to touch base with my boyfriend, to be part of his life again, to feel like I belong somewhere.

'I'll do Arval's flat for you,' I say to Dad. 'If there isn't any hurry, I can take the keys with me now to Spain and come back to London in a few weeks, when I have a day or two's lapse.'

'It's a very big job, you know.'

'It's easier for me, I'm sure. Less painful. I'll box up his personal things and bring them back here so you can go through them when you're feeling up to it. And you hate travelling in London anyway.'

He frowns. 'I'm sure my manager will give me a day one side of a weekend to sort it out.'

'But it'll need sorting to sell or rent out, too, and you don't know any painters and decorators in London. Or estate agents. I'll do it, Dad, I want to.'

Actually the task holds very little appeal for me; I imagine having to sort through my uncle's sock drawer and worse. But I figure I can just fill up a lot of bin liners and chuck anything that looks personal straight into boxes. I've done enough clearing in the past few months that I'm a pro. I've never been to Arval's flat – I always meant to, since we were in the same city and all, but Highgate was right the other side of London and I never seemed to have the time. Anyway, he always struck me as a tidy sort of chap, despite his penchant for crawling through guano. The flat will probably be in pretty good

137

shape, and if it's not, I can call in a cleaning service without the compunction my father would have about money or privacy.

'Please let me do this for you, Dad.' Otherwise, I'm not needed.

He looks away from the telly and at my face, and my desire to help him must be clear on it, because he nods. 'All right then, if you want. I don't have a key, though; he's got a spare behind the gargoyle.'

*Behind the gargoyle?*

'Uh, okay.'

The matter settled, Dad flicks the channels until he comes up with a show about Brits moving to Tenerife. 'This ought to remind you of home, eh?'

I watch the programme. Television can't capture the Spanish quality of light, or the ubiquitous cigarette smoke, but it can show the sunshine and the sea and the cream and white buildings, the narrow streets. It's not home, not quite yet, but it will be. I'm sure it will.

I wonder where Juan is.

'I'll book a flight,' I say.

'Immy?'

She's come in about half past midnight; the bedroom is dark, but her presence is announced by rustling clothes and the scent of beer.

'What?'

'I'm flying home the day after tomorrow.'

'Good. I mean, good for you, it'll be more interesting for you there.'

That's not what that 'good' meant at all. I hear her dropping things softly on the floor, and then pulling back the duvet to climb in.

We used to talk and giggle. We used to throw our

teddy bears at each other with the lights off and see who could make the most hits.

*Why do you dislike me so much that you can't wait to see me gone?* I want to ask her, across the blank gulf of darkness and discarded clothes. The springs creak on her bed and the mattress settles.

'Good night,' I say, quietly so as not to wake my father.

I t's good to be back. The road to San Nasareo flanks the sea, and with every mile I drive, I feel worry dropping away from me. Woodchip wallpaper, faded carpets, soap operas and dusty tea; it's as if they all flutter off into the salty air, taking with them a worrisome parent and a hostile sibling. Here, in Spain, I have work that people will appreciate. I have my own bed and a circle of if not yet friends, then acquaintances who will become friends in time. I have Juan.

I still couldn't get through to speak to him on the phone, but when I texted him my flight details, he sent a text straight back: *You know I always love you. J*.

That was so, so lovely, and just what I needed. I practically hugged my phone to me the entire journey, tempted to show it to strangers and say, 'See? He loves me.' My elation was only slightly dampened when I got to Alicante and Juan wasn't there to meet the plane. But then again, he'd never said he would, and I'm used to making my own way. I've resolved to grab him the moment I get to the restaurant, take him to bed, and make up for our recent separation. Spontaneous outbursts of passion are always better with Juan anyway. We'll have our anniversary celebration naked during the siesta, with our bedroom windows open to the blue sky.

The streets of San Nasareo in the morning are alive with buzzing, honking, walking and shouting. I drive as slowly as I can, drinking in the atmosphere. Cafés line the pavements and the market glows with displays of fresh fruit and fish. I spot Sergio and his mates around one outside table with coffee cups and cigarette packets in front of them. It feels like months since I've seen them, rather than days, and I wave at them as I approach.

Sergio stares at me. He nudges the man next to him with his elbow and says something I can't hear over the engine, and the whole group look at me, fags dangling from their mouths.

Maybe they weren't expecting me back so soon. I smile broadly and cry, '*Hola!*', and by the time I'm level with them I see an answering smile cross Sergio's face, but then I'm past. In the rear-view mirror, they've turned round in their chairs and are watching me go. Juan must've not told them I was coming back today.

I turn off on the road leading to El Flor Anaranjado, which is still unpaved but has had the major ruts filled in, and anticipation begins to tickle my stomach. Everything is going to be wonderful.

I round the corner and the restaurant is surrounded by lush green grass, which makes the building look like a jewel in a velvet setting. They've laid and watered the turf while I was gone. It was expensive, but God, was it worth it. Sergio and his mates were probably in the café celebrating a job well done. I park the rental next to our Jeep and jump out, leaving my bag behind. There'll be time to unpack later, after the joyful reunion. I hear gulls crying to each other as I hurry to the dining room entrance.

The dining room is empty. After my father's bungalow, it feels grand and spacious, every little bit of it carefully chosen for craft and beauty. Probably because I've been away, it feels different. Airier and cleaner. It's also very quiet; I don't hear any cheerful Spanish swearing of workmen.

I draw in a deep breath. Salt, paint, wood varnish. A hint of turf from outside overlaying the sea smell. No cigarette smoke.

I smile. That's it. That's why Sergio was in town; that's why he was staring at me. Juan has sent everyone away, so we have the place to ourselves. It's such a typically Juan romantic thing to do.

'Darling, I'm home!' I cry. There's a faint echo. I go into the kitchen, but there's no Juan among the gleaming ovens and worktops. Also no sign of him in the offices or the walk-ins and storage rooms, though I do notice we've had our first shipment of dry goods. Crates of rice and flour and spices sit unpacked in the store, their colourful labels seeming to exude the promise of deliciousness to come.

Of course he's not downstairs. He's upstairs, waiting in our private space. I climb the stairs, the flutter of my heart confirming that I love Juan every bit as much as I want to.

'Sweetheart, I missed you so, so much,' I call, and open the door to our bedroom.

The bed is made with its cotton spread, the covers pulled up over the pillows and tucked in just as I like it. Just as I do it, and which Juan never manages. The window is closed, the air stuffy. On the bed there is a white envelope.

My heart stops its flutter.

'Juan?' I say, in case he's in our closet bathroom. But that door is open, and the room is dark.

I go to the bed. I pick up the envelope. *Nina*, it says on the front in Juan's handwriting.

It's a love letter. It's a treasure-hunt clue. It's a handwritten apology for forgetting our anniversary. It's two tickets to Venice for a romantic weekend.

My hands are shaking. I know what it is; every cell of my body knows, all at once, as if I've belly-flopped into an ice-cold pool. I watch my fingers open the flap of the envelope and take out the single sheet of paper inside. It is closely written in blue biro, with wide white margins.

*My dear Nina,*

*I know you are a woman of great heart as well as great beauty. This is the reason why I comfort myself that you will understand what I write.*

*I have found again my Juanita. The few words cannot express the emotion. I feel complete. She has, too, been so very unhappy without me. She knows her supervisor was a grave mistake, one that has cost us both many months of loneliness.*

*Nina, you know what it is to love. You will understand why I must leave you to be with my Juanita, who is and always has been my destiny. True love is the most precious matter in the universe and we cannot pass up the chance to grasp it and hold it. Juanita and I are going far away from here, far from the good memories and the bad.*

*I know you will not begrudge the few euros I take to help us in our new life together. I leave you El Flor Anaranjado, which I know is your dream as much as it once was mine.*

*Forgive me,* querida. *I hope that one day perhaps you will understand that when your love so strong and true returns at last, you will be powerless to resist.*

*Ever,*

*Juan*

'What the *fuck*?' I shout.

I drop the letter on to the floor. I haven't read
it carefully, but I don't need to. Everything is crystal,
blindingly clear.

I run down the stairs and out of the building and
jump into the Jeep. I have to dig through my handbag to
find my keys, which settled to the bottom while I was in
England. When I start up the Jeep and throw it into gear,
I see that the petrol gauge is on empty. Maybe this is why
Juan left it behind – he was so eager to fly off into his
new life with his wonderful, perfect soulmate that he
didn't want to bother to get petrol.

Or maybe he didn't want to be easy to trace through
the vehicle.

I shudder. This is not happening to me, not to me. It's
not. I won't let it.

I fly out of the Jeep and into the rental car, which
starts with a roar because my foot is already revving the
accelerator. The tyres kick up gravel and dust behind me
as I do the most violent three-point turn in history and
speed down the road towards San Nasareo.

Everyone in the main square turns and stares at me
and my screeching brakes as I pull up outside the café
where Sergio still sits with his friends. They nudge each
other as I storm up to them. One of them, Manuel, folds

his hands on his lap and leans back in his chair as if he is about to watch a fascinating movie.

'Where's Juan?' I demand. Sergio just shakes his head. Around the corners of his mouth there is a faint smile, which infuriates me.

'*Dónde está Juan?*' I nearly shout it. If anyone in the square wasn't staring at me before, they are now. Sergio shrugs and raises his hands in a gesture of helplessness. I turn to the others, and they do the same.

'When did he leave?' I can't scrape together the Spanish for this question; I'm too upset. Again, Sergio shrugs, but the slight guy with the moustache, who I haven't seen as often as the others but who I think is called Jesus, mutters, '*Martes.*'

Tuesday. The day after I flew to England. He could be anywhere, absolutely anywhere in the world by now.

No. I refuse to believe that he's disappeared. This cannot happen to one person twice in one lifetime. The odds are phenomenally against it. He's got to be somewhere I can find him, and talk to him, and convince him to . . .

To what?

That's not what I need to worry about now. Now, I need to concentrate on finding him. I whirl away from the men and run back to the car, pulling out from the kerb without bothering to check my mirrors. I hear horns beeping behind me but I don't care. I weave down the street as fast as I can, and when I get away from the town traffic I put my foot down.

I've never driven to Juan's family's farm by myself, and after I'm about ten miles out of town all the turn-offs start to look the same. I take what I think is the right one, and then decide after a few miles that it's the wrong one and go back to the beginning and take the turning before, which looks even more wrong, and then try a third, which at first looks more familiar but after half an hour doesn't.

I stop at a petrol station for directions, but as I'm not one hundred per cent sure whether *izquierda* means left or right, I'm not much better off. I put my foot down on the accelerator again and speed off.

I don't know why I'm driving so fast, especially as I'm probably going in circles. Juan is gone. He's not going to be any less gone if I hurry. But driving gives me a purpose, it makes me feel like I'm doing something about the situation, and looking for the right turn-off keeps my mind busy enough so that I don't have to think. About being abandoned. About being a distant second best. About emptiness and silence and humiliation. About those half-smiles in the square.

And now I'm thinking about it. I'm dizzy and I feel sick and as I speed past I see a sign I recognise. I screech to a stop, turn round, and take the correct road at last.

I've spent so much time getting lost that when I arrive at the farm it's siesta time. Usually there are various cousins and other more distant relatives driving tractors and things around, but the wide dusty yard is abandoned except for a couple of loose chickens. It's probably horrendously bad manners, but I march right up to the door and pound on it anyway. What if Juan and Juanita are here?

Nobody comes for ages, and I'm considering searching the barn in case the absconding lovers are frolicking in the hay when the door eventually opens. Juan's mother stands there, her hair carefully tucked underneath a scarf.

She doesn't greet me, just looks at me. In her face there's patience and pity.

I can see there isn't much point in asking, but I have to. '*Usted sabe dónde está Juan?*'

She shakes her head. '*No lo sé.*'

She might be telling the truth; she might be protecting Juan. I remember that Juanita is an old friend of the family.

'*Por favor,*' I beg.

'*Lo siento,*' she says, and then she repeats in English, 'I am sorry.'

That phrase in English, the first one she's said to me, tells me everything. She really is sorry. But she's not going to help me.

'Okay,' I say, and go back to the car. Once inside, I sit with my hands on the wheel, staring out at the chickens pecking at tiny specks in the dirt.

I don't know where to go next.

When I finally get back to the restaurant, the sun is setting in glorious crimson. The sight of the Jeep makes my heart leap, but then I remember he left that behind like so much unwanted trash. Like me.

I can't go into the restaurant. I don't want to see his note. I walk to the front of the building, to the patio overlooking the sea. Several seagulls perch on the railing and on the tables. They don't move when I approach; they look at me contemptuously, as if they know what's happened.

Scattered over the tiled floor are the shells of the lobsters I'd prepared for me and Juan. Something, most likely the gulls, has already picked them clean of meat, and the shells are faded light pink from the sun.

15

It's the next day, and I'm sitting on the patio again, staring at the sea. After the frantic race to find Juan, it's been very quiet. Nobody comes here, and of course I can't go into town without being stared at and reminded that every single person in San Nasareo, probably even the tourists, knew before I did that I was being dumped.

I've mostly sat here in this chair. I don't feel like sitting here; I feel like either rushing off somewhere to track Juan down, or sleeping for the entire day. But the first is completely pointless. Juan doesn't want me to find him. He's not being coy. He's left because he wants someone else more. I'm deluded if I think I can argue him out of that.

In fact, the more I think about it – and I've done very little but think about it – I can't say I wasn't warned. Juan let me know from near the beginning that he was only with me because he'd lost Juanita. What I'd thought was a guarantee that he'd never leave me was really a guarantee that he would.

I've gone back over every single thing he has said to me, everything we've done and planned together, analysing every detail. Over and over and over. And it doesn't help; it just makes me feel more of a fool. So really I should be sleeping instead of sitting here. I want to sleep; I want to stop thinking and rest and maybe even

149

have some good dreams about puppy dogs or flowers or something. I tried sleeping this morning after a sleepless night, pulling the blinds closed against the Spanish sun, burying my head underneath a pillow that didn't smell of Juan at all because he hasn't slept on it for such a long time. I closed my eyes tight and tried to think about drifting away on a peaceful cloud.

Then I remembered my father with his curtains drawn in the master bedroom of our old house, lying in the bed he'd shared with my mother. Sleeping, tossing and turning, with the tray of food I'd brought him sitting untouched on the bedside table. A hushed, abandoned house, with Immy and me tiptoeing around not knowing what to say or do. In my memory that went on for weeks, maybe months. For ever. Until he couldn't take it any more.

I'm not going to sleep.

Below me, the sea crawls in perfect turquoise splendour and the air smells so fresh you could probably bottle it and sell it. The sun is dancing on the tiles beneath my feet, filtered through the leaves of the trees.

And all of this, at least, is mine.

I sit up a little straighter. I've been so preoccupied with the reality of being dumped that I haven't really thought about the last bit of Juan's letter. *I leave you El Flor Anaranjado, which I know is your dream as much as it once was mine.*

The restaurant is still here. There's nothing to stop me going on with our original plan. I'll have to find another chef, of course. The opening will have to be delayed for a while, too.

But it'll be all mine, everything just exactly the way I want it. No compromises, no consultations. Everything perfect. I picture myself standing on this patio under the evening stars, the tables full of customers, the candles lit. All mine.

I stand up. I can really do this. It'll be more of a challenge, but I'm good with challenges, and then the success is all the sweeter. I head towards the house to get my BlackBerry and reinstate my appointments, to look over Juan's diary.

The rumble of an approaching car stops my steps, and it also stops my pulse. *Juan?* Even though I've got sunglasses on, I shade my eyes with my hands, peering into the distance. It's a battered blue sedan, and there's only one person in it. As it gets closer, though, I see that the driver is too short to be Juan, and that I recognise the car. I wave at it. It pulls up just out of sight around the corner of the building, and a moment later Sergio appears and comes towards me.

I feel a twinge of dread, remembering his knowing smile the last time I saw him. But there isn't a smile on his face now. Instead, he's scowling and walks towards me aggressively, as if he's angry.

'*Buenos días, Sergio,*' I say cautiously. '*Cómo está?*'

'I want my money,' he says to me.

'Um.' This wasn't what I was expecting at all. Sergio has been as laid back about being paid as he's been about starting work on time. And I've never seen him angry like this, not even when he's swearing in Spanish at an uncooperative bit of plastering.

'Didn't Juan pay you?' I ask.

'No.'

I've been in charge of accounts and bill-paying. There were several outstanding bills when I went to England, but I left them in plain sight on my desk downstairs. I'd assumed Juan had paid them all and paid Sergio at the same time. But maybe he was too busy rediscovering the love of his life to bother with silly things like paying people.

'No problem,' I tell Sergio. 'I'll go and get my chequebook.'

'*Cheques? Ni hablar!*' he thunders, and I freeze. '*Los cheques no sirven, joder. Yo quiero dinero contante y sonante.*'

'What?' I say, taken aback by his attack.

He rubs his fingers together violently, the universal hand gesture for money. 'Money! No cheque!'

'Um. Okay, sure. No problem. I'll just need to go to the bank.' Actually it might be a good idea to be around other people; Sergio is looking a little bit crazed.

He stomps beside me to the Jeep, and gets into his sedan whilst throwing me dirty looks. I pull out in front of him; he follows me closely, as if I'll try to escape.

Not that I could get very far anyway: the rental car has gone back and the petrol gauge of the Jeep is still near empty. I'll draw out some extra money while I'm at it and fill up the tank. Then, maybe, after a shower, a trip to see Amanda, the designer. Talking about interior decorating should cheer me up.

I park outside the bank in San Nasareo. Sergio parks beside me and sticks to my side as we enter. He could at least hold the door open for me if he's going to be so surly. I pause to fill out a withdrawal slip.

'How much do we owe you?' I ask him.

He names a surprisingly large amount. 'Is for the grass too,' he explains when my eyebrows go up.

It seems a lot extra for a bit of turf, but I'm not going to argue with him when he's in this mood. And besides, I can decide myself who to hire from now on, and it's most likely not going to be Sergio if he gets this shirty. I can think of it as a final bonus.

I fill out the slip and bring it to the counter. '*Buenos días,*' I say to the teller, smiling and passing over the paper and our chequebook.

'*Buenos días, señora.*' She types rapidly into her computer, and then looks at me with practised pleasantness. '*Lo siento, pero usted no tiene suficiente dinero en su cuenta para sacar esa cantidad de dinero.*'

I shake my head. I've caught something about 'sorry' and 'money', but that's it. I haven't learned much banking vocabulary. '*Hablo muy poco español,*' I say.

'You do not have the money to withdraw this amount,' she says, slowly, as if she's speaking to a child.

I frown. 'Of course I do. There's much more than this in there.'

'No. There was a recent withdraw.'

Juan. I remember another line in his letter, the letter I haven't read since that first horrible moment. *I know you will not begrudge the few euros I take to help us in our new life together.*

He's taken a chunk, then. Bastard. Some of it was his to begin with, but most of it's mine, from the sale of my flat, or ours, from our business loans. Even if he's removed every penny of his own money, though, there should still be more than enough to cover Sergio's bill.

'How much is left?' I ask.

The teller checks her screen. I get the impression she's doing it for effect, because she spends quite a bit of time studying whatever it says.

'*Cuánto?*' I prompt her.

She doesn't look away from her screen. '*Dos euros.*'

My Spanish is bad, but surely not this bad. '*Dos?*'

'*Dos,*' she says, and now she meets my eyes, and I see underneath her pleasantness to the pity. 'Two. Two euros. Is all that is left.'

16

Of course I have a screaming fit. I demand to see the manager and I mangle the Spanish language and at one point I even grab Sergio's shoulders and yell at him for not physically restraining Juan from leaving San Nasareo.

None of it does any good. It's perfectly legal for Juan to withdraw money from our joint account, and even if it weren't, I have no idea how to find him to make him pay it back. The bank manager apologises, but says he's known Juan for years and trusted him. Then he mentions that the account has a minimum balance requirement, and I should make a deposit if I want to keep it open.

I close it and take the two euros and put them in my purse, next to the twenty euros and some loose change that are now all the cash I have in the world.

'*Lo siento*,' I say two days later, and for the hundredth time. The person in front of me is red in the face and he gestures with his hands and spouts a tirade of Spanish. I don't understand the words, but I understand the meaning. It's quickly become a very familiar situation.

'I'm sorry,' I say again, in English this time because I can't even think clearly enough to try it in a different language. 'I can't pay you. I know we owe you money. It's nothing personal, I can't pay any of these either.' I gesture to the pile of bills on the table beside me. Contractors, suppliers, the mortgage and loan repayments, my credit card bills.

'*Coño!*'

I'm too tired to flinch, though he spits the word at me. I don't know what it means, but I can guess. His face is twisted and angry. I'm pretty sure this is one of the people who used to come up here and drink my coffee, who used to laugh and be friendly to me when I was solvent.

He complains for a while longer, and then goes away. I don't watch him leave. I just listen to the waves and look out of the window at the ocean and sky, which are as blue as if this weren't happening.

When the sun is sinking down into a blaze of orange perfection, I get up from my chair and walk around El Flor Anaranjado. My espadrilles whisper against the hand-fired tiles. I touch the Alicante marble top of the bar; it is smooth and cool. Then I run my hands over the mahogany carving. On the end of the bar are the tablecloths I bought with Amanda. Half hidden under the bright woven fabric is a slip of paper. I know without looking at it that it's another bill.

It's all cost so much.

Outside, another car pulls up. I hear footsteps crunching on the path, but nobody comes to the door to yell at me. After a few minutes I become mildly curious and look out of the side window. There's an unfamiliar round man outside with Sergio. They're walking around the grounds of the restaurant, talking to each other, pointing out various features. I see them walk on to the terrace and stand for a long time, looking at the sunset.

Finally they come in, without knocking. Neither one of them looks at me, though they examine the dining room. Sergio is talking. I lean against the bar and they walk past me into the kitchen. I stand and wait for them to come and demand more money I haven't got.

When they re-emerge, they appear to notice me for the first time. 'Is Señor Lopez,' Sergio says to me. 'He say you work good on the restaurant.'

'Thank you,' I say dully.

Señor Lopez says something in Spanish. 'He not see it since before you buy,' translates Sergio.

'Yes, we did a lot of renovation.' Who is this man, some sort of tourist come to gawk at my misery? Sergio is smiling at me, and I've seen that smile from him before. It's the sort of smile that makes you put your hand to your throat to protect it.

'Señor Lopez hear you have trouble. He want to help you.'

'Help?' I look quickly at this new man. Plenty of people have offered to sue me or have me arrested or worse, but nobody has offered to help yet. He's got a shiny scalp under his thinning black hair, and a film of sweat on his upper lip. 'How?' I ask.

Señor Lopez talks to Sergio, and Sergio nods. 'He think is nice restaurant. He buy it from you.'

I close my eyes. Of course I should have seen this coming. I tighten my hands on the marble top of the bar, and then I open my eyes again and look at the men and their patronising, wolfish smiles.

'How much?' I ask.

# Part Three:
# The Temple of Gloom

17

*He's got a spare key behind the gargoyle.*

'Which bloody gargoyle?' I mutter.

I drop my bags on the pavement and gaze up at the building in front of me. Built of crumbling grey stone, with dusty, blank, pointed windows, it squats like a Gothic monster among the neat red-brick Edwardian houses that populate the rest of the street. A precarious turret pokes up from its snaggle-tiled roof. Cobweb tracery sticks to the gables. While the other trees nearby flutter with leaves just beginning to turn crimson and orange, the sole tree here is wizened and its leaves are brown and crispy. It's one o'clock in the afternoon and the British autumn sun is high in the sky, but the house looms in a strange pocket of its own special darkness, which oozes on to the street in a misshapen shadow.

Uncle Arval's building could illustrate the dictionary definition of 'depressing'. Even from the outside it smells musty, like the grave of ten thousand spiders and mice.

And let's not even talk about the gargoyles.

Two carvings shaped like dragons crouch over the thick iron-laced wooden door, glaring bug-eyed east and west as if to frighten off visitors. A twiny-legged stone spider monkey twists around the drainpipe near the first-storey windows. Stone faces project from the walls at seemingly random places, scowling and frowning and gurning and pulling their mouths open with their grossly oversized hands.

You'd think so much sculptured personality would liven the place up a bit, but they just make the building's outline more lumpy and shadowy. The fact that most of them are missing body parts doesn't help.

It begins to drizzle. It's been sunny for my entire journey – in direct contrast to my mood, it's true – but the British September sun isn't up to much compared with Spain even when there's nary a cloud in the sky, so I haven't been in danger of being cheered up or anything silly like that. But now, as I'm standing in front of the only place I can think of where I might be able to crawl away and lick my wounds for a little while, it rains.

The rain gets harder, dripping down the back of my light Spanish jacket. I put my suitcase on the stone step up to the front door, stand on it and, wrinkling my nose, feel around behind the east-pointing dragon for a key. It's definitely slimy back there. Accumulated algae and moss, I try to convince myself. Not worms. Or slugs. Or squished decomposing creatures.

I pull my hand out quickly. I think the black stuff on my fingers is only dirt, so I swallow hard and check behind the west-pointing gargoyle. Its buggy eyes goggle at me as I rummage behind it. 'Don't worry,' I tell it, 'I won't steal your wallet.'

Though if it did have one, I'd be tempted, if only so I could afford a Frappuccino.

Close up, these things should look less creepy because you can see how fake they are. But instead they're more creepy. The chipped-off claws and lichen-blooming stone seem about to move.

No key. With a grunt of disgust, I wipe my dirty hand on the skirt of my floaty flowery dress and step off my suitcase. The house looms over me like a monster in a bad movie.

Who would choose to live in a place like this?

Arval, of course. Batty Arval. The place probably has bats living in it. That would have been the attraction for him. I know Dad hates London these days, but I've always wondered why he never visited his brother, even if he wouldn't visit me. Now I understand. Even if the key floated sparkling clean into my hand on a little pink fluffy cloud, I have exactly zero desire to set foot inside this place.

But I haven't got a choice.

I scan the carvings one by one. I'm tall for a girl but Arval was taller, about six two. There's not much chance that he'd hide his door key somewhere that he had to climb to reach. If you make a show of your hiding place, it's not secret any more. Of course it's stupid to hide a spare key outside in London anyway, but I suppose it's reasonable enough to assume that no burglar in their right mind would want to break into this dump.

Logic rules out the carvings above the ground floor, but there are still quite a few to choose from. Dragons. Imps. Ugly people. Wolves. Yuck.

'Come on, you stone buggers,' I say, 'which one of you is so special?'

A middle-aged, middle-class woman wearing a waterproof and carrying a small white dog under each arm emerges from one of the houses several doors up. She reaches the pavement, puts down the dogs, glances in my direction, and then immediately crosses the street and walks past me with the width of the road separating us. Once she's a good distance away she crosses back over again. I wonder if she's avoiding the house. Considering I'm standing on the pavement in summer clothes in September, surrounded by suitcases and bags and muttering about gargoyles, I suppose she could be avoiding me.

I should be used to it by now. At least she's not pointing and whispering, like the people in San Nasareo.

When I look back at the house, I see it. I must have shifted on the pavement, because it was hidden by an overgrown bush before. The drainpipe snaking down between two dusty windows ends in a wide-mouthed stone bat. Dirty water trickles between its fangs into a muddy puddle on the ground.

It has to be the bat. I bend and reach between its outstretched webbed wings and feel damp metal. I pull out a long, thick iron key. It's the kind you see being carried by hunchbacked dungeon guards. Incongruously, it's attached to a shiny new Yale key by a plastic key ring emblazoned with the triple feathers of the Welsh Rugby Union.

Now that I have the key in my hand, I hesitate. Until very recently I was an attractive, successful young woman with lots of friends, a boyfriend and a business. Surely I must have more options than my dead uncle Arval's cobwebby flat. I can ring a friend. Go and stay with my father. I can borrow some money. I can print up some copies of my CV and try to get a new job. And Edmund . . .

The heavens open and rain pours from the sky.

Pulling my useless jacket up over my head, I bolt for the door, fit the key in the lock and turn it. Instead of the teeth-grinding shriek I've expected, the door opens with a greasy swish. I grab my bags and drag them up the step and into the house.

My footsteps echo in the vast hallway. I drop my bags to the stone floor with a resounding plop and stare at what I've walked into.

The entrance hall has clearly been designed to be soaring and impressive. It stretches three storeys upwards into the gloom. A massive pointy-arched window at the top should let in beams of light, but it's obscured by dust and cobwebs and who knows what else. Down on the ground, stone urns circle the hall and a broad staircase staggers upwards under the weight of complicated black iron banisters.

I breathe in the musty air, poised between going forward and retreating. My mobile is in my pocket. It's been switched off since I got the news about the money being gone, because I haven't wanted to deal with calls from angry creditors. Not yet. And if Juan happened to call – well, I wouldn't be responsible for my actions, so it seems better to avoid the issue.

But now, the phone can be my saviour. All I have to do is turn it on and decide who to call, and I can be out of this place in minutes.

Besides, I should call my father. With all the stuff that's been going on in my life, I've completely forgotten him.

My stomach turns over. He said he was okay, but what if he wasn't really? What if he or Imogen have been trying desperately to get in touch and haven't been able to because I've been too wrapped up in being dumped and left broke?

I turn on the phone with cold fingers and wait, holding my breath, while it retunes itself to a UK network. The screen glows blue in the gloom and seems horribly out of place in the medieval surroundings. It beeps and vibrates in my hand and I count the numbers as they add up: twenty-four text messages, and forty-three missed calls.

Amazing how popular you get when people want their money off you. I scroll through the numbers from the missed calls as quickly as I can with my hands trembling and damp with rain and anxiety. My father's isn't among them. Nor is Immy's mobile. I check the texts, likewise. They haven't been in touch.

I breathe deep of the musty air in relief. Now that I've got sixty-seven missed communications in my hand, phoning someone seems a bit of an overwhelming task. Something to do maybe after having a little sit-down. And a cup of tea.

A creak pierces the stillness and I jump, whirling around.

It's a witch. Her disembodied head floats against the wall of the opposite side of the hallway. I raise my fist to my mouth to stifle a scream.

'Hello,' she says in a raspy voice. 'Nice shoes.'

I realise that her head is not floating; it's poking out of a door. As I watch, she steps through so that the rest of her body is exposed. Her black hair is tangled, her eyes heavily lined with kohl. Her lips are blood red. She wears a leopard-print skirt and a sleeveless top that exposes withered, saggy arms. On her feet are wellington boots.

'Uh,' I squeak.

'Quickly, darling, do you have any fags?' she whispers. 'I—'

'Stop begging for cigarettes, you filthy woman!' thunders a male voice from inside the door. My brain starts working enough to deduce that the door leads to the ground-floor flat. And that the crone and the thunderer must be the occupants.

'Shut up,' she shoots back over her shoulder conversationally, and then turns to me again. 'I'll take a roll-up if that's all you've got.'

'No, I don't smoke.' I remember my last fag, emptying a bottle of Rioja and waiting for Juan. 'Unless I'm very drunk,' I add. Something compels me to be honest with this stranger. Maybe it's fear that she'll cast a spell on me if I lie.

'And are you?'

'Am I what?' I repeat idiotically, noticing that her hair is actually crooked on her head.

'Drunk, darling. Drunk.' She steps forward, gesturing, and I step back.

'No, I'm rather horribly sober.'

'Well, that is a pity. Still, it's eminently curable. D'you need help with those bags?'

'Uh, no. I'm fine.'

'Get back in here, we're not finished!' thunders the voice from within the flat.

'Oh stop being such a fearful tyrant,' she calls back, but she turns and goes inside the flat anyway. The door creaks behind her as she shuts it.

Um. Interesting neighbours.

I shoulder my bags quickly before she decides to come back out and be odd at me some more. Then I realise I don't actually know which flat is Arval's. I look around the hallway again, but I see only the door that the witch came out of.

His flat must be upstairs, then. The tread of each wooden step is worn and sagging. I climb them before I can think twice about it. The first-floor landing runs along the edge of the soaring foyer, guarded by wrought-iron railings. As below, there's only one door leading off it, a heavy wooden thing like the one the witch came through. The staircase narrows and continues upward for another storey and ends abruptly at a smaller door, painted grey as the brickwork.

It looks like there are only three flats in the building, then, which means there's a fifty per cent chance that the first-floor one is Arval's; probably more, actually, because it's got a shiny new Yale lock to match the key in my hand. I go to it, wincing slightly to ready myself for another weird person to pop out, but nothing happens.

The key fits in the lock, and the door opens, without any noise.

I walk into my auntie Claire's living room in Wales.

Well, no, it's not quite that. For one thing, it's much bigger. Claire and Arval had a 1960s semi with Artex on the walls. Here the ceilings are high, arched and pointed, and so are the windows. There's dusty wooden filigree decorating the doorway arches and the floor is wide polished boards, pitted with use.

But the chintz-covered three-piece suite is exactly the one I remember from my childhood visits. And the fringed table lamps, and the round mahogany end-tables with their vases of silk flowers and little china knick-knacks. Even the television looks the same, a small faux-walnut-sided set that stands on an aluminium trolley. None of it suits the room remotely; this room needs vast chandeliers, high-backed chairs, maybe a coffin or two. The furniture looks as if it's been teleported straight from my childhood memories into this odd building, and though the couches and silk flowers are themselves quite homely, finding them here is like seeing a freshly laundered tea towel attached to a zombie.

I drag my bags through the door and close it behind me. I notice that the couches and the tables and the silk flowers are covered with a sparse powdering of fluffy grey dust. Arval has been gone quite a while. From this flat, and from this life. Auntie Claire's been gone even longer.

I bite my lip. Now's not the time to think about this. I promised myself a cup of tea and dry clothes and then I'll get on the phone and try to find a way out of my mess.

I pull another floaty dress and a light cardigan out of my bag and change in the middle of the living room. The bedroom is bound to be full of Claire's knitted blankets, and I'm not quite up to that yet. I hang the sodden dress and jacket from the points of the wooden filigree in the doorway and then look for the kitchen.

It's directly off the living room and thankfully – well, I think thankfully – is decorated more in keeping with the building, which means it doesn't remind me so much of Claire as it does a dusty, disused morgue. The floor is dull green linoleum and there's a big porcelain sink (obviously for washing bodies) and tall cupboards made of dark wood (obviously for hiding horrible chemicals and instruments). There's also a plastic kettle. I sniff it and it smells okay, so I rinse it and fill it up from the tap at the corpse-washing sink and turn it on.

While I wait for it to boil, I look through the cupboards. The first one is filled with bottles and cans. Baked beans, mostly, and tinned fruit. There's a very large bag of porridge oats. I pick up an unlabelled glass bottle and shake it, imagining formaldehyde and other dangerous chemicals, but it looks a lot like corn oil. I smell it: corn oil. There's a tin of tea bags and Auntie Claire's flowered sugar bowl.

The other cupboards are full of crockery, pots and pans, glasses, and other perfectly normal kitchen contents. They're very tall, almost all the way up to the pointed arched ceiling, and I spot a small wooden stepladder leaning in one corner. All the items are arranged neatly on the shelves, logically next to other related items, and though I'm half expecting to see signs of mice, the cupboards are clean and free of droppings or nests. A refrigerator is built into one cupboard, but when I open it, it only contains a jar of mustard, a bulb of garlic and a saucer of bicarbonate of soda.

I make myself a cup of milkless tea in a flowery mug and bring it and a tea towel into the dusty living room. I swipe off a chair and sit on it. Actually it's not too bad in here; it's not dirty, it's just the dust you get from the walls of old buildings. The three-piece suite seems quite well preserved, given how old it must be. If I were staying here, I could get it clean in a few minutes with a vacuum cleaner.

But I'm not staying here. I'm going to ring people and . . .

And ask for help.

'How do you ask for help?' I say out loud.

Well. Obviously I'll call my father first. I'll tell him I'm at Arval's, and he's not to worry but things with Juan didn't quite work out as planned.

I groan. Great. Yes, that's a great idea. Remind my father of his dead brother, and then tell him that I've been abandoned by my partner, who's vanished into thin air with another woman, taking all my money with him. That won't rake up bad memories at all, will it?

No. I'm supposed to be protecting my father, not causing him even more pain. And being back in the bungalow would only bludgeon me with the reminder that the exact same thing that happened to my father has now happened to me.

In comparison with that, this temple of gloom seems almost cheerful.

So who else can I ring? Not Edmund, obviously, although the thought of him makes my heart thump with longing. That's what I was running away from in the first place. I could ring Pet, maybe.

But I remember that moment in the toilets during my leaving party, when she turned to me and told me that she envied me. Me, ordinary Nina Jones, who'd once been disgraced and abandoned. I shudder at the thought of telling her I've been disgraced and abandoned all over again. It's not that I think she'd be cruel about it. But all the equality I worked so hard for, all the making up I had to do for past failures, and that one, precious moment of her envying me . . .

I can't ring Pet.

Likewise anyone else who was at my leaving party. I was so triumphant that night, beaming all over the place, certain I was going to make something amazing of my life and that Juan and I were going to be one of the all-time great couples. It was hubris or some other abstract concept that my English teacher in school tried her best to beat into my brain when my brain was interested in much more important things, like what I could make for tea for three people out of a packet of rice and half a tin of tuna. Anyway, it was a major character fault, and I indulged in it that night along with far too much champagne.

So if I can't ring any of my friends, or any of my family, who does that leave me with?

No one.

A wave of weariness sweeps over me. I've done enough today: fled one country, got soaked in another, rummaged around behind gargoyles and confronted a witch. I get up off the chair and go in search of the guest bedroom.

The corridor leading off the living room is lit by a bare and dim light bulb and is lined with too many wooden doors. The first leads to a bathroom complete with claw-footed tub; the second to a large bedroom that is obviously Arval's, though it's quite spartan and there are no knitted blankets. The third door is to a small box room with a single bed in it. Unlike the other rooms, it doesn't have a soaring ceiling, nor does it have a pointed window; it has plain plastered walls and ceiling and a small square window near the top. It looks a bit like a monk's cell.

I do not care. I haven't slept properly since Juan left.

Or before that, really, since I heard the news about Arval's death. Here in his spare room, I pull back the top blanket and discard it, and climb into the bed. I take one deep breath, smell dust and lavender, and fall asleep with the rain pattering against the monk's window.

I wake up once. It's pitch black and I hear footsteps. I clutch the blanket and listen, holding my breath, until I realise they're above me, not in the same room.

It takes a few heartbeats more to remember I'm in a dead man's bed.

The footsteps walk back and forth. They're unhurried. I focus my gaze on the blank darkness above me, following them from one side of the ceiling to the other as if I could see them through the shadows and the plaster and lath. They pause, as if the owner is doing something, then start again, and fade away like a ghost disappearing into the mist.

It's impossible to tell what time it is. I can't leave. I have nowhere else to go.

Floating in the bed in the darkness, I close my eyes again. *Why why why?* sighs the wind through the eaves. *Why are you here?*

The rain is a thousand little footsteps around me.

According to the small plastic clock on the wooden bedside table, I wake up at exactly 9.16 a.m. I sit bolt upright in bed before I recall I don't have anywhere to go, anything to do, any reason to get up.

Except that I'm hungry. I haven't eaten anything since Spain, and precious little there. Actually, it feels good to be hungry. I feel better rested, too, though to be truthful I could easily lie back down and go to sleep again, even though I've slept, at a conservative estimate, for fifteen hours, only waking that one time to listen to the footsteps.

I glance up at the ceiling, remembering how ghostly they were. In the daylight, that seems ridiculous, of course. Obviously someone lives in a flat on the top floor, and that person was walking around at night. Maybe an insomniac or something, though for all I know it was only ten o'clock and they were getting up to switch off the telly. Even in this weird house, people must do normal things.

Speaking of which . . . I swing my legs out of bed, stretch, and go to use the bathroom. The fixtures are all ancient, but clean enough aside from the dust. The loo is the type with one of those cisterns planted way up on the wall, and a long chain to flush it. The water comes down with an exuberant whoosh, which for some reason is quite satisfying to me. Despite its beauties, El Flor Anaranjado never had brilliant water pressure.

I wander to the kitchen. The flat is chilly and I can distinctly smell damp somewhere, but despite these concrete sensory impressions I feel a bit as if I'm in a dream. Probably because I never thought I'd end up here, in this place, alone and penniless. You'd think a good night's sleep would make me feel better about the whole thing, but it's going to take more than that.

I make myself a bowl of porridge from the big bag, and a cup of black tea. I pour white sugar into both of them; what's the point in watching my diet when I'm reduced to eating a dead man's cereal?

After my breakfast, though, I do feel better. The oats sit in my stomach reassuringly, as if anchoring me to reality. I make myself another cup of tea and sit at the kitchen table, considering my options.

Though really, there's only one.

'I'll stay here for a little while,' I say out loud, because I want to hear something other than the sound of rain. 'I'll sort out Arval's stuff, like I told Dad I would. And then I'll wait for things to calm down.'

It sounds reassuring. I don't ask myself, out loud, how waiting for things to calm down could possibly solve anything. One step at a time, that's the way to do it.

And the next step is obvious. I can't possibly stay somewhere this dusty. I dig around underneath the corpse sink until I find a pair of rubber gloves and some cleaning cloths, and I check all the doors in the long corridor until I find a cupboard with a vacuum cleaner in it. Thankfully, and somewhat surprisingly, it's a brand-new one.

Cleaning is good. It keeps your body busy and gives you something to think about. It gives you small goals that you can feel pleased about achieving. I start with the living room, where I vacuum the floors and upholstery, dust everything in sight, stand on a chair to suck up the nests of cobwebs in the corners of the ceiling. I polish the wooden tables and carefully wipe the porcelain sheep. I bring in the stepladder from the kitchen to wipe down the many-paned windows. When I'm finished, the room is nearly as spotless as my auntie Claire kept it, back when it was in another house in Wales. Then I go for the kitchen, where I scrub down every surface. When my mouth gets dry, I drink a glass of water. Then I go back to cleaning. Keeping busy. Not thinking.

In the living room, my mobile beeps and buzzes on the table where I've left it. I'm much too absorbed with wiping out the empty refrigerator and bleaching the already-white sink. My mind is kept carefully blank.

When I finish, I look up at the tall window. It's stopped raining, but the sky is darkening into twilight. Everything seems very quiet without the rain or the swish of my cleaning cloth. Extremely quiet for London, even some godforsaken corner of it. As I listen, a door closes somewhere above me and I hear footsteps walking downstairs. They're deliberate, purposeful, and though they're not heavy, I get the impression they're made by a big person. Not someone small, anyway. Or an insubstantial ghost.

They continue downwards past the first-floor landing, and in the distance, I hear the massive front door shut with a muffled boom.

It's the only human sound I've heard all day except for my own, and it should be comforting, I guess. It's not, though. It only reminds me that other people have lives, other people are going out and about their business. Whereas I . . . well, I'm here.

I peel off the gloves, suddenly conscious of the dust in my hair and the grime on my bare knees beneath my skirt. I've been doing so much cleaning that I've neglected to clean myself. I wash my hands, go back into the living room to pick another floaty dress out of my suitcase (I really wish I'd kept my jeans when I went to Spain), and head for the bathroom.

There's a large spider in the bath, of course. I should have expected it. We regard each other warily for a little while. It's brown and hairy, nearly the size of my palm. I can distinctly see its jaws.

I retreat and close the door.

Instead of bathing, I find the linen closet and change the sheets on the bed I'm using. When I finish, I sit down on it to consider what to do next. I start yawning, so I lie down for a minute, and the next thing I know, I'm waking up and it's dark again and somebody is walking around over my head.

The little plastic clock has a light on it if you press the button, and it tells me it's after midnight. I'm chilly. I pull my dress over my head, crawl beneath the blankets, and fall back asleep.

I'll do something worthwhile to solve my problems tomorrow.

'What's the attraction of a bath?' I ask the spider. My voice echoes off the black and white tiles on the floor and walls. 'I mean, I can understand a nice dark corner full of flies. But why a bath? What good is it to you?'

The spider sits there, being hairy.

'I'd like to take a bath, actually,' I tell it. 'Three days without bathing is verging on the ridiculous, not to mention disgusting. Especially with all the crawling around in cupboards I've been doing. I could grow vegetables in my hair.'

I swear the spider is thinking about all the cobwebs I've destroyed in the past few days. And planning revenge. It must be quite a complicated revenge, with lots of cunning plans to think through in detail, because the damn thing hasn't moved more than three inches in forty-eight hours. Or maybe it goes zinging around the entire flat while I'm sleeping, but I don't want to think about that.

I've been using the loo as quickly as I can, angling my body ready to bolt out the door if the spider moves. I've been brushing my teeth in the kitchen sink. But enough is enough. It's not like I'm planning on going out or entertaining visitors or anything, but I can't stand myself this dirty, and I am not going to climb into the corpse-washing sink for a sponge bath.

'I really don't want to squish you. Or touch you. Or think about you lurking in the bathroom while I'm naked and vulnerable. How about I open the window for you, and you go outside?'

This seems reasonable to me, but who understands spider logic? I go to the long, narrow multi-paned window and open it, a process that requires unscrewing this bit and pushing out this other bit. It only opens a couple of inches, and it's begun to rain outside. The fresh air is cool and smells slightly greasy.

'There, doesn't that look appealing?' I say to the spider. It is, I know, quite possibly the only creature in existence which has less desire to go outside than I do. I haven't set foot outside this flat in three days. I thought, initially, that I might run out of things to clean, but after I'd done my bedroom and Arval's bedroom I discovered the library. It's got faded velvet curtains over the windows that create a suitably gloomy lack of light. One tall wall is lined with bookcases, and another is a cluttered collection of files and photo albums. There's a desk piled high with odd bits of electrical equipment, tools and wire. I didn't know that Arval liked electronics. I wonder what he was building. A radio or a toaster?

This is the sort of thing I should be sorting out for my father, but sorting out requires thought, and so what I've been doing is pulling the books out one by one, dusting them carefully, and then putting them back, without reading much besides the title. There are a lot of books about bats, of course, and shelves of travel books too. One or two volumes about chartered accountancy, which is what Arval did before he retired. There's also a good collection of popular fiction and older novels with titles like *The Mysteries of Udolpho*, titles that make me shiver slightly. I don't want to know about other people's dark secrets. My own are quite enough to be ignoring at present.

'Have fun out there in the big wide world!' I tell the spider, and then retreat from the bathroom and close the door after me again. I go back to the library, where I've removed a shelf-ful of books, and begin dusting them and replacing them.

It's comforting to think that maybe the spider problem will resolve itself. Perhaps if I leave my own life well alone for a while, it'll resolve itself too. It's certainly very good not to think about it for a while. While I'm here, cleaning, the creditors will go away . . . my father and Imogen will win the lottery . . . all my friends will forget I ever existed . . . Edmund and Caroline will have their baby and be blissfully happy . . .

A stab of something, jealousy or pain or loneliness, goes through me and I gasp.

Clearly these books aren't taking up enough of my attention. I need something more energetic to do.

I go into the living room and move the three-piece suite several feet clockwise so I can hoover underneath it. The couch is pretty heavy and I have to heave and grunt to push it across the carpet. On the plus side, this is several minutes when I don't have to think about anything. On the minus side, I'm now all sweaty.

I suck up the teensy tiny dust balls and replace the couches. Now I really need a bath. Plus, I could clean the bathroom and that would use up quite a bit of time, especially if I used an old toothbrush or something. Maybe I could use the vacuum cleaner to suck up the bath spider. That would solve my problem.

I picture the spider lurking in the vacuum cleaner bag. Planning an even worse revenge. Maybe laying eggs for thousands of baby spiders. Then, when it's dark and I'm asleep, slowly emerging from the plastic tube, coated in sucked-up dust, and picking its way across the hallway to my bedroom . . .

Ugh. No. I cross my fingers and open the door to the bathroom. Please be gone, please be gone, please—

It's sitting in the bath. It's moved slightly to the left, away from the window.

'Please go away,' I whisper to it. I want to be clean. I want to be safe. I want to have something to do.

It doesn't budge.

Tears of frustration prick at my eyelids, but I can't cry because if I do I'm not sure if I will stop. I slam the bathroom door shut and go to the kitchen, where I try to sit down at the table and relax for a minute, but as soon as I sit down I stand back up again. I pace to one side of the kitchen, and then the other, and then back and forth. I straighten the chairs. I open the fridge and close it. I teeter on the edge of having nothing to do, on the edge of a deep black hole of nothing.

I close my eyes. 'Go away,' I whisper to the deep black hole.

It doesn't.

*It's not the same*, my father says in my head. *Your mother left me, but Arval just left. There's quite a difference.*

*Your mother left me.*

*Left me.*

I lift my head from the kitchen table and jump up. I can't sit here thinking. I open the cupboards and find a pint glass and, in the back of a drawer, a long-handled spatula. I put on the rubber cleaning gloves.

I go to confront the spider. Because even an eight-legged monster is better than those two words.

*Left me.*

I kick open the bathroom door with my bare foot. This would be suitably dramatic if the door burst open, slamming against the tiled wall, but actually it just swings a bit. I push through and the spider is, of course, still in the bath ignoring the open window, which now has rain water puddled beneath it. I hold up the pint glass ready, and approach the bath.

God, it's so big. I'm not really sure the glass will cover it. Maybe I should just squish it with the spatula. But squashed spider guts are even more disgusting than a live spider, and besides, killing spiders is supposed to be bad luck, right? It's supposed to make it rain.

I snort. Like I could possibly be given any more bad luck or rain.

I lean quietly over the high side of the bath. There's a trail of limescale from the cold tap to the plughole, which I could really enjoy cleaning once I get rid of this spider. Focus on that, Nina. Not how hairy the legs on this thing are. Not on its beady eyes, millions of them, looking murder at me.

I aim the pint glass and slowly, carefully, unobtrusively bring it down.

The spider bursts into movement and I jump back, screaming. It runs inhumanly fast to the other side of the tub, where it crouches in wait.

Gulping down several deep breaths to calm my heart, I reposition myself. It's not going to leap on me and rip my throat out. It's just trying to run away. Ugh, what if it tries to run away *up my arm*?

I move the pint glass more quickly this time, but the spider dashes towards me. I scream and flinch and at the same time bring down the glass, more in self-defence than anything else. When I look down, I see that I've caught one of the spider's legs under its rim. The rest of it scrabbles on the porcelain, trying to get free. I can hear its little claws.

'Eeegh,' I gasp. The spider twists and pulls. I shudder, drop the glass, and retreat several steps away, flapping my hands to shake off the imaginary feel of spider. Of course the spider immediately frees itself and bolts over the edge of the tub and halfway up the tiled wall, where it perches, defying gravity.

I clutch my hands together and look at it. I cannot let it escape into some dark corner where I can't find it, because that would be even worse. Before I can think of all the disasters that could happen, I rush for the tub, pick up the glass, scramble on to the side of the bath and stand on it, the porcelain cold against my bare feet. I aim the glass and bring it down. It clinks against the tiles. The spider is beneath it. I can't spare the breath to cheer, but I can afford to move more slowly now. With my other hand I slide the spatula underneath the rim of the glass. The spider adjusts itself to stand on the spatula. And then it's trapped.

'Yes!' My exultant cry echoes in the room. Carefully I climb off the bath and bring the glass to the open window. I hold it outside as far as I possibly can, and then pull the spatula away and shake the spider out. I don't look down to see if it lands okay. It's on its own now. There are plenty of gargoyles to catch hold of on the way down, anyway.

I shut the window firmly, put the glass and the spatula into the bin by the sink because I can't picture myself ever using them, and then get to work cleaning.

It's blissful. It takes ages. The bathroom's not actually that dirty, but there's limescale on the fixtures and there's all that grout to scrub. When I'm done, I climb into the tub and have a long, long shower. Normally I'd have a bath, and this is a beautiful big tub for it, but that requires lying still and also waiting for the bath to fill, so a shower is better. Then I get to wipe down the tiles and the bath, and comb my hair and pick up each loose hair that's fallen on the floor, and then I go into the living room to get some clothes out of my bag. I put on a halter top and shorts, and then because I'm cold I put on a little T-shirt over the halter top and wrap a lime-green pashmina around my waist like a skirt. I bought the pashmina in San Nasareo on a cool day, actually on the day when Juan and I went to look at the hotel bar, but I'm not thinking about that. I just want to be warm.

And now I have nothing to do.

Except . . . except I could look for how to turn on the heating. There are ancient iron radiators in every room, but they're stone cold and I haven't seen a switch anywhere. That's a good project. It should eat up some time. And then . . . and then . . .

I look around for the heating controls. There isn't anything obvious here. I go to the airing cupboard in the corridor, but there's nothing there, nor in the bedrooms, nor in the library, and I know it's not in the bathroom, having just been over every inch of it with an old toothbrush, but I check anyway. I search the kitchen, and am crossing the living room just to look in the airing cupboard again when I notice there's a small cupboard built into the wall near the front door, painted white to blend in, like a secret door. I haven't opened that one yet, even in my cleaning frenzy; it looked like a haven for spiders and mice. But I'm a Mighty Spider Conqueror now.

I go over to it and open the door. That's where the controls are all right; they're mounted on the wall near the top of the cupboard. But that's not really what I see.

There are shoes in here. Boots, mostly: hiking boots with crusts of mud, weathered wellingtons, lightweight boots with spikes in the soles. But there are a couple of pairs of trainers too, some moccasins and a pair of scuffed dress shoes. A waft of leather and dirt and rubber assails me, and with it a memory.

I was fifteen years old. My mother had been gone for two days, leaving the house under a stunned hush. My father was asleep, Immy was watching telly downstairs. I was doing the laundry and needed clothes hangers for our school jumpers, because surely we would be going back to school soon, me to St Hilda's and Immy to Highgrove Primary. I walked into my father's room, where he was a shape under the blankets, to get some hangers out of the wardrobe, as I had done dozens of times before without ever thinking about it. I was annoyed, actually, that Daddy hadn't brought his empty hangers into the laundry room, as Mummy always did, as Immy and I always had to. Even though I was annoyed, I crept quietly; I opened the wardrobe carefully, so as not to wake him.

I reached up to take down the empty hangers, and then I saw them. All of Mummy's clothes, still hanging there in the wardrobe next to Daddy's suits and shirts. And on the floor of the wardrobe lay the jumble of her shoes.

Beautiful shoes, delicate shoes, high heels and satin and leather and sparkles, every one of them imprinted with her foot. Smelling of fine leather and perfume, curled into the shape of her arch and toes, left behind like so many insect shells because she was never coming back.

Here, now, in front of Arval's shoes, I stagger backwards and press my hand to my mouth. But the noise comes out anyway, the high keening scraped deep from my stomach, a ragged noise of sadness and loss, the noise of the person who is left.

I put both hands to my mouth and mash them against my lips, hard enough to hurt, but that's when the sobs start. They rip out of me and my legs collapse beneath me and I land curled up on the wooden floor, crying.

I think about my mother, but mainly about the hole she left in my life when she abandoned us. I think about Edmund. I think about my father and fighting with Imogen and the red-brick house we had to leave and the bags of fifty pences. I think about the whispers at school, in San Nasareo; my beautiful vision of success, which was always empty and now is gone. I think about Arval and Claire and how they smiled at each other over flowered mugs of tea. I think about Juan and all the things he told me, that I was beautiful and desirable and lovable and how all of these things were lies, how I thought I had it all and had nothing, how even at the height of my triumph I was disposable and worthless.

And then I don't think about anything; I just cry and cry, with the tears smearing my face and my lungs heaving as if my body has decided that crying is what it does now, that all my breaths will be sobs and my arms will be permanently welded around myself as protection that doesn't protect at all.

Above my shuddering breaths and sniffles I can hear, in the distance, the door to the top flat open and those footsteps come down the stairs. They pause on the landing, not far from my door.

Oh God, whoever it is can hear me crying. Embarrassment adds itself to the mix of emotions, but that doesn't make me stop. In fact it brings up a fresh wail and a new round of sobs.

Time passes. I cry. There's a well of tears somewhere inside me and I can't stop until it runs out. But slowly the sobs subside, my body relaxes. I can breathe.

I sit up. It's quiet. My breath hitches once, twice, but it seems to be over. For now.

On the landing, the footsteps shift, then hesitate. Then they walk away, down the stairs to the ground floor. The outside door opens and closes.

I stand, but my knees are wobbly, and my chest feels as if I've run a marathon or smoked a thousand cigarettes. I wipe my face on the pashmina, which has come loose from around my waist, and stagger to the couch to lie down. The soaring windows tell me that outside it is getting dark.

Empty and exhausted, I close my burning eyes.

\*

I'm ashamed to admit that I wake up in the middle of the night and can't stop thinking, and to keep myself from crying again, I hoover the entire flat.

I stand in the corridor outside the flat door and try to control my heartbeat.

This is absolutely ridiculous. All I'm doing is going down to the shop for a pint of milk. I can't believe I'm actually afraid.

It's because I haven't been out of the flat in so long, not once since I've been here. I've lost track of the time; I don't think it's been a week yet, but it's hard to tell because the days and nights merge together. It's occurred to me that television might be distracting, but I can't concentrate enough to understand the schedule yet, so that doesn't help with orienting myself. The only thing I can help tell the time by is those footsteps; they always go out at dusk and return sometime in the night, when they walk around upstairs. During the day, they're quiet.

Anyway, this morning I decided enough was enough and it was time I had a proper cup of tea instead of drinking it black, so I should go outside before I withered away to nothing more than an ashen shadow in a halter-neck dress. It took a little while to get ready to go out. Of course I have to take my time doing everything, stretch it out to fill up as many thoughts as possible. What took the longest was finding something to wear. I've finally unpacked my clothes and hung them up in the wardrobe in the monk's-cell room, and out of the suitcase they look incredibly garish, and far too insubstantial. They were fine for Spain, but in this atmosphere they look like butterflies in a crypt. Not to mention they're not half warm enough for an English autumn. That damn charity-shop worker was right: I should have kept my clothes and shoes. But I can't think about that too much, because it brings the risk of crying.

And I don't want to cry again. Not like that, ever again.

In the end I put on a flowery dress over a T-shirt, added a little linen jacket and wrapped the lime-green pashmina (which I've washed since my crying jag) around me. I'm a little wary of shoes at the moment, so I grabbed the first pair that came to hand, which happened to be pink strappy kitten heels. I found a battered black umbrella hanging up in the kitchen. I put the house keys in my handbag, and stepped out the door.

And now I'm standing here, unable to move. And this is far too stupid.

'Nina Jones,' I say aloud to myself, 'are you trying to tell me that you would rather stay inside a freaky haunted house talking to spiders than walk down to the shop and get some milk?'

I consider it and I'm appalled to learn that yes, I would.

I reach out behind me until I can touch the wooden door. Then I push myself off it, hard. The momentum carries me forward down the landing. Once I've started, it's easier to continue and I stomp down the wooden stairs. I stalk across the tiled hallway, past the marble urns and the fluttering cobwebs. My kitten heels clatter. I open the front door, step outside into the drizzly afternoon, and begin to march down the street without looking back.

This is a much better idea than staying inside. I'm much less likely to think if I'm moving. I walk briskly down the street, past all the rosy Edwardian houses with their bushes and gardens and net curtains and clean paintwork. It all looks so middle class and safe and normal that I can't help glancing over my shoulder as I walk to check that Arval's house really does exist.

It does. A misshapen Gothic lump glowering behind a dying tree.

The road curves round, sloping downwards, and there's a shop at the end, next to some run-down-looking tea rooms that seem to feature orange vinyl prominently in their decor. This was my destination, the shop for milk, but now that I'm here I don't want to stop yet. I walk on, though my heels are slipping on the wet pavement, uphill this time, past the shops and the pub and past the green, where the leaves are beginning to yellow. Mostly I focus on my feet, one in front of the other; the purpose isn't to see, it's to move. The rain picks up and I open the umbrella, noticing only when it's open that it's broken and half the spikes stick out, bare, like skeleton fingers. I hold the intact side over my head and keep going, though my skirt gets wet and sticks to my bare legs as I walk.

Houses, neighbourhoods, down the hill and back up again. At one point I'm suddenly surrounded by children in school uniform, chattering loudly to each other. The words are a meaningless jumble of sound, and they disappear as quickly as they've come. Then I'm alone again, hearing the rain and my skirt swishing and my breath in my ears. It's hard to believe I'm in the same busy London I used to live in.

I don't usually walk for walking's sake. I'm more of a cab sort of girl. The last time I just walked was after Edmund and I—

No. Just walk. Concentrate on one foot. The other foot.

I have no idea how far I walk, or where I go, or how long it takes me, but eventually I notice that the rain is letting up and it's getting gradually darker. I pause, looking around, and see to my surprise that I'm only a few metres from the corner shop and the orange vinyl tea rooms at the end of Arval's road. I wonder if I've done a big circle, or a zigzag, or maybe several circles. I search my memory for any landmarks, but aside from the children, it's all a blur of red and green and grey and wet.

And my feet hurt. Beneath the pink straps, my skin is chafed and red. Kitten heels aren't really the best thing to wear on epic depressed walks.

I blink. Is that it? Is that why I'm acting like this? Am I . . . depressed?

I don't want to think about that. I need milk, that's what I came out for. I push open the door of the corner shop. Inside, it's steamy and warm, colourful with packages. The man behind the till is talking to a customer and doesn't notice me as I wander around the aisles, bemused. I should probably get something to eat; I've had nothing but porridge and things out of tins for days. But I'm not hungry, and I can't imagine wanting anything in particular. In the end I pick up a pint of semi-skimmed milk, a loaf of wholewheat bread (even now, I can't think about white bread, Edmund's edicts are so crammed into me) and, in a nod to five-a-day, a carton of UHT orange juice. I bring them to the till.

'I'm glad to see you've managed it,' says the customer who's been chatting with the shopkeeper.

I put the orange juice on the counter, and only realise from the pause that the customer was speaking to me. I look at her for the first time. She's in her seventies or thereabouts, with bright orange dyed hair in a twist at her neck. She's slender, wearing a forest-green suit in soft wool; if it's not Chanel, it's a good knock-off. She's looking at me as if she expects me to know what she's talking about.

'Uh . . . excuse me?' My voice is rusty.

'Getting drunk, darling.'

She sounds familiar somehow. I look at her more carefully, wondering if I've blacked out at some point in the past few days and had a conversation about drinking. Her skin is powder-white and softly wrinkled around her mouth and eyes, which are grey. She wears red lipstick, and for some reason I recognise the shade. Her voice, while throaty, is unmistakably posh and plummy, and I wonder if she's the mother of one of the girls I knew at St Hilda's. But I wouldn't have been talking with a friend's mum about getting drunk, and besides, she's speaking to me as if resuming a conversation only recently interrupted.

'Or perhaps you haven't,' she says. 'William, does she smell of alcohol? Michael tells me I have killed off most of that particular sense.'

The shopkeeper sniffs loudly as I stare. 'Don't smell nuffink,' he says.

'Oh, I do apologise, darling. I try so hard not to jump to conclusions, but you seemed so desperate for it before, and so deserving of it somehow. But never mind, it will come. William sells spirits, if you're so inclined.'

'Um. No thank you, this will be fine.' I touch the milk, as if it will save me from surrealism.

'Arval never kept much on hand, I know, though I do believe he had a bottle of sherry for emergencies. Have you checked over the cooker?'

'Oh.' The voice and the blood-red lipstick suddenly click into place, though not the hair and the suit. 'You . . . you're the downstairs neighbour.'

'Yes, of course. Evangeline Clegg.' She holds out her hand, and I don't know what to do except take it. Her grip is soft and warm and somehow businesslike, although we're in a corner shop talking about getting drunk.

'Nina Jones.'

'Oh, I did think so. Arval's niece?'

I nod. 'I thought . . . You had black hair before.'

She lets go of my hand and flutters her own around her head. 'Wigs. Terribly useful.'

I'm not sure if she's talking about the black hair or the red at first, but then I remember the black hair had been crooked.

'Three pound ten,' the shopkeeper tells me. I reach into my handbag for my purse. My stomach sinks as I realise I only have euros, and precious few of those. Not that I particularly want the bread or milk or juice, but this was my project for the day, and I seem to have failed.

'Do you take these?' I ask, holding out one of the few notes I've got left.

'Sorry, love.'

I droop. 'That's all right.' I put the euros back in my purse and reach for the things, to put them back on the shelf.

'Don't be silly, darling,' Evangeline says beside me. She puts one hand on my arm to stop me, and with the other hands William a note.

'But . . .'

'You can pay me back when you've got those changed.'

'But that's—' I stop. I can't explain to a stranger that finding a bank, going in, asking to change euros, counting out three pound ten and then returning the money to her seems far too insurmountable a task. Even thinking about it makes me tired and gives me a little flutter of panic.

'We're neighbours. Never fear, darling, I know how to

find you. And when.' This seems to amuse her, and she chuckles deep in her chest.

'Yes, but . . .'

'If you're really determined not to accept a small kindness, you can do something for me at the same time. The usual, William.'

'Evangeline, Michael will—'

'*The usual*, William.'

He sighs, and takes a red packet of cigarettes down from the display behind him. He puts it beside my milk.

'There,' says Evangeline happily. 'You just take those with you, and *hide them*, darling, and hold on to them for me until I've got a spare moment to pop up and see you. Favour repaid.'

William shakes his head at her slightly, but gives her her change and then puts everything in a blue plastic bag for me.

'Well thank you,' I say, though I don't really mean it. Now I have to find a bank. And I'm going to have a visitor. Both prospects fill me with dread. I'd rather have gone without the milk.

'Not at all, not at all. Toodles, William.'

I don't know what else to do, so I follow Evangeline out of the shop.

'Well,' she says briskly, 'it is charming to meet you again. Would you care for a cup of tea?' She indicates the orange vinyl tea rooms next door.

'I . . . um . . . thanks, but no, I'd better be getting back.'

'Of course, always something to do. I shall see you soon. And remember' – she taps the side of her nose with a finger – '*hide them*.'

'Right,' I say, and scurry off as fast as I can.

I'm so eager to be by myself again that I don't even notice how gloomy the house is in the gathering dusk. I unlock the door, dart inside and close it behind me, leaning against it and breathing hard. My left foot is throbbing more than my right, something I've only been dimly aware of up till now, but in the silence and lack of movement it's more obvious. Maybe I twisted my ankle or something while I was walking. I pull off that shoe, wincing at the lines of blisters across my skin. Then I begin to limp up the broad wooden stairs, dangling the spiky umbrella and the blue plastic bag from one hand, holding the shoe underneath my arm, and gripping on to the cold banister with the other hand, watching my feet as I have done during my entire walk.

I don't know why I'm such a hurry to get back into the flat. I have no more tasks for the day, nothing more to scrub and polish, no more plans but to turn on the television and try to fall asleep. I can make tea with milk, but how long will that take?

'I hate this place,' I mutter. 'It should've been knocked down years ago as a crime against good taste. It's creepy and cold and I hate it.'

'Ahem.'

It's a soft, deep noise, half a clearing of the throat, half a deliberate warning. I stop stock still and raise my head.

A man is standing on the landing above me. He's tall, or at least he looks it from this angle, and angular and dark. He's wearing an old-fashioned black hat and a black raincoat that's voluminous enough to look a bit like a cloak. The collar is up around his pale-skinned face, so all I can really see is a straight, severe nose, a wide, grim mouth and a flash of his eyes in the shadow cast by his hat. His foot, clad in a black boot, is poised over the top step on the flight I'm walking up.

I stare at him in surprise, and he stares back. Something about his eyes, half in shadow, roots me to the spot. I hear him draw in a breath.

'Excuse me,' he says. He sets his foot down on the step and then continues down the stairs towards me. His footsteps, deliberate and measured, are the same ones I've heard every evening. He doesn't look at me as he passes, but I see that he's carrying a big black rucksack. The air in his wake smells vaguely of cedar.

I stay where I am, and turn to watch him reach the bottom of the stairs and then open the front door and go out without glancing in my direction again.

Well. I've met all the neighbours now. At least this one doesn't seem inclined to become better acquainted.

Thank God.

22

The phone ringing takes me by surprise, which is the only reason I answer it.

Every now and then my mobile has given me a beep or a ring, and aside from glancing at the screen to make sure it's not my father or sister trying to get in touch, I haven't paid it much attention, just left it on the polished side table next to the couch, beside a vase of silk flowers. But this time I happen to be passing on my way to the kitchen to make a cup of tea, an important stage between showering and getting dressed, and one that helps make this simple task last as long as possible, preferably all morning. The phone rings, it's near my right hand, and without thinking, from years of habit, I pick it up and press the answer button and put it to my ear.

'Hello?' The second syllable falters as I realise I've made a mistake.

'Nina, sweetheart!'

It's Pet. Her loud, high-pitched voice is exactly the same as always, as if I've spoken to her two hours ago instead of nearly two months. It feels odd to hear it standing here, wrapped in only a towel in Arval's living room, in the 'after' part of my life. In every way, Pet belongs firmly in the 'before' section.

'How are you, Pet?' I ask.

'Oh, fine fine fine, you know how it is, been

super-busy with this and that, having some photos done, been on a bit of a jolly to Cornwall, south of France, that sort of thing. How's the fabulous restaurant and the fabulous Juan?'

'Fabulous.' It comes out without me thinking, and it sounds hugely unconvincing to me, but Pet doesn't seem fazed.

'Wonderful. When's the opening again, I've forgotten?'

'It's . . . been put back a little bit. There's still so much to do.'

'I really don't understand this restaurant lark, it seems like so much hard work, and in the end, what do you get for it? People get hungry, you have to do it all again. It takes up so much time. Still, though, it's all passion, isn't it? Like you and Juan?'

Has Pet always been so manic in the way she talks? Or is it because I've barely spoken to a human being for days? 'How's it going on the man front for you?' I ask her, sidestepping the Juan-and-passion issue. Asking Pet a question about men can keep her chattering for hours. I perch on the edge of the couch, anticipating a long time of listening.

'Oh, you know, this and that. Listen, babe, I was wondering, I thought basically I might pop over to Spain soon and see how you're getting on, see this beautiful place and everything, maybe get you to show me the night life. Pet and Nina hit the Costa Blanca, what do you think?'

'Um. I . . .'

*I'm not on the Costa Blanca. I'm broke and dumped in Highgate.*

Like I'm going to say that.

'Actually, Pet, it's not a good time right now. Would you believe the contractors found a gas leak under the floor, and we've had to take the whole thing up. Juan and

I are staying in a hotel in town, and we're up at the restaurant day and night trying to get it sorted out quickly. I've learned how to lay tiles myself!'

'Oh. So you're busy.'

'Exactly. But once we're back on schedule again, I'll send you a VIP invitation to the opening!'

'That's wonderful. It's just that I . . .' She sounds hesitant suddenly.

'What is it, Pet?'

'Oh, nothing, babe, nothing, everything is tickety-boo. It's the weather here, that's all, you wouldn't believe the rain we've been having. London in the autumn is basically desolate. I'm ready to top up my tan. Hoped you'd be up for some partying at night, sleeping on the beach by day, but of course you and Juan are busy living out love's young dream.'

I restrain myself from snorting. She's got half of that right: *Juan* is busy living love's young dream.

'Not still reciting poetry, is he?' she continues.

'Probably. Listen, Pet, I've got something urgent on right now, so can I call you back?'

'Of course, of course, wouldn't dream of interrupting you. *Hasta la vista!*' She rings off, leaving me with the urgent task of making a cup of tea as slowly as possible.

I go to the kitchen, rinse out the kettle and carefully refill it, cursing myself for answering the phone. In one fell swoop, and almost by mistake, I've gone from discreetly not mentioning my problems to my friends, to out-and-out lying about them.

It shouldn't make much difference. Everybody thinks I'm in Spain anyway; where's the harm in confirming their beliefs? Since I'm not going to tell anyone about what's happened.

*Yet*, I amend myself quickly. Not yet. I will, eventually. I'll have to. Sooner or later everyone will start to wonder why the restaurant hasn't opened. But that time seems so impossibly distant, an abstract idea far in the future, like the day that, according to scientists, the sun will explode.

And nearly as catastrophic.

I grab the kettle before it's finished boiling and pour the water into my mug, splashing it in my haste to have something to do. I wasn't this afraid of people finding out when I first got here, was I? I was actually considering ringing people, and I decided quite rationally not to because I needed more time before I faced it. But now I've had more time, and the idea has become more terrifying rather than less.

That's not supposed to happen. I'm supposed to get better, not worse. I put my hand on the top of the towel I'm wearing and hold it to my chest, suddenly short of breath.

There's a knock on the door.

I shouldn't answer it; I don't want to talk to anybody, and besides, I'm not exactly dressed. But I need something to make me move, something to help me breathe, so I hurry to the door and open it.

It's Evangeline. Her red hair is in the same twist and she's wearing the same lipstick, but she's got on a strapless green cocktail dress, a fake-fur shrug and a string of pearls. 'Thank goodness you're in, darling,' she says in her raspy voice. 'I'm gasping.'

So am I. I stand back to let her in, because I don't know what else to do. 'I don't have your money, I'm really sorry,' I say.

She waves her hands dismissively. I notice she wears several rings on each. 'Money is nothing between friends, darling. You hop off and get dressed, I'll make us a drink.'

Um. I hesitate, but Evangeline heads straight for

the kitchen, obviously confident of her way around Arval's flat, so I go off to the monk's cell to pull on some clothes. It's another floaty dress and the pashmina, though I'm sticking to flip-flops while my blisters heal. I comb my hair and twist it into a wet plait down my back, since I'm not going to have time to sit waiting for it to dry. I do this all much more quickly than I was planning to, but when I get back to the living room Evangeline is already settled on the couch, her legs curled up beneath her and two steaming mugs on the coffee table in front of her.

I sit down warily on one of the chairs. Evangeline looks like she wants to have a good natter, and therefore I'm going to have to do some more lying.

'I'm very sorry about your uncle Arval,' she says, handing me a mug.

'Oh. Thank you.'

'How's your father doing?'

I blink. 'Better than I expected, I think. I should, um, ring him.'

'We never met, of course, but Arval did talk. We shall miss him horribly. Your uncle, of course, not your father, who I daresay is a very good man, but we don't know him, after all. Drink up.' She takes a deep drink of her tea and I sip mine. My eyes widen when I taste the whisky in it. Quite a bit of whisky, actually.

'I was mistaken, it wasn't sherry, it was Scotch.' She sips again. 'Arval was up in the Orkneys last summer. Not a big drinker himself, worse luck. Have you been there?'

'Not to the Orkneys, no.'

'I can't stand the smell of fish. Poor Michael has to turn the fan on and open all the windows when he wants a fish-finger sandwich. I had a nanny who used to serve me the most appalling fish pie. Ruined me for it for life.'

I try to put this together, and deduce that she's saying

that the Orkneys smell of fish. I have no idea whether this is slander or not.

'There are lots of bats, though,' I say. 'In the Orkneys. I assume.'

'Unusual habitat, apparently. They have a unique vole as well. Of course I only pick these things up by listening; I wouldn't know a vole if it hit me in the face. Would you?'

'No.'

'Oh good.' She raises her mug to me and smiles as if we have discovered something significant in common, something that will make us soulmates for ever. 'Were you horribly close to Arval?'

'Not really,' I say. 'I mean, he was my only uncle, but I always favoured Auntie Claire more, before she died.'

'Why was that, dear?'

'She was very motherly. Comfortable, like this furniture.'

'This was hers, of course.' Evangeline nods as if approving, and I wonder why that makes me feel pleased. She takes another sip of tea, and I take one too. The whisky warms my throat all the way down to my stomach.

'I meant, why did she die?' she says suddenly.

'Um. Uh, cancer. She had breast cancer.'

'Ah.' Evangeline nods again, in a different way this time, her ringed fingers stroking her rather sharp chin. 'Of course. That would make it difficult.'

'It was a long time ago,' I hasten to tell her, because she looks somehow as if she's going to get upset about my aunt.

'Oh yes.' She stands up. 'As I was saying, darling, I'm gasping. Do you mind?'

I stare at her stupidly for a moment before I realise she's gasping for a cigarette, and that's why she's come up here. 'Um, yeah. Just a second, I'll get them for you.'

I've hidden the fags in a rice steamer in the back of one of the kitchen cabinets. It was quite enjoyable finding a hiding place, actually; it reminded me of stashing my sweets at school so they wouldn't be confiscated by the teachers. When I return with the packet, Evangeline's face lights up. 'Ah, *thank you*,' she says. She looks ten years younger, proving the potency of nicotine as a drug, if the mere prospect of it works better than Botox. She takes the packet from me and scampers to an armchair beneath one of the tall windows. Perching on the back of the chair, she opens the window and leans her elbows on the sill as she unwraps the cellophane from the packet.

'You've done this here before,' I say.

'Oh, many, many times. Arval didn't like my little habit, but he was kind enough to tolerate it. I don't smoke much, but I so enjoy it when I do. And Michael absolutely won't hear of it.' She extracts a silver lighter from the bodice of her gown and lights her cigarette. At the first drag she closes her eyes in utter pleasure and holds the smoke in her lungs for a long moment before she blows it in a thin stream out of the window.

I remember that voice thundering at her through the door the first day I arrived. What was it he said? *Stop begging for cigarettes, you filthy woman?*

'Michael is your . . . husband?'

'Mmm. Non-smoker, always has been. Frightfully tiresome about it. Oh, I am sorry, forgive me for being rude.' She offers the packet to me, and I shake my head.

She called him a tyrant before. He sounds rather horrible. Is this why I've had to hide the fags so thoroughly? Is he in the habit of going through the neighbours' cupboards? And then William was so reluctant to sell her fags in the shop, too. Obviously Michael is one of those bullies who keeps his wife on a tight rein and makes everyone else afraid of crossing him too. I don't like smoking either, but I've suddenly got a lot of sympathy for Evangeline.

'One does need to take one's pleasures while one can,' she continues. 'Speaking of which, you do have the most glorious tan. Where have you been?'

'Spain.'

'How wonderful. I remember climbing in the Pyrenees in my youth. My parents were very interested in healthful holidays, you see. Do you live in Spain?'

'No, I . . . Not any more.'

'Pity. But there is nothing like England. I was born and bred here in Highgate, myself. The air here is quite extraordinary; it feels more like a village than part of the metropolis. People come and go, of course, but for some people it gets into their bones and they can't possibly leave. Will it be that way for you, do you think?'

Ack. The thought fills me with panic. 'I haven't experienced much of the air.'

'Of course, you've only been here a few days yet. And you are staying here in Arval's flat for . . . ?'

'I'm sorting things out for my father. We're not sure whether we're going to rent it out or sell it, yet.'

'Oh, so you're not staying yourself?'

'I'm . . . it depends how long it takes me to sort everything out.'

'So you've somewhere else you should be?'

'Um.' I bite my lip. 'Not exactly.'

Evangeline takes one last deep drag of her cigarette and then leans out of the window and puts out the butt on the side of the building. I imagine there's a collection of black smudge on the grey stone, from packets and packets of fags smoked in secret. 'Well,' she says, 'you are certainly welcome. I do hope you'll enjoy it here.' She picks up her mug and raises it to me in a toast. We both drink. There's a lot of whisky in there; I bite my lip to stop from grimacing. This woman has enough troubles, hiding from her tyrannical husband. She doesn't need me to not appreciate her drinks. She's probably desperate to talk to anyone, actually. That's why she was spending so much time chatting in the corner shop.

Evidently my self-restraint does no good, though, because she hops off the back of the chair and puts her mug down on the table. 'I know, it's rather horrible, isn't it? I've never been fond of spirits, except for gin, which hardly counts. Listen, do you have any plans?'

'Well, a couple of things.' Cleaning, and a bit of skulking.

'Are they urgent?'

'I suppose not.'

'Wonderful. Do you like wine?'

'Well . . . yes.'

'Sit tight then, darling, I'll be right back.'

She leaves the flat door open behind her and clatters down the steps, leaving me in a faintly smoke-laced room, which suddenly seems rather cavernous and empty. I drink the rest of my boozy tea, and by the time I've got to the bottom of the cup, I realise that in the past half an hour or so I've lied to my best friend about where I am and what I'm doing, and told a complete stranger the truth. Nothing like the whole truth, granted, but not an out-and-out lie.

Evangeline reappears at the door with a large paper shopping bag dangling from her hand. She's breathing slightly heavily and her cheeks, under their make-up, seem to have lost some of their colour. I jump up in alarm and take the bag from her. My hand touches hers for an instant, and I feel how papery the skin is, see the blue veins standing out on the back. She's been so sprightly it's been easy not to think of her age.

'Michael may be right about the cigarettes,' she says wryly. 'They do tend to reduce one's lung capacity. Still, Nina, I've a treat for us.'

She leaves the front door ajar, settles on the settee and takes the carrier bag from me. The colour returns to her cheeks as she triumphantly takes out a biscuit tin and a bottle of red wine. 'I've got far too many sandwiches,' she says, extracting a waiter's corkscrew from a pocket. 'Pop this open while I get us some glasses and plates, will you?'

By the time I've opened the bottle, Evangeline has returned with two wine glasses and two plates. She levers up the top of the biscuit tin, picks out a triangular quarter sandwich, and gives it to me on a plate.

I pick it up. It's on white bread, and I can see a thick smearing of butter on each slice. Between them is something pink. I sniff and remember packed lunches at school, end-of-the-month teas.

'Corned beef?' I ask. 'Out of a tin?'

Unbelievably, my mouth is watering. My diet has consisted of mostly porridge, and lately dry toast, since I haven't got any butter.

'I know, it's hugely nostalgic, isn't it? There are far too many for me here, so please help yourself.'

I bite into it. The bread is soft and bland and the butter and corned beef fatty and salty. There's a hint of hot English mustard. Compared to porridge it's incredibly tasty, and before I know it, the sandwich is gone and I'm licking my fingers.

'Oh, lovely, you liked it. Here, have a glass of wine.'

She's filled the glass nearly to the brim. Faintly embarrassed by my unthinking gluttony, I sit on the end of the couch and sip in a much more delicate fashion at the wine. It's dark, rich with tobacco and berries, and strangely quite complementary to the corned beef and white bread. I take a second sip to appreciate it and Evangeline puts another triangle on my plate. This one goes down nearly as quickly as the first one did, but as soon as it's gone, I find another in its place, this one filled with grated Cheddar cheese and tomato. Evangeline has been talking about something all this time, though I haven't actually caught any of it because of the food and drink. I swallow the third sandwich, wash it down with a divine gulp of wine, and say, 'I'm sorry, what was that you were saying?'

Evangeline smiles at me. She's got her own wine glass in her hand and has left faint lipstick prints on its rim. 'Merely reminiscing. When you reach my age, you'll find it becomes as involuntary as breathing. Please help yourself to the tin.'

I do. There are more triangles, stacked on top of each other, two apples and a packet of crisps. I take another corned beef sandwich and bite into an apple. It's sharp and sweet and I have to close my eyes for a moment, it's so good.

'Arval had a weakness for fruit. It must run in the family.' She sips her wine. 'What else runs in your family?'

Being left alone. 'Arval and I are both tall,' I say, knocking back some more wine.

'You are so lucky. It is a plague, being petite. My brother Edgar, bless his soul, always called me a "minimus of hind'ring knot-grass made". He could quote the most annoying bits of Shakespeare.'

'My sister usually sticks with normal everyday sarcasm.'

Evangeline shudders. 'Treacherous, aren't they? Is she a younger sibling?'

'Yes.'

'They are born specifically to torment you.'

'I'll drink to that.' We clink glasses, and I realise that mine is nearly empty. Evangeline refills it, and tops her own up. The wine and the food are spreading warmth through my entire body. My fingers and toes are tingling a bit, as if they're being suffused by an unaccustomed blood supply.

'The thing about my sister,' I say to Evangeline, feeling as if my tongue has become unstuck after God knows how long, 'is that she acts so damn superior, she thinks I'm so bossy, just because she's there. She doesn't have a job, she doesn't have a house, she spends all day lurking in her room and yet she's so fucking—'

I realise I've both sworn and started on a rant, and I blush.

And exactly who is jobless and homeless and lurking in a room these days, anyway?

'Oh darling, don't I know it. Edgar never had a job, spent his days swanning about being charmingly feckless, and yet he was always the favourite. Unfair, but I'd never change him, of course. Cheese sandwich?' She passes one to me.

'Aren't you having any?' I ask her, glad of the change of subject, but she shakes her head and takes out another cigarette.

'My sustenance is the noxious weed.' She goes back to her perch near the window and lights up. The noxious weed actually smells pretty good, which should tell me that I've had too much to drink already, after the Scotch and the one glass of wine. Of course I haven't drunk in some time, and more pertinently haven't had much of an appetite either. The last thing I ate was . . . was . . .

I'm not sure. I eat the sandwich Evangeline gave me because it's bound to have an alcohol-dulling effect. And take another drink, to balance it out.

'Oh!' Evangeline throws her cigarette out of the window and starts to her feet, so abruptly that I nearly spill my wine on the couch. 'How could I be so thoughtless? Here we are in his flat and we haven't toasted Arval yet!' She holds her glass up, and I stand and clink mine against hers.

'To Arval.'

'To Arval and his Ozark big-ears,' I say. We both drink deep. 'It's a hell of a way to go,' I add, forgetting my previous qualms about swearing.

'Have you spoken with Viktor about it?'

'Who's Viktor?' As soon as I ask, I know I didn't need to: there could only be one person called Viktor. 'Oh, you mean the brooding dark night-walker upstairs?'

'That's certainly one way of describing him,' Evangeline says, going back to the window and lighting a third cigarette.

'He only comes out at night,' I tell her. 'What do you think he does in the day?'

'He sleeps, I should imagine; it's what creatures of the night generally do while the sun shines.' She blows a curling stream of smoke, seemingly unconcerned about the bizarre habits of her neighbours. But I'm feeling the effects of alcohol and of not having spoken to another person for days.

'It's strange. This whole house is strange.'

'Do you think so, darling?'

'It's so . . . creepy. All the gargoyles and the wrought iron. I mean, no offence because you obviously live here, but doesn't it feel to you like it should be full of ghosts?'

She smiles, deepening the gentle lines in her cheeks. 'Have you seen a ghost or two, Nina?'

I think of the empty shoes, footprints of the dead and gone. 'Not . . . not a literal one.'

Evangeline taps her chin with her finger and sips her

wine in between puffs. 'We did hear some screaming the other day from this direction.'

'That was probably me catching this ginormous hairy spider in the bath.'

'Oh, so you've met Fifi?'

'Fifi?' I gasp. 'You mean . . . you've got a *spider* as a sort of a pet?'

Then I notice that her grey eyes are sparkling and she's trying to suppress laughter. I can't help it; I giggle, and she joins in with a raspy, full-throated chuckle. It feels as good as the wine and the food.

'No pet spiders,' she says. 'I can't give you a definitive answer about the ghosts. Highgate is famous for them, of course.'

'Really?'

'Oh yes, all sorts of supernatural creatures. Don't you remember the Highgate Vampire, or was that before your time?'

In the distance, downstairs, I can hear the door scraping open. A voice booms up the stairs, echoing all the way: 'Evangeline?'

Evangeline jumps up and hurriedly puts out her cigarette. 'Must go, darling,' she says, knocking back her wine and scurrying to the kitchen. I hear water splashing in the sink and the rushed sound of cabinets opening and closing as she hides the cigarettes again. She comes out wiping her hands on her skirt, and gives me a peck on the cheek. Her face is slightly damp.

'Do I smell of smoke?' she asks.

I sniff. Wine and perfume. 'No.'

'A triumph.'

I stand up to see her out, and maybe peer down the stairs at her thundering husband, and I wobble. 'Oops, I think I might be a little drunk.'

'That's precisely the idea, Nina darling. You finish up

that bottle and then take a nap; you'll feel better for it. Thank you so much for the fag break, see you later, bye bye!' She hurries out of the flat, slamming the door behind her.

'The mighty tyrant calls,' I murmur in the sudden absolute silence. I pour another glass of wine. It's mid-afternoon and this is probably the slippery slope to something horrific that will land me in a gutter somewhere, but her advice about drinking and then taking a nap sounds very good.

In the end, though, I only manage half the glass and half the other apple before my eyes begin to slide out of focus. Before I can fall asleep on the couch I cork the wine, close the biscuit tin, and bring everything back to the kitchen to keep until I can return it later.

On the counter, near the refrigerator, are half a dozen eggs, a loaf of bread and a pineapple.

23

There really isn't another word for it. I'm lurking.

I've got everything that Evangeline left for me in her cloth bag, and I'm hovering outside her door, wondering whether to knock and also listening as hard as I can for what's going on inside her flat. I haven't heard anybody leave the building, but I don't hear anything from inside, either. I don't really want to knock on the door and possibly get Evangeline into trouble, but maybe she's in trouble anyway? I think back, trying to discern in memory whether the voice booming up the stairs had sounded threatening, or just loud. It's hard to tell, especially with all this wine sloshing around inside me.

I tried to take a nap, but I kept tossing and turning. I'm not used to complete strangers secretly giving me food. I'm not sure why this one did. All I can assume is that she noticed, when she was rummaging around for the whisky, that there wasn't much to eat there except for a bit of porridge, the end of a loaf of bread and a few tins, and she put the empty cupboards together with my lack of cash in the shop and drew her own conclusions.

The thought, when I had it, made me sit up bolt upright in bed, feeling queasy. Never mind that the conclusion is correct; this is pity. This is charity. I do not take pineapples from people who feel sorry for me.

So I bundled everything, even the mostly drunk bottle of wine, back into the bag and came down here. But how do you return an awkwardly shaped bag of food if you don't dare knock on the returnee's door? I can't fit it through the letter slot, and leaving it on her doorstep seems incredibly rude. And there are eggs in there, they could get broken.

Actually, scrambled eggs on toast would be very nice.

I think back over my conversation with Evangeline. She was a little bit curious, but she didn't probe, even when I started spouting off about Imogen. And she was odd. But not at all pitying or condescending. In fact, if she hadn't left the food in the kitchen, I'd never have guessed that her object all along was to feed me, despite my having scarfed most of her lunch while she never had a nibble herself. She just made it seem that she was enjoying my company and the chance to smoke.

I stop lurking and climb back upstairs with the bag. I unpack everything in the kitchen, leaving the bread and eggs and wine on the side and putting the pineapple on the table like a centrepiece. I keep the biscuit tin to return later. Then I roll up Evangeline's cloth bag, pull on a pair of turquoise capris underneath my dress for extra warmth, get my own handbag and the broken umbrella, and leave the flat again, this time to actually go outside.

There's a bank down the street, which I didn't see before on my epic trek of the neighbourhood. I open the door and have to pause for a minute because suddenly I can't breathe.

*Dos euros*, the Spanish teller says in my mind.

I swallow. I close my eyes and count to fifty. I clutch my handbag, go to the counter and change my euros for the grand total of eighteen pounds thirty-seven, which is officially all the money I have in the world. The change reminds me of my bags of fifty pences for the electricity meter, a lifetime ago. I separate out three pounds ten and put it in Evangeline's bag.

Then I go for a long, long walk. Concentrating on my wet feet in their wet flip-flops, on the sound of the rain on the umbrella, on my breathing and my heartbeat, on an errand achieved, and not on the absurdly small amount of money in my bag. I don't see much except the pavement, although at one point, at the top of a climb, I glance behind me and see London spread out below, the houses and the mists and the towers and temples, everything I am missing and everyone I am hiding from.

I don't look up much after that.

It's growing dark when I reach the corner shop and the orange vinyl tea rooms, and once again I'm soaked through. The red wine has worn off and so have the sandwiches, and I discover, as I hurry up the street towards the house, that I'm shivering. I let myself in, then put Evangeline's money wrapped in her bag through her letter slot. I press my ear against the door and listen for a moment, but don't hear anything except for some faint talking that could be the television.

When I straighten up, the man from upstairs is standing on the steps.

Viktor, his name is. He's got his cape-like mac and wide-brimmed hat on, and he's carrying a black canvas bag big enough to lug a corpse around. His eyes are very dark, and his eyebrows are drawn together in a frown.

'What are you staring at?' I snap.

He stands there without answering for a moment, his hand on the wrought-iron banister. At last he clears his throat and says, 'You have rather eccentric fashion sense.'

'You're one to talk, caped crusader. When's that hat from, the nineteenth century?'

'It does keep the rain off,' he says, looking pointedly

at my lower half. I glance down at myself: sopping wet flowered dress over sopping wet turquoise capris, feet and legs splashed with mud.

He may have a point, but I refuse to be criticised for oddity by a creature of the night. I step exaggeratedly out of his way and gesture for him to pass.

'If you want to speak to Evangeline and Michael, you should probably knock,' he says, not budging.

'What, you mean you consider it *rude* to stand listening outside someone's door?'

To my satisfaction, his mouth tightens and he stomps down the stairs, past me and out the door.

I go upstairs for my eggs on toast.

'Dad? How are you?'

'Oh hi, Nina, how nice to hear from you. I'm fine, fine, and you?'

'I'm' – I hardly hesitate at all – 'great. I'm sorry I haven't rung in ages, it's been so busy here.'

'Well, you like to keep busy in your line of work. How's the weather in Spain?'

'Beautiful.' I cross my fingers and hope there haven't been any Spanish hurricanes, or if there have that they haven't been destructive enough to make the BBC news. 'I just wanted to make sure you were all right.'

'Oh yes, you know me and Immy, ticking along.'

'Are you sure? Because I can always come to see you, it's no problem. If you're . . . you know . . . lonely.'

'Of course I'm sure. Thought of you the other day, though, saw that boss of yours on the telly. Edward?'

'Edmund.' I swallow hard.

'Edmund, that's right. He's got that new programme now. Funny food he cooks, it's all like little pills. Well, must go, we're about to go out to the pub to meet Immy's new young man.'

'Oh.' I twist my fingers in my flowered skirt. 'Well . . . have fun.'

'Thank you. Oh, before I forget, do you remember Arval's flat?'

'Um, oh yeah, that place. What about it?'

'There's no hurry for you to get to it, seeing you're so busy. I rang the owner of the building and they say they'll keep an eye on it for as long as we need them to.'

Shit. Now I have to worry about someone snooping around and discovering I'm here. 'That's very nice of them.'

'Right, Immy's tapping her foot at me, best go. So don't worry about the flat, all right, love?'

'No. Of course not. I won't worry at all.'

24

'It's all the usual sort of thing. Small animals – cats, squirrels, foxes – found dead and drained of blood. Young girls attacked by spectral entities, corpses appearing in vehicles, sightings of hideous apparitions, crazed mobs storming the cemetery, et cetera. This was in the seventies, though, darling, ancient history to someone your age, I daresay.'

Evangeline sucks on her cigarette and blows a stream of smoke out of my window. We're on our second cup of tea, with no Scotch this time. She's been up here for the past three afternoons, puffing her way through her packet of fags. Today her pineapple is ripe and I've gained some of my dignity back by grilling it and serving her sweet, smoky slices with her tea.

'What happened?' I ask.

'Well, I always thought that if it was a vampire, it must be a very timid and slender one. Imagine being surrounded by millions of people and eating nothing but fox blood! You wouldn't, would you? But that's what the newspaper headlines said: Highgate Vampire. Then someone claimed to have staked it through the heart. Though if I'd staked a corpse through the heart, I'd be quite eager to conceal the fact, don't you think?'

'So you don't believe in all this supernatural stuff?'

I'd think living in a building like this for long enough could make you believe whether you wanted to or not. I'm vaguely surprised I haven't strung the dried-up garlic in Arval's fridge on to a necklace.

'Oh, I wouldn't say that, darling. As far as I know, the vampire is still walking around exsanguinating the wildlife.' Evangeline puts out her fag, stands and stretches. 'Well, time's up, darling, Michael's home from work any minute. I'll just replace these in the rice cooker.'

After she's gone into the kitchen, I wait a few seconds and then follow her. Just as I suspected, she's trying to sneak a packet of custard creams from her handbag into the cupboard.

I stop her with my hand. 'Evangeline, you've got to stop giving me food. It's very kind of you, but it's not necessary.'

'Oh darling, humour me. I haven't got any children or grandchildren to feed, and at my age it's one of the few biological urges I have left.' Gently she extracts the packet from my hand.

'But it makes me feel . . . You're giving me so much and I haven't given you anything in return.'

Her eyes widen in surprise. 'Nina! You surely jest. You are my secret vice maiden, allowing me to smoke my cigarettes up here. And besides, I so enjoy our little chats.'

'I do too.' Today I found myself storing up things to say, just to hear her throaty laugh.

'Well then, let's hear no more of it. Anyway, I'm glad you reminded me, I was going to ask you a favour.'

'What?'

She opens the packet and passes me a custard cream, which I absently put in my mouth. 'Well, tell me if I'm going senile, darling, but I seem to remember you said you have done work connected with the food service industry.'

'Yes,' I say cautiously. I have mentioned only this fact, and changed the subject quickly afterwards.

'I've not told you this before, but my husband Michael owns a sort of little café, very bijou, and we are absolutely short-staffed at the moment, more customers than we can handle. One of his employees has left to have a baby, another's moved away – you know what the business is like, I'm sure – and of course I've volunteered to help, but he says I mustn't give up the lifestyle to which I've become accustomed. I was wondering if you'd consider perhaps helping him out just the tiniest bit, a few mornings a week, with all your expertise.'

I swallow my biscuit, which seems very dry. On the one hand, it would be good to help Evangeline after she's been so kind. On the other, I'm not sure I'm up to working for Michael the tyrant. On the third (if that's possible), this is my time. I'm supposed to be licking wounds, not serving coffee, even in a very bijou café. Anything like a job seems like far too permanent a decision, since I'm really not going to stay here for much longer, only until I've recovered a bit.

'I'm sorry, Evangeline. It's not that I don't want to help you, it's just that . . .' I search for an excuse, and can't find any, 'I've got too much on.'

'Of course you do, darling, don't we all, but it would help us so much. It goes without saying that we'd pay for your time; not what you're used to, I'm sure, but a token of our appreciation.' She hands me another biscuit.

I shake my head. 'I'm so sorry.'

'Oh well, do let us know if you reconsider. Toodles, darling, see you soon.' She air-kisses both my cheeks and for a moment I lose myself in the scent of perfume and tobacco. Then she's gone.

Miraculously, it's not raining this afternoon, although outside the clouds are low and grey, and Evangeline's open window has let in a very cold draught. I wrap myself up as well as I possibly can and head out for my daily walk.

Like my afternoons, these have become slightly more structured, in that I consciously decide whether I'm going to go uphill or downhill, north or south or east or west. Today I go downhill towards Hampstead Heath, where the leaves are yellow and sparse, though the grass is green. Amazingly, someone is swimming in the Men's Pond. I pause to watch him for a moment, but then he dives and I see naked buttocks. So I turn and walk quickly away.

The road back up the hill is lined by trees and high walls, and is shadowed like a tunnel. The narrow pavement winds upwards. You'd think I'd be in pretty good shape from all the cleaning and walking I've been doing, but I'm breathing hard when I round a corner and am confronted by a mess of Gothic arches, pointed ceilings and crenulations. At first I think I've stumbled upon a back entrance to Arval's house, but then I realise this place is more tasteful, more like a church than a nightmare and with substantially fewer gargoyles. It's set slightly back from the road on the left, behind chained-off car-parking spaces. In the stone over the wide doorway are carved the words 'London Cemetery'.

Highgate Cemetery. Home of dead people and, according to Evangeline, at least one fox-sucking freak. This must be the gatehouse or the chapel or something. Despite myself, I wander up to the massive closed wooden door, where a sign says that the west cemetery is only open for tours by appointment, but that for an admission fee you can traipse around the east cemetery all you want.

I'm not going to pay money to surround myself with melancholy and decay; I can do that at Arval's house for free. Still, for a moment I linger at the gate, imagining night-time and a shadowy figure gliding past the tombstones. Fangs shining, eyes dark and hypnotic. Wearing old-fashioned grave clothes, maybe a Dracula cape. Or an ancient hat.

A creature of the night.

I walk on, but my mind is ticking over in a strange way. This place really isn't that far from the house. And if you were a supernatural monster with an appetite for blood, wouldn't you prefer to spend your non-sucking hours of daylight in a centrally heated attic instead of a damp, draughty old catacomb?

I shake my head. Mist has gathered on my hair and it drips down my neck. I must be going as batty as Uncle Arval if for one minute I think that the man living upstairs from me is a vampire. I've got real things to worry about, like money and food and the owner of the house popping in to make sure the flat's all right and discovering me there already. Like not having any appropriate shoes and the likelihood of that spider reappearing. Like a broken heart.

For a moment I let myself think about Juan. It's like testing a broken tooth with your tongue to see if it's healed yet. First I try remembering the night we met, how he rescued me from the chair. That doesn't hurt, so I try something more difficult: the first night we made love. I remember how I flung him down on the floor and practically ravished him, just so he wouldn't get the chance to do that endless foreplay. Or so I wouldn't have a chance to have second thoughts.

I keep on toiling up the hill. That memory should

hurt, but it doesn't. Instead it seems sort of stupid, to treat sex like something to get over and done with. Maybe I feel that way because I'm most likely never going to have sex again. Unless I'm desperate enough to go on the game to get some money.

The thought makes me stop walking. Dear Lord, have I just compared my relationship with Juan to prostitution?

No, that's nearly as silly as thinking my upstairs neighbour is the undead. I have feelings for Juan. I went into a relationship with him because I honestly wanted him, not because I was using him for what he could give me: affection, safety, an escape, an excuse. And even if I was using him the littlest teensy bit at first, as I got to know him better I came to love him. To prove it, I remember the moment I found his note on the bed saying he'd left me.

Searing pain, humiliation and despair. I clutch my stomach and feel sick.

There. I must love him.

Unless, of course, this pain is from being left, and not from being left by Juan specifically. If it's leftover pain from being abandoned by my mum and, effectively, by my dad all those years ago when I was a teenager. Pain I've pushed aside for all the time since because I've been too busy getting on with my own life. The crying-over-shoes incident sort of makes me think that might be true.

There's a bench by the side of the road, and I sit on it while I try out another thought, this one a fantasy rather than a memory: Juan coming back to me, apologising and saying he's made a terrible mistake.

My fists clench, but I make myself imagine it in detail. Here he is, in front of me, holding a dozen roses and begging for my forgiveness. Two dozen roses. Am I glad?

Of course I'm glad. Because now I can dump him properly and use my money that he stole to get some of my life back.

I jump up off the bench and start walking again. If anybody happens to be watching me, they probably think that I am insane, but I need to puzzle this out and movement helps. Right. Wanting to dump him doesn't mean I didn't love him. There are things that are unforgivable even if someone is the love of your life, and running off with Juanita is one of them. I'd be stupid to take him back.

But what does it mean that my second thought was about my money? Do I want my money and my dignity more than I want Juan's apology? Did he really mean that little to me? Does that mean I really was using him?

I'm frowning furiously, and striding so fast that I nearly bump into a lamp post, a pillar box and a woman with a pram. Before I've figured it out, I'm standing in front of the Temple of Gloom. I stare up at the windows of the top floor; blinds are drawn down over them, like shut eyes blocking off the weak afternoon sun.

What is he *doing* up there?

Walking around at night and sleeping during the day is very odd behaviour, even if Viktor isn't a vampire. He might be doing shift work or something – but in a cape and hat?

Okay, I'll make a deal with myself. It is an absolutely totally ridiculous idea that I might have thrown myself into a relationship with someone I didn't care about because I wanted what he could give me, and that I care more about money than my erstwhile life partner. The chances of my being that shallow are roughly the same as the chances of my upstairs neighbour actually being a vampire.

So: if Viktor is a vampire, then I'm a bad person.

Easy.

\*

I'm not a big horror fan, but I've seen a few films during sleepless nights. So I know the protocol if a woman thinks she's met someone who might be a vampire. Her first action should be to go online or go to the library or befriend Anthony Head and learn all about what vampires are like. To get a checklist to tick items off on. Yes, he hates garlic, yes, he avoids crosses, yes, he has two-foot-long slavering teeth that thirst for my blood.

My strategy is simpler. I sit in the living room and wait for the sun to go down. When I hear the upstairs door open, I get up and at the exact moment that the footsteps reach the first-floor landing I open the door and step out.

Viktor glances at me, then quickly away, and walks by as if to ignore my very presence. He's not wearing his hat and I can see that his hair is dark brown and slightly long. It's thick and wavy and dishevelled as if he's pushed it back from his face with his hands.

With his hair showing and his face not concealed, he looks more human. I can see high cheekbones, dark eyebrows, the shadow of beard stubble on his chin and jaw. His mouth is wide and turned down at the corners, as if he is displeased about something. Maybe the shortage of tasty animals.

'Hey, strange man upstairs,' I say to him, and this does make him look up, though he doesn't pause. 'Are you a vampire?'

'Yes,' he says. He goes downstairs and out the door into the gathering darkness.

## 25

I open my eyes to blackness, my heart racing. For a moment I don't know what's woken me up, but then I hear it again: a tapping at my door.

I sit up. I'm not in bed. The tapping is light but insistent; it continues for several seconds and then stops. I grope around me, encounter upholstery and cushions, and remember that I couldn't sleep so I lay down on the couch, lights on, curtains drawn, to watch some telly. But the telly isn't on, and neither are the lights, and I have no idea what time it is, but it's surely too late for someone to be knocking at the door.

I fumble for the lamp on the side table, but then think better of it. What if it's the owner of the building, knocking to see if someone's moved into the flat? Wouldn't it be better to keep quiet?

But then the owner would have a key and wouldn't need to knock.

*Tap-tap-tap*. It's louder now.

The reason I've been sleeping on the couch is that I spent a good chunk of last night looking through my uncle's library for books about vampires. There were several. Including one with a scene where a child vampire hovers outside the window of a friend he knew in life, tap-tap-tapping at the window to be invited in. After I read it I had to hide the book in one of Arval's desk drawers, and then turn on some mindless television to try to blank my mind out.

*Tap-tap-tap.*

I shrink back against the couch cushions. The darkness is total, far too dark for London, and it occurs to me that maybe the tapping is coming from somewhere inside the flat, because ghosts and the undead can walk through walls. I reach out for the lamp, not caring if I give myself away, because without light I'm stuck inside my own thoughts and I think I might scream.

I find the switch and click it.

Nothing.

*Tap-tap-tap.*

'Nina?'

The voice is hushed and muffled through the door, but it's gravelly and plummy and I recognise it and start breathing again.

'Evangeline?' I stand and stagger for where I think the door must be, and next to it the light switch. I reach the wall somewhere clear of them both and feel around the cold plaster for a landmark. But when I flick the switch, nothing happens.

'What's going on with the lights?'

'Open the door, darling.'

I do. The landing is dark, though not quite as dark as the flat. I can just about make out Evangeline's slight form in what looks like a long white nightdress. Her skin looks chalk-pale, her eyes like glittering holes. A kerchief covers her hair. She seizes my wrist in her hands, which are cold.

'What's wrong?' I ask.

'I need you to help me. It's Michael.'

My stomach flips over. 'What . . . has he done?' I try to draw her into the flat, to safety, but she resists.

'You've got to come downstairs, darling. Quickly.'

I step on to the landing. My feet are bare and the floor is freezing. Evangeline tugs me along by my wrist to the stairs. There are no lights on here either, but the tall windows let in a vague milky light that outlines the banisters and the edges of the steps.

'This isn't right,' I say as we descend. My voice is hushed, but it still echoes in the silence. 'This is London, it should never be this dark.'

'The electrics are off. Hurry, Nina, please. You're a slip of a thing, aren't you? I hope you'll be enough.' She's sure-footed, but her voice sounds very worried. She guides me across the hallway, our bare feet whispering on the marble tiles, and through the cavern of her door. It's darker in here, but my eyes have adjusted somewhat and I can see the cracks where the curtains don't quite meet, the irregular shadows of furniture, and a faint flicker from through a doorway. Our sounds are more muffled in the enclosed space, and there's a soft carpet underfoot. I smell perfume and the sulphur of a match.

Despite Evangeline pulling me onward, I hesitate. I didn't sign on to get involved in the lives of strangers. Especially not strangers with rather scary husbands, in the middle of a power cut, in a flat where I don't know the escape routes. It's utterly silent, and in the split second I stop moving I can imagine about a dozen different things that might be beyond that next door, every one of them something that would haunt my dreams for years afterwards. Even if I did get out unscathed.

'Evangeline,' I whisper, 'let's just call the police.'

'Don't be ridiculous, darling.' I'd take more comfort from these words if her voice weren't so shaky. Still, it's enough for me to let her draw me further into the flat, further into her life, down a carpeted hallway and into a bedroom.

A thick white candle sits on the bedside table and throws a circle of yellow light that makes the shadows even darker. The bed is huge and tall, its white sheets rumpled, its four carved posts rising up into the darkness. On the floor lies a man.

He has curly black hair and a beard shot through with grey, and his shoulders are broad in their striped pyjamas. There is a blue tattoo on the back of one of his large hands. From the chest downward he's covered with a blanket. To my relief (I think), his eyes are open and they fix on Evangeline, and then me.

'You must be Nina,' he says. 'Evangeline's told me a lot about you.'

He speaks, in his booming voice, as if he were at an afternoon tea party.

'I . . . um . . . likewise.'

Evangeline flits to his side and kneels beside him on the floor. She lays one hand on his forehead. 'Are you cold?'

'Of course I'm not bloody cold. I'm lying on a carpet.'

She touches his wrist and the tips of his fingers. 'That carpet is merely a thin layer between you and a polished marble slab.'

'I told you, woman, I'm perfectly comfortable and content to spend the night right here. There was no need to get people out of their beds.' He looks past Evangeline's shoulder at me. 'I'm very sorry, Nina. This silly woman won't do as she's told.'

'I . . . it's all right.'

'You can't stay here, darling,' Evangeline tells him in a low and gentle voice.

'Nonsense. Done it a hundred times. In the army we used to sleep on snow.'

They are completely absorbed in their argument with each other, so I look around the room to try to find some clues about what is going on here. Now that it seems there's no immediate danger, I can see I've missed one vital aspect of the room: in the corner there is a chrome and black wheelchair. I glance back at Michael; it's impossible to tell for certain because of the blanket, but his bottom half does appear to be substantially less strapping than his top.

'Did you fall out of bed?' I ask.

'Minor problem,' answers Michael. His accent is considerably more estuary and less plummy than Evangeline's.

'He made the most enormous crash, darling! Woke me up with the worst start. And he's got a lump on the back of his head the size of a goose egg. You have got to have a headache, Michael.'

'My head's as hard as a rock.'

'We need to get him back into bed,' Evangeline tells me. 'But I can't quite handle it myself tonight.' She wrings her hands together and I can see the lines of worry and fatigue in her face, how slight she appears in her voluminous nightgown. With her hair covered by the kerchief, the angles and bones of her face seem more defined, and she is at once more aged and more beautiful. Especially now that I know that her anxiety wasn't for herself.

'No problem at all,' I say cheerily. 'You can't possibly weigh any more than my auntie Claire's sofa, and I've been heaving that around all week.'

'So that's what the noise was.' Michael levers himself up on to his elbows. The movement drains the blood from his cheeks. Evangeline immediately props him up with both arms, biting her lip. 'Stop with your clucking, woman,' he tells her, though I notice that he finds her hand and grasps it.

After a moment he's collected himself. 'Right, we

might as well get this over with. Nina love, if you come behind me and get your hands under my arms, you and I will do the heavy lifting and my doting wife can steer. Once I've got a grip of the bed I should be able to do it myself. Bloody ridiculous bed, it's far too tall.'

'Michael Clegg, do not dare to slander such a priceless heirloom. Both my parents died in that bed.'

'All the more reason to throw it on the tip. Now make yourself useful and get rid of this bothersome blanket. Ready, Nina my love?'

I get behind him as he's instructed, and put my hands under his large arms. I have absolutely no idea how to lift a person, but both husband and wife seem brisk now that the decision's been made.

'Don't worry,' he tells me. 'It only takes brute strength.'

'I'm not sure how brute my strength is, now that I think of it.' I have a vision of dropping him like a stone back to the floor. 'Maybe . . . maybe it would be better if we asked the guy upstairs to help. He looks strong enough.'

'I tried Viktor first; he's out,' Evangeline says. 'He'll be wanting to take advantage of the power cut, no doubt. Just give it your best shot, darling, no one can ask more than that.'

'All right.'

'On three,' Michael says. 'One, two, three.'

I heave upward as hard as I can and Michael grapples for the bedstead while Evangeline pushes his waist and legs. He is very heavy, but I can feel his muscles bulging under my fingers as his hands reach the headboard and hold on tight. 'I've got it,' he grunts, 'if you don't mind helping Eva with my legs.'

One push, this time on a thigh thin and lifeless under cotton pyjamas, and he's lying on the bed. I step back, gasping. Evangeline stands, her forehead resting on Michael's chest, her hands rising and falling with his breathing. He strokes the cotton of her kerchief and her narrow shoulders.

It's too private a moment; I shift on my feet and watch the candle gutter for a few moments. Then I hear Michael murmur, and Evangeline busies herself rearranging the blankets and pillows for him.

'For God's sake, stop fussing, old woman. If you want to make yourself useful, go and make us all a hot drink. There's a torch in the bedside table. I can't think why you didn't use it when you were creeping around the corridors.'

Without a word Evangeline takes the torch from the drawer and leaves the room. I take a step after her, to help her in the kitchen, but Michael waves at me to stay. When her light footfalls recede he says quietly, 'She's always been strong enough to help me before.'

'Oh.' Even in bed in pyjamas, having recently been on the floor, Michael looks so much bigger and healthier than his wife. I'd guess he's at least ten years younger, if not more.

'She'll pretend it doesn't bother her, of course. I don't fall out of bed often, thank God.' He rubs the back of his head. 'And I can do most things for myself, though it pleases her to do them for me. Glad you were here tonight, though. I don't mind the floor, but she'll be happier with me tucked up here.'

'I'm glad I was here too.'

Now *there* are some words I never thought I'd say about being in this place.

He shifts himself in bed, rearranging his legs with his hands. 'What's this rubbish I hear about you not wanting to work in the café?'

I wasn't expecting this. 'Oh, well, I'm . . . I mean, I'm

sorry I can't help, but like I told Evangeline, I'm quite busy.'

'Hmph. I suppose it does take up a lot of time, vacuuming a flat three times a day.'

My mouth falls open. I've been rumbled.

'Eva would work her fingers to the bone, bless her, but I won't let her set foot in there until she's got some of her strength back. Besides, she keeps bothering the customers for fags. You'd be doing us a favour.'

'Evangeline said it was to help you, not her. She said you were too busy.'

'She would. We're not that busy, but I've had two people leave. I'm sure it won't be much of a challenge for you, especially compared with moving couches and screaming at spiders, but it might pass the time. Eva would rest a little easier knowing I'm not short-staffed.'

'I'm not planning on staying here,' I say, since he's demolished my pat excuse.

'And I'm not planning on hiring you permanently. I doubt I could pay what you'd ask for anyway; you look a bit high-maintenance.'

I look down at my flowered dress, wrinkled from sleeping on the couch, and I laugh. Evangeline reappears carrying a silver tray with the torch and three steaming cups on it. 'The gas is still on, thankfully,' she says as I take the tray. 'We haven't had a good power cut in ages; it's always so very cosy, I think. Nina, you take the armchair just there. I'll sit here on the bed.' She perches beside Michael, curling her legs up underneath her nightgown, and sighs happily. 'It's like a midnight feast at school! Except without all the ghastly horrid girls.'

'Well, only two,' says Michael.

The cocoa is rich and creamy. Evangeline looks as if she's settled down for a good chat, but I drink quickly, feeling superfluous now. Besides, I need to make my escape before Michael can go on about the café any more.

'So it's sorted,' he says. 'You'll start tomorrow morning. If you knock on our door at seven, we'll walk down together.'

'But . . .'

'Oh, that's marvellous!' Evangeline puts her cup down on the bedspread and claps her hands. 'I'm so glad you agreed to help, Nina. You'll be able to keep an eye on Michael for me and make sure he isn't overdoing it. Or flirting with the pretty customers.'

'You're one to talk, woman, you're on your third husband. Besides, I can spend the day flirting with Nina now.'

Evangeline hops off the bed. 'Best go off to sleep, darling, you've got an early start. Nina, you take the torch until the lights come back on, and I'll help you through the maze of this flat so you don't bark your shins.'

I'm bundled out of the flat within moments, and before I know it, I'm standing on the moonlit stairs, the torch cutting a swathe of light, wondering what on earth has just happened.

## 26

'*This* is the bijou café?'

I can't help it. Last night, before dropping off to sleep, I swore I would be as cheerful as possible this morning. Evangeline thinks Michael needs my help; Michael thinks Evangeline needs my help; between the two of them I'm bound to do some good anyway, and just because I'm miserable that's no reason to let other people down. So this morning I dressed in a very cute sleeveless fifties-style floral dress with a nipped-in waist and a full skirt and a pair of butter-yellow heels, ready to spread sunshine despite the unrelenting rain.

Which is why it is particularly confusing when Michael stops his wheelchair in front of the orange vinyl tea rooms.

' "Bijou" is an Evangeline word,' he says. He unlocks the glass door and wheels himself over the threshold. I follow him as he snaps on the lights (power was restored at six minutes past five this morning; I know because I was awakened by the television and all the lights in the flat turning on).

Inside, it's worse than I thought. Sure, I'd anticipated that all the chairs would be upholstered in orange vinyl, and the tables covered with wood-replicating plastic. I could have foretold the glassed-in counter at the back, ready to hold a selection of tired-looking cakes and wilting sandwiches, and the collection of well-worn white catering mugs and stainless steel teapots. And the Artex walls, so thick with peaks and swirls that they make the room appear to be sitting inside a casing of whipped cream. But I never could have imagined the plethora of paper doilies, sitting on every table underneath the sugar bowls, stacked in teetering piles on the back counter ready to be used for God knows what. Or the spider plants. They hang from the ceiling, perch on the edges of the counters, crouch on shelves, dripping leaves and little baby spider plants.

I've walked into the 1970s. And not in a funky, retro way; in a shuddery, has-this-place-had-a-lick-of-paint-since-Edward-Heath-was-prime-minister way.

'You can take the front, and I'll take the kitchen,' Michael tells me, gesturing towards a doorway dangling with plastic beads. 'Don't think you're dressed for washing dishes anyway. Eva tells me you've done this before?'

'Uh . . . sort of.'

'Well, if you can make a pot of tea you can't go far wrong. Help yourself to anything you'd like to eat or drink; it's one of the privileges of the job and Eva will be asking if I've fed you.' My misgivings must be showing themselves on my face, because he winks at me and smiles. 'You'll be fine, love, a trained monkey could work here, and when I'm on my own, you'd swear one does.'

He wheels himself through to the kitchen, the beads clicking behind him. And I'm alone, in charge of the shop. I look around at the Artex, the vinyl, the everlasting doilies, and I remember the sleek chic of Jett, the glorious light of El Flor Anaranjado.

The door opens and two old ladies with wheeled shopping bags come in. 'Two teas, love, and a bacon roll,' one of them calls, and they seat themselves in the front window.

Like a trained monkey, I switch on the urn.

*

Evangeline might have misled me with her use of the word 'bijou', but she wasn't kidding about the busy part. The two old shopping ladies are the start of a flood of customers that continues without a break from half past seven onwards. They're not queuing outside the door, as they used to at Jett, but they steadily fill all the tables. All of them seem to be regulars, as I discover from the protests when I try to serve tea without placing a doily beneath each cup. As long as I remember the doily, though, they all seem happy enough and I hear the exact same conversation about the reason for the power cut about seventeen million times.

Michael brings out cakes for the glass display, makes sandwiches, washes dishes, and calls out contributions to the power-cut discussions from the kitchen in his boom-ing voice. Mid-morning he gives me a grated cheese and cucumber sandwich, which he claims he's made by mistake; when he tries the same trick some time later with a ham and tomato toastie, I suspect he's lying but I eat it anyway, between making tea and filter coffee and clearing tables.

I lose count of how many times I feel something tickling the back of my neck and whirl around only to discover yet another breeding spider plant. Fortunately the crockery is made of some improbable substance that doesn't shatter when you drop it on the floor.

When Michael emerges from the kitchen with three hot buttered scones slathered with jam and pulls a chair away from an empty table so that he can wheel up to it, I look at the clock and am surprised that it's half past two. 'Tea break,' he tells me, and I make us a pot. I've no sooner put the obligatory doilies on the table than the front door opens and Evangeline comes in.

'Darlings!' she calls and joins us at the table, kissing Michael and perching on one of the chairs. He puts a scone in front of her and pours her a cup of tea. 'How's your goose egg?' she asks him, leaning around and rummaging through the thick hair at the back of his head. He rolls his eyes at me and demolishes half a scone in one bite.

'Stop clucking around me like a hen, woman.'

'You must have a very thick skull. I've never heard such a crack.'

'Need to have a thick skull to put up with your prattle day in and out.'

'You'd do well to pay attention to the prattle, if you don't want to go the way of my first two husbands. So, Nina darling, how was your first day?'

'Fine.' To my surprise I've finished my scone and tea already. I've forgotten how fast time can go and how hungry you can get when you're busy.

Michael reaches over and plucks a metal dish from the counter near the till. 'Not bad for tips,' he says, and dumps the contents into my hand. It's mostly coppers and ten-pence pieces, but when I quickly count it, it's over two pounds. 'It's yours,' he tells me, and I could argue with him, but two pounds quite substantially increases my ready cash, so I pile it next to my tea cup to take away with me.

'Oh, darling,' Evangeline cries, looking downwards, her cup held delicately between thumb and forefinger, 'you've absolutely ruined those gorgeous shoes.'

Hmm. I have. Butter-yellow leather is fine when you're sitting on a sunny veranda, but not so good when you're carrying tea slops. 'A bit of shoe shopping this afternoon, then,' I say, poking at my coins.

To my surprise, Evangeline seems to take me seriously. 'Wonderful, darling, nothing brightens the spirits like a pair of new shoes. Off you go, then, you deserve it.' Michael nods.

So I scrape the coppers and tens into my handbag, where they jingle as I wave goodbye.

It is, of course, raining outside and I step straight into a puddle. I wander up the street, looking at the shop fronts for the first time since I've been here. I open the door to a charity shop and step inside, mostly to escape the rain, but partly because of what Evangeline has said. It smells of wool and washing powder. A young woman in a pinny sits behind the counter, chewing gum and reading *Hot! Hot!* magazine. I gravitate towards the rack of shoes at the side. Most of them aren't in bad shape, though some are of such breathtaking ugliness that I can't believe anyone would buy them second hand, let alone new. My gaze skips over grey loafers and plastic sandals and alights on a pair of brown ankle boots on the bottom shelf. They're lightweight with rubber soles and are so utilitarian as to bypass fashion considerations altogether. I slip off my ruined heels and try the boots on. My soles sing out with unaccustomed comfort.

I check the price tag: £2.50. Cheap, used, and they will look awful with the floaty flowery dresses that comprise my entire wardrobe. I tuck them under my arm and browse through a rack of jumpers. This one's acrylic, this one's hideous, this one has a suspicious stain on the hem, but there's a soft grey woollen one that looks about my size, on sale for one pound. I take it up to the till.

And then I see them. In the glass case under the girl's *Hot! Hot!* magazine is a pair of Jimmy Choos. Black, slender, exquisite, and incredibly familiar.

'Where did these come from?' I ask, stabbing my finger at the glass.

The girl looks up from her magazine. She shrugs.

'Could be from anywhere. We distribute donations between shops.'

'Could I see them?'

She opens the case and gets the shoes out for me. I hold them in my hands like the precious things they are and examine the buckles, the toes, the tip of the heels, the soles. There's no question about it. These are the shoes I bought to greet a prince when he came to Jett.

And then I turn one over and I see the price tag.

'You're selling these for *forty-five pounds*?' I screech.

She shrugs. 'I know it's expensive, but they're designer.'

'Expensive? Forty-five quid? Do you know how much these cost new?'

'They're not new, though. You can get new ones down Primark for a tenner.'

'They're Jimmy Choos!'

'Are you going to buy them or not?'

'They're—' And then I remember the loose change in my purse, the small notes.

'No,' I say. 'I'll just take these boots and this jumper.'

I'm too weary to clean. I plop down in front of the television and put on any old mindless crap to distract myself while I twist the sleeve of my new jumper between my thumb and fingers and think about my old life, the one I carelessly discarded and am never going to get back.

Now that I've entertained the thought, I can see it's obvious: I never loved Juan. I chose him because he was there and convenient, because he was available and I thought he was in love with me. I chose him because he wasn't Edmund but he was close enough to being Edmund that I thought my heart would never know the difference. And looking back at what Juan said to me, I can see now that he chose me because he thought I was safe too – someone like him, pining for an unrequited love, someone desperate enough to stick with second best. And he was right.

That not only makes me a bad person, but a pathetic one.

You know, it's not my salary I miss so much. It's the sense of belonging and control. How respected I was as Edmund Jett's PA, how I could walk into any club with Pet, how I could decide to buy something and have it. Though people respected Edmund, not me, and let me into clubs because I was Pet's friend, and whenever I passed over my credit card I was spending money I didn't have.

None of it ever really existed.

So what am I left with? A dead-end job at the ugliest café in the universe and a social life that consists of watching an elderly lady smoke cigarettes? Is this all I deserved in the first place?

Suddenly I hear a voice so familiar that my heart throbs and I sit up like a bolt.

'I'm passionate about quality,' Edmund says. For a split second I think he's here in the room with me, and then I realise he's on the television. Standing just beyond the screen, wearing a snow-white shirt and dark trousers. 'Passionate about food,' he continues. 'Passionate about perfection.'

It's an advert for his new series. I eat him up with my eyes.

Maybe I never had anything of my own in my old life. But at least I was close to something, someone that mattered.

'Watch *Jett Stream* tonight at nine, here on Four.'

*Jett Stream*. That's what they're calling the series he's made. The one I helped with, that night that Juan and I were supposed to sleep together for the first time. It's all happened without me.

I turn the television off.

There's a knock at the door. Probably Evangeline, I think, and I go to answer it as an escape from my own head. But when I open it, the man from upstairs is standing there.

'Oh,' I say.

He's not wearing his hat or cloak-coat. He's in jeans and a dark blue jumper. In normal clothes he looks less hulking. Except for his near-permanent frown and his brooding eyes, he seems almost human.

'Can I come in?'

'Um. Okay.' This has me flummoxed. It's not like I really, *really* believe he's a vampire. Or even that he's dangerous. But he hasn't exactly tried to make friends with me up to now. Still, it's worthwhile to find out how his mind works, so I step aside and let him into the flat. He stands just inside the door, looking slowly around him.

'Don't you usually go out at sunset?' I glance at the window, where the light is beginning to fade.

'I've got a few minutes.'

He shows no sign of taking a seat, or of saying what's on his mind either. He's quite tall, taller than Edmund. If I were standing close enough to him, I'd have to look up at his face. Of course I have no intention of trying that out. And he's got a big frame, but he's not bulky. I recognise his cedar scent from him passing me on the stairs. Maybe a cedar coffin keeps the moths out of your clothes while you're sleeping the day away.

'I'd offer you a drink,' I say, 'but I happen to be using all my blood just now.'

'Hm.' He frowns and crosses his arms on his chest. 'You haven't changed much in here.'

'I'm . . . not staying long.'

He draws in a long breath, and lets it out. 'I haven't been in here since Arval left for America.'

'Oh.' I remember something Evangeline said. 'You and Arval were friends, weren't you?'

'Yes.'

'I'm sorry.'

'Hm,' he says again. I wait for him to elaborate, but he just keeps looking around.

'At least he got to see the Ozark big-ear.'

His frown deepens. 'Do you know what an Ozark big-eared bat is?'

'Not really.'

Abruptly he sticks out his hand. 'I'm Viktor Goran.'

'That's quite a name.' I shake his hand, though. His skin is warmer than I expected and his hand pretty much engulfs mine for a short moment, before he lets me go and crosses his arms again.

'I'm Nina Jones.'

'Arval's eldest niece.'

'Everybody seems to know this. Did he talk about me or something?'

'Yes.'

I perch on an arm of the couch; I might as well make myself comfortable, even if he wants to just stand here. 'What did he say?'

'He said you were some sort of a secretary in Chelsea and you had more shoes than anyone he'd ever seen.'

'I wasn't a secretary, I was a PA. And good shoes are totally necessary in order to make the correct impression.'

'I'll tell Arval that the next time I see him.'

'Listen, if you came down here to criticise my footwear, you can turn right around and suck on a fox.'

His lip curls. 'Why are you here?'

'I . . . I'm going through the flat and sorting out his things. Deciding what to keep.'

'Do you understand anything that you've found?'

Right. I've just about had enough of this. I've had a shitty day; I don't need a creature of the night interrogating me. 'What the hell do you mean by that?'

'I mean look at you. You don't exactly seem like the appropriate person to go through Arval's things to decide what's valuable. To say nothing about the jokes about vampires and Ozark big-ears.'

'I'm not making jokes.'

'If you're taking it seriously, that's even worse.'

'And what gives *you* the right to criticise *me*?' I practically yell it. 'I'm his niece, I'm family, I'm *normal*. I've had a *proper* life. I don't live in some grotty attic in a house that time and taste forgot, lurking in bushes all night wearing some awful cloak! I don't hide keys in gargoyles, I don't spend all my time chasing after bats, I'm certainly never totally rude to strangers and eavesdrop outside their doors listening to them having a private moment of crying!'

'I didn't mean to eavesdrop,' he says, but there's no stopping me now, and his admission makes me even angrier.

'As far as I'm concerned, you can go through Arval's stuff yourself, I don't care. I just want to get out of this horrible place as fast as I can. I don't *belong* here, this house is the ugliest thing I've ever seen and you have to be a weirdo even to think about living here.'

'That's what you think, is it?' He sounded a little bit contrite a moment ago, but now his voice is low. I didn't think he was dangerous, but suddenly he's all large, powerful anger. I keep on going anyway.

'And I think it's totally hypocritical that you're

condemning me for asking you if you're a vampire when you're the one who answered yes!'

'What would *you* answer if someone asked you such a ridiculous question?'

'I don't know, I don't sleep all day and act like some brooding freak.'

'No, you just spend all your time obsessively hoovering and waking up your neighbours.'

'I like things to be clean.'

'Nothing needs to be that clean.'

'Okay, so now I see the reason you have no friends.'

'I had a friend. He died. And I don't see it as compensation that he got to see his favourite bat.'

I open my mouth to reply to that one, but I can't. His eyes are glinting, there is a red spot on each of his high cheekbones, and he's practically spitting out his words.

'As far as I can see, you've been spending all your time here traipsing around in inappropriate clothing, criticising everything you see and generally thinking you're above everybody and everything. You don't understand your uncle's passion, and what's worse, you think it's a waste of time. Seems to me you don't want to be here, and the sooner you bugger off back to Chelsea, the better.'

'I can't think of anything I'd like more.'

'Good.' He turns, stalks to the door and yanks it open. Then he pauses. 'You know, the real reason I came down here was to thank you for helping Michael and Evangeline last night while I was out. But now that I know we're all weirdos, I don't think I'll bother to thank you after all.'

He slams the door behind him. I can hear it echoing in the high hallway.

I'm leaning on the glass counter, drawing on a doily, during a lull between customers. Michael wheels up beside me. 'Cuppa?' he asks, lining up the pot and cups.

I nod. I've been feeling very guilty for the past several days, since making the weirdo comment. I was angry when I said it, striking back at Viktor, and it was mostly aimed at him anyway, but his parting shot made me realise I'd been condemning the Cleggs too. And yes, they're not exactly run-of-the-mill people, and they wouldn't fit into my old life, but they've been nothing but kind to me. It's sort of got me thinking about whether they might need more help than just a hand in their café.

'Have you ever thought about updating your menu?' I ask Michael.

'What, you mean getting in that trendy foodie stuff like rocket and sun-dried tomatoes?'

That's exactly what I mean, but I backtrack a little bit. 'You don't have to go trendy, no, of course not. And your baking is brilliant; you make the best scones I've ever had. But maybe a little more variation? For example, you only use Cheddar in your sandwiches, but there's a deli just down the road with all sorts of beautiful things in it. Maybe you could offer a choice of cheese, or try a couple of interesting salads instead of iceberg lettuce and tomato.'

'In other words, rocket.'

'Rocket isn't even trendy any more, and it's really nice. Or you could get some different bread in from a local bakery; venture beyond white and brown sliced.'

Michael rubs his beard. 'Mildred,' he booms across the café, 'would you eat your egg sandwiches on fancy bread if I had it?'

Mildred adjusts her headscarf and considers. 'Might do,' she concludes. 'If it didn't bother my dental work.'

'What about rocket?'

'What have spaceships to do with egg sandwiches?'

Michael turns back to me. 'You can look for some different bread if you like. No new vegetables.'

'Maybe if you ask someone other than Mildred . . .' Mildred, who has an egg sandwich and a cup of tea every day at 12.35, is not exactly an advocate of change.

'Mildred has been eating here since 1953. You have been here five minutes.' He mashes the tea bags in the pot. Michael likes his tea well and truly stewed.

'I just thought that a more modern menu might help you reach out to a wider client base.'

He rolls his eyes. 'Women. Is nagging built into you with the extra X chromosome?'

'No, but you and Evangeline did say that my experience in the food service industry might be useful to you, so it seems worthwhile to suggest a few things. For example, I've been thinking about your decor . . .'

'What about the bloody decor? Don't tell me I need to clean it better.'

Actually, the café is very clean; that's one thing I can say for it. 'No, but it is a little bit, uh, retro, isn't it? The thing is that first impressions are so important. You could do some things, they wouldn't take much money, to make the place seem brighter and airier, maybe appeal to a more upmarket customer, as well as your regular clientele.'

'Nina, this is a caff, not the bloody Ivy.'

'I know, I know, and I'm not suggesting much, just maybe a lick of paint and something different instead of lace curtains? Weed out the spider plants a little, source some local artwork, consider a change from linoleum on the floor? I've done a quick sketch . . .' I offer him the doily.

He ignores it. 'Nina, love, the last remodel this café had was by my father, three months before he died. This is the way it looked when I inherited it. It's how it looked when Evangeline came in here for a cup of coffee and a cigarette after her second husband's funeral and spoke to me even though I was a surly, bitter cripple with nothing but this place to my name, and how it looked when she came in here every day until I made her my wife, and how it's looked every day since, lace curtains and all. It's not changing.'

'Right. Right. I'll . . . I'll look for some bread this afternoon. Nothing too chewy.'

The door opens and Evangeline comes in. She's wearing a bright pink ruffly blouse, which clashes with her red hair. 'Darlings, guess what I got today, at last?' She waves an envelope in the air.

'A party invitation?' I guess.

'Oh, better.' She hands it to me and I pull out a heavy sheet of paper. It's hand-lettered in elaborate curlicues, decorated with little drawings of bats. *You are invited to a celebration of the life of Arval Jones*, says the top line.

'Arval's funeral,' I say.

'Wonderfully appropriate, don't you think?'

'My sister Imogen designed it.' I recognise her style. A few weeks ago I would've thought the whole Gothic imagery was over the top, but knowing where Arval lived, now it seems pretty understated in comparison. 'The funeral's this Saturday,' I say in surprise.

'Of course, you've known for ages, haven't you? I must say, it's very naughty of you not to tell us, Nina.'

'Oh, I . . . wanted you to wait and get the invitation yourself.'

'Where is Hedegogllygoden?'

'It's the village where my father and his brother grew up. Do you mind if I nip out and make a phone call?'

'As long as you don't come back with any sun-dried tomatoes.' Michael takes down another cup.

I've been brave enough to keep my mobile with me, though I've turned off the ringer. I walk a little bit away from the café before I dial my father. As usual, he answers at the last possible minute. 'Hello?'

'Hi, Dad, it's me, Nina.'

'Nina, lovely to hear from you, did the post get to you in Spain?'

'Um, yeah. Imogen did a good job with the invitations.'

'I'll tell her you said that, she'll be pleased. I don't suppose you're coming?'

'Well, it is a bit late notice, Dad.'

'Yes, the invitations took some time, and then I didn't get to the post office until the day before yesterday. I'm very impressed by the speed of the postal service to Spain. But we should have a good turnout. I've had a few of Arval's conservation friends on the phone, even some from America.'

'What are you doing about catering?'

'It's all in hand, all in hand. Service at the church we were christened in, then back to the hotel for a knees-up. We should pack it out, sent out at least a hundred invitations. All arranged by me, and Imogen of course, she's been very helpful.'

Oh my God. My father and Imogen couldn't arrange a piss-up in a brewery. And they're dragging a hundred people to a hotel in an obscure corner of Wales?

'All we have to worry about is picking up Arval's ashes from the airport the day before,' he adds.

And they're going to be in charge of fetching a dead body?

'I probably will be able to come after all,' I say.

'Well that's wonderful. We'll look forward to seeing you there.'

A crowd of schoolgirls on their lunch hour push past me, chattering at the top of their voices in very English accents. 'Must go, see you Saturday,' I say quickly, and ring off.

This, of course, leaves me with a whole new set of problems. I go back to the café frowning, because I'm going to have to do something I really don't like to do.

Luckily, Michael and Evangeline are sitting in their usual corner by themselves. I slip into the extra seat and Evangeline immediately pours me a cup of tea.

'Michael thinks we should wear black, darling, but I think black is such a terrible cliché for funerals. What do you think?'

'I think whatever you wear will be fine.'

'What will you be wearing?'

'Um . . . I haven't thought about it.' Oh God. A halter-neck dress and a second-hand jumper are not going to cut it.

Evangeline taps her chin. 'I do believe I have an idea.'

I don't know how to say this, so I just spit it out. 'Michael, I'm really sorry, but would you mind paying me for the work I've done already so I can buy a train ticket to Arval's funeral?'

'Oh!' exclaims Evangeline. 'Nina, of course you must come with us in the car, I wouldn't dream of anything else.'

'But . . .' I try desperately to think of an excuse. 'I'll probably need to get there early.'

'Then we'll get there early too, darling. It's no trouble, we'll be shutting the café, and why waste money on a train when we're going anyway?'

'The thing is . . .' I swallow. 'The thing is, my dad thinks I'm still in Spain. So I can't arrive with you.'

'That's no problem at all, we'll drop you off at the station if need be. No worries, we are the souls of discretion.' Evangeline mimes zipping her lips closed.

'And I'll give you your wages now,' Michael says. He wheels over to the till.

'I love a bit of subterfuge,' whispers Evangeline.

She turns up at my door that evening holding a garment bag. 'It was a long internal struggle, but I've decided not to wear black,' she announces. 'But of course that leaves me with a horrible dilemma, because I have this stunning suit that hasn't had an airing in far too long, and I simply hate the thought of it languishing at the back of my wardrobe. And then I thought that with your figure, it would look perfect on you.'

I eye the bag. I have been fretting about what to wear, but knowing Evangeline's dress sense, her 'stunning' suit may be stunning in a way she doesn't quite mean. Right now, she's wearing a blood-red kimono, the same shade as her lipstick, over what look like pyjamas.

'That's very kind of you, Evangeline. Please come in and let me try it on.'

She hands me the bag. I wait, expecting her to go straight to the kitchen to get her cigarettes, but she's looking at me expectantly, and I realise she's waiting for me to look at the suit.

'I haven't actually decided to wear black yet,' I say to her. 'As you say, it's such a cliché.'

'Ah yes, but always so chic and elegant.' She perches on the arm of the couch, and holding my breath, planning excuses already, I unzip the bag.

It is a black woollen dress and jacket, short-skirted, nipped in at the waist, simply and exquisitely cut. The label says 'Mary Quant'.

'Oh,' I say.

'From younger days, obviously. It will be much shorter on you, of course, but that's never a bad thing with legs like yours, is it? Go on, nip to the loo and try it on. I'll wait here.'

I hang the suit from the shower rail while I get undressed. It looks small, but when I step into the dress it slithers up my body with no problems at all and the zip does up smoothly. I've lost weight over the past few weeks. I put on the jacket and look at myself in the mirror over the sink, which is the only one in this flat.

The dress and jacket fit as if they were made for me. I twist and turn, checking myself from all angles. It's perfect: sombre and yet stylish. If I put my hair up, I will look like a sixties *Vogue* cover model – or, more importantly, a successful business owner. I push my hair up experimentally and catch sight of my face. I haven't looked at myself properly since I've been here, and it's not a pretty sight. I'm not wearing make-up, of course, and my skin is pale and I've got circles around my eyes.

Oh God. I look down at my bare legs. I'm pale all over. Not good.

'Don't keep me in suspense, darling,' I hear Evangeline call from the front room. I go in to show her, and at the sight, her face lights up.

'Nina! You look fabulous! I don't care what you were thinking of wearing, you simply must wear this suit or I will be horribly offended. It could have been made for you.'

I do a little twirl for her, and run my fingers over the wool. 'It's beautiful.' And with her praise, I feel beautiful too. Except for the skin, which is a major problem.

'Yes, they certainly don't make clothes like that any more.' She shakes her head, a wistful smile on her face. 'If that dress could talk, the tales it could tell.'

'All I need now are shoes.' In my head, I rapidly go through an inventory of the shoes I've got left, but that's not good either. I've ruined several pairs, and a suit like this wouldn't work with strappy summer heels.

'I can't help you there, I'm afraid. I've got frightfully small feet. Michael is always comparing me unfavourably to a doll.'

I nod. 'This suit is more than enough. I think I may have an idea.'

'I've come for the Jimmy Choos.'

It's the same girl at the charity shop, and she's drinking tea out of a chipped and tannin-stained mug, sorting through a pile of clothes draped all over the glass case and the till. She looks up at me without a hint of recognition, and I'm hit by sudden panic.

'You haven't sold them, have you?' I kneel in front of the case and push aside a blouse. No, they're there, behind a brooch shaped like a pirate ship. My wonderful, wonderful shoes.

'Oh, the black high heels? No, we've had quite a bit of interest, but they're rather large.'

'I'll take them, please.'

She gets them out of the case for me and I immediately pull out the exact money in cash and give it to her. It doesn't take everything I've got, not quite; I won't be buying any rounds at the funeral, but I've still got some left over for sundry expenses, and for one more necessity. 'Don't you want to try them on?' she asks.

'I don't need to. Where's the nearest chemist where I can buy fake tan?'

I read the instructions four times before I begin. I only have a very little tube of exfoliator left, so I use it all on my face, and just give the rest of myself a good rub with a towel. And I do everything it says on the back of the tube: I use moisturiser on my knees and ankles and elbows, I start from the bottom up, I apply the brownish-orange gunk in a brisk circular motion, trying for an even coat all over. Then I stand naked, with arms and legs akimbo, in the centre of the bathroom until the stuff has dried.

Then I go to bed. Tomorrow night, Friday, I will do a second coat so I will be properly, healthily, Spanishly bronzed on Saturday.

When I wake up in the morning, I poke my legs out from underneath the duvet, then clap my hand to my mouth to stop myself crying out.

My legs look as if someone has thrown a container of orange paint on them and let it drip in great gobs to pool around my feet.

I jump out of bed and look down at the rest of myself. My forearms aren't too bad, but my upper arms are just as streaky as my legs, and my chest is one big orange blotch.

'Oh shit, oh shit, oh shit.' I run to the bathroom and jump under the shower, where I scrub and scrub and scrub. My skin goes pink, but the fake tan does not budge. When I finally climb out of the shower, I look like . . .

Words fail me. Suffice to say I could have got a more natural-looking tan sunbathing under a road-painting truck.

I can't go to Wales looking like this. There's only one

thing for it. I haven't rung this number for a very long time, but my fingers pick it out by themselves and Pet answers within two rings.

'Nina,' she says. Her voice is subdued, but then again it is early in the morning, especially for her.

'Pet, I need your help. I have a serious fake-tanning emergency. I wanted a top-up and I used this cheap stuff because it was all I could find, and now I look like a streaky orange slug, and I don't have any exfoliator because I used it all on my face, and I've got to look decent for a big meeting! What can I do? Should I try to wash it off, or should I just apply another layer? Or what about bronzing powder, do you think that would help? Or a scrub brush?'

She doesn't reply.

'What are you doing, are you looking for a magazine or something that has advice?'

'No,' she says. 'Tell me again, why are you using fake tan if you're in Spain?'

'Well, it's autumn and I just, you know, wanted a top-up.'

'And this is for a meeting?'

'Well, sort of a party thing, sort of a meeting, yes.' I don't want to tell her about Arval's funeral, because if she thinks I'm in the country, she might ask why I'm not coming via London.

'And this would be about the restaurant? Your restaurant, which you're about to open any day now?'

'Yes.'

'Your restaurant, in San Nasareo, called El Flor Anaranjado? Where you are right now?'

She's speaking very carefully. A thread of a chill creeps up my spine. 'Yes.'

'That's interesting,' she says. 'Because I was at El Flor Anaranjado, in San Nasareo, two days ago, to give you a surprise, you know? And I don't speak Spanish all that well, but I'm fairly confident that I was told by a horrible fat man that you had sold the restaurant to him a few weeks ago, and then disappeared.'

The chill has transformed into whole-body goose bumps. 'Oh.'

'Oh.'

I know she is waiting for an explanation. But I don't know how to give such an admission of failure: as a businesswoman, as a lover, as a friend, as a person.

'Try a long hot bath for the fake tan,' she says at last. 'And then scrub with salt. Goodbye, Nina.'

On Saturday morning I knock on Evangeline and Michael's door, having already run to the shop to get a pair of semi-opaque black tights. Evangeline answers the door with a cheerful 'Good morning, darling!'

I blink. 'Evangeline, you're blonde.'

She touches her platinum hair, swept back into a Grace Kelly chignon. 'Yes, Arval always liked me blonde. You look marvellous, darling. It almost makes me wish I'd worn black myself, it looks so divine with your hair. I'm quite envious.'

She is in ankle-length blue satin, tightly fitted to her tiny waist, and of course the omnipresent red lipstick. 'You look wonderful,' I tell her, following her into her flat.

It's the first time I've seen it in daylight, and it is something to see. The living room is larger than Arval's, but absolutely stuffed full of heavy mahogany furniture. Red velvet flock papers the walls, hung with convex mirrors and yellowing portraits; an enormous potted palm fills one corner. There's an actual marble bust over the fireplace.

'Wow, this really . . . fits the house,' I say.

'Doesn't it perfectly? Modelled on Walpole's Strawberry Hill, though of course on a smaller scale. Let me pick up my wrap and we can go down to the car.

Michael's already loaded in. He so loves to drive.' She takes a brightly patterned paisley shawl and a plastic rain hat from the back of a horsehair sofa. 'I will warn you, though, that he likes to go fast.'

'Fast isn't a problem,' I say as we leave the flat and she locks the door. Though if I'm truthful, I'm not really in any hurry to get to Arval's funeral and the biggest deception I've yet tried to pull off. Especially as the phone call with Pet has been dragging very heavily on my conscience.

At least her salt advice worked. My legs are still streaky (hence tights) but my arms and chest are looking much better, especially after another application of fake tan. With a bit of bronzing powder, my face looks nearly natural. With any luck it'll be raining as hard in Wales as it is here in London, and the lights won't be too bright in the hotel for the wake.

Michael's behind the wheel of a long black Volvo sedan parked in front of the house. He's sitting in the driver's seat, and I can see that the controls have been modified for him. 'How did you get the chair in the boot?' I ask Evangeline as we walk towards the car in the rain.

'She had a hand.'

I jump at the voice. It's Viktor, standing under a black umbrella, off to one side of the pavement. In his black suit, he half blends into the shadows under the dying tree. He steps forward and opens the front passenger door for Evangeline. Then, once she's in, he reaches for the back door as if to open it for me, but I open it and slip in before he can perform this obligatory, and totally insincere, act of gallantry.

Then, to my dismay, he comes around and gets into the back seat on the other side.

'You're coming too?'

He regards me with a grim face. His suit, with white shirt and dark tie, emphasises the angles of his body, and here in the back seat with me, he feels very large, as if he is taking up all the space and the air.

'Arval was a very good friend of mine,' he says. 'If you recall, we spoke of it the other day.'

'Buckle up, darlings!' Evangeline cries and we're off, threading through the London traffic. She's right: Michael is a fast driver, probably too fast for Highgate, but I've got more urgent things to worry about, like the big man emanating hostility from the other seat. As a matter of fact, when I look, we've got a foot or so of space between us, but I feel crowded, too warm, too close.

He waits until we're well under way, and Evangeline and Michael are bickering about the best route to take to get to the M4, before he speaks again, in a low voice.

'I'm very surprised to see *you* here.'

'Arval was my uncle,' I protest.

'I expected you to be at the funeral. I didn't expect you to be here, in this car.'

In his emphasis of the last words, I remember what he believes I think of Evangeline and Michael, and I blush. 'It was very kind of them to offer me a lift.'

He raises one eyebrow. I set my chin. Evangeline and Michael know I like them. I don't have to prove it to Viktor.

Then I remember something else.

'Um, I have to ask you a favour, though,' I say.

'What favour could I possibly do for you?'

He really is laying the sarcasm on thick. I ignore it and say, 'Once we get to the funeral, I need you to pretend you've never met me.'

Both eyebrows go up this time.

'I don't see it as being that much of a hardship for you, since you hate me anyway.'

'I see.' He leans closer and whispers, 'You don't want to be associated with the weirdos?' His breath tickles my ear, and his cedar scent is stronger. I bite my lip.

'Just . . . please. I can't explain it. It would . . . mean a lot to me.'

He looks me straight in the face. His eyes are dark and very keen. I am suddenly much, much warmer, my cheeks flushing, my palms damp.

'Fine,' he says, and settles back in his seat. I cross my arms and lean against the car door, as far away from him as I can get.


'It's left down this road, I think, and the lane to the church is about half a mile down. You can drop me at the bottom and then drive up.'

'But your shoes, darling. It'll be an utter mudbath.'

'I'll be fine. These are Jimmy Choos. The mud wouldn't dare to touch them.'

Viktor snorts beside me. He's barely said a word the entire journey, which is fine with me. Michael reaches the lane and pulls up at the end, and after checking the way is clear, I get out. It's not actually raining here, which is a bonus. Evangeline rolls down her window and I lean in to give her a kiss on her powdery cheek. 'Thank you,' I say.

'Never fear, Nina, we'll pretend we've never even heard of you,' she says. 'Sixty years in amateur dramatics, I'm a perfect person to be in on your secret.'

'I have one condition,' Michael adds. 'I won't give you away as long as you nudge someone and point at me and say, "Who is that incredibly handsome man over there?"'

'You've got a deal.'

'It has to be loud enough for lots of people to hear.'

I hear a car approaching. 'Yes, yes, now go!'

The wheels kick up mud and gravel as Michael hits the accelerator and heads for the church. I begin to pick my way up the lane. I don't think it's far, but it's been many years since I've been here, and my memory's not great. For example, I didn't remember it being quite so steeply uphill.

But the smell is the same, grass and earth and manure, with a faint tang of bonfire. I hear the bleating of sheep, and beyond that the burble of a stream and the distant roar of the motorway. Wind scuds the clouds overhead and reveals patches of blue. There's a raised grassy track in the middle of the lane, and I keep to that, walking on the balls of my feet as much as possible to save my heels from sinking into the dirt.

I ran up here, once, with Imogen a lagging toddler tugging on my hand, and Claire and Arval laughing behind. We had a picnic in the cemetery. I think it was my idea. I remember telling my aunt and uncle that as long as we brought flowers for the graves, the people inside wouldn't mind if we sat on them to eat our lunch.

*Maybe that's the key*, I think, walking as quickly as I can, my attention half on placing my feet on tussocks. *You have to offer the dead something, so that they won't feel left out.*

Have I offered anything yet to Arval? Or Auntie Claire?

Abruptly I'm at the top of the rise and the church is in front of me. It's relatively modern, with a squat tower, made, I recall, of the grey stone from the original church, which collapsed in a freak earthquake in the 1930s. No gargoyles, no Gothic arches, just large, airy stained-glass windows that look out over the green hills. Should be a blessed relief. I see that Michael has parked among many other cars at the side, and that though the wheels of his chair are sunk in the gravel, Viktor is pushing him with little difficulty towards the entrance. None of them even glance my way.

I dawdle until they've all three gone into the church, and then I go to the entrance. I take a moment to refresh my lipstick, make sure my hair is tidy, my suit and shoes are unspotted with mud or fake tan. As prepared as I can be, I walk inside.

My father stands inside the door with Imogen beside him. He's wearing a dark charcoal suit and a blue striped shirt, polished black shoes and a dark red tie. His hair is brushed back, exposing clean, shiny skin on the top of his head. There is a white rose in his buttonhole.

I stop. After all this time on my own, seeing him well and smiling is like a glass of cool water when you're thirsty.

'Nina,' he says, and I go to him and hug him. He smells of an unfamiliar aftershave. He kisses me on the cheek.

'You look nice, Dad. Is it a new suit?'

'No, same as always. I gave the shoes a bit of the old polish, though.'

'And you cut your hair.'

'Oh well, time to grow old gracefully and all that.' He lets me go so I can greet my sister. She's wearing a pair of wide trousers, a long-sleeved indigo top, unscruffed Doc Martens and an armful of bracelets.

'Nina,' she says, and it sounds completely different from how my father said it. I hug her anyway. She bends briefly, then drops her arms.

'I loved your invitations,' I tell her. That gets me a smile, though a grudging one.

'This is for you.' My father picks up a white rose from the side and gives it to me. I notice Imogen has one, too, in her hair, which has been combed. I pin it on the lapel of my suit, then glance into the body of the church. It's full of people, some sombrely clothed, some in brighter colours. To my relief, I can see a bronze urn of ashes on the altar.

'We're nearly ready to begin,' my father says, 'but there are a few people still to come who you can help us to greet.' His Welsh accent is more pronounced, maybe because of the landscape, maybe through habit. This is the church where he and Arval were baptised.

At that moment several of Arval and Claire's former neighbours arrive, and I'm glad of the distraction. If we'd stood there for much longer, Dad was bound to ask how my flight was, and . . . Well, this isn't the time or place for the truth, and I'm not quite ready to lie yet. Not after Pet's silence on the phone.

My dad pokes his head out of the door of the church and checks for incoming traffic, then glances at his watch. 'I think we're ready to roll,' he says to Imogen, and she nods and goes down to the front of the church, presumably to talk to the vicar.

'Shall we?' He offers me his arm. I can't remember if I've ever been arm in arm with my father. Together we walk down the aisle. The pews are nearly full, and people turn their heads to look at us as we pass. It's like a strange parody of how my father would give me away at my wedding, except the organ music is a muted hymn and the altar, while crowded with white flowers, also holds a brass urn containing my uncle's mortal remains.

We slip into the first pew, next to my sister. I haven't been in a church for a very long time. We were never a religious family anyway, but I've been kept so busy working for the past few years that I haven't even had time to go to the usual things even a non-religious person goes to church for: weddings, christenings, funerals.

I do remember Auntie Claire's funeral, though. We sat in the first pew then, too: my father much bigger; my

261

sister much smaller. Along with Arval, and my mother. I remember looking down at my mother's legs next to mine on the smooth wooden seat. She wore a tight black skirt, sheer black tights, and high-heeled shoes. She handed me a tissue when I sniffed.

My legs, now, could be hers.

The vicar greets us, and after a short preamble and prayer we stand to sing a hymn. My mouth follows the words automatically, programmed some time long ago in my childhood. Did we sing this song for Claire? Probably. I glance to the side and recall Arval standing there dressed in a black jacket. He had a lot of hair back then, and it was brown. He sang out in a loud tenor that rang through the church. There are a lot of people singing now, some loud and in tenor voices, but the sound is less rich without him.

We sit back down and the vicar talks some more, in a strong Welsh accent. Surprisingly for a funeral, this church is quite cheerful. The white flowers stand out against the grey stone and fill the aisles with scent. The sun has broken through the clouds and casts patterns of red and blue and gold through the stained-glass windows. Ironic, really, that this place where we're mourning Arval's death is more uplifting than the place where he lived.

Funerals are odd things anyway. They're so clean, so final, not like life, which is messy and leaves all kinds of loose ends. For example, where is my mother now, the woman who sat beside me last time I was here? The woman who dried my tears and kissed me every night at bedtime and left without a word, for ever? Is she even still alive, out there somewhere, not thinking about us at all?

If she'd died, we'd have been able to say goodbye. We'd have known she'd struggled to stay with us. We'd have kept a little piece of her with us, like Arval living with Claire's furniture. Instead of clearing the house, moving away, and the long years of nothing. The three of us left revolving around each other, not really touching.

I sniff. My father hands me a tissue.

I gaze at the brass urn on the altar. Of course I can't wish that my mother was in one of those. Arval's hair, his quick gaze, his laugh, his voice, his eccentricities and his memories, all are reduced to ashes inside. It's better to be out in the world somewhere, even far away. That's what you want for the people you love, even if they don't love you back.

We stand and sing another hymn, and then, when we sit down, the vicar steps to one side. A tall, dark figure separates from the congregation and walks to the front. He moves quietly, head held high, his footsteps somehow significant on the stone floor in the silence. I register his height, his movement, the elegant cut of his suit and the red and blue lights gleaming on his hair before I realise that it's Viktor.

He puts his hands on the podium. We all hear him draw in a breath.

'I first met Arval Jones half an hour before twilight,' he says. 'I was in Brazil and it had taken me three days to travel to the Caverna da Meia-noite, with a local guide to help me. There had been sightings of *Saccopteryx gymmura*. I had set up my equipment, waiting for the bats to emerge, when I heard a rustling in the bushes. I thought it was an animal, maybe a bear. Maybe a giant rat.'

There's a ripple of laughter in the church.

'It was Arval Jones. He had a Brazilian guide too, but he didn't have any equipment except for a home-modified heterodyne bat detector. He settled down beside me, said hello and then kept absolutely quiet for the next four hours. Didn't even change position. He just watched and listened for the bats, with his knees up near his ears.

'I think this tells you everything you need to know about Arval. The man had a passion that had nothing to do with recognition for himself, and everything to do with the conservation of something that he cared about. Arval and I became friends in Brazil, and a couple of years later, when I was looking for somewhere to live in London, he found me a flat upstairs from where he lived, in an extraordinary building full of extraordinary people.'

Yikes. That comment should be aimed at me. I feel as if it is aimed at me. And yet he doesn't glance in my direction; he focuses on the flowers in front of him, speaks with vehemence as if he is speaking from the heart. Of course he's not talking about me. He's talking about Arval.

'My own family were far away, and I was in a new place, but Arval let me into his life without hesitation or reservation. I think most of us are here for the same reason. He was a man of passion and feeling. I'll miss him as if he were my own brother.'

He pauses, and we can hear him drawing in another deep breath. For a moment, as he looks at the flowers, I think he's going to cry, and I will him not to. Because if he does, I will cry too.

'To tell you the truth,' he says at last, 'I've been very angry at him for leaving me, and doing something so stupid as to go climbing around in caves looking for Ozark big-eared bats instead of seeing a doctor. I've been stomping around rather sullenly for the past few weeks. But here, remembering him, I'm not angry any more. I'm thankful for the time he gave to me, and to all of us here.' He pauses again, and looks at the urn. 'Goodbye, Arval.'

Then he steps down and goes back to his seat. I watch him as if I've never seen him before. Someone else stands up to talk, a woman from the conservation charity Arval left his worldly riches to, but I don't really listen to her because I'm looking at Viktor and Evangeline and Michael, the denizens of the Temple of Gloom, all sitting in a row. I knew that Arval had been part of their lives, but didn't quite understand how big a part; how long and probably complex their friendship was. That inside that absence in Arval's flat there were memories of years and experiences and the daily rubbing along of living close together with other people. A whole life I know nothing about. And the same could be said of every person in this church, everyone who knew Arval, so many people he connected with and touched. All of it gone, except for what we all remember.

Like how he gave me a life-size Javanese fruit bat toy for my seventeenth birthday and I hid it under my bed, certain it would come to life and suck my head like a cantaloupe. Like how he and my father used to listen to the cricket together on the radio, drinking tea and nodding their heads at shots they approved of. Like how when my mother left and his wife was gone, he said nothing, but when he visited he would give me a long, warm hug. Like a father.

Everyone stands up to sing another hymn, and then it's finished. My father goes up and gets the urn, and he and the vicar lead everyone outside the church. Imogen and I tag along behind him. The sun is bright now, and the wind brings the scent of sheep. We stop in a corner of the cemetery, the plot where Auntie Claire was buried all those years ago. It's sort of strange looking at the plot, which is covered over with grass; last time I saw it, it was open and lined with that AstroTurf stuff. The mourners all circle the grave in a ring several people deep.

To my surprise, Dad pops the top of the urn. 'Arval asked to be laid to rest here with his wife,' he says, 'but I thought that since he loved being outdoors so much, it would be better for us to scatter the ashes instead of burying them. And I think he'd want everyone to help.' He reaches into the urn and takes out a handful of grey ashes, which he sprinkles over the grass on my aunt's grave. Then he passes the urn to me.

I put my hand in and take out some ashes. If you'd told me this morning that I was going to be handling my uncle's burned-up dead body, I would have been even more reluctant to come here. But in fact, it's not bad at all. The ashes are gritty, sort of like sand, and a fine powder lifts into the wind when I scatter them. It's not really Arval; what remains of Arval is here, in the people around the grave. I give the urn to my sister.

The ashes run out before we run out of people, but that's okay. Once it's over, everyone moves off in a low buzz of conversation towards their cars, to drive to the hotel for the wake. Imogen doesn't move, though, and I stay with her as Dad walks slowly away, talking to some people.

Imogen is looking at our aunt's gravestone. 'Do you remember being here for Claire's funeral?' she asks me.

'Yes.'

'I don't. I must have been too young. I sort of remember afterwards, drinking Vimto and sitting on a flowered couch. I'd never had Vimto before.' She pauses. 'Was . . . she here?'

My sister never mentions our mother, but I know instantly that that's who she means. 'Yes.'

'I don't really remember her either. I actually remember drinking Vimto more clearly than my own mum.' She sounds disgusted with herself.

I touch her shoulder. Her hair, dancing in the wind, tickles the back of my hand. 'That's okay.'

'Do you think she's dead?'

'I don't know. I hope not.'

She slants a glance at me. 'Why do you say that? Do you hope she's coming back, even after all this time?'

'No,' I say. 'She's not coming back.'

'No, she's not coming back,' my sister repeats. 'I don't really miss her; it's more the idea of having a mother that I miss. You miss her, though, don't you?'

'Yes. I do.' I remember the shoes, the crying, the emptiness. How eleven years of mourning came awake and ripped a hole out of where I'd been keeping it hidden inside. Right now the wound isn't so raw, though. It feels like it's scabbing over.

Imogen sighs. 'I'll miss Arval. He was cool.'

'Yeah, he was. I'm sorry I didn't know him better.'

'Girls?' our father calls from the cemetery gate. 'Are you coming?'

Imogen starts off. I linger for a moment, to touch Claire's gravestone. It is smooth and cool. 'Goodbye, Claire,' I say. 'Goodbye, Arval. Goodbye, Mum.'

My words are borne away by the wind towards the fields and the sky.

The Pack Saddle Hotel is more upmarket than one would expect in a village the size of Hedegoglly-goden, but nevertheless its interior design is based around horse brasses. We go directly to the function room, where people are already milling around in conversation and a cold buffet is laid out on tables. My father takes two glasses of wine from a passing waitress and gives them to my sister and me. 'Fortification,' he says, lifting a pint of lager from the same tray.

I sip my drink, amazed. 'Did you arrange all of this, Dad?'

'Yes, had to give Arval a proper send-off, didn't we? Excuse me, I've got to have a word with the vicar.' He hurries off. My sister has already made a beeline for two young men in black skinny jeans, lounging against the wall. One of them kisses her rather self-consciously on the mouth. I assume this is the young man my father mentioned she'd met.

Directly across from me, between me and the bar, there is the back of a tall person in a black suit. He's standing angular and straight, with a pint of bitter in his hand, in a small circle of people I don't know. Above the chatter in the room, I can hear a low, deep laugh. It seems so incongruous a sound that I'd assume it was coming from someone else, except that Viktor's shoulders are shaking and I can see him tilting his head back.

If I were smart, I'd stay away. I'm bound to ruin his good mood, for one. But I head straight for him, and tap him on the shoulder.

When he turns around there's still a smile on his face, the remnants of the laughter. It makes him look like a totally different person. It lifts his face, softens his mouth, carves creases into his cheeks.

Of course, when he sees me, his smile begins to melt away. Before it can go completely, I hold out my hand.

'Hi, Mr Goran, isn't it? I'm Nina Jones, Arval's niece. It's really good to meet you.'

He shakes my hand but doesn't speak, and the man next to him says, 'It's Dr Goran, don't let him be modest.'

'Dr Goran. Is that . . . you're a medical doctor?' Shift work. That's the strange hours.

'No, a zoologist at the University of London. I did my PhD on *Saccopteryx gymmura*.' His voice is cold.

'The Brazilian bat,' I recall. 'And do you still study bats? At night-time?'

'Recently I've been out most nights observing them, as part of a research study.'

'We're the bat crowd,' says the man next to him cheerfully. 'Or the London contingent anyway.'

Viktor hesitates, then indicates the people in the circle one by one. 'This is Harris Levy, Cindy Wood, Fliss Mithrani, all of the London bat group; Professor Bill Grammer of the University of Glasgow, and Ethel Wan, secretary of the Bat Conservation Society.' Each of them shakes my hand and says a word or two in sympathy for my uncle.

'I wanted to thank you,' I say to Viktor after I've finished doing the rounds.

'*Thank* me?' I have to give him credit, he's playing

along with the stranger charade more or less, but I sense the rest of the group going silent, observing our conversation, as if they know there's a subtext underneath it and are trying to figure out what it is.

'Yes. I was really touched by what you said at the church. It made me think about saying goodbye. And it helped me to understand my uncle a little better. You were obviously a good friend to him, and I wanted to thank you for that too.'

'It was easy to be friends with Arval Jones.'

*Though not Nina Jones*, he means, but I carry on anyway. 'So if you're out all night watching bats, you must have to sleep a lot during the day.'

'You mean like, oh, say, a vampire?'

'I mean you're probably very busy and wouldn't have time to help me with something.'

'Help you?' His eyes narrow slightly, but he must realise that others are watching and he's obliged to be civil back.

'My dad has asked me to go through Arval's flat and sort out his things. When he asked me, I thought sure, how hard could it be? But I was wrong.'

'You were?'

'Yup. Totally wrong. I don't really know where to begin. I didn't know him well enough, and he had all this equipment and books I don't know what to do with.'

'It's . . . a big job.' He is clearly taken aback by the line I'm following here.

'It's too big for me. I don't know if Arval told you, I'm a personal assistant, so bats are right out of my league. And I know the things that are important to his family, but not to his friends or colleagues. So I wondered if you might help me with it, since you live upstairs and everything.'

'You want me to help you sort through Arval's flat?'

'Yes. Please.'

He stares at me. I look steadily back at him. He has quite an impressive stare, but now I've seen him smile, too.

'But not if it makes you too sad,' I add.

'I . . . no, I would . . . like that.'

'Have you seen Viktor and Arval's building?' Harris asks me. 'It's way out there, isn't it? Like a Hammer Horror set.'

'They have really big spiders too,' I agree.

'I think it's wonderful,' pipes up Fliss, who hasn't said much so far. 'Especially Viktor's flat and its view over Highgate. He's got a balcony, too, with little gargoyles carved in the railings.'

'Built in the 1840s during the Gothic revival craze,' Ethel says, in a ponderous voice. I have the feeling she's the type who knows everything and doesn't mind sharing it. 'The house was originally the residence of Sir Neville Clarke, split into flats in the fifties, I believe.'

'We're going out to the grounds in a few minutes to see if we can spot some Daubenton's bats over the pond,' Harris tells me. 'It's nearly dusk. Would you like to come?'

I hesitate. Across the room, my father finishes speaking with the vicar and shakes his hand. 'I'd love to, but actually I need to talk to my father for a minute. Excuse me.'

I'm a few steps away when I hear Harris say, 'Whoa, she's a looker, Vik, and was I imagining it, or was that serious eye contact going on between you?'

'You were imagining it,' Viktor says.

I catch up with my father. 'Can I talk with you somewhere in private, Dad?'

'Of course, sweetheart, of course.' We begin to make our way across the room, though on the way people keep stopping us to offer condolences, or just say a word. My father shakes everyone's hand. Mostly he says, quietly, 'Thank you,' and then he introduces me. We speak to conservationists, cavers, accountants, residents of Hedegogllygoden, two reps from the Welsh tourist board and Auntie Claire's two sisters, Catherine and Clarissa. Neither one of them looks much like how I remember Claire – Claire was cosy and plump, and Catherine is rail-thin and Clarissa rather masculine. But Catherine shakes my hand in a limp grip and says, 'Oh yes, I remember you as a girl, Nina. You were such a happy, carefree child.'

'Was I?'

'Oh yes, full of sunshine. I remember telling my Stuart so. So imaginative. I only met you a few times, but you would sit on my knee and tell me story after story, all made up out of your head. I told Stuart I thought you would turn out a writer or an actress maybe, with that blond hair and those blue eyes. And very fond of cakes.'

'That hasn't changed, at least,' I say, laughing to be polite.

'Yes, she always used to tell stories and be pretending,' my father agrees. 'Grew out of it, I suppose.'

Maybe. I bite my lip.

Not any more, though. I decided on the drive over here from the church that enough is enough. The little charade with Viktor was fun, and anyway I pretty much did feel as if I were meeting him for the first time, he seems so different away from the Temple of Gloom.

But I'm still feeling awful about my conversation with Pet. And that one moment of honesty, of connection with my sister in the churchyard felt good, healing in a way. Lies could never do that. Lies separate. Juan lied, and so did my mother, and I've just said goodbye to all of that. Time to suck it up and tell the truth.

Besides, I think as we say goodbye to Catherine and Clarissa and slip through the door, my father has . . . changed. I haven't seen him anywhere except surrounded by the walls of that horrid bungalow for so long, so maybe it's because we're somewhere new. Maybe it's all the people at the funeral, who are inspiring him to make an effort, come out of his shell. Whatever it is, he's got a confidence to him that I haven't seen for years and years, not since the day that changed all of our lives and took my sunshine.

Quite suddenly, he looks like a man who can handle the truth.

There's a little chintzy sitting room down the corridor and we go in there. 'I think it's going really well, don't you?' my father says.

'It's great, Dad. The service was beautiful and I liked the idea of scattering the ashes on Claire's grave. I thought you handled that really well.'

'This is a good place for a reception too, isn't it? We used to come here for a meal and an evening out. Arval used to like it.'

'You've done an amazing job. You've thought of absolutely everything.'

'Do you think the food looks good? I've been talking too much to try any.'

'It looks delicious. Really delicious, Dad. And you're a gracious host. I'm so impressed by all of this, it couldn't be better.'

'Well, Arval would have liked it.'

He's smiling to himself with satisfaction. How long has this person been inside my father's body?

'Now, Nina, I know you wanted to arrange it, and I'm sorry I didn't let you help. But it was important for me to do this for Arval myself. I wasn't sure if I could, you know. I've been out of things for so long, and this place,

I haven't been here since . . . you know.' He gestures to the air, meaning grieving and abandonment and failure, all the things we don't talk about. 'I'm sorry I didn't ask for your help. I do know you wanted to.'

'You didn't need my help, you've done really well on your own.'

He nods. 'Don't take this wrong, please, Nina. But I don't think I could have done it if you'd still been here. So it's been . . . it's been good for me that you went to Spain. I know you were worried, but it's been the making of us both, hasn't it?'

'Dad, I've got to tell you something about that.'

'All right, but let me finish first. I've been meaning to say something to you for a long time. I'm not sure why I didn't, maybe I thought it was obvious, but these things need to be said. You're beautiful, such a beautiful girl. And you've struck out on your own, you have your own business, your own new life in a new country. I think you're very brave.'

'Oh Dad, no, I'm not brave at all. I—'

'You're very brave. Look at me. I've had one . . . setback, and I hid myself away, hardly looking around from one day to the next. But you, you've gone out there and made a success of it. And you saw how your mother . . . how our marriage didn't work out, and yet you still believe in love. Everything you do turns out so well, sweetheart, and it's not luck, it's your own beautiful nature and your heart. I'm so proud of you.'

My throat closes up and my eyes prickle at the corners. I try to say something, but nothing comes out. My father takes me in his arms and hugs me and I cling to him.

We stay like that for a long time.

Eventually he sniffs and loosens his hold. 'Well now, what was it you wanted to say to me before I started wittering on?'

He's got a gentle smile, and a tear in his eye. I can see the pride he was talking about on his face. I've craved it for so long.

'Nothing. Never mind. It's not important.'

'Are you sure?'

I'll tell him later. I can't give this up just yet. Surely a few more hours won't hurt.

'Definitely. Do you think it's time for another drink?'

'About that time, yes.' We leave the room, my father's arm around my shoulders as we walk down the corridor. Horse brasses glint in the light from the wall sconces.

'Have you checked in yet?' Dad asks me. 'Imogen and I already have, so don't worry about us.'

'Check in? You . . . are you staying here?'

'Yes, we thought we'd like to relax a bit and not worry about getting home tonight. I think quite a few of the people here are staying, making a night of it.'

'But I didn't know, I didn't reserve a room.'

'Not to worry, I reserved one for you when I booked ours. I thought you'd be tired out. I'm surprised you didn't arrive earlier to get settled. Did you come straight from the airport?'

'Uh . . .' Oh, this is hopeless. I'm doomed to a life of deception. 'Yes.'

'Well maybe you'd best go check in now then, get it out of the way. Lobby's to the left.'

'Oh. Right. Okay.'

Dad gives me a peck on the cheek and goes off back to the wake. I proceed to the lobby, chewing my lip. There's a young woman in uniform behind the desk.

Thankfully Dad hasn't suddenly become efficient enough to notice I don't have any luggage. With any luck, if the receptionist notices she'll be too tactful to mention it. Though this is a small town, probably prone to gossip. I take a deep breath and spread a wide, assured smile on to my face, the smile of a woman who's so self-sufficient she doesn't need any luggage and loves to wear the same suit two days in a row.

'Hi,' I greet her. 'I'd like to check into my room? Nina Jones?'

'Of course, Miss Jones, and I'm sorry about your uncle Arval.' She gives me a form to fill in. 'You're in Room 312; may I have a credit card?'

I freeze in the middle of signing my name. 'My father didn't pay when he made the reservation?'

'No, Mr Jones paid for your sister and himself when he checked in. If it's a problem, madam, we can—'

'No, no, no problem. What's the nightly rate, please?'

She tells me. It's not expensive, not by London standards, but it's substantially more than the twelve pound thirty-seven I have in coins in my purse and which needs to last me until Michael pays me again.

I notice there are some people standing behind me, and I make a show of digging through my handbag. 'I'm sorry, please go ahead and attend to these people. I think my card's fallen to the bottom of my bag.' I shift to one side, pretending to search. Of course there aren't any credit cards. The credit cards are all cut up and are lying in some landfill in Spain.

'I apologise, sir, madam, but we're fully booked,' the receptionist is saying to the people who were behind me.

'Oh. Well, we should've known, we flew over here last minute. Where's the nearest place we could stay?' The man has a distinctly American twang.

'There isn't anywhere local, unfortunately, sir, and I believe there's a function at the pub in the next village, but maybe if you try Newport . . .'

I grasp the chance and jump in. 'Oh, there's no need for that. Of course you must stay here if you came all this way. Please, take my reservation. Is 312 a double?'

The receptionist nods. 'But where will you stay?' the American woman asks.

'It's no problem, my sister wanted me to double up with her anyway, like a girlie sleepover. Or there's a chance I may need to go back to London tonight. Really, please, take it. My father, Owen Jones, is Arval's brother, and he'd be gutted if Arval's friends had to go all the way to Newport to get a bed.'

'Well if you're sure . . .'

'I'm very sure.' I crumple up the check-in form and beam at everyone, the picture of altruistic satisfaction.

Right. Well, this is no big deal. I'll just tell my father I had to get back, and hitch another lift with Evangeline and Michael. Unless . . .

When I get back to the wake, a crowd has gathered around an upright piano in one corner of the room, and they are singing a rousing version of 'The Gas Man Cometh'. My sister is there with her boy in skinny jeans and the other one who must be his best mate or brother, and I'm not surprised to see that Evangeline is right at the centre, playing the piano with relish.

I join the circle as they've got to Monday, when the gas man comes again. They finish with a flourish and I add my applause. Evangeline is smiling broadly; her piano-playing has dislodged a strand or two of blond hair from her chignon. 'Arval did so love his Flanders and Swann,' she says, and then she spots me and hops up from the piano bench.

'Darling!' she cries. 'I've been simply dying to meet you. You're dear Arval's other niece, aren't you, Bridget, isn't it? He did tell me oh so much about you.'

Her voice is stagy and loud, and she clasps my hands in both of hers. 'It's Nina,' I say. I really might as well go along with the charade, now that I've committed to it. Besides, more than half the room is watching us meet for supposedly the first time. 'I'm very sorry, you must forgive me, I've met so many people today, Mrs . . . ?'

'Oh, it's Ms, I'm a feminist, darling. Ms Evangeline Clegg. I was your uncle's neighbour, and so fond of him.'

'That's nice to hear. Did you have a good journey from London?'

'Marvellous. Though my husband will drive too fast, and doesn't allow cigarettes in the car. Do you happen to have one, by the way? A ciggie?'

'No, I'm sorry, I don't smoke.'

'A pity. Oh well, I think there's some hope to be had from the vicar; he looks a kindred spirit.'

'Will you be going back to London tonight?'

'Oh no no no, we're staying here. Michael is absolutely shocking behind the wheel when he's had a sherry or two, and it's such a treat to stay in a hotel, don't you think? Those little cakes of soap, et cetera. And it feels so naughty, like a dirty weekend.'

'Stop talking rot, woman, we've been married far too long for that.' Michael is over by the buffet, but his voice thunders effortlessly across the room.

'Ah, so you say, so you say, but you haven't seen what I've got packed in my valise.' Evangeline winks at me.

Okay. There's that question answered.

Basically, I'm stuffed.

I take a glass of wine from a passing tray, and ask Evangeline, 'Do you know "Madeira M'Dear"?'

30

Wine doesn't solve my problems, but it does make them easier to ignore. As the evening progresses, Imogen's boyfriend's mate gets out a guitar and one of the Americans produces a harmonica, and soon there's a small but dedicated party of dancers in the corner of the room.

I have no intention of dancing, and the Jimmy Choos forbid it anyway, even after several glasses of wine. Or *especially* after several glasses of wine. But I gravitate to the corner and plunk myself down next to my sister, who's swigging cider and talking vehemently to her boyfriend.

'Of course Deeanna's going to tell Harvey that the baby is his, she's not bloody stupid, is she? It's going to come out, though, Beryl saw that whole argument with Aloysius through the back window, remember.'

'I don't think she will,' the boyfriend says. 'The whole idea behind Deeanna is that she's the likeable victim, and if she starts lying now it will turn the viewers against her.'

'I agree with Immy,' I cut in. 'Harvey's been hinting at wanting a family anyway, so Deeanna will just think it's what he wants to hear. If she lies for his sake, the viewers won't mind so much, and she thinks Aloysius is gone for good anyway. The thing is that Nicky saw

Aloysius when she went to Portugal to look for Bryan, didn't she, so he's going to turn up again and everything will go pear-shaped.'

I stop, because they're both staring at me.

'You've been watching *Emerly Street*?' my sister asks.

'Um.' Have I? There has been quite a bit of mindless telly in my life lately, and I must have absorbed some of it without noticing. 'I've caught an episode or two.'

Immy beams. 'Wow. I never thought you'd do something I asked you to do.'

'Well I . . .' She's looking so ridiculously happy because of a television show that I can't deny it. I make a mental note to watch *Emerly Street* on purpose a few times. 'You were going on about how good it was. And you're right, the storylines are definitely gripping.'

'Have you visited the street corner?' the boyfriend asks. I say, 'The street what?' at the same time that Imogen nudges him hard in the ribs with her elbow. 'Um . . . I'll go talk with Wizzo for a bit,' he stammers, getting up and leaving.

'Now that I've watched your favourite soap, do you think I'm worthy of being introduced to your boyfriend?' I ask Imogen.

'Oh. Sorry. That's Andy. He's a good guy, when he's not being clueless. And that's his cousin Wizzo, playing the guitar.'

'And what's the street corner? He's not also your pimp, is he?'

To my relief, she laughs. 'No. He's talking about thestreetcorner.com. It's a . . . it's a fan website that Andy and I set up.'

'An *Emerly Street* fan website?'

'Yeah. We've got chat and inside info and things. It's just . . . we had an idea one time, we thought it would be fun.'

She's acting embarrassed about it, which tells me it's important, because I haven't seen her self-conscious about anything for ages. 'And you run it all yourself? Is that what you've been doing on the laptop every time I see you?'

'Yeah. I do the chat and research stuff, and Andy runs the tech side. We were voted the best soap site last month by *Soapmonthly* magazine.'

'Wow. You never told me, Immy.'

'You never seemed interested in anything I do except for looking after Dad and applying to university.'

'Well, I'm also sort of interested in whether you comb your hair.' I touch her arm. 'That's brilliant, Imogen.'

'We're attracting quite a few advertisers and starting to make some money. Which I'm putting away for uni, before you ask.'

'Wow,' I say again. I lean forward and kiss her on the forehead, the way our mother used to, the way I used to do when I dropped her off at school.

But that's wrong. My little sister isn't a little girl any more, and she doesn't need me to take care of her either. I raise my glass to her, and she clinks her pint glass against it, and we drink together.

'I'm sorry,' I tell her. 'If it helps, I've been more interested in what I should be doing too, instead of what I'm actually doing.'

'That's okay. Thanks for talking to me about Mum.'

For a moment we sit quietly and watch Andy joking with his cousin and the American impersonating Bob Dylan. Evangeline catches our eyes and waves at us cheekily, and I wonder how we look to her, if we look like real sisters.

I remember the excuse I gave to the desk clerk, about sharing a room with my sister to bond with her. Suddenly it seems almost possible. We haven't got teddy bears to chuck at each other, but we could make do with pillows.

'I'm really looking forward to tonight,' Imogen says suddenly. 'Andy lives with his parents too. We've never had a night together without having to be deathly quiet. And Andy is really loud when he—'

'Please.' I hold up my hand. 'I appreciate the new honesty, but there are some things I really don't need to know about my little sister's life.'

She giggles. As if on cue, Andy appears and holds out his hand to Immy. 'Forgive me for my slip-up yet?'

'You'll be lucky,' she says, but she takes his hand and stands up with him and they join the other couples dancing, swaying to a rhythm of their own.

For a few minutes I watch the two of them. This day was supposed to be about death, but instead, for some people at least, it seems to be about love. Evangeline and Michael are having a dirty weekend of it, and then there's my sister and Andy. She looks so young, and her skin is radiant. She's just starting out.

I can't begrudge her happiness, especially as she's just shared some of it with me. But for a moment I imagine myself on the floor with her, dancing with someone tall and blond, golden and beautiful, a perfect Prince Charming. Then I drop the dream and crush it beneath my foot like one of Evangeline's spent cigarettes.

It's not going to happen. Edmund will never be mine, and I'm a spare wheel spinning in her own rut. The best I can hope for tonight is a space on someone's floor, and a minimal loss of dignity.

There's a lot of wine in my glass, but I drink it down. If I'm drunk enough, maybe I won't mind sleeping in the bushes. I head to the bar for another.

Someone has got there before me, someone tall and dark-haired in a black suit. 'Howya doin', neighbour?' I drawl, leaning against the bar next to him.

'Shh, someone might discover your deep dark secret,' Viktor says.

'Who buried your sense of humour? I meant you're my neighbour at the bar, of course. Did you see any bats?'

'Quite a few.' He drums his fingers against the bar, obviously impatient to leave, but he hasn't got his drink yet.

'What is it about bats, anyway? Why are all of you so crazy about them?'

'For one thing, they're endangered. But they're also incredible creatures, one hundred per cent adapted to their natural environment. They can navigate in pitch darkness using the most subtle sonar in existence, they contribute immeasurably to their ecosystem, and even their shit is useful.'

'Wow.' I nod. 'That's something. Useful shit.'

He clears his throat. 'Were you being serious about my helping you with Arval's flat, or was that part of your show?'

'I was being serious. You were right. I was wrong. I apologise. Though I still defend my right to hoover whenever I want to.'

'I can see I need to invest in earplugs.'

He is still grumpy, but I sense a certain softening after my apology. Not enough for him to actually like me, but enough maybe to help me out. 'Listen, are you staying here tonight?' I ask.

'Yes.'

'Alone?'

His eyes narrow. 'What are you trying to ask me?'

'I'm just . . .' I look quickly around to check if the coast is clear. Everyone seems involved in their own conversations, singing or dancing. 'Do you think you would mind if I slept on your floor?'

His drink arrives. He doesn't even look at it. 'What the hell is going on with you, Nina Jones?'

'A glass of white wine, please,' I say to the barmaid. Once she's gone, I sigh. 'I can't think of anyone else to ask. My sister and my father don't know about my . . . situation. And everyone else here would think it was strange that I didn't just share a room with my family. Except for Evangeline and Michael, and they need their privacy for obvious reasons. You're the only other person who already knows I've got a secret.'

'Why don't you just get your own room?'

'I can't afford it.'

'I thought you had this wonderful job in Chelsea. And weren't you moonlighting at Michael's place?'

'I don't have the Chelsea job any more. And I spent all the money Michael's paid me.'

'Let me guess. On shoes?'

'Shoes are important. And I didn't know we were staying the night.'

Viktor shakes his head, and looks to the heavens as if for strength. 'Arval told me your side of the family was dysfunctional, but I didn't think it reached this level. All right, if you're so desperate, I'll lend you the money to pay for your own room.'

'The hotel is completely booked up.'

'Vik?' One of the bat women appears at his elbow. She's slim, petite, nervous, and doesn't acknowledge me. 'Do you think you could bring me another vodka tonic when you come back?'

He looks down at her and something flits across his face. Might be guilt, might be pain, might be passionate desire for all I know about the guy. 'All right, Fliss.' She lingers, fidgeting from one foot to the other, still not looking at me, until he says, gently, 'I'll be a minute, okay?'

'Yeah, all right.' She moves off reluctantly, casting several backward glances, to join the others.

When Viktor turns back to me, his manner is considerably less kind. 'Fine. You can sleep in my room, under one condition. You are going to tell me the truth about what you're doing in Arval's flat and why you're deceiving your family. Every little thing, no lies or evasions or arguments about shoes to divert me.'

I nod. It's not as if I've got a choice. 'Okay.'

He raises a hand for the barmaid's attention and mutters, 'I'm going to be in so much trouble for this.'

'Thank you,' I say, but then I see the vicar making a beeline for me, and take my wine to go and meet him.

I can't work out if I'm feeling more anxiety or relief that I've got to tell Vampire Viktor about my messed-up life. Something is fizzing in my stomach and adding a little bit of extra sharpness to my senses, though come to think of it, that could be the alcohol. Anyway, we've agreed I'm sleeping in his room, though I have no idea which room that is or how I'm going to get into it. It's not that I'm scared that people will think we're getting off with each other. I couldn't care less about that, quite honestly; the whole wake can think I'm Susie Sexpot if they want. No, the thing is, I don't want it to get back to my father, because he believes I'm blissfully in love with Juan.

So I have a bit more wine, and sing some songs with Evangeline, and eat some of the food on the buffet, and point out the rocket salad to Michael, and get involved in discussions about Clarissa's bunions and the vicar's hall carpet. I take a toe-crunching turn on the dance floor with Wizzo, who tells me how brilliant my sister is and how Andy used to spend all his time at the computer but now thanks to her he's got a social life. At one point

Harris, the guy who invited me out to see bats, comes across, sloshing beer over the top of his pint glass.

'So,' he says, tumbling into a chair beside me, 'what's up with you and our Dr Viktor? Are you planning on doing some hot monkey loving?'

'No, no loving, monkey or otherwise. He doesn't even like me much.'

'Ah, but these things are deceptive.' He tries to waggle his eyebrows, but they get stuck halfway up his forehead.

'Not in this case.'

'So do you think maybe you and me could do some hot monkey loving? Or maybe just lukewarm rabbit loving?'

'Uh, I don't think . . .'

'How about a coffee sometime? Not even a rabbit coffee?'

'Harry, I think it's time you went to bed.' Viktor is there, his tie slightly loosened. Nothing wrong with his eyebrows; he quirks one at me as if to accuse me of trying to seduce his friend.

'Yeah, probably,' mumbles Harris. He gets to his feet and wavers. 'Yikes.'

'Here.' Viktor puts his arm around his friend's shoulders. 'I'll give you a hand up there, as I'm going. You're right next to me; I'm in Room 206.' He looks significantly at me as he says this, and I take it as a hint.

I wait until they're gone, and a sufficient length of time has passed for Viktor to have settled Harris in his room and gone to his own. Then I kiss my dad, who's embroiled in a discussion with Michael about . . . well, it's hard to say, but it sounds like seersucker. Evangeline, dancing with one of the Americans, waves to me as I go.

The hotel is one of those buildings that started out, in the mists of time, as somewhere quite small and then was built on to by succeeding generations, which means that the corridors wind narrowly up and down several levels and the doorways don't quite match. Paintings of horses line the walls and there is a saddle hanging near the stairs. I reach Room 206 and tap lightly on the door.

Viktor answers it. His tie is gone. Silently he steps back and lets me into the room.

It's small and has a brown carpet, and a brown-and-green bedspread on the double bed. The bed, a small table with one chair, and a dresser with a telly on it take up most of the available space. There are, unsurprisingly, horse brasses on the walls.

'Thanks,' I say as soon as he's closed the door behind us. 'You've saved me from sleeping outside somewhere.'

'A fate worse than the truth.' He turns his back on me and goes into the en suite bathroom. I suppose I could lie down on the floor and try to go right to sleep, but that seems a bit rude and I'd sort of like to wash my face first. Instead I perch on the chair, and within minutes he's back with two plastic cups, which he puts on the table beside me.

'I borrowed this from Michael,' he says, drawing a silver flask from his inside breast pocket. He unscrews the cap and pours us each an inch of what is, from the smell, whisky.

'You think I'll tell the truth better if I'm drunk?'

'I think I'll hear it better if I'm drunk.' He sits on the bed across from me and takes a drink. 'So go ahead. Tell me Nina Jones's big secret.'

Even though I don't like whisky, I take a sip to stall. Viktor is sitting dead still, watching and waiting. I briefly consider waiting him out, but as he apparently crouches in bushes spotting bats for a living, I don't think I'd win.

'Um,' I say, and then stop. He watches me for a while longer. I can hear his soft breathing, and my heartbeat.

'Is it really so much easier for you to lie than to tell the truth?' he finally asks.

'I don't lie,' I say quickly. 'I mean, I don't normally lie. This is an extraordinary situation.'

'You mean that normally, outside extraordinary situations, you're a truthful person.'

'Yes.'

'Completely honest and transparent, forthcoming about everything about yourself.'

'Yes.' Then I remember how I kept my feelings about Edmund a secret from everyone. How I never told anyone in Holybrook about why we'd moved there. 'Well, when I can be. Sometimes you have to keep things in, you know? So you won't hurt someone.'

'Right. So you only lie if it's to save someone's feelings.'

'Yes.' Then there was Pet, and what I hid from her without even thinking. The pain in her voice before she hung up the phone. 'Sort of.'

'Sort of. Basically, what you're saying is that you're a compulsive liar.'

'No! I'm . . . There are things you don't tell people. Things that are private.'

'So private you have to lie to your family, leave your job, squat in your dead uncle's flat and piss off all your neighbours.'

'Yes. I mean, I didn't intend to piss off the neighbours.'

'Well that's all right then.'

He takes another drink, and keeps on staring at me. Dammit. He may be patient, but he's got one hell of a forbidding expression. Deep dark eyes, thick brows, high cheekbones, stern mouth. If I were a bat, I'd hide in a cave every time he came lurking around to spy on me.

'Okay,' I say. 'If I tell you, will you leave me in peace?'

'I'd like nothing more. The last thing I need in my life is another woman with problems.'

'No lectures about it?'

'Not unless I really want to.'

'Well the first thing you should know is that I'm not ashamed of knowing Evangeline and Michael. I like Evangeline and Michael. They've been really kind to me. The only reason I asked you all to pretend not to know me is because nobody except the three of you knows that I've been in Highgate.'

'Well, that's better. Twisted, but better. So why are you in Highgate?'

'Right.' I take a deep breath and a sip of whisky. Before the burn leaves my throat, I say, 'I went to Spain with my boyfriend to open a restaurant and he ran off with another woman and all our money and now I've got nothing.'

There's a pause.

'That's it?' he says.

'That's not enough?'

'Well, it's tough, but I was expecting something much worse. I thought you'd killed someone and you were on the run or something.'

'And you think I have an active imagination because I said you were a vampire.'

'Maybe not killed someone. But something bad, something shameful.'

'It's not bad and shameful to be abandoned and robbed by someone you thought loved you?'

My anger makes him draw back a little. 'Okay, I get it. You're nursing a broken heart for this guy who ran off.'

'No, I'm not. I didn't love Juan. I love someone else.'

'Someone other than your boyfriend?'

'Yes,' I say defiantly. 'Someone perfect and wonderful.'

'O . . . kay.'

I stand, my fists clenched. 'Listen, is it so unbeliev-
able that I might be in love with someone? And because
I can't have him, because he truly loves someone else, I
might have taken my chances with another man?'

'And made a bad decision. Is that what you're so
ashamed of?'

'No! I mean, yes! I mean . . . it's not that bloody
simple.'

Viktor shrugs off his jacket, and tosses it on the bed
beside him. 'Hot in here,' he says. Then he splashes
more whisky into our cups. I'd hardly noticed, but mine
was nearly all gone.

'It's all a bit melodramatic, though,' he says. 'We've all
made bad decisions in our love lives; we don't go and
hide out in empty flats and have minor breakdowns.'

'Oh, is that what you'd say happened to me, in your
expert opinion, Dr Goran? A minor breakdown?'

'The crying, the hoovering, the talking to yourself, the
screaming. Yeah, I'd say that was about right.'

'The screaming was because of a *spider*.'

But the rest of it. I remember scrubbing the bathroom with a toothbrush, even the clean parts, running
and running away from the black hole inside me. Being
scared to go outside. I sit back down on the chair.

'So what are you going to do now?' Viktor asks me.
'You can't hide inside Arval's flat for ever.'

'I don't know.' I can't think about it. Whenever I do,
the whole concept just slips away from my mind, as if it's
wrapped in grease.

'Do you think eventually you'll start telling people
the truth?'

'It's not as easy as that. I need to pick the right time,
when it will do the least damage. My father, for example:
he's fragile. I don't think he's ready to hear it.'

'Looks to me like he held up pretty well at his brother's funeral.'

'You don't know him like I do.'

'He's an adult, Nina. So's your sister. So are Evangeline and Michael, come to that. You can't just delay telling them the truth until it's convenient.'

I sink my whisky angrily. 'Who made you my judge, all of a sudden? I thought you said you wouldn't give me any lectures.'

'I said not unless I felt like it. And I feel like it. It makes me angry to see you playing with people, because you're afraid to admit that you failed.'

*You failed.*

I gasp and close my eyes as that black hole swims back, as the scab rips off the wound it left. I can say it to myself, I've been saying it to myself, but so stark and blunt in Viktor's voice, it's much more real.

Distantly I hear footsteps, and water running.

'Here. Drink this.' Something cold presses into my hand and I lift it to my mouth automatically. It's a plastic cup of water. I gulp it, feel its everyday coolness. *This is me, drinking water, this is normal, there is nothing so very wrong.*

I open my eyes and Viktor is frowning down at me. It's a different kind of frown, though. Softer. Closer.

Oh God, he feels sorry for me. I put the cup down, push my chair back as far as it will go and stand up. Even with the Jimmy Choos I'm quite a bit shorter than him. Still, it makes him step back a little, and that's something, though I could do with him stepping back a whole lot more.

'What about your bad decisions, then?' I shoot at him.

'We're not talking about me.'

'You're having such a good time ripping me to pieces, I might as well get to join in the fun.'

He crosses his arms. This is sort of a relief, and sort of

a disappointment, though I don't know why. What was I expecting him to do, hug me and make it all better?

'What about that nervous girl who didn't like you talking to me?' I pursue. This offence is so much easier than defence. 'What was her name?'

'Fliss.' He says the name with that same emotion I saw on his face downstairs.

'Am I right? Was she a bad decision?'

He rubs his forehead with his hand, disarranging his hair. 'You could say that. She's downstairs drinking herself stupid because I won't let her keep on believing she's in love with me.'

'Did you lead her on?'

'Not on purpose. She . . . we got involved, but there were some issues. She's got some problems, things I tried to help her with, but I couldn't.'

'Ah, so this is how you know all about breakdowns. You caused one.'

His jaw clenches. He brushes past me to an open bag on the dresser, to pull out a pair of jeans and a long-sleeved T-shirt.

'Let me guess,' I say. 'Bats are little things, endangered, you said. They need a big strong brooding hero to champion their cause, someone to study them and understand them and protect them. That's you. You like bats, but you like the way they make you feel even more.'

He's ignoring me. He goes into the bathroom, but I follow him and stand in the doorway. His white shirt and his dark hair, reflected in the mirror in the fluorescent light, are almost blinding in their contrast. He grabs a toothbrush from the side of the sink and puts it into his shirt pocket.

I should stop, but I can't. After being pinned down and prodded, it's too tempting to turn and aim something back.

'I reckon that behind all that grimness you're a bleeding heart. You like the girls with the problems, because you've got the answers. They need you. That's your type.'

He's facing the mirror, leaning on the sink, with his hands fisted on the porcelain. In the mirror, his eyes meet mine. They frighten me, and that makes me even more determined to stand my ground.

'And what's your type, Nina Jones? The men you can't have, or the men who leave you?'

'Well, your Fliss can rest easy, because I can tell you what's not my type: big grouchy men who can't get off the moral high ground.'

He whirls around, and in the same movement grabs my shoulders.

'That's good,' he says, 'because blonde bimbos with legs up to their armpits who can't even tell a bat from a moth aren't my type either.'

He glares at me. I glare back.

Then he crushes me against his chest and kisses me.

My head whirls with shock, then my head whirls with the kiss. He's so much taller than me, so much bigger, stronger, warmer. His lips are softer than they look. He smells of cedar, he tastes of whisky, his mouth presses hard against mine and I open for him, I don't know why. For an electric split second our tongues touch.

Then he lets me go and steps away and I'm left staring, open-mouthed, heart thumping. His shirt is crumpled where I've clutched it without knowing.

'Not my type at all,' he rasps. He steps past me, through the gap I've left in the doorway. 'I'm sleeping in Harry's room,' he says, and I hear the door close behind him.

I sleep in Viktor's bed, because I might as well, but I lie on top of the blankets and stay fully dressed except for my shoes. It's not like he's been in the bed, or that he's going to come back into the room, but it feels less intimate.

I can still smell him on the pillow.

When the sun's in the sky, I get up and leave the room. I go downstairs to the lobby and sit in an armchair pretending to read yesterday's *News of the Globe*. The receptionist, a different one from last night, kindly brings me a cup of coffee and doesn't ask why I'm up so early, alone.

The paper's no distraction, nor the coffee. The same thoughts as last night are still buzzing around my head. The biggest one being, *What the hell?*

Where did that kiss come from? One minute we're at each other's throats, and then bang, we're tongue-wrestling. It makes no sense at all.

Maybe he wanted some lipstick on his mouth so he could go downstairs and make Fliss jealous. Though that doesn't seem like something he'd do, and he could've just asked to borrow my tube of Lancôme. Maybe I was hitting a nerve and he wanted to shut me up, keep my mouth busy, knock me for six. Though that assumes he had some control and purpose, whereas when we broke apart, he looked just as surprised as I felt.

Maybe, after hearing my story, he simply couldn't resist his desire for screwed-up women and grabbed the nearest one handy. This seems the most likely.

Though there was something happening when we were touching that felt like him and me, not abstract, not impersonal.

I shake my head and drink lukewarm coffee, black. Obviously I have not been kissed for a while. Not like that, anyway. It was desperate, almost unwilling, and very physical. There wasn't a touch of romance in it at all. Not my kind of kiss.

Except that my lips still burn with it, despite the coffee, despite the Lancôme, despite the glob of toothpaste stolen from his tube to rub over my teeth this morning.

Anyway. No good worrying about it. I have other things to think about, like the possibility that I've had a little breakdown.

Actually, the certainty that I've had a little breakdown. All alone, in that flat, maybe the breakdown I should have had back when I was a teenager. It's strange I couldn't see it while it was happening, but maybe that's the nature of breakdowns; you only understand them in retrospect, when you've got over your irrational urge to clean and never think.

And yet I learned some things during that time, or at least I've come along far enough so that I can consider seeing things with a slightly different perspective. Viktor called Juan a 'bad decision', as if he were an unflattering haircut or an unwise investment. A 'bad decision' sounds so trivial, so much like something anybody could make. Looked at that way, Juan's almost done me a favour by running away. What if I'd committed to someone I didn't really love, and then he stuck with me? I'd be living with my bad decision for a long time, maybe for ever.

Whereas now, I'm living with gargoyles and deception.

'I didn't know you liked that sort of thing,' my father's voice says beside me. I start, and realise I've been staring at page three of the *News of the Globe* for the past ten minutes. A topless woman with a football scarf draped strategically over her nipples smiles up at me. I quickly close the newspaper and greet my father.

'I'm hungover,' he says cheerfully. 'Haven't felt this way in years. Let's celebrate with a fry-up.'

When the fry-up comes, though, I can't touch it. There's too much going on in my head. Imogen comes into the dining room holding hands with Andy, and immediately nicks both my pieces of bacon. I thought being in love was supposed to take your appetite away; I lost half a stone when I started working for Edmund. Then again, rampant sex all night long tends to make you hungrier, and Immy has a love bite on her neck barely concealed by her again-tangled hair.

'Nice one,' I whisper to her, and she blushes. I wonder what she'd say if I told her I spent the night in another man's bed, alone. She'd probably roll her eyes and think I was rather pathetic.

'Good morning, darlings!' Evangeline wafts into the dining room, trailing perfume and Michael. She heads straight for our table and kisses my entire family and Andy on the cheek. 'I hope you all slept well, or not, as you please. What fun it was to be in a strange bed! I so rarely get the chance these days. Pity it was with my own husband, but even so.'

'Don't worry, I'll be taking her home straight after breakfast,' Michael tells us, and shoos her to their own table.

My father finishes his last sausage and rubs his

stomach. 'That's better. Imogen and I were going to spend some time this morning wandering around Hedegogllygoden. She doesn't remember it well, so I thought I'd show her the places Arval and I grew up, the old house, our school, that type of thing. Do you want to join us?'

'Oh, Dad, I'd really love to.' The thing is, I would. It would be good to see my father connecting with his past, to learn more about him and his family, especially the ones I never met. But Michael and Evangeline are leaving, and I need the lift.

'But you have to go.'

'Yes.'

I'm not watching the door, but I know when Viktor comes into the room. It's like an itch on the back of my neck, the faintest whiff of cedar. I pour myself another cup of coffee and watch under my eyelashes as he crosses to join Evangeline and Michael. I can't help but glance around until I see Fliss; she's at a big table of bat people, sunk down in her seat, watching Viktor.

I wonder what happened between them. I bet it was messy. Especially if Viktor had to resort to kissing me to keep from talking about it.

He isn't looking at either me or Fliss; he's looking at a menu, and talking to Michael. 'Black pudding,' Michael booms, but I can't hear Viktor's reply, just the low thrum of his voice.

*What are you going to do now?* I hear him ask in my memory. *You can't hide inside Arval's flat for ever.*

Dammit, he was right about that, too.

'What are you doing now?' my father asks me. 'Train to Heathrow?'

'Actually,' I say, 'I think I'm going to get started on sorting Arval's flat soon. You've inspired me by your efficiency.'

'Oh. Well, that's good.'

'After I'm done, I was thinking I'd come and visit you. I'd like to talk a few things over with you. I . . . could use some advice.'

'Well you know you are always welcome, sweetheart.'

So that's it. I'm committed now. I'll do Arval's flat, and then I'll come clean.

Then I'll figure out the rest of my life.


I meet Evangeline and Michael around the back of the hotel; they've brought the car there specially to be secretive, and Evangeline is actually wearing sunglasses and a kerchief over her hair, as if that would keep anyone from recognising her. 'Thanks,' I say to them, slipping inside the car.

Viktor is there, in the back seat, glaring moodily out the window. 'Sleep well?' I ask him blithely.

'As well as could be expected. You?'

'Very well, thanks, I had an extremely comfortable bed.'

His frown deepens. I imagine he kipped on Harris's floor, and Harris was probably drunk enough to snore like a bear. But really, I wasn't the one who kicked him out of his room. He decided to do that all by himself, just like he decided to kiss me.

Michael revs the engine and we shoot on to the road with a rattle of gravel. I rub my lips together at the thought of the kiss. How warm Viktor was. The restrained power in his body. He wasn't so gloomy then. When I glance up, he is looking at me, but he quickly turns his head away.

That's how we're playing it, obviously: avoiding the issue. But I can't resist pushing it a little. He was the one who accused me of not facing up to reality, after all. Evangeline has turned on Radio Two and is singing along with the Arctic Monkeys.

'Anything interesting happen to you last night?' I ask Viktor.

'It's an intriguing behavioural experiment,' he says. 'Putting a whole lot of people together and giving them unlimited alcohol. All sorts of unexpected things occur.'

'Are you speaking as a zoologist, or as a participant?'

'Animals don't drink. It's one of the very many ways they're more sensible than humans.'

'Where'd the expression "drunk as a skunk" come from, then?'

'I don't know about the skunks, but I was absolutely hammered, darlings,' calls Evangeline from the front seat. 'What laughs.'

Viktor's cheek creases slightly. I wonder what it would be like to see his full smile, head-on, aimed at me. If he smiled at me, I think I'd be able to tell him that he was right about some of the things he said last night. But the smile fades away as quickly as it began.

'What sort of unexpected things occurred last night, from your perspective as a scientist?'

'Several. Drink loosens tongues.' I see a sudden tightening of his mouth as he catches the implications of his last word. He refocuses out the window.

'Let's put it this way. You can always tell if you've had a good night if there are people you'd rather avoid the next morning.'

'There are one or two of those,' he says, still looking outside. 'Some more than others.'

'Female or male?'

'In my experience, these little conflicts tend to focus around people of the opposite sex.'

'Sex!' sings Evangeline from the front seat. 'People getting off with each other left and right last night. Wouldn't be surprised if there were several cases of corridor-creeping after lights-out! Arval would have loved it.'

Viktor glances at me again, then away. 'Do you think so, Evangeline? Arval never struck me as being interested in intrigues.'

'That's because you never had a good gossip with him, darling. Did you know he was a secret soap-opera addict? Used to tape the omnibuses for him.'

'Soaps are wonderful things,' I pursue, 'but I'm more interested in real life.'

'Oh, darling, so am I. So much more scandalous.' She picks up a chorus of a Beach Boys song and warbles away.

'So,' I say under cover of the music, 'did you do anything you regret last night?'

He shifts in his seat. 'I think it's time for me to ask a question. Did *you* do anything you regret?'

This time he doesn't look away from me. It's not as intense as the way he looked at me last night, before he kissed me; it hasn't quite got the urgency of anger and frustration and whatever else behind it. But his gaze still has the power to make me feel pinned, interrogated, and I know he's talking about the kiss.

'I wasn't the one who started it,' I say.

He's silent for a long moment, which is filled up with Evangeline singing about California girls. I do my best to keep my face unreadable under his scrutiny. It was his idea. He gets to talk about it first.

'No,' he says at last, 'you didn't start it. So it's not up to you to regret it.'

Then he turns toward the window again with what I know is finality.

I look out of my own window, at the M4 slipping away from Wales into England.

Once I decide to do something, I don't hang about. I used to think that was a virtue, but the Juan thing has given me pause. Anyway, in this case I've delayed long enough, and besides, it will be a pleasure to do something for Arval at last.

Michael has given me a stack of flattened cardboard boxes from the café, which once housed coffee and tea and doilies, and I've hauled them up to the flat, opened them up, and labelled them, things like 'Charity' and 'Family' and 'Bin' and 'Bat Group'. I start with the easiest room, the bathroom, binning Arval's prescriptions and hairbrush et cetera, until the medicine cabinet is empty except for a small box of dental floss, which I don't think he'd mind my keeping. Then I begin on the rest of the house, dealing with the obvious things first. I put one of Auntie Claire's crocheted afghans in the box for Imogen, a multicoloured one that reminds me of her. I make a mental note to put the sugar bowl and crockery in storage, for one day when I might once again have a home of my own. I put the framed photo of my grandparents' wedding away for Dad. Then I tackle the rest of the photos, looking through them one by one.

Evangeline comes up for her cigarette around four. Her hair is black again, and in long Pocahontas plaits, and she is wearing a muumuu. She claps her hands in delight when she sees what I'm doing, and immediately joins me among the albums and boxes.

'Do show me your baby pictures, love,' she says. To my faint surprise, Arval has a collection of them, an album dedicated to me and Imogen from birth upwards. Evangeline takes it into her lap, and I sit beside her on the floor to look through it.

'Your sister does so resemble you.'

'God, no, not at all, we're chalk and cheese, and I'm about half a foot taller.'

For answer she folds back a page in the album, so that two-year-old Imogen stands next to two-year-old Nina. We are identical: blond hair, blue eyes, rosy cheeks, quizzical expressions. 'I guess we started out more similar than I thought.'

'Things happen to make us different.' She touches Immy's photo, which has been cut in half. 'Someone was cut out?'

'My mother, I suppose.' Several of the photos are cut up this way, though they've been carefully remounted into the album. 'Arval must have done it out of loyalty to my father.'

'Ah. The wronged party, was he?'

'We all were.'

Evangeline pats my knee with her beringed hand. I turn the pages. The last photo is of me aged fourteen on a bicycle, legs far too long for my body and hair escaping my ponytail. That was about the age I started to get spots. I felt ugly and clumsy all the time. About four months before Mum left.

'Do you have any children?' I ask Evangeline.

'Oh no, darling, it just never happened. First husband wasn't eager, second wasn't able, and by the time I met Michael, I was past it. We lost my brother Edgar very early, too, so you're looking at the last of the line.' She sighs. 'At least it sounds horribly romantic. Fortunately, I've always been able to adopt people.' She links her arm in mine and squeezes it.

I put the album into the box marked for Dad, and rummage through the other photos. There are several cardboard boxes stuffed with pictures of bats and groups of people, some familiar from the funeral; I set these aside in a corner of the living room where I'm putting stuff for Viktor to look at. When he surfaces and decides to speak to me again. Since we've returned from Wales I've heard nothing more from him, not even nightly footsteps. Which is fine by me. I think.

For every photo that has something to do with Highgate and the Temple of Gloom, Evangeline has a story to tell. There are photos of moving in, painting, parties, what was apparently a fancy-dress barbecue on a balcony flanked by gargoyles, presumably the one upstairs. Evangeline is dressed as Cleopatra, Michael appears to be Harry Potter, and Arval is, I think, Einstein. Viktor is wearing a toga made out of bed sheets, which exposes his bare shoulders and half his chest. I put the photo aside quickly.

'We love celebrating Hallowe'en here,' Evangeline tells me. 'We must start thinking about running you up a costume. With a bit of powder you'd make a wonderful ghost of someone who died tragically young. Or a sexy witch.'

'You know, when I first saw you, I thought you were a witch.' I blush when I say it, but Evangeline just laughs.

'Oh, don't worry, darling, when I first saw you I thought you were an alcoholic. Isn't it good that first impressions are so unimportant?'

'Um. I . . . yes.'

'Now, this is hungry work. What do you say I nip

downstairs and get some grub? Michael's left me a tonne of sandwiches, as usual.'

I leap up. 'No, it's my turn to feed you for a change.'

In the kitchen, I put on the kettle and make sandwiches. Gloria the local baker sells me baguettes at a knock-down price because I've set her up to supply Michael's café. Chicken livers are cheap, and make an easy and tasty pâté. I've even made flapjacks with the last bit of Arval's porridge oats. I put together a feast and bring it out to Evangeline on a tray with what is probably inordinate pride. But it's the first meal I've been able to offer for a very long time, and Evangeline was right: feeding people satisfies some basic instinct, some need for connection and comfort. It doesn't matter what the food is, as long as it creates a feeling of home.

We eat it as a picnic on the floor, surrounded by scattered memories.

Late Thursday morning I'm stacking freshly washed teacups in the café and humming. Sorting out the flat has given me a sense of purpose. Not like the frantic cleaning I was doing a few weeks ago; this is calmer, more necessary, and requires thought instead of banishing it. I'm actually looking forward to visiting Dad, bringing the boxes of his brother's things for him.

Beyond that, I haven't really thought yet. It's enough to slowly bring order to what's left of my uncle's life. Mine can wait.

But a stray thought has crossed my mind, about maybe asking Dad if he minds me staying in the flat for a little while, once it's cleared. Until I find my feet again. Maybe I can get a job around here, join a temp agency or something.

Six months ago, I could have had my pick of jobs anywhere in London. I wouldn't even have to give a CV;

I'd just mention Edmund Jett and the door would be open. I'd had a few offers. If I'd been smart I would have taken up one of them, instead of jumping ship and going to Spain. I could be in the exciting heart of London right now, in my old flat, with all my own clothes, planning an evening out with Pet and the girls. The whole idea has a sort of golden glow around it, in my mind.

Some day I will go back. I'll build myself up again from the bottom; I've done it before. And when I'm ready, I'll swan back into Chelsea and treat myself to dinner at Jett, with the handsomest male company I can find. Some day I'll be so happy I'll even be able to look at Edmund without feeling the pain of longing, without betraying any emotion on my face at all.

Today, however, if I had to go back to Chelsea, I'd be best off wearing a Hallowe'en costume to disguise myself.

The thought reminds me of something I've been idly wondering for several days now. No one in the café wants serving, so I go through the beads into the kitchen to help Michael, who is making up a bowlful of tuna mayonnaise. I pick up a J Cloth and start wiping down surfaces. 'What colour is Evangeline's hair?' I ask him.

'It changes more often than I change my socks. What colour was it last time you saw her?'

'Black. But I mean, what colour is it really? The blond and black were wigs, right?'

'They're all wigs.' He finishes the tuna, pops a plastic cover on it, and swivels his chair slightly to start grating a block of Cheddar. 'She's got dozens of them in a closet. Every time I go in it, I think I'm going to be attacked by disembodied hair.'

'Ew.'

'Yeah. I'm trying to convince her to get rid of them once her hair grows back enough, but I think she's developed an addiction. And it's less messy than dying, I suppose.'

'Once her hair grows back?'

'Mm. The chemo did a number on it, so we used my electric razor in the end. Still, it's longer than it was, and in a few months—'

I stop wiping the prep area. 'Chemo?'

'Breast cancer.'

I sit down on the plastic chair by the door. I suddenly feel all shaky and weird. 'Is she going to be all right?'

Michael shrugs. 'This is her second time round, but she's a fighter. She's got no tits left, so it'll have to come back somewhere else, if it wants to. I wish she'd stop smoking.' He wraps the cheese block in cling film and wheels it over to the fridge. 'I take it she didn't tell you.'

'No. I knew she was frail, but not . . .'

'She doesn't talk about it. Prefer if you didn't mention it to her, quite honestly. Now get up and serve some customers, will you, or I'll have to hire another girl.'

I wander into the front of the café and serve tea and clear up without noticing what's going on around me. Poor Evangeline. Poor Michael. And yet they don't seem to be scared of it, or hiding from it, even though they don't talk about it. They're just dealing. Living life. Collecting wigs. Sneaking fags.

The café door opens; it's about time for Mildred to come in for her egg sandwich, so I call, 'Hi, Mildred,' with my back still to the room. I grab a metal teapot and a couple of doilies for the tray, and then, because Mildred hasn't answered, I glance over at the door.

It's not Mildred. It's two people: a young woman, short and slender, with spiky brown hair and a nose stud and eyebrow studs and a black leather jacket. And another woman, in a tweed overcoat and a pink knitted hat, whose face I've examined so many times without wanting to, wishing it were mine.

I drop the teapot with a clatter and bolt for the kitchen. Michael is reaching for the eggs and one of the baguettes I've started ordering.

'Michael, I've got to go, can you take care of this customer for me?' I gasp, grabbing for my jumper where it's hanging up by the back door.

'Did Mildred say something mean?' he asks me, but I've already escaped, out the back alley and round the corner towards the Temple of Gloom.

By the time I reach the front door I'm already feeling foolish. Here I am, thinking about how my new friends aren't hiding from things, and what's my first instinct when I'm faced with a problem? To hide.

I'm about to put my keys back in my pocket and return to the café when the door opens under my hand. Evangeline stands there, a beret perched on her black wig. She smiles at me in surprise. 'Hello, darling, did the slave-driver let you out early today?'

She is old. It's hard to tell how old; smoking adds years, make-up erases them, but she gives the impression of being well preserved. The skin on her hands is slightly waxy and the blue veins show through. It is easy to see the shape of her skull beneath her face, but this is part of her beauty.

'I'm being a coward,' I tell her. 'And I'm not a good friend, either. Can I talk to you for a few minutes, Evangeline? I've got something to tell you.'

'Of course.' She leads the way back into her flat. Once again I'm struck by how it's like stepping back a hundred years or more. I get distracted by a glass case on the flocked wall, holding a small stuffed bird. A handwritten card in the case tells me that it is a song thrush.

'My grandmother's,' Evangeline tells me, and sits on

the horsehair sofa, patting the seat next to her. 'Would you like some tea?'

'No thank you. Evangeline, I've been lying to you.'

'Really? Do tell.' She leans forward, interest plain on her face.

'I've . . . I didn't come here to sort out Arval's things. Well, I did, but that wasn't the real reason. The real reason I'm here is because I've messed up my life and I'm hiding from my problems. I had a business in Spain, but it went under. I'm bankrupt. My boyfriend left me. I've lied to all my friends and family.'

'Oh, is that it, darling? I've known that for ages.'

I sit back. 'You did?'

'Of course I did. Your father rang me weeks ago and said I should be expecting you sometime in the future, but of course you were already here. He rambled on about you at some length, very proud of you I'd say, and it wasn't difficult to read between the lines and figure out what had happened to you. Something similar happened to my brother Edgar. Your father hadn't the foggiest idea of the truth, of course.'

'You didn't tell him, did you?'

The look on her face tells me she didn't.

'Thank you,' I say.

'Oh, darling, don't thank me. You've brightened up this place no end. It's been so empty without Arval upstairs, and with Viktor stomping around everywhere. You've been a breath of fresh air. And so helpful at the café, too. It was dreadfully kind of you to volunteer to work for us.'

I have my doubts about who's been dreadfully kind here. It seems more to me that if Evangeline knew I was broke, she was doing me a favour by asking me to work for Michael.

She'd never admit it, though. A wave of affection for

her sweeps through me, and I give her a hug.

'Wait a minute,' I say. 'Why would my father ring you? You said you'd never met him.'

'Well I own the building, don't I? It's been in my family for yonks.'

'Oh.' I blush furiously, remembering the first time she came upstairs for a fag. 'I . . . I think I was horribly rude about it to you. I called it creepy . . .'

'But it is, darling. Wonderfully creepy. My great-great-grandfather was a lovable eccentric. He built the place in order to impress a rather distant ice queen – we suspect she was his mistress at the time – and he installed her in here until his first wife died and he could marry her. We've rather come down in the world since then, though I've made a point of it myself to marry my lovers whenever possible. At least I can keep up the moral standards, if not the architectural ones. Why did Michael let you out early, by the by?'

'He didn't. I was running away from someone I didn't want to see.'

'Do tell.'

'It was Gretchen, who was the bartender at the restaurant where I used to work. And Caroline, my boss's wife.' I bite my lip. 'I don't know what they're doing here. They didn't seem to be looking for me; maybe they just walked in by chance.'

'Are these people you're hiding from?'

'Yes. I'm also in love with Caroline's husband.'

'Ah, now that's a story! Fantastic. Sorry to be a pest about this, but does Viktor know about the husband and the hiding out?'

'He knows everything.'

'Yes, I thought so.'

'You mean the way he refuses to talk with me because I'm a horrible queen of deception?'

Evangeline laughs. 'Darling, I'm not a bad queen of deception myself, and he's unfailingly charming to me. No, I think it takes something out of the ordinary to ruffle our Viktor's temper.'

'Could have fooled me.'

The telephone rings on its spindly side table and Evangeline gets up to answer it. Anachronistically, it's a very new digital phone in a sleek cradle. 'I'll tell her,' she says into it and covers the tiny mouthpiece to speak to me. 'Michael says the coast is clear and Mildred wants her egg sandwich.'

It's past two o'clock in the afternoon and he's probably asleep. I listen for a couple of minutes, but I don't hear snoring or anything, so I knock softly on the door of the upstairs flat.

Nothing. I wait, consider knocking again, then turn to go down the stairs. Before I reach the first step, I hear footsteps approaching, and the door opens.

Viktor has evidently been taking a shower. He's wearing a pair of boxer shorts and a T-shirt and is holding a white towel. He's barefoot and his hair is wet. 'I thought you'd be in your coffin,' I say, which wasn't what I meant to say but I find myself being distracted by a drop of water travelling down his neck. There's a slight golden tone to his skin that I've never noticed before.

'Even the undead have to wash occasionally.'

I shift from foot to foot on the landing. 'Listen, I know you hate me and everything, but I've been looking through Arval's things and you said you'd like to help. So I'm going out for a walk, and I thought you might want to have a look around while I'm gone. Seeing as you don't like being in my immediate vicinity.'

'I never said that.' But I notice he doesn't invite me in.

'Here.' I hold out the Yale key to him. 'I'll be a couple

of hours. Just leave it behind the gargoyle near the front door when you're finished. I left a pile of things in the front room for you, but there's lots in the library that you're welcome to sift through. I've pretty much set aside everything that's important to the family, and Evangeline has already taken some photos, so you can have whatever you like for yourself or the bat group.'

'Thanks,' he says, and takes the keys. His movement wafts a faint scent of shampoo in my direction. I hear music behind him in the flat, something sort of acoustic-guitary, sounding like summery afternoons.

'No problem.' I turn away and begin to clump down the stairs in my second-hand boots.

'Nina?' he calls. 'Which gargoyle should I leave it behind?'

'Don't worry. You'll know.'

I take an epic trek through Highgate Woods, and then wander around the park near the Temple of Gloom. There are a lot of dog-walkers in Highgate. And women pushing prams. I don't remember ever seeing so many dogs and children in Chelsea or Kensington. Maybe it's easier to have these things here where it's less busy. Maybe I just never noticed them. Hard to say.

When I get back, there are no keys behind the bat, even though I've been gone over three hours, which is surely more than enough time. I shake the rain out of my hair and go up to the flat. The door is slightly ajar.

I know better now than to expect ghosts, vampires or axe murderers in this house, especially at half past five in the afternoon, but I've lived in London long enough to be wary of an unlocked door. I push it open gingerly with my muddy foot and see Viktor sitting on the flowery couch with his nose buried in a paperback novel.

'Oh good, you've made yourself at home,' I say,

entering. He starts up guiltily and closes the novel, which I can see is *'Salem's Lot* by Stephen King.

'Arval was always telling me to read this one, and I found it in one of his desk drawers.'

'Yeah, I hid it there because it was too scary. Cup of tea?'

I head straight for the kitchen because I need a cuppa even if he doesn't. But I'm a bit surprised to hear him say, 'Yes, thanks.'

I have no idea how he takes his tea, so I pour the milk into Auntie Claire's china jug and put that and her sugar bowl on a tray with the cups. I'm hungry myself, so I add the leftover flapjacks from the other day. When I get back to the living room, Viktor has abandoned the novel and is standing next to several boxes in the corner.

'I thought the trust would like some of his detectors,' he says, indicating several boxes he's labelled in neat block capitals. 'And he's got some books they could find a home for. They'd probably like his expedition journals too, but I'd like to look them over first and make some notes of his data.' He's labelled another, smaller box with his own name.

'Did you see the photographs?' I put the tray down on the table and curl up on the couch, adding milk to my tea.

'Yes. They're great. Thank you. There was one that I think got mixed up with the others by mistake.' He picks up a photo from the top of his box and brings it over to me, then sits at the other end of the couch to pour milk into his own tea.

I stare at the photo, which is a Polaroid, fading slightly around the edges. I definitely didn't see this one the other day. It's of my family. We're standing in front of the bungalow in Holybrook, on grass that's brown with summer. Imogen wears her school uniform of gingham dress and jumper. I remember it extremely well because it was her first school uniform and she never wanted to take it off. I had to sneak it off her floor at night after she'd gone to bed in order to wash it and iron it for school the next day. In the photo she is eight and her hair is in the plaits it would take me ten minutes to do each morning.

I'm fifteen. I've got a hand on Immy's shoulder, and while she's smiling, gap-toothed, at the camera, I'm turned towards my dad, who is standing a foot or two away from us. I'm wearing plimsolls, little white shorts and a striped T-shirt, and my legs look like those of a wobbly colt. Gouged between my eyebrows there is a line of worry, far too deep for a young girl.

I touch between my eyebrows and feel where the line has embedded itself in my grown-up skin.

And then I look at my father and I gasp.

'What?' Viktor is immediately sitting close beside me.

'It's . . .' I'm about to say *nothing*, but it's not nothing. My father in the photograph is a nightmare memory. His clothes hang off him, his eyes are shadowed by dark circles. His hair is lank and thin and his skin is grey. Not only is he not smiling; he looks as if he has never smiled, not once, in his entire life.

'I'd forgotten he looked this bad,' I say.

Viktor takes the photo from my fingers and turns it over. Arval has, of course, labelled it; the date is about three months after my mother took off. I don't remember him visiting then. But it's not surprising – this photo shows me what I was most preoccupied with, why I couldn't afford to notice anything else.

'Was he sick?'

'No. Not really. I mean . . . well, yes, sort of, he was.' I touch my father's face.

'He looks much better these days.'

'Yes, he does. He really does.' I haven't fully realised how much better he is, until now, when I see what he used to be like. 'It's like a ghost story in reverse. He's come to life again.'

What's done it? Not the bungalow, or the job, or the telly. Not a new relationship, or closure on the old, or anything immediately obvious as being fulfilling. Not anything I've done for him, not for the past several years, anyway.

Just time, I guess. Time and nature and life and maybe my sister, a little bit, too.

'I need to trust them more,' I say.

Viktor looks a bit puzzled, but he nods. He picks up his tea and reaches for a flapjack, apparently reassured that I'm not about to burst with some sort of emotion. He takes a bite, and then looks surprised. 'This is good.'

'I must have learned something after years of working for a chef.'

'Or maybe I've been doing nothing but sucking foxes for too long.'

That makes me smile, and he smiles back at me. His smile is quite literally transforming, like sunshine breaking through dark clouds.

'We haven't really got off to a good start, have we?' he asks.

'Not unless you like continuous arguing, no.'

'Well, it's been fun, but I'm open to trying something else.' He finishes off his flapjack in a single bite. 'It'll be dusk soon, and I've got some observations to do. Would you like to come with me?'

'Wow. Do you know, that's the most exciting social invitation I've had in weeks, aside from my uncle's funeral.'

He shrugs. 'You don't have to come if you're not interested. I just thought . . .'

'I am interested,' I say quickly. I'm not one hundred per cent sure why I'm interested. Maybe it's because everyone else seems so gung-ho about the little critters, or maybe it's just in the interests of burying the hatchet. 'I'd really like to,' I add. 'Are you sure you want me to, though? I mean, you've been avoiding me, ever since . . .'

'I've been in California, at a zoology symposium. I was the keynote speaker.'

'Oh. I thought . . .' I clear my throat. 'Never mind.'

'Do you have any appropriate clothes, do you think?'

I look down at myself. I'm wearing my grey jumper over, of course, a flowery dress, with a pair of Arval's socks. 'What, something darker?'

'Something warmer. I'll bring a pair of tracksuit bottoms down for you, and a coat.' He gets up and goes to the door, hoisting one of the big boxes under his arm on his way. 'I'll be five minutes.'

He's less than five minutes, actually; I barely have time to finish my now lukewarm tea before he's back, wearing a jumper and his black cloak-like coat and with his big black bag over his shoulder. He holds out a bundle to me, which I take to the bathroom to change into. The grey sweats are long enough so that I have to roll them up around my boots, and I have to cinch the drawstring tight around my waist so they won't fall down. He's also brought me an extra jumper, which I put on over my own.

It's strange to wear his clothes. They smell of him, and when I look at myself in the mirror, they provide a sort of map of all the ways his body is bigger than mine. The shoulders of his jumper hang down my arms and the sleeves flop around past my hands. The jumper is made of good-quality wool, and the sweat pants of soft, heavy cotton, and they feel a contrast, too, to the light cottons and silks of my Spanish wardrobe. Warmer, more real.

'All ready,' I say, rejoining him in the living room. He looks at me, for more than the second or two needed for acknowledgement, and then he shakes his head and says, 'Let's go.'

'What?' I ask as we're going down the stairs.

'What, what?'

'Why were you staring at me?'

'I haven't seen a woman in my clothes for a long time.'

'Fliss didn't wear them?'

'Fliss . . . was different. And besides, that was in the spring.'

I'm not sure what that has to do with it, but I pull on the extra jacket and fall into step beside him on the pavement. We cross the road at the bottom of our street and head for the park. It's still light outside, but the sun is sinking down towards the horizon. 'I never really noticed this before so much in London,' I say. 'The way the shadows get longer near the evening. Do you think it's because we're on a hill here?'

'Could be.'

'Or maybe because I have time to notice.' I bury my hands in the pockets of his coat. They're warm. 'What went wrong with Fliss, anyway?'

'You were right. I was trying to be a hero.'

This makes me smile. 'You mean I'm not a totally clueless bimbo?'

'I'm sorry I said that.'

'That's all right. You also said I have legs up to my armpits, which isn't a bad thing. And I really can't tell a bat from a moth.'

'Not yet.'

We enter the park and begin to cut across it, past the formal gardens laid out in boxes and curves.

'I'd say I'm sorry I called you grouchy, but you are actually grouchy.'

'Not usually, you know. I have quite a few friends, hold down a job, people come to my lectures, I'm the apple of my mother's eye, things like that.'

'I must have got you on an off month. So what happened with Fliss?'

He sighs as we pass the eagle statues that flank the bottom of a flight of stone stairs. 'Fliss is a joiner. She likes to have things outside herself to hold on to. She came into the bat group about a year and a half ago because she'd gone on a bat walk and decided that bats were going to be her next big passion. Before that it was dancing, and before that it was church, and I think before that it was a variety of recreational drugs. I met her during one of her high periods, and she's very charismatic then. Sparky and exciting. Attractive.' I have to walk quickly to keep up with his long strides. 'Then she slid down, as I found out she always does. I tried to get her help, but . . .'

We walk under trees half bare with autumn, and across a bridge over water. Yellow leaves float on the glassy surface. 'What kind of help?'

'Well, counselling mostly. But she said all she needed was me.' He turns up his collar, not from the cold, and not even to hide from me, I don't think. It seems like he's doing it to shelter from something, maybe himself. 'I should've known from the beginning. All the clues were there, but I ignored them, like a fool. I thought I was stronger than that. So I ended up breaking her heart.'

'And you hate yourself for it.'

'Hate's a strong word, but . . . I shouldn't have done it. Shouldn't have got involved. It was my fault, in the end.'

'Because you couldn't love her?'

'Well. Not enough.' We cross another swathe of grass and then come out through a gate on to a road.

'We're going *here*?' Across from us is the grey chapel thing, the Temple of Gloom's more cheerful sister, the entrance to Highgate Cemetery.

'Tonight, yes.' He takes me across the road, right up to the big door.

'You can't just go in, though, can you?'

'I've got permission from the Friends of Highgate Cemetery, for a scientific project.' He unlocks the door with a big key. Disappointingly, it doesn't screech on rusted hinges, but instead swings rather discreetly open. It leads to a short arched passage, opening out to a courtyard.

'We're going to a cemetery to watch bats.' I shake my head. 'You couldn't make this up.'

'I don't always come here. This is one of several sites I'm observing. Wait here a minute.' He goes off, around the corner of the building, and I stand waiting. A curved brick wall encloses the courtyard, arches cut out of it like a weird wedding cake. There are plaques on the walls. Graves. I shiver.

Viktor returns, carrying an aluminium ladder over his shoulder. I hope we're not going to be climbing down into any graves.

'You've brought me here in revenge for my vampire comments, haven't you?' I ask.

'Of course not. Well, maybe a little bit. Up these stairs, here.'

The stone stairs in the curved wall climb upwards, and are pitched in such a way that I can't see to the top of them. 'Are we the only people in this place?'

'The only living people, yes.' He smiles at my hesitation and that's enough to get me moving up the stairs. At the top, I gasp.

Trees loom over the gravel path, forming a canopy. And between them, behind them, around them, *through* them, is a city of graves.

'Holy crow.' I wander forward. You can't hear the city, only a rustle of trees and our feet on the gravel. The gravestones crowd together, some spiky like jagged teeth, some elaborately carved, piled on top of each other as if jostling for position. In the deepening shadows I see a stone angel, a shrouded pillar, a weeping woman without a hand.

'This way,' says Viktor, leading me up the path. Leaves crunch and whisper. They are orange and brown, and the foliage around us is a muted curtain of colour in the fading light. Against this, the graves are subtler hues of grey and pink and brown stone, greened over by lichen and moss.

'It's beautiful,' I murmur. A slow riot of life and decay. I try to read the inscriptions but it's difficult in the shadowy light; anyone could lie here, deep beneath, sleeping.

It's definitely getting darker as we ascend, but my eyes adjust to it and so I can see adequately, within the tunnel of trees at least. It feels as if the cemetery stretches in a labyrinth for miles around us.

'Last week I was spending most of my time in an alley behind a dry cleaner's,' Viktor tells me. 'This place has more perks, if you don't mind it being a little spooky. Speaking of which, here we are.'

'Oh, wow.' Suddenly, out of a wall of trees, there's a big stone gateway, flanked by improbably elaborate pillars. 'It looks like a set for an Indiana Jones film.' I point through it, to an upward-sloping stone corridor. No roof, just doors either side, their entrances pitch black. 'You can so imagine a big ball rolling down through there to crush us both.'

'Want to take a chance?'

'Sure.'

This is creepy. This is really creepy. I don't need to be told that these are crypts. There are skeletons lying behind these doors. Skeletons, rotting grave clothes, and lots and lots of spiders. Our footsteps echo slightly and the air has grown distinctly colder.

'Are you scared?' Viktor asks me. The fingers of his free hand brush my arm.

The hairs on the back of my neck are standing up. My heart is pounding. Every shadow seems poised to leap out at us.

'I'm not scared.'

And it's true. I'm not frightened, just excited. Viktor shakes his head in disappointment and leads me to the end of the corridor. Here, we're facing a curved wall of mausoleums, the outside of a great circle of stone. A path leads between the inner and outer circles to both left and right. It's like being inside some weird city, where the houses are for corpses.

'Oh, wow,' I say again.

'It's called the Circle of Lebanon,' he says. 'It was very desirable real estate for rich dead people in the nineteenth century. We'll set up here. I'm pretty sure this is where Lucy and Willie are roosting.'

'Lucy and Willie?'

He sets down the ladder and takes the bag off his shoulder, and then kneels on the path as he unpacks a variety of metal boxes and equipment, what looks like a GPS, an electronic organiser and a thick, battered notebook. 'My project is tracking individual Natterer's bats around this area, to try to determine their roosting habits, why they abandon one roost for another, why they form colonies or roost individually; to identify all the different factors that might go into an individual bat's movements in an urban environment. I'm collecting data in conjunction with two other teams in Paris and Berlin. I think two of my females are here in these crypts.'

'How can you tell?'

'Tracking devices. Arval helped me develop them.' He hands me a black plastic box, about the size of a chunky mobile phone. He turns a switch and I hear a very faint sound of static. 'Hold on to this while I try to pinpoint the bats.'

'Are they out already?' I look overhead, but see nothing but sky, leaves and the bare fingers of trees.

'Natterer's usually wait until after sunset. Be quiet for a minute.' He fiddles with his equipment, frowns, then smiles. 'I thought so. Come here.'

He scoops up his equipment and sets off down the avenue. It's curved in such a way that it's impossible to see what's ahead. The doors of the crypts are embossed with upside-down torches. In my hand, the box suddenly flares to life with a series of rapid clicks.

'What the . . .'

'There's a Natterer's. She's probably coming out of a crypt. They can find the tiniest entrances. Up here.' Viktor leans the ladder against the curved inner wall. 'After you,' he says.

I refuse to be a fussy female, so I scramble up, to the top of the mausoleum, but where I expected a crumbling stone roof, there's a vast, perfect circle of grass, and in the centre of it, an enormous tree.

'They're roosting in the cedar of Lebanon,' Viktor says behind me. We hurry to the base of the tree.

'Is this safe?'

'Relatively.' Quickly he sets out his equipment, and I sit next to him on the cool earth.

The cemetery lies beneath us in a round pool of shadow, and rises around us in points and human-like figures. The sun is no more than a pink streak in the west; through the fan of the cedar above us, I can see a sliver of moon. 'I'd roost here if I were a bat,' I say.

'It's perfect, really. I'm interested in how many will choose it as a hibernaculum.'

The bat box clicks and whirrs again. Viktor points upward. I see a dark shape, like a small bird, hurtle from the tree across the open sky.

'That was Lucy,' he tells me. 'We got lucky.'

'What's she doing?'

'Eating her own body weight in insects. The clicks you hear are the sounds she makes for echolocation. They're too high for us to hear with the naked ear.'

More clicks, and Viktor points at more shapes. I can see now that they don't move like birds; they dip more between wing flaps, and change direction more often. He enters some information in his PDA, but by now I'm looking and listening so hard that I hardly notice what he's doing. The bats' calls speed up to a frenzy, then slow down; the dark blobs dip and circle. There seem to be dozens of them. Once I feel one whirr close by my face, too fast for me to react. The light drains from the sky, but I squint and look harder until I can't see anything but the trees silhouetted against deep indigo.

'It's a good colony,' Viktor says at last, sounding satisfied. 'There aren't just Natterer's bats roosting here, either.' He reaches over and adjusts the dial on my machine, and I hear a slightly different series of clicks, louder and more regular, crowding one on another. 'Those are pipistrelles.'

'Are they rare bats?'

'They're all rarer than they should be. Natterer's bats are considered scarce. But in the scheme of things, no, they're not exotic. Arval was the collector of rare bat sightings; I'm a behaviourist.'

I'm aware of so much going on around me: the intricate flights and clicks, the tiny world of predator and prey, all the life whizzing around amongst darkness and death. I'm in the heart of something. A perfect circle.

'I never suspected any of this,' I say.

'And you're sure you're not scared?'

'Don't sound so disappointed.'

He laughs. It's become so dark that he's a shape beside me. I hear the rustle of cloth, and the tearing of a wrapper. 'Chocolate?'

'Mm.' I take it and bite into it by touch and smell. Fruit and nut. I give it back to his waiting hand, and hear him take a bite too.

Without most of my sight, my other senses feel sharper. The tree has its own presence behind and above us, a solid shadow, and I'm breathing in essence of crushed needles and wood. It's an echo of Viktor's scent.

'I like it,' I say.

'Don't tell me you'd rather sit on dead people watching flying rodents than go out clubbing at some trendy place.'

'Well, this is fun too.'

'Yeah. It is.' He passes me the chocolate again. 'I think I owe you an apology.'

'Another one? I might faint.'

'I shouldn't have given you such a hard time about hiding from everyone. It's your decision and you're a grown-up. I shouldn't be so judgemental.'

I take the largest bite I can out of the chocolate before I pass it back. 'Actually I think you were right,' I say. 'I do need to be more honest. I do need to get this whole situation into perspective. I did have a breakdown.'

'Oh. I'm sorry.'

'It's okay. I really think I'm better now.' I let out a

short laugh. 'Or are you used to hearing this sort of thing from females, since your tragic ex?'

'Not really. Then again, I don't think I was ever as hard on Fliss as I was on you. I don't think she could have taken it.'

I shiver, though it's not particularly with cold. It's this new sense of freedom, that I can say what I feel here in the dark.

'I've been thinking about it for the past few days while I've been away,' he says. 'I was so busy being judgemental about your choices that I never asked you something more important.'

A bat clicks and flutters past us, the machine translating the sounds it's making beyond the limits of our hearing.

'What didn't you ask me?'

'Why can't you tell anybody who matters what's really happened to you? Why is it so difficult to admit that you've failed?'

It isn't a challenge. It's a question, fairly asked.

I take the rest of the chocolate from his hand and eat it all. I need it. I have never said this before.

'My mother left us when I was fifteen. She took all the family's money, and my father was so devastated he lost his job and had to declare himself bankrupt. We lost our house, our car, Imogen and I had to move from private school, all quietly during the holidays. We moved to a bungalow and I took over running the house. My father was a zombie and couldn't deal with the day-to-day things. And then one day I found him dead.'

'What? But I saw him . . .'

'You remember that photograph you found today? It was about a week after that was taken, I think. Imogen had a new friend and I'd taken her round there for a birthday tea. I was supposed to stay too but I was bored of being with children so I went home. It was so quiet, I thought Dad was out. Then I went into the bathroom and found him lying on the floor between the toilet and the bath. His lips were blue and there was an empty bottle of vodka beside him.'

'Nina.' His arm goes around me.

'I didn't know what to do, but we'd had first aid at my old school, so I hit him as hard as I could on the chest. Trying to do CPR, I think. Anyway, it did something, because he was immediately sick and started breathing again. He threw up a whole load of pills. I don't know what they were; actually, when I think about it now, he must've just swallowed whatever we had in our medicine cabinet. Probably it was all indigestion remedies.'

'What did you do?'

'I cleaned him up and got him into bed. He kept on apologising. I was going to call an ambulance, but he wouldn't let me and I didn't really want to; it was like if other people knew, it would all be too real, if that makes sense? I rang Immy's friend and arranged for her to stay the night there, and I spent the night sitting beside my father's bed making sure he kept on breathing.'

'You were a kid.'

'Yeah. And we never, ever talked about it again.' The memories, though, are still clear, playing themselves out in the darkness in front of my eyes. But less powerful, out here in the open. How'd that happen?

'I was terrified, but more than that, I was ashamed. That's not right, is it? That I should blame my own father for being weak?'

'You were a kid,' Viktor says again.

'I hated him for it. I couldn't believe he would be so selfish as to try to leave us like that. I never wanted to turn my back on him for a second in case he tried it again. I knew from that moment that I was going to have to be responsible for everything, for ever. And I hated him for that, too.'

'Do you still hate him now?'

I bite my lip. 'I never really hated him. I loved him. I still love him. But I've never wanted to be like him.'

The grass is damp and it's getting cold, but Viktor's arm squeezes a little tighter around me and keeps me warm. I can feel him breathing.

'Did Arval know?' I ask him.

'I don't know. He said his brother had had a hard time, but he didn't go into details.'

'I've been angry at him, too, for running off after bats when he could have helped us. But it's entirely possible he never knew. We probably did too good a job of hiding it. Imogen still doesn't know, I don't think. Do you have any more chocolate?'

'No.'

'Damn. Anyway, I never told anybody else this before.'

'Why are you telling me?'

Good question. I decide to go for the literal answer, rather than try to figure out my reasons.

'Because you asked me why I'm afraid of failure, and that's why. Failure means that everything falls apart.'

'But you held it together.'

'You're disappointing me, Viktor. You're supposed to tell me I'm a melodramatic bimbo who needs to get a grip.'

'I think you're got a grip already, Nina. Seems to me you're a melodramatic bimbo who needs to let go.'

But he says it with a smile in his voice.

'Well, if you're going to give me advice, I'll give you some right back. I think you should drop the guilt about not being able to love Fliss enough. You can't choose who you fall in love with. Believe me, I tried, and look where that got me. Dumped and broke.'

'I'll keep that in mind.'

'See that you do.'

'Thank you for trusting me with your secret.'

'That's okay.'

We fall silent. Another bat flutters by and I look up automatically. I can see stars. I never see stars in London. Like I never thought I'd tell anyone about my dad's suicide attempt. But now that I have, the shame isn't as crushing as I thought it would be. Maybe it's the photograph I saw earlier, the concrete proof of how much has changed. Maybe it's just the act of saying it out loud. I feel lighter. It doesn't feel like such a big deal any more.

Viktor is also looking up at the stars. He murmurs something. I can barely hear it, but it sounds like 'What's the worst that could happen?'

'We could crash down into a century-old grave and land in the lap of a corpse,' I answer straight away.

I feel rather than hear his small laugh. 'No,' he says, 'I meant, what's the worst that could happen if I did this again.'

He puts his hand under my chin and tilts it towards him. Then he bends his head and kisses me.

I'm surprised. But not all that surprised. My body curls itself up towards his as if I've been waiting for this very thing to happen again. I thread my fingers in his hair.

We start out much gentler than last time. But soon I feel his tongue softly nudging at my mouth and I open for him. He tastes of chocolate and he makes a sound deep in his throat that sends a bolt of lust through me.

And then it's all bets off: I want more than anything to know what's the worst that can happen. I pull him downward, closer as I sink backwards; he presses me into the earth with his body on top of mine, the hard length of him against me, hot even through all our clothes, his heart hammering against my breast and our mouths devouring each other.

His chin and jaw are close-shaven but still faintly rough, and he's big and warm all over, wonderfully, overwhelmingly male. I slip my hands inside his cloak-coat, underneath his jumper, to touch his stomach. His skin is smooth and firm and there's a line of hair, enough to be satisfying.

That groan again. He sounds like a man on the edge of control, and that's sweeping away my own control, too. He palms my breast through the jumper and takes a handful of my hair to tilt my head back so he can kiss my neck.

He is so intensely sexy. How'd I miss this? I gasp as his mouth reaches my ear and I wrap my legs around him. 'Nina,' he says, pulling his head away slightly, a movement that only serves to press his torso harder against mine from chest to crotch. 'We're in a cemetery.'

'I don't care.' I kiss his cheekbone. I can't see him in the dark, aside from an outline and the gleam of his eyes. But I can feel all of him. He doesn't feel like he cares, either.

'We can't do this here.' His voice is breathless.

'I don't think the people beneath us will mind.'

He kisses my lips once again, lightly. 'I will. I don't want our first time to be fumbled in the dark and the cold without a condom.'

*Our first time*. The confidence that implies, that we will be having sex with each other, tonight and more than once, should probably make me want to hit him. It makes me want to melt.

'And,' he adds, 'I don't want you turning to me halfway through and asking me if I *vant to suck your blood*.'

'I think I've got over that,' I say, but I unwrap my legs from around him and we both sit up. I push back my hair, which seems to have got very messed up.

'Let's pack up the stuff and go home.'

'Are you done with the bats for the night?'

'I'm done with everything except for you.'

That melty feeling again. He produces a torch from his bag and puts it on the ground so we can see enough to pick up his equipment.

'You're very sure of yourself,' I say, giving him his bat detector.

'Right up until the minute you kissed me back, I was convinced you were going to slap me.'

I can't see if he's looking towards my face, or smiling at me, but I know he is.

We don't say anything else as we pack up and cross the circle to the ladder. Viktor goes down first and holds the torch for me so that I can see, then he collapses the ladder and carries it while I hold his bag. The path between the crypts has become a dark tunnel, enclosed by looming stately stone. Here, level with the graves, our footsteps sound loud and close. We could be anywhere: ancient Egypt, silent Rome, or here in this cemetery a century ago when the bodies were fresh.

He doesn't ask me if I'm frightened this time, though this place in the dark is straight out of a horror novel. Our visibility is a single yellow circle ahead of us, isolating details of the path and the crypts. The doorways are surrounded by chunky square pillars that are wider at the bottom than the top, so that they appear vast and stately.

But I'm not thinking about any of this. I'm thinking about my lips burning and my body humming. I'm thinking about how strange and unpredictable sexual attraction can be. I'm thinking about getting more of Viktor's kisses.

I'm feeling alive.

He takes my hand and tucks it under his arm as we reach the corridor leading out, which is even darker than inside the circle. The air is musty. When we emerge through the arch, there's a sudden movement in the circle of torchlight. A bushy tail vanishes into the undergrowth at the side of the path. Up ahead, I catch a glimpse of reflective eyes. I see a cracked urn and the wing of an angel, and then we're going down the stairs out of the cemetery into the courtyard.

'I'll return the ladder,' Viktor says, quietly enough to not break the spell, and I stand under the arches, waiting, counting time by the beating of my heart.

It's not until we step out on to Swain's Lane and a car drives past, far too fast, thumping bass through its windows, that I remember we're in the real world.

We start up the hill, going by road this time instead of cutting through the park. It's quite a climb. The last time I came up here I was thinking about Juan and whether I'd used him. And now I'm side by side with a virtual stranger who seems to know all my secrets and with whom I'm planning on having sex.

The idea suddenly seems totally foolish. Too fast, too embarrassing. My last sexual relationship, to be honest here, was a bit of a mess. And it wasn't even as if Juan wasn't fanciable, or that I didn't have flashes of desire for him. But making love to him was a little like holding my nose and plunging into the pool so quickly I wouldn't have time to worry about how cold it was. And now here I am, on a long, deliberate walk through Highgate with someone else, someone I never even noticed as sexy until about a week ago. On the contrary, someone I seriously considered as being undead.

When we pass under a street light, I glance at Viktor. He let go of my hand back in the cemetery when he put away the ladder, and he hasn't taken it again. He's looking ahead, up the hill, and there's a faint frown between his brows. Maybe all that closeness was in my imagination. Maybe he's regretting this. I remember what he said before he kissed me: *What's the worst that can happen?*

He's not exactly going into this with romantic optimism. And we're not exactly being swept away by the moment any more, either.

We pass the green, go downhill and head for our street. I think about how I can get out of this before it becomes a disaster. I could crack a joke, or say something to annoy him. Either one of them should be easy enough, but my tongue seems stuck to the roof of my mouth.

He unlocks the door and holds it open for me, and we walk, side by side, past the dusty urns and up the stairs. We reach the first-floor landing and this is my chance. I could say good night and thank him. This is all so sudden, he couldn't blame me for changing my mind.

But my lips are still tingling from his kiss and I can feel him pressing me into the vast circle of grass. The fluttering and the warmth and the stars. I keep my mouth shut and I walk up with him, past my door and to his. He opens it and flicks on a light. I step in, and it feels as if I've come much further than a single flight of stairs.

I have to blink. The lights are very bright, and this wasn't what I was expecting. The outside of the Temple of Gloom looks distinctly medieval; Evangeline and Michael's flat is pure Victorian; Arval's furnishings haven't changed since the seventies. But the furniture here in Viktor's flat is spare and modern enough to make the soaring ceilings and the huge pointed windows and the unfinished floors look as if they were built yesterday. It's like going in a time machine in reverse from past to present. There's a black leather couch and a long workbench with a new computer on it. A small but decent stereo system and several shelves of CDs. Red and orange rugs scatter the floor.

'Welcome to my lair,' Viktor says. We both stand there, near the door, not touching. He doesn't make a move towards me, but he doesn't make a move away either. We just look at each other. It would be hard to believe that not long ago we were kissing passionately under an ancient tree, if I didn't remember it so vividly, and if he didn't have several cedar needles in his hair.

'I have to warn you about something,' I say.

'I know. You're still in love with that unattainable man.'

'I always will be.'

He nods. 'So if you have sex with me, it will just be sex.'

'Which is fair enough, because you don't really like me anyway.'

His cheek creases with a suppressed smile. 'Good thing you're so perceptive about people. I might have missed that otherwise.'

He doesn't move, though.

'So, um, are we going to . . . ?' I ask. I'd sort of expected him to grab me and start snogging by now.

'That's up to you. Do you want to?'

Saying yes seems too strange, given what I've just admitted about Edmund. Instead I step forward, put my arms around his neck, and stretch up to kiss him. He meets me halfway. It's a long one, a slow one, a very sexy one.

'Do you?' he asks me, in a low voice, when we're done. His eyes are half closed, his mouth near to mine. I've got my hands in his hair and his are spanning my hips. He's making me dizzy.

'Yes,' I whisper.

And then I find out how this man can kiss when he really wants to kiss. I hang on to him and my bones turn to jelly and the two of us begin to walk, locked together, across the flat to the bedroom, me backwards, our knees colliding and our feet narrowly missing each other. But I don't care if it's awkward. His mouth feels so fantastic and his hands on me feel even better. I push off his coat and it falls behind him somewhere, and I immediately start pulling up his jumper. By the time we get to his bedroom door he's bare-chested and I'm running my hands all over his skin. I will admit I've peeked at the photo of him in the toga, but in real life he's much better. He's lean, but his shoulders are strong. I press my lips to his collarbone and the hollow of his shoulder and breathe in his woody scent.

He pulls his jumper up over my head and starts to work on the drawstring of the trousers he's lent me. 'I should be much better at this,' he mutters, and I reluctantly stop touching him to help him out. But our hands, working together, are just as exciting as any bare flesh. The minute we solve the knot, the trousers drop around my ankles. I stand on one leg, trying to reach my bootlaces.

'Here.' Viktor picks me up and puts me on his bed. It's a double, low to the floor, with a white duvet, and it's rumpled and unmade. This slovenliness should be a turn-off, but actually it's gloriously sexy, and as he bends to tackle my boots, I turn my head to the side and sniff the pillow, imagining him curled up warm and cosy here, lost in dreams. Imagining me tucked up under his arm.

He chucks my boots in the corner and I hear his follow them. Then he strips me of his trousers and Arval's socks, and his big, warm hands stroke their way up my legs. I lie back on the pillow, enjoying the sensation and watching his dark head coming upwards. 'I lied,' he said.

'Mmm?'

'I absolutely adore your legs, even if they are up to your armpits.' He's reached my knickers now. They are plain white cotton, though thankfully not dingy. He kisses me through them, and I have to close my eyes and groan. I feel him taking off my jumper, and I wiggle enough to help him do it, in the process brushing my naked belly against as much of him as I can. He has much less trouble with my bra than with my drawstring and I take advantage of the time to get rid of my knickers too, and soon I am naked, with his hands and mouth on my breasts, which is . . . oh dear God, that's so good.

'Trousers,' I gasp. Viktor makes an enquiring sound, though no more than that because his mouth is busy. 'Take your trousers off,' I clarify, reaching down for them and popping the top button.

He does. Then he lies down next to me, his body touching mine from head to toe, arms and legs twined around each other, and now it's all instinct and desire and pleasure. I could touch and explore for ages but I'm very glad when, at the perfect moment, Viktor reaches into his bedside cabinet and comes out with a condom. I watch him putting it on, biting my lip with wanting, amazed by the sure-handed way a man touches his own body, and then we're reaching for each other.

I watch his face as I pull him inside me. He has half a gentle smile and he looks as surprised as I am. Then we're kissing again, kissing the whole time, holding on to each other as hard as we can.

It takes me some time to catch my breath afterwards. Viktor rolls us both up in his duvet, skin to skin. I trace his face with one of my fingers. The straight dark brows, soft and glossy, the high cheekbones, the strong jaw, the wide mouth relaxed and kissing my fingertip. Under the duvet he lazily strokes my side.

'Where did this come from?' I say, running my finger down his nose.

'The nose? My father's family are Russian.'

'No, I meant this.' I tighten my leg around him, which brings us more intimately close. 'You and me, in bed together.'

'Oh. I . . .' I wouldn't think it possible, with the way we've been touching, but Viktor blushes. 'I've been attracted to you for a long time.'

'Really? Since when?'

He looks sheepish, which should be hard for someone with a face like his, but he manages it. 'Pretty much from when I first saw you.'

'You hid that well.'

'I didn't want to like you. You seemed to hate everything I care about. And you were acting totally out of your mind.'

'Though we've already established that you're crazy about crazy girls.'

'Don't want to be. And in your case, I think it was the legs anyway.' He wraps mine tighter around his hips, for emphasis. 'And your eyes. And you're very sexy when you curl your lip in scorn. I had to argue with you in self-defence.'

I try to take this in. All this time he's been rude to me because he's been struggling against his raw sexual urges. It would be flattering, if he hadn't been struggling because he thought I was both insensitive and insane.

'Wow.'

He pushes back my hair, which has become pretty tangled in the melee. 'What about you? Were you arguing with me to stop yourself from ripping my clothes off too?'

'No. I honestly did think you were some horrible Gothic creature. But I've been pretty deluded. About lots of things.'

'Are you deluded now?'

'That's what I'm trying to figure out. I'm enjoying it, if I am.'

'How much are you enjoying it?' He strokes my bottom, cups it in his hands, and I feel his cock hardening against my thigh. Good recovery time. I like that in a man.

'Definitely enough to use up some more of those condoms,' I say, and reach downwards.

In the morning, I wake up before Viktor. I'm in his arms, snuggled up close to him, and sunshine streams through the high windows into the bedroom. It smells of sleep and sex and cedar. His face is relaxed, his hair falling forward. Somewhere along the line I've absorbed his features in my memory: smiling, scowling, watching, biting his lip in pleasure. Last night, when he came, he looked straight in my eyes as he shuddered into me, as if he were giving me his orgasm.

He lets out a muted snore, and I smile and carefully creep out from his embrace. I sit on the edge of the bed and stretch. My muscles are stiff, but my body is refreshed. I find my knickers and bra on the floor and put them on, followed by my grey jumper, which is long enough to cover me to mid-thigh anyway. The walls in the bedroom, like the main room, are painted white, and they soar all the way to the wooden vaulting of the roof. I pull the heavy drapes closed, so the sun won't disturb Viktor, and the room subsides into twilight.

The wooden floor is rough against my feet, but not cold, and the scattered rugs are soft. I wander into the main room, where the windows look out on the blue autumn sky and the chimneys of the neighbouring houses. Fliss was right: there are some very good views of gargoyles. But as there's so little furniture and clutter, the gargoyles look almost stylish. In a weird, ghoulish way, of course.

People's living spaces should tell you so much about them. I pause just inside the room, rubbing my bare foot up and down my bare leg.

I could walk around Viktor's flat, look at the spines of his books and the music next to his stereo. But do I want to? I know some things about him, but there's much much more I don't know. It's an enormous blank space right now and it would be an investment of time and feeling to fill it. I don't know if I'm up to it.

For example, what if I went over to the other side of the room and saw that he had the same CDs I did? Would we then have to have a long conversation about, say, Rush and how much we loved or didn't love *2112* and what was the best song off the Greatest Hits CD? Or what if, as is more likely, he doesn't have any of the same CDs at all, and we have to argue about whether our favourite bands are any good or not?

This might seem like a little thing, and it is. But it's the millions of little things like this that are involved in getting to know someone, every one of them an opportunity for me to worry about him looking down at me for what I like, or me being disappointed with him for what he likes. I'm not ready for any disappointment. Or hard work. It's hard enough work getting to like myself again.

I hover there, rubbing my foot on my leg, torn between the big unknown in front of me and the warm, sexy bed behind me. Because no matter what Viktor and I say about it being only sex for sex's sake, if I stay much longer, it's going to start being new conversations and learning and worry.

But the sex for sex's sake was so good that I can't quite bear to go just yet.

I'll have a cup of tea. That won't teach me too much to bear, and if Viktor hasn't woken up by the time I've finished, then at least it looks as if I waited around for a bit to be polite. There isn't a separate kitchen, it's built into a cranny in the wall of the main room, and though it's also modern, it's fairly basic. I fill up the kettle, find the tea bags and bend down to look in the refrigerator for milk. There's a bottle in the door, but when I pick it up, it has only a thin film of white on the bottom.

Hands clasp my waist and I jump. 'Boo,' says Viktor, and I turn around into his embrace. He's got on a red dressing gown, his hair is messy and he's warm from sleep. I didn't think he'd have a red dressing gown.

'Why do you put an empty milk bottle back in the fridge?'

'Mm. I forgot what it's like having a woman around. I've been up for thirty seconds and you're nagging me.'

He smells so sexy. We're having one of these new

conversations already. 'I just don't understand what it is about men and milk bottles.'

'I come from a long line of scientists. It's an experiment.' He kisses my cheek and then my neck, breathing me in. I step on to his feet, so that I'm standing with my naked skin on his. This still doesn't bring me up to his height, but it means he can kiss my neck more easily.

'You've got huge feet,' I say.

'You're one to talk.' He steps backwards with my feet on his, and then forwards again. I hang on to his arms and wiggle my toes. Back and forth, moving together, barely balanced. I wonder if our footsteps are audible downstairs in the monk's-cell bedroom.

'I thought you'd be long gone by now,' he says.

Yes, because when you have sex for sex's sake, you disappear before the first bit of morning light. I'm obviously not very good at this. I loosen my hold on his arms. 'Um . . .'

'It's nearly half eight, and I thought you started at Michael's at seven.'

'Oh! Yes, I do.' I've forgotten all about it. I step off his feet, on to the floor, which feels cold now, and head straight for the door. 'I'll see you . . .'

'Hold on, I'll come with you.' I must look a bit panicked by this, because he adds, 'To have breakfast at the café. I'm out of milk, remember? And we skipped supper.'

'Oh, sure. I'll, uh, meet you at the front door after I'm dressed.' I open his door.

'Nina?'

I pause.

'I'm not going to make any demands on you. I heard what you told me last night before we went to bed together. I honestly want breakfast.' He smiles, digging those lines in his cheeks that make it look like he smiles a lot. 'Though I'll go to bed with you again whenever you like.'

I smile back. Suddenly I sort of want to know if he has any Rush CDs. 'I'll meet you in five.'

Downstairs in the bathroom I have a quick wash and look at myself in the mirror. My cheeks are flushed and my eyes sparkle with the afterglow of good sex. I pull on a dress with more than a little red in it and take a few minutes to put on some make-up and brush out my hair. When I go out on to the landing, Viktor's waiting for me, holding my boots and wearing a blue jumper and a green scarf. Neither one of us says anything as I put on my boots, and we go down the stairs together and out the front door.

It's a glorious autumn day, one of those days you see in films about glorious autumn days where glorious things happen. Viktor picks up an orange leaf from the pavement and gives it to me. I tuck it behind my ear like a flower. The colour reminds me of Evangeline's auburn wig.

'I have a bone to pick with you,' Viktor says.

'Uh oh.'

'You're letting Evangeline smoke out of your window.'

'I wouldn't say I'm letting her. She seems to take it as her birthright. Besides, Arval always let her.'

'Not for the last three years he didn't. She's taking you for a mug. And she shouldn't be smoking in her state.'

I frown. 'How ill is Evangeline?'

'She's in remission, hopefully for good, but the chemotherapy took a lot out of her.' He glances at me. 'She didn't tell you, did she?'

'Michael did.'

'I worry about them. I'd never tell them, though. After the other night when Michael fell out of bed, I've made sure my mobile is always with me. I think they should consider a lift in the bedroom, or getting a lower bed. But they're the two most stubborn people I know.'

'They're perfect for each other.'

He doesn't answer, and I realise I've strayed into talking about relationships. I shut my mouth.

'Where the hell have you been?' Michael thunders at me as soon as we walk into the café. The tables are nearly all full and he's pouring water from the urn, making tea. I quickly take his place.

'Sorry, Michael, the time got away from me.'

'I see you brought in another hungry mouth to feed, too. Get to making tea, you useless girl, and I'll start on the bacon butties.'

He wheels away and I smile. Being insulted by Michael is like a badge of honour. I glance up and see that Viktor has joined Evangeline, who is sitting at her usual corner table under the biggest monster spider plant, sipping tea and reading a doorstopper of a paperback novel.

I wonder how long it will take until Evangeline and Michael figure out what's happened between me and Viktor. They're bound to, eventually. To my surprise, the idea doesn't bother me that much. They know everything else about me anyway.

I hum under the chatter filling the café and make tea, feeling the steam from the urn curling the ends of my hair. What's going to happen tonight? Will I go and watch bats again with Viktor? Or should I just give him the key to the flat, so that when he's finished with his work for the night he can sneak in and join me in bed? I run through an inventory of my underwear; thank God I didn't get rid of any lingerie before I went to Spain. In fact, I added to my collection a great deal. Maybe red lace . . . maybe black silk . . . maybe nothing . . .

'Hello, Nina.'

The voice comes from a million miles and a million years away, and my heart flips over before I even consciously realise who it is. My hands still, holding doilies, and I lift my eyes to see a golden god, wearing a spotless woollen jacket and a Burberry scarf.

'I'm rather surprised to see you,' Edmund says.

## 35

'Edmund?'

It comes out as halfway between a gasp and a squeak. I drop the doilies and take a step back, which upsets a small tower of metal teapots. They hit the linoleum floor with a clatter.

'What are you doing here?'

'I could ask you the same thing,' he says. His voice is exactly as I remember it, cultured and with that note of authority that rings so perfectly across a busy kitchen. I can hear it particularly well because the café seems to have gone completely silent.

'I . . . I'm helping out a friend.'

'And I came to look for you. Gretchen said she saw you here.'

'*You* came to look for . . .'

'And I'm extremely glad I found you. You look beautiful, Nina.'

I touch my face, which is burning from his gaze. 'Why did you . . . ?'

'Do you think we could go somewhere more private?' He makes a small gesture to the rest of the café and I look around in some confusion. Sure enough, everyone is watching us. My eyes focus on Viktor. The monster spider plant casts a spiky shadow across his eyes.

'Nina?' Edmund prompts me.

'Oh. Yeah. I . . . uh . . . Michael?' I turn, expecting to find him in the kitchen, but he's right there behind me in the doorway.

'You go ahead, I can handle things here,' he says.

'Right, I . . . okay.'

I come out from behind the counter. Edmund watches me. I notice him looking down at my feet, in their second-hand boots. My mouth is dry and my head is spinning and I can't catch my breath. He opens the door for me and puts his hand under my elbow to guide me out.

He hasn't changed a single hair since the last time I saw him. The sunlight outside makes his eyes an even brighter blue. 'I live . . . I'm staying just round the corner,' I tell him, and he puts his arm around my shoulders as we walk.

'It's wonderful to see you,' he says. 'I've missed you.'

The weight of his arm, his face close to mine, his familiar scent of spices. 'I've missed you too,' I say, hoping he won't realise what a massive understatement that is.

'I was hoping you'd say that.'

I swallow. 'Uh, here we are.'

Edmund gazes up at the Temple of Gloom. At least with the advancing autumn, the dead tree in front isn't so obvious. I unlock the door and we step in. As we cross the foyer, I can't help but see the place as Edmund must be seeing it. The passing days and events have made me used to the dusty urns, the creeping staircase, the swaying cobwebs, but Edmund is so perfect, so stylish and glossy that all the dinginess seems even worse. We go up the stairs in silence and I feel him looking around.

'This is . . . different,' he says.

'That's one way of describing it.' I let him into the flat. 'Is it yours?'

'No, it belongs to my dead uncle.'

'Oh, that's a relief.' He takes off his coat and scarf and tosses them on an armchair, revealing a spotless pale shirt. 'Is Juan here with you?'

'No.'

'That's also a relief.' He smiles, and my heart thumps.

'Would you like a cup of tea?'

'No time, I've got to get back to Jett before they start prep.' He sits down on the couch, which immediately appears horrendously out of date. I hover, until he beckons to me to sit next to him. So I do.

'Why are you here?' I ask.

'I told you, I came looking for you. I could hardly believe it when Gretchen said you were making tea in a Highgate greasy spoon.'

'But why did you come looking for me?'

'You've got a bit of something dead behind your ear.' He removes the leaf from my hair and tosses it on the coffee table, where it lands with a brittle whisper. Then he takes both my hands in his.

'I need you, Nina,' he says. 'And I think you need me too.'

'You . . . what do you mean?

'When I heard you were in London, I made some telephone calls.' He lowers his voice. 'I know you had to sell El Flor Anaranjado.'

'You do?' Oh God. Panic curls in my chest.

'And I heard a rumour that Juan ran off on you, too. Is that true?'

'Y . . . yes.'

'My poor Nina.' Edmund pulls me towards him and takes me in his arms. 'Juan was a fool,' he murmurs into my hair. 'No, I was the fool for letting you go.'

I can't think or breathe or move. 'So you're offering me my job back?'

He pulls away slightly so that he can look into my face. So close, he's dazzling: faultless skin, brilliant eyes, shining teeth. 'Nothing's been the same since you left. Oh, it's ticked over, of course, and Jennifer is fine. But she doesn't have your energy, your panache, your devotion. Your love.' His voice lowers to a thrilling timbre.

'I loved . . . that job.'

'You once said you loved me too.'

I sit up straighter, away from him. 'Edmund, we've been through this. The situation with Juan doesn't change anything. I might have some feelings for you, but you're married. I won't break up any marriage, and certainly not one as perfect as yours and Caroline's.'

'Caroline and I split up.'

My breath goes completely.

'You say we had the perfect marriage. It may have looked that way from the outside. But we've been drifting apart for years. Caroline is a wonderful person and I'll always love her, but she doesn't share my dreams. Not like you do.'

'You . . . you're not married any more?'

'We're not divorced yet; these things take some time. But we're finished, Nina. Absolutely. She moved out nearly a month ago.'

Edmund Jett has been single for nearly a month? How did I not know this? All this time, while I was losing everything in Spain, while I was having a breakdown in Highgate, why didn't some primal part of me sense the change in the air, the fundamental shift in reality?

'In some ways you helped me see what was going wrong,' he adds. 'You pointed out to me that I was worried about us having children, and when I thought about it, you were right. I couldn't have a family with Caroline, not when my heart wasn't in the relationship.'

'Oh no. I didn't mean to split you up, Edmund.'

'Nina, Nina, you didn't split us up. We'd been heading that way for some time. And it wasn't only babies that were the issue. I couldn't feel the way I should about Caroline, not with the way I feel about you.'

'You . . .'

He pulls me to him again, so that my face is crushed against his chest and I feel his words travelling through my entire body. 'I want you, Nina. I want you to be with me. I love you.'

He kisses me. I am so stunned I can't move.

*This is it*, I think. *This is my first real kiss with the man I love, the man who is now mine. My first real kiss in my real new life, where I have everything I ever wanted.*

It's over rather soon, and I stare at Edmund, breathless.

'So you'll come back with me?' He smiles, that smile of pure confident sexiness.

'When . . . ?'

'No time like the present, is there? I'm sure your friends in the café will understand that you've your own life to live now. Besides, I'd think you'd be desperate to get out of there. And this place, too.'

'I'll have to pack.'

'Of course. You can take a cab to Jett once you've finished, and I'll see you there.' He kisses me again, and stands. 'And Nina, can I just quickly ask about your shoes and your jumper?'

'Oh.' I look down at my boots. 'These are what I wear to the café. And the jumper – I got rid of all my winter clothes when I went to Spain and this is the only warm thing I have.'

'Well, that's easy to take care of, and fun besides. Here.' He takes out his wallet and hands me a wodge of cash, all twenties and fifties. 'That should help you with an outfit for tonight, at least.'

'I . . . I don't believe this.'

Edmund grins. 'I know. It's like a fairy tale, isn't it? And I quite like being Prince Charming.' He kisses me swiftly on the cheek and then picks up his coat and scarf. 'Don't be late, my love.'

36

I leave my bags outside my door and go up to knock at
Viktor's flat. The sound is hollow, and I wait and wait
but he doesn't answer. Maybe he's still in the café. Or
maybe he's pretending not to hear.

I snort. If Viktor wants to avoid me, fine, he can avoid
me. It's not like I didn't tell him how I felt. Right?

Right.

I march downstairs, pick up my stuff, and go down to
knock on Evangeline's door. There's no answer there
either, which does make me think they're still at the café.
I should give in my notice there, anyway, too. And if
they're not there, I'll just leave a note or something with
Michael.

Like Juan's note. *Forgive me*, querida. *I hope that one
day perhaps you will understand that when your love so
strong and true returns at last, you will be powerless to
resist.* Except less cheesy and in better English, of
course. And I'm not running off, and there's nothing to
forgive me for. I'm just going back to where I belong.

'Bye bye, Temple of Gloom,' I say, and it echoes
around in the usual way. Just imagine: in the time it takes
a taxi to get to Chelsea, I'll no longer live in a morose
dump of a castle. I'll be in the centre of things again, with
a lot fewer cobwebs.

I slip out the front door and it closes behind me with

a final bang, which would probably sound more important and life-changing if I didn't simultaneously run straight into Viktor's chest. The wool of his jumper is soft and his body is hard and I step back quickly, rubbing my nose, which has bumped against his collarbone.

'Leaving?' he says.

'Um . . . yes. I tried knocking on your door.'

'Who was that?' Evangeline is standing next to Viktor, practically on her tiptoes. 'That divine man in the café, darling. Was that your lost scandalous love?'

'Edmund,' Viktor says.

'Yes. Edmund Jett, the chef and owner of Jett in Chelsea. He's offered me my job back.'

'He's offered you more than your job, I'm guessing.'

I tilt my chin up. 'He's split up with his wife.'

'Oh! Goodness! What interesting times. So it's straight off to the arms of your lover, how romantic!'

I smile at Evangeline, strictly avoiding looking at last night's lover and his arms. 'Yes, I think we're going to try to make a go of it.'

'How thrilling. I shall miss you dreadfully, though, Nina. It won't be the same here without you.'

The daylight makes Evangeline's eyes twinkle, but it also makes her skin look papery and her black wig look false. I drop my bags and give her a hug. She is bony and frail and the closest thing I have had to a mother for a long time.

I squeeze my eyes tight shut and hold her and let her hold me. 'I'll be back,' I promise her. 'I'll visit. And you can use Arval's flat whenever you want to smoke a cigarette.'

'Oh, there's no point if there's nobody to talk to. Maybe I'll give up.' She pats my back and gives me an extra squeeze, then we let each other go. I wipe my eyes.

'I really will visit. Soon.'

'Of course you will, darling.'

I hear Viktor grunt. I've never known anybody to pack so much weight of scorn, doubt and cynicism into one small non-verbal sound.

I turn to him. 'Don't be like that. I told you about this beforehand, remember? I didn't promise you anything.'

'Do I look surprised?'

He doesn't. He looks tall and forbidding and granite-faced.

'Well,' I say, 'I've got to go. It was . . . nice, Viktor.' I'd like to say more, or hug him, or even kiss him, but I can't. Not here, in the sunlight, in front of the Temple of Gloom, in front of Evangeline and the gargoyles. I hold out my hand to him, this man I've instinctively trusted, in whose arms I've slept. 'Thank you,' I say.

He shakes my hand. Then he opens the front door and goes inside. This time, the boom does sound final.

'Michael says don't worry about the café, he'll get one of the local girls to come in and help,' Evangeline says.

'Oh.' Amazing how quickly things can go back to normal, as if I've never been here. It's reassuring, really. It means I'll adjust very quickly to being back at home in Chelsea. 'I'll be on my way, then,' I say, and kissing Evangeline on the cheek, I pick up my bags and head for the high street to hail a cab.

I go back to Jett via Selfridges, where I get myself some suitable clothes and spend some time in the ladies' changing and doing my make-up and hair. When my cab pulls up in front of the restaurant, I'm as flawless as I can make myself and my stomach is jumping around with nerves. Edmund, in his chef's whites, meets me at the plate-glass door.

'You look wonderful,' he says, kissing me on the mouth and guiding me through the dining room with his hand in the small of my back. 'Welcome back. It's not changed too much, has it?'

You can't change perfection. I look around at the linen, the crystal, the silver, the beautiful lines of the tables and chairs, the tasteful lighting and the expensive wallpaper. The waiting staff are scurrying around, making adjustments. Jennifer, my replacement, is hovering by the kitchen door. She's wearing a rather beautiful suit and very high-heeled shoes and she goes straight to Edmund when we hove into sight.

'Edmund, the people from Rombauers' have—' She stops. 'Nina?'

'Hi, Jennifer.'

'What are . . . are you back on a visit?'

I look at Edmund, confused. 'Haven't you told her?'

'Told her what, my love?'

'That . . .' I lower my voice to a whisper. 'That you're giving me my job back.'

'I'm not giving you your job back.'

'But . . .'

Edmund takes me slightly aside, under the fronds of a statuesque fern. 'Nina, sweetheart, I don't want you back as my PA, I want you back for you. You don't need to work for me.'

'But I don't have any money.'

He bursts into laughter. 'You've seen my tax returns. I make more than enough for both of us. Besides, it's a full-time job just being the love of my life.'

*The love of my life*. I can't argue with that.

'Now, let's go back to the house. Jennifer, I'll be back during the dinner service. Can you hold all messages till then and have everything set up for the conference call with Japan? I'm absolutely not to be disturbed.' He winks at me, and with his hand in the small of my back again ushers me to the front of the restaurant, where he picks up my bags.

A cab comes along right away, and Edmund flags it down and hands me into the back seat. 'Rombauers' haven't stopped ringing for the past week,' he tells me, settling in beside me. 'They've somehow decided that it's a good idea to bypass my agent and appeal directly to me for sponsorship.'

I nod and listen, struggling to remember who Rombauers' are. The name rings a bell, surely it's someone I've dealt with before as Edmund's PA, but the facts have disappeared from my memory. Once upon a time I used to know every little detail of Edmund's professional life; I used to live and breathe his appointments, his successes, his media image, and schedule his every working day down to the last minute.

I'm sure that will come back soon. Even if I'm not his

PA any more, I'm going to be even more intimately involved in his life. I don't stop listening to Edmund, but I look at his knee so close to mine. I think about all the times we rode in cabs together and I wasn't supposed to touch him. All the frustration and longing.

I lightly rest my hand on his knee. He covers it with his.

'Here we are,' he says. I'm surprised to see we're already at his house, though it's hardly any distance from the restaurant. I guess it's because I'm so used to walking now. He helps me out and pays the driver, and carrying my bags, leads me up the herb-lined walk to the front door, gleaming with new paint and polished brass.

No sooner are we through the door and in the hallway than Edmund drops my bags and turns to me. 'Now, my beautiful girl, I've got you to myself at last.'

He takes my face in his hands and kisses me. It is lovely, unhurried and romantic, just as I always dreamed being kissed by Edmund Jett would be. I close my eyes and throw myself into the moment. *It's a dream come true,* I tell myself.

It's weird. I open my eyes again and look at a close-up of his golden hair and the side of his face. Edmund stops kissing me and looks into my eyes, still holding my face in his hands. 'What's wrong?'

'Nothing. Nothing's wrong. It's just . . . this is a little hard to get used to, that's all.'

'Come upstairs. I promise you'll get used to it very quickly.' He steps backwards towards the wide, graceful staircase, catching my hand and tugging at it.

I stop, my heels sliding slightly on the tiled floor. 'No.'

Edmund frowns. 'There is something wrong. What is it?'

'This is Caroline's house, Edmund. I can't . . . make love with you here, in her bed.'

'I was planning on going to the guest room.'

'That's nearly as bad. I'd feel like a guest.'

'Well, there are four bedrooms upstairs, two bathrooms, and the entire ground floor to choose from. What do you prefer?'

He's speaking very patiently, and I shift from foot to foot, feeling foolish. 'It's not just the rooms, it's this whole house. I've only ever been here when Caroline was here too. It's hard enough to adjust to the idea of you being single. I don't think I can do it here.'

He kisses me gently on the forehead. 'Of course, Nina, I'm being insensitive. This is all new to me too.' I watch him thinking. 'What about the flat above Jett?'

'That might be better.'

'Right then!' He picks up my bags again. 'Back we go.'

In another cab, Edmund is no longer talking about work. Instead he is holding me close to him, stroking up my arm, touching my hair. It's very difficult to believe that in less than ten minutes we will be making love for the first time. None of it feels real. Especially as this morning, I was naked with another man.

I push the thought of Viktor away and cuddle up closer to Edmund.

The cab pulls up to the rear entrance of Jett, and Edmund and I tiptoe up the back stairs, careful not to let anyone see we're here again. He unlocks the door to the flat, drops my bags, and immediately sweeps me up into his arms and carries me through the living room into the only bedroom.

The eaves are low in this flat, so I have to duck my head while he's carrying me. He puts me down on the double bed, lies down beside me, and reaches for me. 'Oh my darling,' he murmurs.

'Wait a minute,' I say. He stops, his fingers a mere inch from the top button of my blouse.

'What is it now, my love?'

'This bed looks familiar.'

He looks up at the headboard. 'We brought it here when we redecorated the house.'

'It's from your bedroom?'

He doesn't have to answer. I sit up. 'I'm sorry, Edmund.'

He sits up too. 'What about the couch?'

'Have you and Caroline made love there together?' He thinks about it, then nods reluctantly. 'I'm sorry,' I say again. 'I don't mean to be awkward, it's just that I want things to be new between you and me.'

'The house is on the market already. But that doesn't help us right now.'

'Maybe we can get a hotel room.' Yes, that would be good. Somewhere tasteful yet anonymous, with no memories for either of us.

He checks his watch. 'I don't have enough time for that. I've got to be in the office in a couple of hours for this thing with Japan.'

'Oh.'

Edmund gives me his charming grin. 'Oh. Exactly. Anyway, it can't be helped. And waiting will just make it better when we finally are together.'

'I've been waiting for a very long time already.'

'I know.' He kisses me gently on the cheek. 'But I promise I'll make it up to you. We'll get a suite at the Savoy and spend all Sunday in it.'

'Sunday? But it's Tuesday.'

Edmund shakes his beautiful head. 'How long have you been living with the Addams Family? You've forgotten how much devotion this job takes. It's not like making tea for pensioners.'

'I guess the pace of life was different in Highgate.'

'You'll soon be back in the swing of things.' He stands

up and straightens his clothes. 'I might as well get downstairs and sort out this thing with Rombauer's before things get too crazy. Where would you like to stay, Nina? At the house, or here? Or shall I reserve that suite for the week?'

'I don't need a suite to myself. The flat will be fine.'

'Perfect. It will be good to know you're so close while I'm working, at least.'

'But . . . won't you stay here with me?'

'Nina.' He strokes my hair, which even after my rapid Selfridges grooming is considerably wavier than he's ever seen it. To say nothing of all the split ends, since I haven't been able to get it cut. 'If I stay here with you, I won't be able to resist making love with you. And you're right, things should be new between you and me. I'll stay at the house.'

'Oh. I . . . well, all right.'

'Good girl. You know where to find me, right? And I'll have something sent up for you to eat.' He checks his watch again, and runs his fingers through his hair. 'Oh, and Nina? I haven't told anyone about you going belly-up in Spain, or where I found you. I thought you'd prefer to keep that between you and me.'

'That's very considerate of you, Edmund.'

'Only what you deserve.' He kisses me swiftly on the lips. 'I can't wait until Sunday,' he says, and leaves.

Nothing ever changes on the King's Road; shops might come and go, but the shoppers still prowl, looking for the perfect outfit. Always a new perfect outfit, to replace the perfect outfit bought last month or last week or yesterday.

Edmund has given me his credit card and told me to have fun. So I'm using this morning, while he's in a meeting, to invest in a more appropriate wardrobe. Or rather, I'm supposed to be. So far I've bought one pair of tights, which I put on right away because my legs were cold.

I just can't get into it, somehow. I've wafted into loads of shops, and I've looked in lots of windows. But nothing appeals to me. Neutrals are everywhere this autumn, very classy and chic on the mannequins in the windows, but bland when contrasted with the bright oranges and reds of the leaves all around me. It doesn't seem to be bothering anybody else; wherever I go, credit cards are being brandished like magic talismans to pleasure. There's obviously something wrong with me rather than the clothes. Maybe I've been wearing the same ratty old jumper for so long that I've lost all the fashion sense I ever had.

Going into a Starbucks raises my spirits. I have been several months without a mocha Frappuccino, which is cruel and unusual punishment in anyone's books. I queue for one and curl up with it in a purple armchair in the window. I wonder if I've ever been in this particular Starbucks before. It's hard to tell; I've definitely been in one of these purple armchairs, but they pepper London and the world. It's not the Starbucks where I let Edmund see that I loved him, anyway; that Starbucks will forever be enshrined in my memory as the place where the seeds of my new life took root.

Though this one looks an awful lot like it.

I draw deep on my straw. The first sip is pure memory and heaven. The second sip, though, is quite cloying. And the third is unbelievably sweet. I put down the plastic cup.

Somewhere along the line I have lost my taste for mocha Frappuccinos. Edmund will be pleased. *At least there's something new about me that will please him*, I think, and then immediately banish the thought as unworthy.

I squirm in the purple armchair. This could be much more fun if I weren't alone. I think about all the afternoons I used to spend with Pet, swanning in and out of shops, talking over our wish lists and purchases, gossiping over changing room walls. I try to remember what I bought on these outings, but that seems less important now than the outings themselves.

And I suddenly know what I should be doing instead of shopping. I should have done it days ago. I should have done it weeks ago.

I'm out of Starbucks and heading down the road right away. My watch says I've got about an hour before Edmund's out of his meeting and wants to meet for coffee. Though this should only take a few minutes, if Pet slams the door in my face.

*Goodbye, Nina.* I ring the bell for Pet's mews house and stand on her doorstep chewing my lip and remembering how she sounded the last time I talked to her on the phone. There was such finality in that 'goodbye'. Like she never wanted to see or talk to me again. Sort of like the door to the Temple of Gloom slamming behind Viktor.

'Yeah?' she says over the intercom. She sounds half asleep.

'Pet? It's Nina.'

There is a long pause, during which I savage my lip some more. Then she opens the door, steps out, and shuts it behind her.

She is wearing skin-tight jeans and a T-shirt without a bra underneath, looking beautifully mussed from bed even without her make-up. 'I didn't think I'd see you again,' she says.

'Pet, I am so, so sorry. I'm not sure what to say to you. I lied to you and I'm really sorry.'

She tilts her head as if considering. 'And that's

supposed to make it all better, is it? An apology on my doorstep?'

'No. I don't know if I can make it any better. But I've been afraid to try. I've felt horrible.'

'The thing is, Nina, I actually thought you were different.'

'Different how?' *As in, successful? Well-off? Socially confident? From a normal family?*

All of these were lies, more or less. They were bigger lies, if she only knew it, than the lie about being in Spain when I was really in Highgate.

Pet runs her hands through her hair, mussing it further. 'You always seemed more real than the other girls I know. Like, that you cared about more than how much money I have or what new bloke I'm shagging or what new club I can get us into. You seemed to like me for me, you know?' She purses her lips. 'Do you remember that afternoon we spent together just reading the papers? I haven't had a day like that ever, with anyone else. Like we could just relax and not be perfect or anything. And then . . . when I got to Spain and found out you'd lied to me, I was like . . . well, that's it. Another person who's not really my friend.'

'You *liked* that day reading the papers?'

'Yeah. I hoped we could do it again.'

'Oh God.' I twist my foot into the carpet. 'I . . . thought you'd be horribly bored.'

'Yeah, well I guess we didn't know each other as well as we thought we did.'

No. And it was much worse than she thinks. Because I *did* like Pet for her money, and her new blokes, and her clubs.

Or at least I thought that's why I liked her.

I sigh. 'Pet, can I come in? I have a really long story to tell you, and I'm not sure you're going to want to be my friend after I've finished. But you need to know all of it, from the beginning.'

'What, you mean what really happened in Spain with Juan?'

'Yes. But it starts way before that, back when I was a kid. Can I come in?'

She considers. Then she opens the door.

38

I hover in the doorway of Edmund's office. It's empty; Edmund is downstairs, in consultation with his sous chef, Red. I've been out for a walk around Kensington Gardens and now I'm at a loose end. I don't feel like shopping, Edmund doesn't need me, *Emerly Street* isn't on until seven and I've already rung Evangeline once today. Talking with Evangeline on the phone is just like talking to her in real life, but without the cigarette smoke or the view of exotic clothing; I sat on a park bench next to a statue of Peter Pan and had a good natter about everything except Viktor. I'm not sure if she was avoiding the subject, or if I was. Anyway, the topic didn't come up.

I look around the bright room, trying to decide where to sit. Edmund's chair is sleek black leather, dominating his big glass desk. Beside it is what used to be my desk, and is now Jennifer's. It's more cluttered than it used to be when it was mine, and she's perched a small teddy bear on it. Caroline's chair sits in the corner, and I won't sit on that in principle, but there's another armchair next to it, an unassuming white one that Edmund sometimes uses for visitors. I sink into it, rubbing my eyes.

I never used to be this tired when I worked here, and in those days I used to get a lot less sleep. Maybe I got used to my early nights and late mornings in the Temple of Gloom. Maybe I'm older. Maybe I'm just running on less adrenalin these days.

Maybe I'm tired today because of the dream I had last night, alone in the double bed of the flat next door.

I was under a cedar tree at nightfall. It was a complicated shadow in the dusk above me and behind me. I could smell its wood and its sap, and I could feel its rough bark behind my shoulders. I leaned back on it and it wrapped needled branches around me, but they weren't hurtful. They curled around me like a duvet. Like sex.

I woke up with the scent still in my nostrils, my body longing, a feeling in my stomach half nostalgia, half desire. It stole my sleep and it's been with me ever since, even though I tried to get rid of it with that brisk walk through the park. It makes it hard to concentrate on anything.

My phone beeps. Pet has texted: *How u doin? Pxx.*

This is a good sign. Texting is safer for fragile relationships; it builds communication in small, easy bites. Next time I see her, next week probably, maybe we can be a bit more normal together. Normal and better, because I'm not hiding from her any more, and because I think that this time we can really be friends.

*I'm sexually frustrated*, I text her back.

It's true. Why else would I be dreaming of my night with Viktor when that's all over? Though trust me to dream of a tree instead of actual sex. It's not as if I don't remember the sex. Because I remember every single sweet second of it. If I'd known it was going to end the next day, I wouldn't have let Viktor sleep.

I shake my head. It feels like regret, but it's sexual frustration. It's built up very quickly since my last orgasm, not because Viktor awakened a hunger in me, but because I've only had snatched moments with

Edmund. On Sunday, Edmund will banish for ever any thoughts about past lovers. Nobody could follow Edmund. The man uses his hands for a living, for God's sake.

Dreams don't matter. Not dreams you have at night. What matter are the dreams you have during the day, your goals and hopes. Night-time dreams are just your body's way of saying 'Please drink less caffeine before you go to bed.'

Jennifer comes in, bustling in her heels, and immediately opens her laptop and starts clicking away. I tuck my phone into my pocket to wait for Pet's reply, and take a magazine out of my bag. Surreptitiously I watch Jennifer. Her blond hair is piled on top of her head. Her heels make her appear taller. She looks very much like me. How odd that I never noticed it before.

Edmund said, that first day he found me, that Jennifer didn't have my energy and devotion, but she certainly seems to be hard-working and efficient. She dogs Edmund's steps everywhere he goes. I've barely had a moment with him on my own in the days I've been here. She does things slightly differently from the way I would do them, but I've bitten my tongue.

I flick through the magazine, trying to get interested in easy winter make-up tips. I remember Caroline sitting in this corner, reading her book, out of the way yet easily found. I wonder if she ever got bored.

'Coffee?' I ask Jennifer and go to the espresso machine.

'Thank you.' She clicks away until I bring her the coffee, in a delicate cup. Then she sits back in her chair, giving me a look that is blatantly assessing. 'So the rumour is that Gretchen saw you in Highgate.'

I stand, rather than going back to the armchair. I'm taller than Jennifer, that's one thing. 'Yes, she did, I've been staying there for a little bit, sorting out some family business. Where is Gretchen anyway?'

Jennifer shrugs. 'She resigned just before you reappeared. I think she was offered a job at Claridges.'

'She was offered a job at Claridges last winter and didn't take it.'

'Yes, well, I think she was spending too much time with Caroline for comfort. They'd got to be quite good friends through this whole thing.'

'I thought . . . it was my impression that Edmund and Caroline's break-up was quite civilised.'

'Civilised? If you call walking out on your husband the night before his TV premiere civilised.' She sniffs.

'*She* walked out on *him*?' I would never have thought it possible that someone could walk out on Edmund. I pull Edmund's chair over, and sit down next to Jennifer, putting my coffee cup near hers. 'You know, I always thought they were the perfect couple.'

'Apparently she says she wasn't happy for ages,' Jennifer says. 'She wanted more time with him, according to Gretchen. I don't think she ever really supported his career.'

'Yeah, I guess that whole spending-time-together thing can get annoying in a marriage.' I say it jokier than I really mean.

Jennifer glares at me. 'I would've thought *you'd* understand. When you were training me you never stopped talking about how brilliant and visionary Edmund is.'

'He is. Totally brilliant and visionary. He's the most amazing man I know.'

Though even as I say it, I'm thinking of Michael and Arval, preserving what they've loved. Viktor tracking tiny, miraculous bats. Even my father, who came back from the dead.

'Anyway,' Jennifer says, 'he's due to be finished with Red in five minutes. We'd better go down.'

'Right.' We abandon our coffees and file down the narrow back stairs. 'I've reserved you and Edmund a suite at the Savoy for Sunday afternoon,' Jennifer says over her shoulder.

'Oh. I . . . thanks.'

Edmund is striding through the dining room when we get there. His face lights up when he sees me. He pulls me towards him and kisses me on the lips, tilting my body backwards slightly in the manner of an old-fashioned movie kiss.

The dining room is half full of people lingering over lunch. I can feel the weight of all their gazes on me.

'Can't wait for our suite,' he whispers to me when he's finished, and he sets me on my feet and winks at me. Then he heads back to the kitchen, rubbing his hands together, stopping to exchange a few words with customers as he goes.

I straighten my dress. Jennifer hurries after Edmund. In my pocket, my phone beeps and I look at it, largely to avoid seeing the expressions of anyone in the restaurant.

*Roll on sunday and dream come true eh m8? Pxx.*

My fingers are shaking as I text back. *Yes, problems all solved sunday. Nxx.*

On Saturday evening I do the works. Soaking, exfoliating, waxing, shaving, plucking, buffing, conditioning, all of it with the best products one can buy on the King's Road. I don't do fake tan; I've cured myself of that particular desire. I play a newly downloaded *2112* at the highest volume possible through the dinky MP3 speakers, which is nowhere loud enough, but which causes sufficient noise inside my head. I go through all these motions of beautification with as little thought as possible, especially not the thought of the last time I tried thinking as little as possible.

It takes me a long time, and when I'm done I decide to go to bed, because tomorrow I won't be doing much sleeping. I slip between Egyptian cotton sheets, prepared for my lover, with my skin feeling as smooth as a baby's. I close my eyes and try to find the sleep of the innocent.

It doesn't come. I'm too excited. My muscles are tense, my jaw is aching, my head is throbbing, my stomach is churning. If I didn't know better, I'd say this was fear, not anticipation.

The wide, soft bed is desperately uncomfortable. Maybe I should go and put on Rush again. Maybe I should clean the spotless flat.

Maybe I should just think this one through, for once.

Why would I be afraid of sleeping with Edmund? He's everything that I ever wanted. Or at least he always has been.

Several times over the past few days I've caught myself watching him, trying to figure out how he's changed. Why there aren't little clouds of joy floating me around underneath my high-heeled shoes. The thing is, other than being single, and in love with me, which should make him even more perfect, Edmund hasn't changed at all. He's still as successful as ever, still as talented, still as confident and sexy and stylish and charming.

I'm clenching my teeth and curling my toes. I feel like I did on my first day at Holybrook Comprehensive, when everyone stared at me and wondered where I'd suddenly come from. Or how I felt after realising Pet knew I'd betrayed her. Sick with myself, sick of myself, wrong in my pampered and preened and perfumed body.

This is not sexual frustration. This makes no sense at all.

I squeeze my eyes tight shut. If I sleep I'll feel better, and by the time I wake up it will be daylight on Sunday and Edmund will arrive to take me to the Savoy and I'll already have started my new life so it will be too late to worry about anything. I concentrate on the feeling of the cool sheets on my body, on the smell of the bunch of lilies Edmund had delivered to me, underlaid with the scent of cooking that never quite goes away in this flat. I listen to tyres swishing on the road outside and dead leaves rattling against the bricks and the pavement. I picture myself in a narrow single bed, closeted in a cell like a monk with a window far up, held safely in by thick walls. I breathe slowly, relaxing into gravity, warming a pocket around me. Safe. This is better.

As I drowse, the room shifts and I hear something

more. Footsteps overhead, walking back and forth in the night. The whirr of small flying creatures calling to find their way home.

The thought wakes me up completely and I sit up in bed, staring at the low, sloped ceiling. For a minute I thought I could hear someone walking around. But that's impossible. Viktor is in Highgate, and besides, this shallow, expensive flat is on the top floor of Jett's building.

If I stay here I can't get any higher.

'I don't think this is my happily ever after,' I say out loud.

I never really unpacked, which probably should have told me something. Anyway, it's the work of a few minutes to get my things together. It takes me longer to decide what to write to Edmund. I can't wait around for him to turn up, and it's too late to ring. But I remember so well the feeling of finding Juan's note. Or wishing for one from my mother.

My pen pauses over the paper. There's too much to say. Maybe that's why my mother never left a note – not because she didn't care, but because she did and the task of writing it down was too daunting. Maybe that's why Juan's was so dramatic and clichéd.

Maybe I've just changed enough to see the possibility of forgiveness.

I always thought that leaving was an act of cowardice, running away before you can see the hurt you've caused. But now that I'm doing it myself, I can see that there's another fear behind the secret flit: the fear that if I don't go now, while the dream of those footsteps is still echoing in my ears, I might never go. It would be easier to stay with what I know, my older, smaller dreams.

In the end I just write, *Sorry, Edmund, I have to go,*

*please call me.* I put my mobile number on the bottom in case he's lost it and Blu-Tack it to the door even though he's got a key to the flat.

The street lights and the cars passing ensure that it's not really dark outside, even though it's late. I flag down a cab.

'Where to, love?' the driver asks.

I hesitate, but the darkness makes the decision for me. And besides, I should have sorted this ending out a long time ago.

'Holybrook,' I say. 'In Bedfordshire. Will you take a credit card?'

*I'll pay you back*, I promise Edmund in my head. And then I start trying to figure out what I'm going to say.

The neighbourhood is sleeping when the cab pulls up in Halcyon Close nearly an hour later. The engine rattles loudly in the silence, though not for long; a plane passes overhead and drowns out the noise and the cabbie's goodbye. I let myself in the front door and leave my bags in the hallway while I go to the kitchen to put the kettle on.

I hear shuffling, and my father appears in the kitchen doorway, wearing crumpled blue striped pyjamas, his hair standing on end and his eyes bleary, and a cricket bat in his hands. 'Oh!' he gasps when he sees me, and lowers the bat. 'Dear God, Nina, you startled me. I thought you were a burglar.'

I go straight to him and hug him. He's warm from his bed and he pats me on the back. 'What's wrong, sweetheart?' he asks.

'I'm sorry to have woken you up,' I say to his shoulder, which I've laid my head on. 'I just needed to talk to you.'

'Well of course you can talk to me any time you like,

dear. But are you in trouble? It's such a long way to come, from Spain, just to talk.'

'I don't think I'm in trouble, not any more. But Spain is what we need to talk about. Is Imogen here?'

'No, she's spending the night with that boyfriend of hers. He lives just in the other close. We can ring her if you want, though it's nearly two in the morning.'

'That's all right. I'll tell her later. Please sit down, Dad, this might take a while.'

I make us both a cup of tea. I sit down across from my father. And then I start to tell the truth.

It takes more time than I'd have thought, because although the truth is simple, there have been so many people and feelings involved, and I've learned so much, that I find myself explaining everything that's happened during the past year or so, from my hopeless crush to my ruination in Spain to my breakdown over shoes to my leaving Edmund again. I don't think I've ever said so many words to my father all at once. For so long our conversations have been restricted to trivialities and practicalities.

He sits and listens, drinking his tea, making us more, waiting when I pause because a plane is going over. He doesn't say a word, just watches me with his blue eyes. And then I finish and I look back at him.

'What do you think?' I ask.

He reaches across the table and takes my hand in his. 'I'm so sorry, Nina. So sorry you had to go through all of that pain.'

'You're not angry at me for lying to you?'

'I think I understand why you had to.' He rubs his free hand over his face, as if the conversation has made him weary. 'I haven't been much of a father to you. With Imogen, she's younger and I could make it up to her. But you . . . I . . . I've let myself lean on you. It's been too easy for me to do.'

'I never minded,' I say quickly.

'No, maybe you didn't, but it's not the way things should be, is it? I used to tell myself it made us closer, and maybe it did, in a way. But the fact is that I was too concerned about my own problems to help you when you needed me.'

'You were ill.'

He shakes his head. 'Maybe so. I wonder sometimes if it all started a long time before that. Your mother and I used money to paper over the cracks. Or credit, really. We weren't good role models for you. And then when she left us and I thought I'd lost everything . . .'

Every instinct tells me to jump in and change the subject, tell him it was okay, do anything not to talk about this. I stay quiet and wait.

'What I lost,' he says finally, 'was nothing compared with what I kept.'

I squeeze his hand hard. He squeezes mine back. We sit there together as the tea goes cold in our mugs.

My father clears his throat. 'Well. What are you going to do now?'

'Actually, I need your help, Dad, on a few things. The first is that I need to borrow your car. I have to get to London before the sun comes up.'

It's still dark when I hit the M1, but by the time I reach the lights and buildings of north London the sky is turning indigo, hesitating between night and sunrise. I drive as fast as I can, sitting on the edge of the seat with my hands clenched on the wheel and my bottom bouncing up and down on the seat, urging the car to go faster, faster, past the sleeping buildings and the stretching streets, faster through the waking traffic and the zombie pedestrians. I tap my fingers at red lights. As I drive up the hill I look in the rear-view mirror and see gold and pink light creeping upwards in the east.

I screech up in front of the house and park on a double yellow line. I jump out and stand on the pavement, looking up at the Temple of Gloom.

It's still a grey, misshapen lump with a turret sticking up like a snaggle tooth. The rising dawn picks out the wings and beaks and talons of all the stone creatures who have found their home here.

Like me.

I sit on the step in front of the front door and pull my legs up under my coat. Daylight comes gradually, as slowly as discovery, and I wouldn't be able to see the stages of dawn, except I can pick out the details of the spider monkey gargoyle just above me better every minute. It's scowling.

I'm not sure what's going to happen. But I do have one thing that I didn't have when I last arrived here, sodden and wearing a Spanish dress: hope. Maybe not that much of it, but a little. Hope and the knowledge that if I need to, I can start over.

I hear footsteps on the pavement and I know who it is right away, but I keep on looking at the spider monkey because despite everything I tell myself about hope, I'm scared. Finally, though, the desire to see Viktor outweighs anything else. He's wearing the cloaky coat, but he's got the hat in his hand. It's light enough now so I can see his face, but he's very good at showing a mask. He stops about a metre away and watches me, as he would a not particularly interesting specimen of mammal.

'Hi,' I say.

'Morning.'

The grim face is a defence. He confessed it to me in

bed, with his arms around me, and I'm almost sure of it now. Almost.

'How are the bats?' I ask.

'Ironically enough, they're mating.'

'In the autumn?'

He puts his bag down on the pavement, and sits down next to me. He rests his elbows on his thighs, his hands dangling between them, and sighs. He looks tired.

'Did you come here to find out how long bat sperm can survive? Because I can tell you, but it's very early in the morning and I haven't slept yet.'

*Can I come to bed with you?* It might work. But it also would put us right back into the sex-for-its-own-sake pattern, and that's not why I came back here.

'I don't love Edmund,' I say.

Viktor is silent and still. Then he sighs again, and this time I hear more anger than exasperation. 'I'm not your confessor, Nina.'

'No. You're one of the truest friends I've ever had. You, and Evangeline, and Michael, and Pet, though I didn't know it. But mostly you.'

'And this is what you came back to tell me?'

He's not angry, though. More cautious. I like the caution. It means there's a feeling to protect.

'No. I came back to tell you that my father has lent me Arval's flat for as long as I need it. I'm going to stay here. I'll look for a new job.'

'I can't be with someone who enjoys the drama of being messed up,' he says. 'Or someone who'd rather be somewhere else.'

'I'm finished with being messed up. And I don't want to be anywhere except for here.' I swallow. This is it. Don't be a coward, Nina. 'With you.'

He's frowning. 'And why should I believe you're not going to change your mind again?'

'Look at me.'

He does. He looks straight into my face in the way only he can, and I look straight back. In the distance I can hear traffic, a bird creaking, the whole world waking up. But close up, it's only him.

Viktor reaches out and pulls me into his lap. He wraps his arms around me and I bury my face in his neck. 'Daft cow,' he says into my hair.

Then I kiss him, and that's the beginning.

You can buy any of these other
**Little Black Dress** titles from your
bookshop or *direct from the publisher*.

## FREE P&P AND UK DELIVERY
(Overseas and Ireland £3.50 per book)

| | | |
|---|---|---|
| Improper Relations | Janet Mullany | £5.99 |
| Bittersweet | Sarah Monk | £5.99 |
| The Death of Bridezilla | Laurie Brown | £5.99 |
| Crystal Clear | Nell Dixon | £5.99 |
| Talk of the Town | Suzanne Macpherson | £5.99 |
| A Date in Your Diary | Jules Stanbridge | £5.99 |
| The Hen Night Prophecies: Eastern Promise | Jessica Fox | £5.99 |
| The Bachelor and Spinster Ball | Janet Gover | £5.99 |
| The Love Boat | Kate Lace | £5.99 |
| Trick or Treat | Sally Anne Morris | £5.99 |
| Tug of Love | Allie Spencer | £5.99 |
| Sunnyside Blues | Mary Carter | £5.99 |
| Heartless | Alison Gaylin | £5.99 |
| A Hollywood Affair | Lucy Broadbent | £5.99 |
| I Do, I Do, I Do | Samantha Scott-Jeffries | £5.99 |
| A Most Lamentable Comedy | Janet Mullany | £5.99 |
| Purses and Poison | Dorothy Howell | £5.99 |
| Perfect Image | Marisa Heath | £5.99 |
| Girl From Mars | Julie Cohen | £5.99 |
| True Love and Other Disasters | Rachel Gibson | £5.99 |

## TO ORDER SIMPLY CALL THIS NUMBER

## 01235 400 414

or visit our website: www.headline.co.uk

Prices and availability subject to change without notice.